I0710246

# THE EVER RISING
## BOOK TWO

# MISFORTUNE GILDED IN GREED

### CHANTEL BURNHAM

EVER RISING BOOKS LLC

Copyright © 2024 by Chantel Burnham via Ever Rising Books LLC

All rights reserved.

No part of this publication may be reproduced, distributed, or transmitted in any form or by any means, including photocopying, recording, or other electronic or mechanical methods, without the prior written permission of the publisher, except as permitted by U.S. copyright law. For permission requests, contact Ever Rising Books LLC via everrisi ngbooks.com or chantelburnham.com.

The story, all names, characters, organizations, and incidents portrayed in this production are fictitious. Any references to real places or incidents, real people, and real brands and corporations are used fictitiously. Other names, characters, places, organizations, and events are products of the author's imagination, and any resemblances to actual events, places, persons or organizations, living or dead, is entirely coincidental.

First paperback edition 2024

ISBN: 978-1-962158-02-2

Imprint: Ever Rising Books LLC

Book Cover by My Lan Khuc Valle

# ALSO BY CHANTEL BURNHAM

**The Ever Rising Series**

*Magic Feared and Furious*

# Content Warning

This book contains descriptions that may be upsetting to certain readers, including: discrimination, violence, and cruelty to mythical animals. It also deals with themes of slavery and captivity.

To my parents, who gave me a rich childhood.
This book would not exist without the lessons you taught me.
Thank you, and I love you.

# PROLOGUE

Concealed in the shadows of a dense copse of trees, the black sedan waited. The driver peered through binoculars at the enormous gated property across the street. A woman sat beside him, reading a stapled stack of papers embossed with a sigil of a flaming dragon.

"Ma'am, we've got movement turning up to the front drive," the man with the binoculars said as he shifted in his seat, damp with sweat despite the breeze wafting through the open windows.

A second man snoozing in the back seat perked up from his doze with a nasally snort. The woman cast a glare over her shoulder at him as she lowered her papers, then stared toward the gated entrance, her expression hard. Through the trees a floral-patterned delivery van pulled into the drive.

"It must be for the party tonight," the driver continued, lowering his binoculars to look at the woman beside him. She didn't respond.

The delivery van squealed to a stop before the closed gates, the driver leaning out his window to talk into a black speaker box. A moment later the gates slid back, allowing the van to enter.

The woman clicked on a recording app on her phone and relayed, "April twenty-fourth, Weston, Massachusetts. A van labeled, *Spring Gardens Florist* approached the McKenna residence at eleven-fourteen in the morning. Further action will be reported." She ended the recording and tucked her phone away.

"It's just another flower delivery," the driver said with a sigh, his shoulders sagging.

"Probably," the woman replied, turning back to the papers in her hand. "But keep watching, just in case. We don't want them to pull any funny business and dispose of the M.A.s before we can get to them."

"I don't think we have to worry about that," the guy in the back seat drawled, settling back now that the excitement was over. "The transition went smoothly. They didn't even notice. These Everbleeders have no idea what's about to hit them."

# Chapter One

"You sure your mom is okay with me catching a ride home with you?" Hillary asked, biting her lip and running her hand over the plush interior of the backseat. "I can take the bus." She gestured out the window to the long line of buses filling with students, the enormous crest of Marchand Academy splashed across the vehicles' sides.

I laughed, pulling my long brunette hair away from my uniform jacket. "That's ridiculous. It's no problem taking you," I lied, meeting my chauffeur's steel-gray eyes through the rearview mirror. I ignored his reproving look and turned to my best friend as she read a text on her phone, her backpack on the soft leather between us.

The truth was my mother would throw a fit if she learned I was giving friends rides home from the academy, but so long as Santeri kept his mouth shut, she would never know.

"And you really don't think she'll let you hang out this afternoon?" Hillary asked. I rolled my eyes, leaning into the seat and staring at the ceiling.

"I don't know," I sighed. While it was Friday, it would be a battle convincing my mom to let me out of Maddock Duty just to hang out with friends.

"Oh please, Mallory, you have to come!" Hillary begged, her blonde curls bouncing. "Felicity said she can get us into a private screening of that new Grayson First movie before it even comes out! I want to see it with you! Paz and everyone already said yes to going! Marcus too," Hillary said in a knowing tone.

I could feel my face growing hot as I pictured Marcus' beautiful, floppy black hair, and the dimpled grin he'd cast at me earlier today. The new kid in school had caught my eye, along with half the girls in our grade. And that included Felicity Davis. I didn't like hanging out with Felicity—she took every opportunity to exclude me and gave me backhanded compliments when no one else was in earshot—but she was Hillary's cousin, so we tolerated each other. Until now. Any civility between us was now left behind in our race to win over Marcus.

I considered the flirtatious moment Marcus and I had shared in history class today. During Silent Study, I'd been bored while reviewing the notes on the Irish Potato Famine of 1845, having known the material since I was eight, as my own some-odd-great-grandmother had come over from Ireland to America during that time. I had been looking around the room when Marcus and I made eye contact. His smile and roguish wink had made a butterfly volcano erupt in my stomach, and they were still fluttering like crazy even an hour later.

But, it was because of my ancestor that I wouldn't be there to sit by Marcus in the movie theater this afternoon. My great-great-great-grandmother had brought more than just history with her to the United States: she'd brought the start of our family's fortune.

And my personal misfortune. My thoughts flashed to Maddock, and I grimaced. No one would believe me if I told them the truth. No one believed in magic these days.

"It depends on the time. My mom always has chores for me right after school," I said, inwardly gritting my teeth at the thought. Hillary would freak out if I told her what my *chores* entailed.

"Which I still think is stupid, as you have all those live-in maids," Hillary said, rolling her eyes as she pulled out her phone.

"They're not *live-in*. They go home every night," I replied, annoyed. My mother would never be *that* generous. "Besides, they all quit like, a week ago. My mom has been freaking out about it." I didn't mention that our cooks, gardeners, pool boys, and other utility workers had quit within the last week as well, so my mom had been in hysterics for days.

I didn't understand why. Sure, it was a shock, but more employees could be easily found with one look on the internet.

I was upset about it because much of the staff had worked in our home for several years, and had been my friends. Or so I thought. Now they were gone, leaving me alone in that house. My only hope was that they left because they were offered better jobs. I certainly wouldn't want a person like my mother as an employer. My mom must have cut their pay to make them quit all at once. The only person who stayed out of our original staff was Santeri, our faithful butler and chauffeur.

"But anyway, my mom says it builds character and patience, so I have chores," I said, gritting my teeth.

"Well, if *my* mom had a maid," Hillary laughed, "I don't think she'd care at all if I built character or patience, just so long as the toilets got scrubbed without her having to always yell at me and my brothers to do it."

I wanted to reply that my socialite mother didn't *really* care if I built character, but I held back. What would my friends say if they learned that many of the replies about my home life were rehearsed lines?

"Here, smile," Hillary said, turning her phone camera onto me. We pressed our cheeks together as she snapped several pics.

"Ooh, we look so classy in these," Hillary said, looking through the pictures. "I guess being in a Rolls helps. Ugh, I hate my chubby face." Hillary puffed out her cheeks. While she was slightly plump, she was gorgeous, with curly blonde hair, blue eyes, and full lips. And even though she was beloved by everyone for her bubbly personality, she was still very touchy about her weight. "No way Tom Anderson would ever want to go to the spring formal with a cow like me," she sighed with a self-deprecating laugh.

"Hey!" I snapped, exasperation flushing through me, "What did I say about you saying stuff like that? I'm serious, stop it."

Hillary glanced at me with a shy smile. I gave her a soft shove. "If Tom doesn't say 'yes' to you, he's a blind idiot! You are a gorgeous goddess, okay?"

Her smile strengthened. "Okay."

"Say it."

"He's a blind idiot, and I'm a gorgeous goddess," she said with a timid laugh.

"You better believe it," I replied, stern. "We'll plan how you're going to ask him, and he's going to say yes!" I looked at the picture of us on her screen. I was the exact opposite of my best friend: rod-straight brown hair, super pale Irish skin that was prone to sunburn, and a rail thin body, no curves whatsoever. My mother was curvy, so I prayed the benefits of puberty were just taking their sweet time. "He will."

"And Marcus will say 'yes' to you," Hillary teased.

"We'll have to see," I sighed. "If Felicity claims him tonight, I won't get the chance." We pulled up to Hillary's house, and Hillary hopped out, dragging her backpack out behind her. She turned, smiling at me as she moved to shut the door. "Bye." She cast a wary glance at Santeri before saying, "I'll text you."

I nodded, giving her a secretive smile. "Bye."

Santeri pulled away from the curb and I could feel his amused disapproval at ignoring my mother's rules, but didn't say anything. We soon pulled into the long, winding drive leading to my house.

The property on either side of the drive was filled with trees and flowering bushes, just getting their leaves and buds in the warm spring sunshine. As Santeri pulled into the enormous circular drive, he had to squeeze between all the delivery vans and catering trucks that filled the driveway in order to drop me off at the front doors.

"Is there a party tonight, Santeri?" I asked, sitting up straighter to see out of the windshield. I hadn't heard anything about a party. My mother was always so loud about them, why didn't I hear about this one? I was better at tuning out my mother than I thought.

Now my mother's dragon-ish mood about the staff quitting was becoming clear. She needed people to help with setting up for this party, and she would have had to shell out a small fortune for caterers and temporary staff to set up and clean afterward.

"There is, indeed, Miss," Santeri said, turning the wheel to pull up beside a black van that displayed a large decal of some inedible shellfish hors d'oeuvres. He put the Rolls in park and shifted to look back at me, staring at me with smiling gray eyes. His young face always seemed to clash with his salt and pepper hair. "I'm picking up your father from the airport tonight. He's coming home just for the occasion."

My dad had been in Japan for the last three weeks on a business trip. If he was coming home for a party, it must be a pretty important one.

"So, no lessons tonight, then?" I made an exaggerated pouty face. While it was nice being able to get a ride anytime I wanted from Santeri, I couldn't wait until I turned sixteen in a few months. I would be getting a car of my own at my Sweet Sixteen, even though I didn't have my learner's permit yet. *Soon*, my mother had said. The time had come and gone for it, and I still didn't have my permit. I had no doubt my mother had forgotten to sign me up, too busy planning parties and jetting off on expensive trips.

Santeri laughed, his expression apologetic as he pushed back his cap a bit. "I'm afraid not. I'll be too busy directing caterers. How about tomorrow evening?"

"Okay. Thanks, Santeri." Before he could be bothered to open my door for me, I hopped out and ran up the shallow steps to the house.

The double doors were wide open and people were making trips to and from the vans parked out front, carrying large vases of flowers, trays of food, tables, and linens inside.

I followed a woman carrying a box of lights inside to the grand foyer, which, now that the furniture had been removed, resembled a small ballroom. The double grand staircases were being strung with lights and garlands of fresh flowers and greenery. Workers were on the three levels of banisters, hanging long streamers off the balconies, and my mother had brought out the four gigantic crystal chandeliers to dot the three-story-high ceiling. Someone was on the roof, visible through the enormous glass cupola in the center of the ceiling, polishing the leaded glass dome until it sparkled.

The rooms were a whir of noises and movement as people set up stands for ice sculptures, food, and music. Men were stringing lights out on the stone terrace that exited off the grand dining room, which led to the lawns and overlooked the large, man-made pond along one side of the property. I could see through the open french doors that a pair of women in a rowboat were setting up floating lights on the pond's surface.

On the other side of the foyer, my mother was speaking with a man in an apron. As usual, she was immaculate. Wearing a skin-tight pencil skirt and frilly blouse with towering stilettos, her makeup was done with the perfection of a goddess, and her long strawberry blonde hair flowed down her back in soft curls. I could only hope that one day I could achieve her effortless beauty. But my mother would never let me borrow Hye, her stylist and the secret ingredient to her flawless looks.

I meandered over and stood beside my mother, waiting for her to notice me as she talked with the caterer.

"And double-check that we have enough hors d'oeuvres and cutlery for dinner. I paid a fortune for your services, and if you run out of *anything*, you won't even be able to cater a child's birthday party when I'm through with you. Do you understand?" My mother asked, tossing her hair, menace rippling through her voice.

"Of course, ma'am," the man replied, a thin sheen of sweat glistening on his pale face as he inclined his head in a sort of bow. I wanted to warn him that if he remained bowed that way much longer, she would chop his head off for good measure.

"Good." My mother's face lightened as she looked at the clipboard in her hand and checked something off. The man quickly backed away.

*Good thinking*, I mused, *don't turn your back on her.*

"Okay, now, to check on the flowers," she muttered to herself, sucking on the end of her pen. She turned and nearly walked into me.

"Oh, Mallory." Her blank expression twisted into horror. "Wait. Mallory? Why are you home? What time is it?" she cried, checking the slender, diamond-encrusted watch on her wrist. "It can't possibly be past three o'clock, can it?" she asked, panic shrilling her voice.

"That's why I'm home," I sniffed. "I get home every day around three-fifteen." I let my backpack drop to the marble floor for emphasis.

"I'm way behind schedule! When I get a hold of those betraying little—" She moved to hurry away, but I saw the thought visibly strike her, and she paused midstep, making my stomach clench.

*Here we go. You can do this, Mallory. Just ask her.*

She turned back to me, eyes widened with implication. "—Oh, have you done your chores today?" she asked.

"No, Mom, I just got home. I will, but," I paused. *Deep breath, and just ask.* "But can I go to the movies today with my friends?"

"Darling, we have a party tonight!" she trilled, still concentrating on her clipboard. "And you have your chores."

"Yeah, I can see that," I said, glancing around the busy room, sidestepping her reminder about the chores. It looked like it was going to be some party, even for my parents' standards. "I don't remember you telling me about a party."

"But I must have!" She gasped, finally looking up from her clipboard. "I've been planning this party for over two months!"

I shrugged.

She exhaled. "You just weren't listening, as usual, with those headbuds in your ears all the time."

I covered a laugh. Headbuds.

"So many important people are coming tonight. We've got the senator and his wife, and that new up-and-coming author, he wrote, oh, what is it called? You've probably read his series. Apparently, all the kids are reading them right now." Her face twisted into a look that said, *though I can't understand why.* "Oh, and Grayson First," she continued. Her face flushed. "And, the *most* exciting guest, Houston Banwell! Can you *believe* that? He—"

"Wait! Grayson First the *actor*?" I interrupted, my pulse fluttering. Grayson was just a few years older than me, extremely famous, and also super hot. Excitement flared inside me, and I reached for my phone, about to text my friends, when my heart dropped.

I wasn't allowed to attend my mother's parties. She said not until I turned sixteen. So it didn't matter that the hottest, coolest actor in the world was coming to my house; I wouldn't be able to meet him. I sighed.

"Yes, he's coming," my mother giggled, and I raised an eyebrow at her. "With his new girlfriend, because he and Hannah Tolin, you know, are *tkk*." My mother clicked her tongue as she made a cutting gesture over her throat. "But I hear he's a lovely man. Except for the whole cheating thing."

"So, anyway, can I go to the movies?" I repeated, wanting to keep her from continuing her recital of the guest list.

"You'll have to do your *chores* first." My mother gave the pointed look she always reserved for me when she said "chores." I don't know why she felt the word needed to be stressed like that because I knew exactly what she was talking about. Taking care of Maddock was the only chore I had. It wasn't an easy thing to forget.

"But can't I do it after the movies today? It will be too late for me to go with my friends if I do the chores first. Maddock will be fine till after."

My statement finally took my mother's attention fully away from her beloved to-do list. She puffed out her chest with the look of an insulted duchess as she stared down at me.

"Young lady. You know the answer to that! Your chores cannot wait. Poor Maddock has been hungry all day, and you need to feed him and clean his *cage*."

Like she cared how dirty her beloved pet's "cage" got.

I glared at my mom, who turned her attention back to her clipboard and was busily sucking on her pen with her perfectly lipsticked lips.

"But I'll miss the movie with my friends!" I insisted, trying to bring her back to our discussion. If I let too much silence fill the conversation, she would forget I existed and wander off to check the menu or something.

"You can go another time with your friends, then," she said, her tone indicating she was already losing interest in what we were discussing.

"But—"

"*Excuse* me! Those lights cannot go there!" My mother burst out, brushing past me to correct the errant man hanging lights along the windows.

I whirled and snatched up my backpack to take up to my bedroom when my mother called to my retreating back, "Mallory, go do your chores, please. Thank you."

Fury bristled inside me, and I bit back the angry words I longed to shout. I was already going! If she had paid any attention to me she would have seen that.

Stomping up the stairs, I kicked a box of lights out of my way, causing it to tip over and almost fall down the stairs. Guilt shot through me as the heavy-set worker with a thick neck beard cried out and caught the box just before it tumbled down the stairs. I was too angry and embarrassed to utter an apology. He shot me a glare as I passed.

"Everbleeder," he hissed under his breath. My face flushed as I continued up the stairs, not sure I'd heard him right, but I shrugged it off as some sort of nerd curse word. He looked like someone who would play *Mages & Magic*. I laughed to myself. That guy would probably die of excitement if he knew what was hidden in our backyard.

# Chapter Two

I stalked down the echoing marble hallway, past the two-story library, office, and my personal game room before coming to my bedroom. I slammed the bedroom doors shut behind me and flumped down on my four-poster bed, glaring at the decorative molding on the ceiling. The curtains on all the windows were open, letting the spring sunshine stream inside, illuminating my desk, the ornate furniture around my fireplace, and reflecting off the vanity mirrors in my ensuite bathroom.

I had expected my mother's answer to be no, but it still made the blood roar in my ears. I stayed out of her way as often as I could, but the one time I wanted her attention, she couldn't give it. It wasn't like Maddock was starving, anyway. He always had extra food. My mother made sure of that.

With a growling sigh, I pulled out my phone and quickly typed, *I can't go today. I have to do my chores right away because my mom is having a party tonight, so I'll be busy all afternoon*, to both Hillary and Felicity.

I immediately got a text back from Felicity.

*Shame*, she had typed. *Everyone else all said they could go. Marcus as well :)*

I stared at that hateful little smiley face, knowing full well that Felicity had pre-typed that reply. She probably didn't even read my full text, her response had come so quickly. Hillary texted me back a moment later, saying she was sorry, but maybe we could do something later tonight, maybe even a sleepover, since my parents would be busy.

My glower melted into a smile, grateful for Hillary. She knew how to cheer me up.

I sat up and stretched, dread creeping into my stomach as I thought about feeding Maddock. It really sucked. I'd been doing it since I was nine, ever since my grandfather had been taken to the nursing home. One would think that doing it for six years would make me used to it, but if anything, it was just wearing me down.

I'd never been able to join any clubs, sports teams, or any other after-school extra curriculars, because Maddock always came first. My mother didn't understand, or even listen, as I tried to explain that I wanted to do normal teenager things while I could. But no. Maddock and the welfare of this family came before my unimportant desires for normalcy.

There was no escaping the imprisonment of my duty. I'd often wondered if I'd be able to go to college at all, or if I'd have to stay at home and be Maddock's caretaker. If I couldn't even go to the movies on a Friday afternoon, my future didn't look good.

With a groan, I slid off my bed. I changed out of my school uniform into old jeans, tennis shoes, and a tee-shirt I wasn't afraid of getting stains on. Pulling my hair up into a messy bun, I wandered down the hallway to the servant stairs that led to the kitchen, and by extension, the back side yard.

As I descended the stairs, the kitchen bustled with hired caterers, and for a moment, I missed our head chef, Tusi, who had been with us for eight years, and always had a plate of his signature nachos and salsa or a smoothie waiting for me after school. Now, a handful of unknown faces dotted the kitchen, and I'd had to make do with packaged after-school snacks.

No one even noticed me slip out of the side door and trudge towards the small, inconsequential garage that was tucked behind the larger, more ornate car garages. I walked around the glassy building that showed off a row of shiny cars inside.

My family owned several luxury cars, the crown jewel being my father's beloved, custom-made Bugatti Aureus. He had commissioned it five years in advance, so that it would be ready for his fortieth birthday. I stared through the glass walls at the gold car in a lineup of over a half-dozen other cars, my faint reflection staring back.

'*We're well-to-do. Every well-to-do family should own a Bugatti,*' he had said. He said that about most of the cars he bought; the sports cars, the vintage, the luxury, and the row of supercars that graced what he affectionately called, "The Car Dealership." The garage I was headed for sat behind The Car Dealership, tucked almost out of sight in the trees. The old building was made up of whitewashed cinder block, and was one of those old-school garages that didn't even come with an electric garage door. I reached into my shirt at the neck and pulled out a small, sturdy chain that held a key at the end of it. I unlocked the heavy padlock and lifted the garage door. Sunlight illuminated the room, no need to switch on the florescent lights to see the enormous refrigerator, chest freezer, and a wall of cabinets, plus a special liquor curio that I was not to touch.

I traipsed over to the four ATV's that were parked in a row along one wall. My friends and I had enjoyed several summers riding these in the woods that surrounded our grounds, but I was sure to keep our fun well away from the forested hill nestled at the far back of the property. I groaned just thinking about it. The hill held more than just unpleasant memories.

On my way to the fridge, I unclipped the special, enormous crates that attached at the front and back of the nearest vehicle.

Expensive steaks, foreign cheeses, crisp vegetables, thick bars of Swiss chocolate, bottles of cider, caviar, white truffles, slabs of tuna, and other delicacies were heaped onto the refrigerator shelves. The cupboards were likewise filled with extravagant snacks. My mother had a grocery service that delivered fresh food nearly every day to our house just for Maddock, and my mother would stock the fridge and cupboards in this garage herself. No way would she let any staffers do it; it would raise questions as to why we had a special garage with food that no one in the house touched.

When my game of Food Tetris was complete and the crate lids could close without crushing anything, I heaved the crates back to the ATV, clipping them in place with care. The one time I hadn't secured them well enough, the crates fell off, bursting open like expensive piñatas, and the scolding I got from Maddock about the soiled and smashed produce alone was enough to ensure I took care to secure everything extra well from then on.

On the other side of the ATV shed was a small path that led to the woods. Across the extensive lawns from my position, I could barely see the men setting up tables at the edge of the pond. I reversed out of the garage and gunned it into the forest. My mother didn't want me running the ATVs over her lawns and tearing tracks into the grass, so I was forced to take the long way around through the tangled woods that encircled our estate. Plus, I had to be careful to sneak away to take care of Maddock when the help wasn't looking, so questions of what I was doing wouldn't arise.

I liked the woods; they weren't perfect, weren't nitpicked at, they were allowed to just *be*. Best of all, my mother didn't step foot in them. My parents owned these woods and several hundred more acres across the hills. Out of curiosity, I once even measured the distance and learned that Maddock's home was almost a mile away. It made me grateful for the ATVs.

I would usually speed around the well-worn tracks through the trees for a bit before heading toward the hill, avoiding my responsibility for as long as I could, but my bad mood wanted this over with as soon as possible. Not to mention, with the party tonight, my mother would skin me alive if I was late retrieving the one thing she really wanted.

The engine whined as I began my ascent up the thickly forested hill, the vehicle's wheels kicking up twigs and dirt as I gave it a little more gas to get up and over the top. Trees extended out in front of me as I crested the hill, but ended in a clearing.

I burst out of the treeline into the warm afternoon sunlight, entering the large, open glade almost the size of a football field. I drove between two weather-worn stone pillars topped with marble Celtic crosses standing like sentinels, guarding the clearing. Six other similar pillars surrounded the edge of the glade, and in the middle of the field stood a small, single-story building.

I guided the ATV up to the door, then killed the engine. Dismounting, I strode up to the building, more of a dilapidated barn, really, and opened the squeaky door.

Inside was what you would expect of an abandoned building that looked like it once held horses. Dusty sunlight swirled through the chinks of the roof, and a few slats in the walls were missing. Cobwebs coated the beams in the ceiling. The floor was the only thing that looked solid, though it too was coated with dust. There were a few stalls still standing, but they were empty except for the stray twig or brown, curled leaf.

Leaving the door open, I went back to the ATV and heaved the crates off the machine one by one, waddling them over to the far left corner, where a small keyhole and an iron ring were inlaid into a trapdoor hidden on the floor. A large Celtic cross was burned into the wood.

Setting down the final crate with a huff, I kneeled down and pulled the key from around my neck again, looping it over my head. I paused, my ear turned toward the dusty floor, listening hard. The band *Queen* played very faintly somewhere below me.

I rapped my knuckles three times on the trapdoor. "Maddock, I'm coming in!" I doubted he heard me, but I still knocked. He wouldn't have an excuse to yell at me.

Unlocking the lock and pulling on the ring, the heavy trapdoor revealed bright lights and a carpeted set of stairs that led deep into the ground. Hoisting the heaviest crate into my arms, I carefully stepped down the stairs, not bothering to close or lock the trapdoor behind me; the lock was more for keeping unwanted guests out than keeping Maddock in.

I counted the steps as I descended because the enormous crate blocked my sight of the illuminated stairs, and I didn't want to misstep and break my neck. Maddock would probably mount my head on the wall in celebration if I did. When I got to twenty-four, there was a small landing and the stairs doubled back on themselves, with a railing keeping me from falling to the floor below. I looked over the banister, scanning the opulent, underground room for Maddock.

The 90-inch flat screen TV mounted above the mantle wasn't on, and the plush couches clustered around the burning gas fireplace were seemingly empty. Many of the pieces of furniture were smaller than the others, as if made for a child. The complete kitchen of white marble and stainless steel gleamed in the bright artificial light from the two crystal chandeliers that hung from each end of the high ceiling. But besides the mountain of dirty dishes piled in the sink, the kitchen was empty as well. Off the kitchen, a door led to a greenhouse atrium, where a terrace overlooked a small pond with a running waterfall.

I noticed crumbs littered the colorful Turkish rugs that lined the shiny wooden floors. More vacuuming for me to do. I exhaled in annoyance, and almost knocked the crate into a framed sketch of four potato grubbers on yellowed canvas. My mother said it was an original Van Gogh. Other priceless pieces of artwork dotted the walls, and real gold statues decorated small tables around the space.

A record player on a table opposite the fireplace was playing "Don't Stop Me Now." Reaching the bottom of the stairs, I quickly glanced into the partially open door off to my right, where Maddock slept; I didn't see him on his four poster bed or at his computer desk, and his bathroom door stood open, dark and empty. Beyond his bedroom was a Jacuzzi tub, workout room, and game room, complete with arcade games and snack bar. He had it better than I did. And he didn't have to deal with my mom very often.

"Maddock?" I called to the empty room. A small hand rose up from a wingback chair facing away from me.

"I brought your daily *basket*," I declared, marching past the chair where Maddock lounged. I stopped briefly by the record player to swipe the record player needle off the vinyl disc, plunging the room into blissful silence. Ignoring his snort of displeasure, I headed toward the kitchen.

"Jolly good," came the thick Irish brogue from the chair.

I stepped behind the counter, setting the crate onto the marble countertop with a huff, and faced the room, looking at the man sitting in his chair.

His hair was as black and sleek as an oil slick, and his personality was just as greasy. His beard was shaved down to just his chin, groomed and curled into a thick ringlet. His face, especially his dark blue eyes, always held a cunning expression, with a broad nose and dimples in his pale cheeks. He was dressed in a red and black silk robe that was tailored to fit his broad frame, with bright green, fluffy house slippers on his feet.

The leprechaun sneered up at me from his chair. "What have you for me today?"

"What you always want," I said, heading back towards the stairs.

"You don't need help, do you?" Maddock asked.

I ignored him as I jogged back up the stairs.

"Good, because I wasn't going to help you anyway," Maddock called after me. I didn't even roll my eyes. I had fallen for that trick only once, the very first time he asked, and ever since, he enjoyed repeating it every once in a while to bother me.

I brought down the second crate and began dumping out the contents, slamming down large sides of salmon and bacon onto the marble countertop.

The dwarfish man slid off his seat and hurried into the kitchen, hopping up onto a stool across from me. Glancing over the contents as I began shoving them into cupboards, he frowned and looked up at me.

"What about my *usquebaugh*?" He glowered. I ignored him and pulled out the bottles of sparkling apple cider from the crate and shook one at his face. Maddock's frown deepened.

I shrugged. "You know my parents don't let me handle the hard liquor. You'll just have to wait until they come for a courtesy visit."

"Well, then, what was the point of you coming at all?" Maddock snapped. Grabbing a chocolate bar, he turned away from the counter muttering, "Useless lump," before going back to his chair and throwing himself into it. He glared at me as he devoured the entire chocolate bar in four bites.

"Good question. Maybe I should've let you starve," I retorted. Like that would ever happen. Though I had to bring him meals everyday, he had a storage room full of canned goods and non-perishable items in case of emergency. But it wouldn't last long. Leprechauns could eat a horse in one sitting if they wanted.

I watched the tiny man with a glare of my own. When I was first introduced to Maddock at eight years old, I had been terrified of him. He had cackled at me as I tried to hide behind my parents. I had been short for my age, and it felt like he had towered over me, even though he was only about three-foot-five. Once we had left his home, I told my mother that I never wanted to go back there: I was scared he would curse my hair to fall out or give me warts. But my mother had told me, rather flippantly, to not be silly, that he couldn't actively hurt those who had captured him.

Though he never did try to hurt me, I had always been wary of Maddock. My grandfather had to go over what we knew about leprechauns several times with me before I felt comfortable knowing we had one in the backyard. My grandpa showed me my great-great-great grandparents' journals, teaching me that leprechauns couldn't use magic to cast spells, exactly, and that if fed well, according to the journals, he had to give up his gold to his captors, fair and square.

I felt better when my grandpa also explained that Maddock couldn't get out of his home, as the magic of the marble pillars kept him bound. My grandpa had even started teaching me how to use magic, and I studied from the family heirloom spellbooks my parents had, but I had to promise not to talk about magic with anyone outside the family. I was fine with that, as I could only work spells when I was near Maddock to access the magic he exuded. I couldn't show off any magical spells to my friends even if I wanted to.

I had studied leprechauns even more when I learned that Maddock had requested that I come to serve him after my grandfather was sent away. My parents were thrilled, and I was terrified. However, as I aged—and grew taller—my fear of him turned to disgust, and now he was nothing more than a pest. A pest that liked to insult me whenever possible.

Once, I was stupid enough to ask him why he didn't look like the cartoon leprechauns that we saw around St. Patrick's day, with orange hair, a cheery smile, and buckled boots.

"Are all Irish people red-headed?" Maddock had snapped.

"No," I'd squeaked, afraid of answering wrong.

"Then I guess not all leprechauns are redheads, either, ye great buffoon."

I had felt stupid then, and had cried at his name calling, but my skin had toughened up since then.

I brought myself back to the present, and my grip tightened on the sides of the crate. "What needs to be done? You better be grateful I came at all. I could've gone with—" I stopped myself. He would only torture me more if he knew what I'd missed out on. But I'd said too much even then, and Maddock eyed me with a sly smile curling his mouth. I ignored his knowing grin as I continued stocking the fridge and freezer with the new groceries. He only had a few leftovers from the load I had brought yesterday on the shelves.

"Ach, did the wee lass have plans? Shame, shame. Well, I'll make sure you're extra busy, so you don't have to dwell on what you're missing. Isn't that thoughtful of me?" he asked, his tone dripping with saccharine sweetness.

"How gracious," I drawled, not wanting to show my temper; it would only entertain the lousy little man.

"Hmmm, what can my little servant do for me today?" he asked, stroking his beard in mock deliberation.

While he made hemming and hawing noises, I looked at the clock on the oven. My phone didn't get reception down here, so I was spared receiving any other gleeful texts from Felicity. At least until I left this cavernous basement. Maddock had a landline phone that only rang my parent's special cell phone number if he had demands to make.

I sighed and looked back at Maddock, who was still twirling his beard.

"Could you hurry this up? I'm sure you want me to be out of your sight as much as I do," I snapped.

"Indeed. So, I'll need the dishes washed, and the rugs beaten, the bathroom scrubbed, my plants watered, the floor swept, and I'll need a massage."

"But I gave you a massage yester—"

"A deep tissue massage," the small man amended, a pleased smile on his thin lips.

I stared stone-faced at him, but underneath my emotionless mask, my blood was boiling.

His skin was tough, and I hated touching him, but he was particularly fond of massages, and when my mother found this out, I was forced to take several summer courses in massage therapy to keep Maddock happy and more willing to part with his gold.

"Do you really have so few enjoyments that you have to punish me?" I asked with thinly veiled annoyance. He smiled his leprechaun leer back up at me, meeting my glare with indifference.

"Now, now, I need your service with a smile, or I'll have to let your parents know I'm unhappy with your attitude."

I hitched a horrific smile onto my face. "I loathe you, Maddock," I said as sweetly as I could, baring my teeth.

"I detest you, too, lass. And don't you ever believe anything else."

*Hateful little imp*, I thought, turning away as the smirking man began humming "Whistle While You Work."

# Chapter Three

Once I had finished all the chores Maddock had for me—including the deep tissue massage while he watched his favorite police procedural, *Murderous Intents*—I shuffled into the kitchen, grabbed a bag of chips, and plopped down into a chair opposite the leprechaun.

"Is that all?" I asked with a groan, having beaten and scrubbed all of the fury out of me. Now I just ached and wanted to go home. I popped open the chip bag and grabbed a small handful, munching the salty snack with a sigh. Maddock, who had been paging through an album of records, lifted his head at the sound of crunching potato chips and thrust a hand out at me. Rolling my eyes, I handed over the bag, where he started stuffing fistfuls of chips into his mouth. Salt and potato crumbs tumbled down his robe to the rug below.

"Careful, you little imp. I just cleaned this floor," I complained, frowning over at him, though too tired to really get upset.

"Well, it'll give you something to do tomorrow, won't it," Maddock retorted through his bulging lips.

"Can I go?" I asked. He ignored me as he continued his assault on the chip bag. This was a game he played sometimes, testing my patience, especially if he knew I was eager to leave. If he didn't supply our family fortune, I would've tipped his chair over.

I watched with an impassive expression as he contemplated eating a large green chip in one hand, or a handful of small chips in the other. He compromised by cramming both handfuls into his incongruously large mouth.

Watching him, I felt a slight pang in my stomach as my thoughts jumped to my grandfather. On a day like today, I wished I could do what my grandfather had often joked about, and just tear down the pillars outside the hut and let Maddock free. But that was before my parents had packed my grandfather off to that nursing home, claiming he was old and a danger to himself. And so off he was shipped to the old folks home, where he died three years later.

That had been a dark time in my life, as my grandpa had been one of my best friends, and I had been set up to take care of Maddock in his stead.

After my grandfather had passed on, I wondered more and more if Maddock was more trouble than he was worth. While I wasn't sure of the exact amount, I knew we had enough money to provide a million-dollar lifestyle for several generations down the line. But he had been in the family for over a hundred years, as my parents would proudly tell me every time I complained about Maddock. He was an heirloom. They found him an absolute treat, but that was only because they didn't have to deal with him every day as I did.

I often wondered what it would be like if my family ever lost Maddock and had to enter the real world. My father, on whose side Maddock belonged, worked a lot to expand what Maddock gave us, and my mother, once she was married to my father, never worked a day in her life. Who would when you got thousands of dollars worth of gold every day, sweat free?

But if we were to lose Maddock, what would happen? Would it make our family stronger? Or would it tear us further apart? Maybe we'd move to Ireland to hunt for another leprechaun.

I shook my head. I didn't know what scenario scared me more. I was used to being alone, with no siblings to annoy me, and I had learned many hard things about life despite my family's wealth. I couldn't be like my parents—thrilled at the idea of having a constant source of gold—because they didn't ever have to lift a finger to acquire it. I did. I saw Maddock for what he really was: a greedy, selfish, lazy chore that would probably turn on us the second he got the chance. My parents only saw an eccentric little pet who supplied them with their hearts' desire.

When I met my more down-to-earth friends at school, I began to learn not to put too much stock in money to be happy. While my friends were fairly well-off themselves, wealth didn't rule them like it did my parents. I often wondered if it was unethical, what we were doing, but my parents would point out that several times they asked Maddock if he wanted to leave, and he said no. He always replied that he was comfortable and happy with his living arrangement. And it wasn't like they were keeping him in a dungeon, after all.

But I wasn't so sure. Wasn't a leprechaun's greatest possession his gold? And weren't we taking it from him, ever so slowly? That had to cause some burning resentment.

If it did, he didn't show it to my parents. I usually got the brunt of his revenge via his sharp tongue.

"What's that sour look on your face?" Maddock asked, interrupting my thoughts.

"Nothing," I snapped, then relented, the ache to talk about my grandpa with someone that also knew him burning in my chest. "Just thinking of my grandpa."

Maddock snorted. "Crazy old codger. He was going soft in his old age."

"What would you know about it? You don't care enough about humans to learn anything about us." Indignation bubbled up inside me as I sat up in my chair, glaring at Maddock, who stared evenly back. "My grandfather was never crazy. He was one of the best men I ever knew. I hate my parents for sending him into that old person's home. He didn't deserve it. He wasn't dangerous."

"Yes he was, in a way." Maddock replied, clicking his tongue as he brushed potato chips from his robe, the bag now empty.

With a sigh, Maddock stretched and yawned. "Okay, you can leave now. My doctor TV show is almost on."

"Anything else you need or want?" I groaned, standing.

"No, you may go."

"Not so fast," I said. He was trying to sidestep giving me what I came for, but I was too used to his antics to be annoyed. "Give it up."

Grumbling, Maddock slid off his chair and went to the fireplace. Opening the screen doors, he reached up into the chimney, his head and shoulders disappearing from view. When he withdrew, he held a handful of very large, lumpy gold nuggets. They glinted dully in the artificial light. Reaching into my pocket, I pulled out a folded drawstring bag and held it open. With the familiar look of pain in his eyes, Maddock slowly lowered the bullion into my bag, and

I tightened the drawstring. It felt like it was probably over three pounds worth.

"Go," Maddock growled, turning away from me. This was the worst part. I always felt so guilty and uncomfortable with his angry dismissal. I was taking his gold, supposedly the only possession leprechauns cared for.

One of the great mysteries of leprechauns that I'd never learned, as it wasn't in any of the journals, was where his gold came from, and how long it would last. My parents, grandparents, and great-great-grandparents had been taking gold from him for generations. What would happen if he ran out? I gathered up the empty crates and hurried past him, wanting to get away from his reproachful gaze as fast as I could.

I tried to alleviate my unease by reminding myself that it was always cool seeing where he would pull the gold out. He'd done the fireplace a couple of times, but most often he would leave the room to get the gold. The coolest was when he pulled great big nuggets out of a transparent glass he had gotten from his cabinet.

The sun was low in the sky as I emerged from the basement apartment, double-checking to make sure I locked the trap door, then hurried to my ATV. I got the crates secured before I pulled out my phone. There were a few texts from Hillary, inviting me over to hang out.

Crossing my fingers, I dialed my mom's number. Hopefully, she would think it was someone important calling and actually answer.

My mother did answer her phone, but she sounded harassed.

"Yes?" she snapped.

"I'm done with my chores now. Can I go over—"

"Did you get Goldie fed?" she demanded.

"Yes, I fed Goldie," I replied, rolling my eyes.

"Good. Get home quickly. I want everything put away before the party."

"Okay, but—"

She ended the call before I could say another word. Shoving the phone into my pocket, I started the engine, gritting my teeth. Maybe she would listen to me if I threatened to throw the gold into the pond.

# Chapter Four

By the time I got the ATV put away and the garage locked up, I could hear my mom's shrieks emanating from inside the house. Obviously, the flowers on display weren't angled the right way, or a waiter had spilled something. I rushed toward the house, and as I came around the Car Dealership, my heart jumped into my throat, choking back my startled cry. Several young catering servers stood outside the kitchen door, smoking. I'd never seen workers taking a break outside of the house before. The servers immediately stopped talking when I came into view, their expressions almost hostile. I quickly hid the lumpy bag of gold behind my back as I avoided their glares, ducking my head as I hurried past them into the house, following the shrill keening. I shook off the chills of shock, worried for a moment that those servers were up to something, but I refocused myself. It was nothing; they just startled me, especially when I had a lot of secret gold in my hand. Wanting to unload the nuggets, I knew I just had to follow the screams. That's where my mother would be.

Sure enough, I found my mother in the foyer, yelling at some of the waiters who were hastily mopping up puddles of water coming from an ice sculpture of a mermaid.

The foyer was gorgeous; soft lights hung from the banisters, which were wreathed in vibrant greenery, and small fairy lights glowed underneath crisp white tablecloths. Flowers were everywhere. The fabric that hung from the towering ceiling drifted softly in the light breeze from the open doors. My mother was already dressed in an evening gown of soft cream and lavender, her hair done up in an elaborate knot at the nape of her neck. Diamonds glittered at her throat, ears, and wrists, and her makeup was flawless, despite her red face. Her words became clearer as I neared the commotion.

"This is what happens when you're stuck with second-rate service!" she was screeching. "Our guests will be here soon and we can't have a leaking mermaid here to greet them!"

"Mom!" I shouted so she would hear me over the noise she was making. She whipped around, eyes fiery and mouth widening, ready to scream some more, but when she saw me, her angry expression dissolved into a look of delight.

"Sweetie!" She rushed towards me, but paused for half a moment to roar at the waiters over her shoulder, "Get that ice mess out of here!" She placed her hands on my back in a motherly way, and steered me through the hallway between the two staircases, into the rooms beyond.

We entered into the kitchen, where platters of food were set up, and people were bustling around, prepping for arrival. My mother piloted me into one of the pantries that held food storage, and shut and locked the door behind us. A hidden door in the pantry led down into our wine cellar, and I followed my mother down the stone steps, taking care to shut and lock this door as well. I stepped into the brightly lit, chilly wine cellar, a sweet smell intermingling with the mustiness of the underground room.

The cellar was enormous, like many rooms in our house, and shelves upon shelves of wines and spirits lined the walls. Shelves ran down the middle of the room, creating several rows of narrow, wine-lined corridors.

We went down one of the passages, making our way to the very back of the cellar. Several barrels of old-fashioned ale sat hidden along the back wall. My mother reached up to a wine shelf above the barrels and pressed a button hidden there. One of the barrels was a decoy, sitting on a platform that rose slightly and swung outward to reveal a set of stairs.

My ancestors loved their trapdoors and secret rooms.

We both headed down into a long hallway that had a circular metal door at the end. My mother hurried to the vault, where she entered a code and had her face scanned. With a beep, the heavy, reinforced steel door opened. Automatic lights clicked on, revealing stairs that descended into a large open room. The middle of the space consisted of several desks with computers. The vault also served as a panic room, so another door led to a room with beds and a full kitchen. The rest of the space was filled with cabinets, drawers, and shelves that housed all of our priceless artifacts, family heirlooms, document files, and of course, mounds of gold.

When the vault door was shut safely behind us, my mother turned to me.

"Well, let's see what we have," she breathed. Every time I came into the vault with my mother, I felt like I was entering a dragon's lair, my mother guarding her hoard with a hungry look. I slapped the bag of gold into her hand, and my mother's smile sparkled.

"Ooh, he gave you a good haul this time. He must've been very satisfied!" my mother cooed, digging into the bag and inspecting the nuggets she pulled out. The yellow light they reflected nowhere near matched the gleam in my mother's eyes.

"Oh, that little darling," she said, admiring every nugget. "Don't you think leprechauns make the best house pets?" she chuckled. "Let me just take them over," she trilled. I watched her click over to a desk which was outfitted with a scale and other instruments for measuring the gold. Putting the gold on the desk, I saw her pause, as if debating whether she had time to weigh and document the dimensions of the nuggets. She seemed to have decided against it, and instead wrote a note, no doubt chronicling the date and time we'd gotten this particular mound of gold.

A sense of disgust rose up in me as she patted the gold fondly, then sashayed back over to me.

"Well, you did wonderfully." Her nose wrinkled as she stared at my sweaty, dusty shirt. "But you better shower before the party starts, dear. I had Hye pick you out the prettiest party dress—"

"You what?" I gasped, interrupting her.

"What?" she asked, her expression blank.

"I have a party dress?" I repeated, mouth agape. "I'm going to the party?"

"Didn't I tell you?" my mom asked, her own frown of confusion turning into a smile.

I shook my head, and my mother let out a small squeal, bouncing on her toes. "Your father and I just figured it was time for your "coming-out-in-society" moment, because, after all, you're going to want to have contacts to rub shoulders with to carry on the family—"

"Can I go hang out at my friend's house instead of going to the party?" I interrupted again. I had to disrupt her ramblings, or I would never be able to tell my mother what I wanted. My mother stopped and looked at me.

"You don't want to come to the party?" she gaped, her tone dismayed.

I wanted to say, "Not really," but the look on my mother's face stopped me. Her eyes had gone all wide, and her full lips were beginning to frown. It looked pathetic.

"I knew you had a celebrity crush on Grayson First. That's why I invited him, so you could meet him!" she said, the hurt expression deepening.

"You did?" I asked, my turn to stare. Realizing my mother was planning on my attendance and took care to invite those she thought I might be interested in made me feel . . . I didn't know how to feel.

"Yes. You're growing up now, and it's time for you to meet people in society, at *our* level, who could help you with your future."

I stared at my mother. Were we really talking about my future down in our secret vault that held the gold of our mythical leprechaun? This was getting weird, even for me. We had never once mentioned my future before. Mostly because I was too afraid to broach the subject, afraid they would tell me I was to be Maddock's caretaker until I died.

"Well, okay," I said slowly. "Could I . . . invite my friends?"

"Oh, honey," she said, her nose wrinkling again. "No, I don't think Harmony should come."

My hopeful expression dropped immediately. She couldn't even get my friends' names correct.

"Not this time," my mother continued, "But you'll like it, I promise. And the dress is so pretty." My mom gave me a genuine smile and put a hand on my shoulder. "And I am grateful to you for taking care of Maddock. I know it isn't easy. I tried it a few times, when you weren't old enough, but he would chase me out. He likes you."

"Seriously?" I stared, a smile tugging at my mouth. Was she just saying that? There was no way Maddock *liked* me, but maybe he requested me because he thought I would be easier to boss around.

My mom nodded, smiling.

I felt like I was in the twilight zone. My mom? Thanking me for taking care of Maddock? What was going on?

My mother turned awkward, pulling her hand away from my shoulder, and she began picking microscopic bits of lint from her dress, her heels bouncing.

"In fact, because you've done such a good job, I was hoping we could, I dunno, plan a girls' trip, just the two of us. Once school is out for summer."

"Really?" I rasped. A girls' trip, just me and her?

"We could go to St. Barts, or a place you've been wanting to visit? And we could plan your Sweet Sixteen while we're there, too." She bit her lip, her expression bordering on hopeful as she watched me. When I stared blankly at her as I tried to process what she said, she shook her head. "Well, we can discuss it later, when you come to the meeting with your father and I—" Her phone rang from the small clutch she held in her hand, interrupting her.

"Oh! What time is it?" she gasped, the warm moment between us vanishing. "We've got a party to go to! What have I been doing, wasting time?" She opened the clutch purse and pulled out a jangling cell phone.

*Yes, wasting time* almost *having a meaningful conversation with your daughter,* I thought, exhaling. My mother started for the door as she answered her cell phone.

"Mallory! Come on, let's go!" she called, waving at me. I hurried after her, my mother closing the vault door behind us.

After a quick shower, another surprise came as my mother introduced me to her personal stylist, a beautiful Korean woman with short-cropped hair and a wavy mohawk dyed a soft lavender. We spent several minutes going over how we should do my hair and makeup, with my mother laughing with Hye as they bickered about the best option. Nervousness began to squirm in my stomach. This must be an important party if my mother was releasing her death grip on Hye's talent.

Once a style was decided on, Hye applied my makeup with amazing speed and smudge-less perfection. She then dried my hair and braided a crown across my head, with soft curls framing my face and trailing down my back. She was done in little over a half an hour. I gaped like an idiot at my transformation reflected in the mirror.

"Hye, I love it," I said, staring at her in the reflection of the mirror and twirling a soft finger around a curl. She smiled as she began packing her instruments away in a stained, bulky makeup bag.

"Good," she said, smiling. "Your mom said if you need me for anything, you can call me. As long as I'm not busy," she added, winking. A smile grew on my face as I stared at her through the mirror.

"You'll have to teach me how to do this stuff," I insisted.

"Sure thing, kiddo." She pulled the chair away from the vanity. "We better get that dress on. Guests will be arriving."

She helped me slip into the gown, a gold dress with a slight shimmer, and helped zip up the back.

"You look gorgeous," Hye said, standing back to admire her handiwork.

"Thank you." I felt pretty. The dress gave me curves that weren't even there.

"Well, if you'll excuse me, I've got to go get ready for a hot date," Hye said, winking again. I nodded. Even though my mom loved Hye and couldn't live without her skills, there was no way Hye would be invited to one of my mom's prestigious parties, and I had a sneaking suspicion that it was because my mother was afraid of someone figuring out my mom's secret to her flawless look.

We left the room together, but split at one of the hallways, where Hye went to go down a servants' staircase, and I headed for the double staircase leading to the ballroom-foyer.

I was descending just as cars began to pull up, and my mother was striding nervously around the room, quadruple-checking that everything was in place. My father, who I hadn't seen for weeks, was snitching hors d'oeuvres from passing platters.

"Ah, Mallory!" my mother called, catching sight of me as I reached the bottom of the stairs and waving me over to her. "Hurry, hurry! They're here! Clark! Stop that!" She slapped my father on the shoulder, an exasperated smile on her face as he stuffed a canapé into his mouth.

Upon seeing me, my father's expression broke into a smile, and he gave me a goofy wave with a happy call of, "Hi, Peanut!" I laughed as we all lined up before the doors, where Santeri was standing, waiting to open them for the guests.

My father leaned behind my mother slightly. "You look so pretty, Mallory," he whispered.

"Thanks, Dad." I cast him a happy grin. Maybe this party wouldn't be so bad.

"After the party, I have some gifts waiting for you in my study." He smiled.

"Thank you." My dad always brought back gifts from wherever his "business" took him, and the gifts were always extravagant and plentiful. To be honest, I never knew what his business even was. I just knew that my mother was always happy to see him. And to see what he reported back about our financial growth.

He nodded and straightened back up, his face composed as he waited for the guests to enter. My mother gave the signal, and Santeri opened the doors just as several couples reached the front steps.

My mother instantly became the most charismatic person on the entire planet. It was amazing to watch. Her face split into a genuinely delighted smile as she greeted the two couples that came inside, calling them by their names. She gave kisses to everyone and then brought them over to us.

"You remember my husband, Clark," my mother said to the two couples, who all nodded and took turns shaking my dad's hand.

"And this is my daughter, Mallory," my mother said, finally turning to me. "Mallory, this is Senator Mitch Michaelson and his wife, Suzy." I shook hands with a stocky man and a plump woman in their early fifties before they drifted further into the house, accepting champagne and small shrimps on crackers from roving platters.

"And this," my mother said, an excited glow in her cheeks, turning to the next couple, "Is Houston Banwell, and his wife, Penina. They're the founders of Banwell Industries. They make, well, almost everything!"

I had seen Mr. and Mrs. Banwell in several magazines, and had even had discussions about them in my economics class at school. From what I remembered, they were super wealthy, super elite, and ran several organizations and charities along with their many other enterprises. They were a handsome couple; Mrs. Banwell, who looked striking in a bright orange dress that complimented her dark skin, contrasted with Mr. Banwell, who was pale in a dark suit that showed off his trim figure, his brunette hair smoothed back. Both were tall and fit, and looked to be in their early forties. Mr. Banwell took my hand with a warm smile.

"A pleasure to meet you," he said.

I swallowed and tried to make my handshake as firm as possible.

"The pleasure is mine, sir," I parroted back. Those etiquette lessons my mom made me take weren't going to go away unless my mother saw *some* proof that they were turning me from an uncouth barbarian to a refined rich person.

Mr. Banwell smiled and looked at my mother, who was just finishing shaking Mrs. Banwell's hand. "What a little lady you have here, Grace," he said with a wink. I hid a frown behind a plastered-on smile, though I felt indignation color my face. I wasn't seven years old.

"She should meet my daughter, Ahni," Mr. Banwell continued. "I think they'd get along well. She's a little older. She will be getting into Cambridge next fall."

My mom looked like she might faint. She nodded eagerly and shook Mr. Banwell's hand again. "That would be lovely. We'll have to get together when your daughter is on break."

I almost laughed. There was no way a college student was going to want to hang with a fifteen-year-old like me. I had no doubt, coming from a family like the Banwells, that the daughter was probably all sorts of rich snob.

My family may have been filthy rich, but we paled in comparison to the Banwells, and everyone knew it. I was surprised my mother had been able to get them to come.

The Banwells moved out of the way. My mother had so many stars in her eyes at the thought of having a real relationship with people like the Banwells that she almost forgot that other, maybe-less-important-but-still-important people were arriving. Seeing the amount of cars arriving out front, I realized with a sinking stomach how long and boring this party was actually going to be.

Waves of people came inside. My mother introduced my dad to those he didn't know, and she introduced me to everyone, but I soon lost track of who went with what name. The one name and face I did remember was Grayson First.

He came swaggering in with a stunning woman clinging to his arm. My breath caught. Grayson filled out a tux nicely, with his dark hair slicked casually back, a small rose pinned to his lapel. I recognized his new girlfriend, Sofia Devon, a reality TV star, and someone who I thought was kind of trashy compared to Grayson.

Upon seeing Grayson, my face grew warm. The high cheek-bones, the cleft chin, the razor-edge jaw; my friends would die if they knew I was about to meet and talk with Grayson First! While he was busy shaking hands with my parents, I snuck a few photos of him with my phone that I'd kept in the stealthy pocket of my evening gown. Maybe he'd even take a selfie with me.

He shook my parents hands, making small, polite conversation, and then my mother directed Grayson and his girlfriend's attention to me.

"This is my daughter, Mallory," my mother said. A million things I could say flashed in my head, each sounding more stupid than the last. But Grayson flashed a smile at me then glanced away before I could think of something cool.

"Cute kid," he said, looking around the room, not paying me any more attention.

*Kid?* The blush bloomed hotter on my face, and embarrassment tightened around my lungs. Grayson First was only a few years older than me! I wanted to sink through the floor. He saw someone he knew, waved, and took his girlfriend across the room.

Immediately, I was done with this party. All my childish fantasies of catching Grayson's eye and having him fall in love with me at first sight made me want to shrivel up into nothing.

I wished Hillary were with me. I wouldn't be so embarrassed—or the youngest person here—if I had my friends to giggle the awkwardness off with. But I would have to endure alone, as the list of people went on and on. It was nearly an hour before the people stopped coming, and both my parents dispersed, going to talk to guests, leaving me standing alone by the open front doors.

Turning to face the foyer, I was amazed by how many people were in here; and that wasn't counting the people that had spilled out onto the terrace and lawns. I stared at the crowds, and a familiar, shy feeling threatened to overwhelm me. The thought of trying to break into a conversation with any of these people was not only scary, but embarrassing. I obviously held nothing of interest for these people. I would have nothing to do for hours except stand around like a wallflower in my own house.

I slipped up to my mother, who was busily chatting with a severe-looking woman in a plunging evening dress. No one, not even my mother, paid attention to me until her conversation ended and she turned to see who else she could corner and coerce into speaking with her.

"Can I eat and then hang out with my friends? They're waiting for me," I said when she noticed me.

"You don't want to chat with Grayson? I saw him looking at you!" she said, turning me to face Grayson, who was surrounded by at least four different women. His girlfriend was nowhere to be seen. Probably off somewhere, stuffing her purse with some of our priceless heirlooms, like I'd seen her do on *The Millionaire Match*. Surprisingly, she didn't get kicked off the show because of it, and instead won. Then she rejected the millionaire bachelor. My friends had talked about it for weeks.

"I don't want to," I said, frowning at Grayson. "I want to go be with my friends."

Pressure increased on my arm where my mother was holding me, with her pleasant expression somewhat frozen, as she whispered through the corner of her tight smile, "Mallory, you need to not be so selfish, and do your part for this family." She immediately smiled at a passing couple, mouthing pleasantries. When the couple was gone, my mom smoothed the front of her gown, glancing around the room to see if anyone else was nearby, listening in. "We need you to start networking, get your foot in the door with Houston, or Grayson. I thought you wanted to start growing up!"

I stared at my mother. She nibbled her lower lip as she stared about the room, as though anxious to catch someone else's attention. I felt sick, realizing my mother wanted me to turn into *her*.

Now that I was getting older, in her mind it was time for me to have connections, contacts, and bigger, richer friends. My friends' families were all pretty well off, but they were like my family was compared to the Banwells: galaxies apart.

As I looked around at all the people here—every single one trying to outdo each other with their influence, clothes, or money—rebellion welled up in me. I didn't want to be with people like this. Even though I was the only teenager here, I was barely looked at. I was graced a small glance, just so as not to offend the hostess, but other than that, I was a nobody; not worthy of a mention in a future conversation. Just because I was young and hadn't made my social impact yet, I didn't matter. And I would *have* to make a social impact in some way to gain their attention. It was like high school, but even worse somehow.

And even if I did gain the attention of these people, they wouldn't be my real friends, like Hillary was. From what I'd seen on entertainment news, one fall from grace, these types of friends abandoned you. I would have to keep up appearances. That was why my mother threw parties that sometimes emptied the vault of gold: you had to continue to show up and show off, or you'd be forgotten.

Which was why my mother had invited me. She wanted me to start socializing with influential people, and Houston and Grayson were some of the more influential, or at least popular, people here. I remembered my mother once saying, "Influence is more powerful than gold."

I'd found that hard to believe at the time, but now, being here, seeing all these extremely influential people, and how they treated each other versus those they didn't see as very important, made it click.

Our gold would run out one day. Maddock couldn't possibly produce gold like this forever, and we needed to get our foot in the Banwell penthouse door before that day came.

Disgust welled up in me.

I didn't want these fancy connections. This social ladder only led to a razor's edge of public opinion. I wanted real friends that would pull me to safety from that edge.

"I'm going to Hillary's," I muttered in disgust, but my mother didn't hear me as she waved at someone and left my side.

The smell of passing platters made my stomach grumble, so before going to change out of my party dress, I slipped into the kitchen. I grabbed an awaiting plate of filet oscar that was probably someone's order and hurried up one of the servant staircases. I ate on my bed, in my party dress, not caring how mad my mom would be if she found out.

As I was setting aside the plate on my bedside table, eager to change and head over to Hillary's, I heard drunken giggling outside my door. At that moment, my bedroom door was flung open, and a teenage boy and girl a few years older than I was, dressed in catering uniforms, stumbled through the door. Upon seeing me, the pair immediately sobered. The girl let out a small terrified giggle and fled the room, while the guy, who I recognized from earlier, who had been outside smoking and had glared at me, slurred over an apology before quickly leaving, shutting the door behind him.

I ground my teeth in annoyance. I hated these parties for more than one reason—and drunk partiers and caterers alike wandering my house, not letting me have any privacy—was one of them.

Well, I would leave this all behind. I quickly changed into jeans and a t-shirt, and as Hillary had mentioned a sleepover, I quickly stuffed a backpack with my pajamas and my phone charger just in case the sleepover actually happened. And sleepovers needed snacks.

I slipped through a connecting door from my room into the game room. Beyond several game tables and a wall of arcade machines, a small pantry and fridge held expensive snacks and drinks. I filled my backpack with more snacks than I and my friends could ever eat, and then, not wanting to accidentally run into my mother by going back downstairs, I climbed out my bedroom window, using the small fire escape hidden by climbing vines.

I leapt down to the lawn, then paused, wondering how I would get to Hillary's. I would've asked Santeri for a ride, but he was busy trying to direct the waiters, valets, and other hired butlers while the party was in full swing. I would have to ride my bike.

Going to the garages, I dug my bike out from behind the many cars and wheeled it to the door, considering how to leave. Cutting through the woods would be best, so that my mom/security cameras wouldn't see me leaving down the long drive and stop me before I even left the driveway. I followed one of the ATV trails through the woods that led to a gate on the far side of the property, leading to the main road.

Opening the gate with fingerprint technology, I pulled my bike out onto a neighboring road and peddled toward Hillary's house, feeling free as I left the party behind.

# CHAPTER FIVE

A pillow in the face woke me, and I sat up with a gasping snort, having forgotten momentarily where I was. Paz and Hillary both started laughing, their hair mussed and snarled from sleep.

Last night had been a whirlwind. When I had arrived at Hillary's house, Paz was already there, and they filled me in on what had happened at the movies that afternoon. The new Grayson First movie had been amazing, apparently, but I had my own news of Grayson First to share with them. And while they were excited as I shared my pictures of Grayson with them, I was way more interested in the fact that Marcus was not, in fact, dating Felicity, despite her best effort at the theater.

In a fit of confidence at hearing that, I had declared that I would fight to get to him first. Paz had offered to help me download the Krazy Ex app to find out where he was. Her sisters used it all the time on their exes, but it was a pretty shady, not well-known app. All we needed was his cell phone number, which Paz had sneakily gotten from Felicity's phone. She suggested that we could use it to find out where Marcus was and go hang out with him, but as none of us could drive, and my chauffeur was busy, that plan fell through. Besides, the thought of using such a sketchy app to spy on my crush made me feel icky. It would definitely be intruding on Marcus' privacy, as he hadn't given me his location. However, I did take his phone number, and, telling myself fortune favored the bold, I texted Marcus first.

When he had texted me back, the shocked squealing lasted for a good five minutes. Especially when he told me that he'd missed me at the movie, which only made me feel more courageous. I ended up texting him all night until we fell asleep in Hillary's theater room around two in the morning.

"What time is it?" I mumbled, stretching the soreness from my back.

Hillary searched through the candy wrappers and pillows, pulling out her cell phone from the mess.

"Oh wow," she yawned, "it's almost one-thirty in the afternoon. And my phone is about to die. I forgot to plug it in."

I searched the slumber party mess for my own phone and finally found that it had been pushed under one of the couches. I pressed the button to check if I had any messages, but the screen remained black, reflecting my wild hair and sleep-starved eyes.

"Mine's dead," I said, trying to run my fingers through my hair, but stopping when I realized I would need a brush.

"Mine too," Paz said, flumping back down on her sleeping bag.

"Ha, my phone is the survivor," Hillary said, pumping her phone in the air.

"Only because you aren't as popular as Mal and me," Paz teased. "We got texts from the outside world."

"Your mom doesn't count, Paz," Hillary shot back, and Paz made a face, then laughed, throwing a macadamia cluster at her.

"What do you guys want for breakfast?" Hillary asked, dodging the chocolate projectile and getting to her feet, kicking a pillow toward Paz.

"Blueberry muffins," Paz said immediately, catching the pillow and adding it to the pile under her head as I pawed through my pile of belongings, looking for my phone charger.

"Breakfast? Shouldn't we be having lunch? Licorice," I called, and Paz threw a half-eaten licorice stick at me.

"I'll go look for muffin mix. But if we don't have any, we'll just have to have waffles," Hillary warned as she left the room, calling through the house for her mom.

"Did Marcus text you again?" Paz asked the ceiling, munching a rope of licorice.

"I dunno. I'm plugging in my phone now."

My stomach fluttered nervously. What if he had texted me this morning? If things kept going on like this, maybe he would want to hang out. My status as a girlfriend could be in the near future. The thought made my hands tremble.

Stepping over Paz, who was still sprawled on her sleeping bag, I plugged my phone into the charger. A second later, a light came on in the screen, telling me the phone was now charging, but didn't have enough juice to turn on yet.

"Hey, come help me make these muffins!" Hillary called down the stairs, and I could hear her younger siblings brawling over which channel to watch upstairs. Every time I came over to Hillary's house, I always came away glad I was an only child.

Grumbling, Paz heaved herself up from her bed and got to her feet. Taking a hair tie from her wrist, she tossed back her inky black hair and twisted it up into a large messy bun.

"You coming, Mal?" Paz asked, her voice muffled from holding the hair tie between her teeth.

"Yeah, just a sec. I, uh, just want to check if there are any messages from my mom," I said, glancing at my phone; it was still too early for the main screen to wake up.

"Ha, yeah right. Your *mom*."

"Shut up and go help Hillary with your muffins," I said, trying not to blush.

Laughing, Paz stepped over the mess and I heard her charge up the stairs.

Small butterflies danced in my stomach as I watched the screen finally have enough power to pull up the phone functions.

My heart rose when I saw I had multiple notifications for messages and missed calls, but the moment was less than a heartbeat, and then my heart dropped to the bottom of my stomach as I saw that all of the messages and calls were from my parents' numbers. Probably to yell at me for not taking care of Maddock yet this morning.

I opened the message app, where I had over twenty messages from my mother. Most of the texts were asking where I was and why I wasn't answering, but several of them didn't make sense, saying I was going to miss the meeting right after the party.

*Meeting?* I rubbed at the tension in my forehead as I stared at the text. *What meeting?*

I bit my lip as I remembered that last night, right before leaving the vault, my mom had mentioned a meeting for me to attend, but since she had been interrupted by something much more important—her phone and the party—she didn't tell me the meeting was going to be right after the party. It wasn't my fault I missed it, but I still felt dread well up in my stomach.

The rest of the messages told me to get home immediately.

My stomach twisted. Just my luck.

My mom had definitely realized I was gone, but I doubted she knew where. She never remembered my friends' names.

I checked the time of the last message. It had come in around three-thirty in the morning, around the time my friends and I had fallen asleep. My parents were having a meeting *that* early in the morning? What the heck about? Their parties usually ended around two in the morning.

Maybe the meeting had been about Maddock. Maybe they were finally taking my complaints to heart and we were selling him? No, my parents wouldn't do that. Maybe they were getting another leprechaun. That would make more sense. Either way, I'd better get back home. I was in huge trouble, if the texts my mom and dad had sent were any indication, and staying out longer would only make things worse.

I unplugged my phone and began throwing all my clothes into my bag. It was going to be a pain lugging it home on my bike. Riding to Hillary's was a breeze, since she lived downhill from me. I considered sending Santeri back for it when I got home, but I didn't know if I would get the chance to speak to him; he could be gone dropping my father off into the city or airport or wherever else my father went.

Heaving the backpack over my shoulder, I hurried up the stairs, through Hillary's large open concept living room and kitchen, where Hillary was shouting at her brothers to turn down the cartoon bunny that was screaming at the top of its lungs from the living room flat screen.

"Hillary, I have to go," I shouted, wincing at the noise of the TV. "My mom called and wants me home."

"Aw, you can't even stay for breakfast?" she cried over the din of the cartoons shrilling on the screen.

"I probably shouldn't. But I'll call you later," I said, waving to Paz, who waved lazily back while licking muffin batter from a spoon. I slipped my shoes on and bolted out of the door. I hurried to my bike that was parked in the bushes nearby, and began to pedal furiously home.

When I finally reached the house, after a long stint of heavy biking up the winding driveway to my front door, I hopped off the bike and dropped it in the driveway. Santeri would take care of it later. There was no use sneaking into the house and pretending I had been there the whole time, so I might as well hurry and get this over with. I ran up the steps to the door and burst inside.

I stopped short in the doorway, my backpack falling to the ground beside me as alarm curdled my stomach.

Shards of smashed porcelain dishes littered the marble floor. The draping fabric from the party was in mangled heaps, and most of the lights and greenery that had decorated the foyer were torn down and strewn about the destroyed room.

There were two dining room chairs in the middle of the foyer, back to back. The dining table in the dining room off to my right was flipped over on its side, two of the legs snapped off, and several of the chairs were in splinters.

The formal sitting room on the right of the foyer was in the same state of disarray, couches shredded, and one chandelier was pulled from the ceiling, crystals and twisted pieces of metal scattered across the rugs.

Fear surged over me as I stepped inside, my shoes crunching against a shattered vase of wilting flowers from last night's party. Bits of food lay everywhere, and the walls were defaced with arcane symbols in fluorescent orange spray paint. My heart stopped momentarily as I stared around at the demolished furniture. The French doors leading out to the back were open, curtains slashed to ribbons, and the tables and lights out back were thrown around the lawns. A few of our statues were lying, half submerged, on the banks of the pond.

My voice was stuck in my throat as I stepped towards the two chairs in the middle of the room, as if they were an altar. My heart started beating wildly again as I saw red smears on the marble floor and pieces of rope that were scattered around the two chairs. I recognized my parents' smashed cell phones beside the chairs.

I finally found my voice.

"MOM? DAD!" I shouted, running through the two staircases into the living room beyond. It too was trashed, furniture destroyed, the flat screen on the wall looking as if someone had taken a bat to it. My feet were taking me through another sitting room and hallway to the kitchen next, where dishes, drawers, and food from the large fridge were hurled everywhere. I ran up a back stairway, searching and calling in every destroyed room, but the chilling silence struck me. My parents weren't here. Santeri wasn't here. There were no cops. There were no bodies. The party wasn't even cleaned up. Where was everyone?

When I finally searched the last of the rooms on the second and third floors, I sank against the wall beside one of the guest bathrooms, which had a neon symbol of a dragon sprayed on the door, struggling not to hyperventilate.

What was going on? Who would've done this? Why? Where were my parents? My mind jumped to the vault where my mom and I had gone only yesterday. It was also a safe room. If the house was ever attacked, the safe room was stocked with food and water and emergency supplies. Maybe they were hiding there. It was the last hope I had. If they weren't there . . . *No*, they had to be there.

I stood and hurried down the hall, this last hope growing in my chest.

Just as I turned to go down the stairs, I ran into the hulking form of a strange man coming up them. He was at least six feet tall, his shoulders broad and hunched under a long black duster coat. He wore a black fedora with a ragged black feather sticking out of the purple trim. He looked as if he had a bad case of acne as a younger man, and his scars were half hidden under a patchy beard and mustache. For some reason, he looked familiar.

I opened my mouth to scream as I looked into his broad face, but the knife I saw in his hand stopped the scream cold in my throat. Seeing me, the man's face broke into a chilling, pleased smile.

"Wow, she was right," the stranger said, rubbing his jaw. "She said you'd be back, but how did you disappear right under our noses? When you went up to your room last night during the party, we had people confirm you were in there, and you never came back out."

I took several slow steps backwards as the man advanced up the last few stairs to the top of the landing, my mind flashing to the two giggling servers who had burst into my room last night. Had they been a part of this? What was all *this* about?

"Who are you," I squeaked, my back finally hitting the wall.

"Can't you read?" he asked, using his knife-point to gesture at the tee-shirt under his duster that spelled out *H.A.M.M.A* in red letters superimposed over an insignia of a curling, flaming dragon. There were words underneath it, but I was too nervous about the knife in his hand to read further.

"What's Hamma?" I breathed. I didn't know what he wanted, but he seemed pretty proud of his shirt. His eyes narrowed in disbelief.

"Don't play dumb. As if you didn't know this was coming," he snorted.

I stared at him. "Where are my parents?"

"Learning a lesson, I hope," he said.

Under my fear, I felt a flicker of irritation. Was there really a need to be so cryptic?

"I don't know what is going on, I swear. Please don't hurt me."

"We only hurt those that hurt," he chanted, as if he'd memorized the phrase.

"Hurt? I haven't hurt anyone," I stammered. He smiled at me as if I were a child lying about stealing from the cookie jar.

"Your parents have taught you the same ig-ignorances they, uh, that they themselves suffer from," he said, tripping a bit over the line.

I narrowed my eyes at him. Why was he talking like that? He sounded idiotic.

He continued, "Your time has come to meet your fate, and I am here to take you there."

I didn't have a clue what he was talking about, but his sneering, know-it-all tone was starting to irritate me more than scare me.

"Where are my parents?" I demanded, a little heatedly this time.

"Somewhere where they can't do any more harm," he recited.

I almost rolled my eyes at that one, annoyance setting my jaw at his lack of ability to give a direct answer. I tried to glance at his shirt to get more information about who this guy was, but he shifted his weight, his duster covering the words.

"Do you have my parents or not?" I snapped.

His face flushed and he bared his teeth with a glare. "Yeah, we have them. Your mother was just as mouthy as you are. Now you tell me, where is it?" The man brandished his knife at me, trying to intimidate me.

It worked, as my annoyance vanished and fear flushed into my body again. I cowered against the wall.

"Where's what?" I spluttered, keeping a careful eye on his long knife.

"Your leprechaun. We've searched every inch of this house and backyard, and we couldn't find it anywhere. But we know it's close."

My heart rapped against my ribs, my blood turning to ice. How? How did they know we had a leprechaun?

"Where are my parents?" I demanded again, fear still making it impossible to move my legs, but if I knew my parents were alive, I think I could function enough to try and make an escape.

"We've taken your parents somewhere to help them refresh their memory of where their creature is. They seemed rather dumb about the subject, or at least think we are." He cocked his head and stared at me thoughtfully. "We captured your other one. If you tell me where your other creature is, we will return you to your parents."

I frowned, my mind whirring. Other creature? We didn't have another creature, we only had Maddock. And "they'd return me to my parents?" The way he said it . . . It sounded as though he was saying he was going to take me with him, to wherever my parents were.

"What will you do to them?" I asked. "To me?"

He exhaled impatiently. "I'm not going to explain myself to an Everbleeder. Tell me where your leprechaun is, and no one will get killed. They'll be hurt for their crimes, but not killed. Intentionally," he amended. He gave me a wide smile and, slowly, held up his knife.

When he said the word Everbleeder, the incident from yesterday clicked in my mind.

"You were stringing lights here in my house yesterday!" I cried, the memory of his scratchy beard and heavyset body now vivid in my mind's eye. I had kicked his box of lights, and he had almost fallen over catching them. I hadn't recognized him with this duster and horrible hat, but now I could see it was clearly the same guy. How did they do all this? And what was an Everbleeder?

"Yeah," he chuckled, tipping the knife back and forth, watching the blade. "I've never had to decorate a house ahead of a raid before. It was a new experience. I liked it. You guys had no idea you were surrounded, did you?"

"Did . . . did you have anything to do with all our staff quitting?" I gasped.

"We couldn't have witnesses when we attacked. Too messy. Money has a way of motivating people."

I felt the blood drain from my face. If they could make an entire household quit, how influential were these people, and how had I never heard of them?

"Anyway, back to the matter at hand. Look, I'll even put my knife away, and we can go get your creature." He slid the knife into its sheath that was strapped to the side of his barrel chest. He held up his hands. "Okay?"

There was no way I was about to go with this fedora-wearing weirdo. He had put away his knife, which improved my chances of escaping. My mind raced through several ideas, each more stupid than the last, but nothing concrete would settle.

"Well, if I take you to my leprechaun, you won't return my parents or leave us alone after that, will you," I said. It wasn't a question since I already knew the answer.

He shook his head. "Sorry. Everbleeders have to pay."

"Okay," I said, my shoulders sagging in resignation. I took the stupidest idea that had passed through my brain and decided to run with it.

Literally.

Before he could register my movement, I charged at him and buried my shoulder into his lower abdomen. It was like hitting a squishy brick wall, and I staggered back as pain jolted through me, but it did the trick. With a choking gasp of surprise, he took several steps backwards, obviously forgetting that he stood at the top of the long flight of stairs. His feet met open air and with a cry, he began falling down the staircase.

Not waiting around to watch his tumble, I darted down the hall towards the servant staircase that was closest to the ATV garage. I considered going to the panic room vault as I charged down the stairs, but I didn't want to get trapped down there with no hope of rescue. My phone was dead, the landline was probably cut, my parents were kidnapped.

I needed magical help.

# Chapter Six

Heaving the garage door up and tearing inside, I grabbed a key off the key rack and leapt onto the nearest four wheeler. Turning the key and gunning the gas, I shot out of the garage. Looking back at the house, I saw the intruder appear in an upstairs window. Seeing me, he began yelling and pounding on the window.

The moron thought I had hidden upstairs.

Flipping him the bird on a whim—and shocking myself—I roared around the garage, just to confuse him as to which direction I was headed, before I turned toward the woods and Maddock's home. I needed to reach it before the man caught up if I wanted to work the spell I had in mind.

I weaved in between the trees, blazing towards the looming hill before me. It was still a ways away. I glanced behind me. There was no sight of the stranger, but that didn't mean he wasn't coming.

The ATV whined as I began my ascent up the hill. I had hoped that the machine would be able to go faster since it wasn't weighed down with crates of food, but the climb was still agonizingly slow. I glanced behind me again, and my heart jolted as I saw a small spec in the distance coming through the trees on an ATV. *Idiot!* I should've shut the garage door behind me. I urged the machine to go faster, and soon I saw the crest of the hill. I blasted out of the woods and into the clearing, jumping off the ATV as it trundled to a stop past the pillars. I had to work quickly.

I took a moment to calm my hammering heart and to recall the lessons that had been battered into my brain, even though I had never really used the magic before.

My mind latched onto a warding spell. It was something simple, just enough to keep the man out while I figured things out and talked with Maddock. Maddock was my bargaining chip, after all, and I didn't want to be rushed into making a bad bet. I just needed time.

My heart did somersaults as I heard a distant motor. Reaching out, I could feel Maddock's magical aura even from out here, and I began to draw the power from him. Walking from the first pillar toward the shed, I repeated the Gaelic words I had memorized years ago. I circled the shed as calmly as I could, all while trying to remember the precise order, and pronounce the words correctly. Despite the approaching danger and my fear, my mind was clear and my voice steady as I made the final turn and came to a stop where I had started. As I pronounced the last of the words, a wind blasted past me, whipping my hair as it traveled around the shed.

Hoping that I hadn't accidentally summoned a demon or something, I turned toward the loud roar that was coming through the trees. The large man was riding a green four wheeler into the clearing. When he saw me, he turned and accelerated straight at me, a vicious grin on his face.

Without thinking, I leaped aside, but there was no need for my pathetic attempt at escaping the oncoming vehicle. Right as the ATV reached the pillars, the machine buckled against a wall of solidified air that I had miraculously conjured correctly. The ATV flipped with a horrifying crunch of metal and the ear-rending squeal of a seizing engine. The large man didn't even have time to react to the crash. While the ATV crumpled, he was thrown off the four-by-four, landing hard on the ground with a dull thud, where he lay still.

I stood rooted to the grass, staring at the prone body of the man with an open mouth, a horrible thought leaping into my mind. Did I just accidentally kill someone?

My knees weakened at the thought. I stared at him with bated breath, and exhaled in relief as I saw that his chest was moving. He was breathing at least. He may be badly hurt, but he was alive. And unconscious, which was fortunate. It would give me a little more time, but he obviously wasn't working alone.

I rushed inside the shed, pulled the key from around my neck, and unlocked the trapdoor in the floor. I pulled open the hatch door and screamed as a small face glared up at me a few stairs down.

"What in the Ever was that dreadful commotion?" Maddock snapped. "Did an airplane fall down on us?"

"Maddock, we're in trouble," I rasped, trying to catch my breath from the scare. But as he glowered impatiently at me, I realized I had no idea where to start. I hated the breathless feeling of a time crunch, but there was so much to explain.

"Really? Did you not bring chocolate with you?" he asked with a steely expression. "I've been waiting all day, and no one has come to check on me. You were supposed to be here at seven a.m. sharp!"

Maddock usually had me arrive early on Saturdays because he liked to torment me.

"Shut up, it's not that kind of trouble," I breathed. Sitting down on the top step, I quickly explained everything that had happened since I left him yesterday afternoon.

By the time I finished speaking, there was a strange glint in Maddock's eyes.

"Your parents are missing, you say?" he asked. I exhaled, glaring at him as he stroked his goatee, no doubt trying to cover a smile. Was that the only thing he took away from this entire conversation?

"You don't have to be happy about it," I snapped.

"I'm not happy, just . . . intrigued," he coughed, no doubt choking on the lie. "And you don't know who this man is?"

"No, he said he's from HAMMA?" I questioned. "Do you know what that is?" I glanced behind me at the open door, wondering how much longer we had till the stranger came to.

Maddock shook his head. "Haven't the foggiest. I've been cooped up in here for the last century or so," Maddock reminded, his voice snide.

"You have the internet," I spat.

"So do you, yet you don't know who they are either. Besides, I have parental controls."

*So do I*, I thought.

Maddock rubbed his chin in thought. "They must be a very covert organization to know so much about magic while avoiding any real internet presence." Maddock's eyes locked onto mine, his face emotionless. "And he didn't say what he wanted?"

"He said he wanted *you*. Weren't you listening?" I fiddled with the key around my neck, trying to steady my breathing.

"Oh." Maddock's expression fell slightly. "That can't be good."

"What do you mean? Were you expecting it to be?" I demanded, my fingers aching from clenching them into fists so hard. "They took my parents! Of course they can't be good! I didn't know if I should call the police or not! Should I?" I didn't care if he made fun of me for seeming so unsure. I *was* unsure of what to do, and I needed advice.

"And tell the police what?" Maddock sneered. "Tell them your parents were kidnapped by crazed leprechaun fanatics?"

He was right, of course. If I splashed my parents' kidnapping all over the news, people would come snooping around, and news of Maddock and magic and *why* my parents were kidnapped might get out. That might put them in even more danger. Not to mention I wouldn't be able to do anything at all to help them, as I would probably be taken away and put in the foster system.

"I mean, if they want a magical creature for themselves," Maddock said, his tone nonchalant as he brushed imaginary specks of dust off his smoking jacket, "then I guess there's no reason to fight them. Let them come get me. One master is just as bad as another."

"What are you talking about, *bud?*" I sputtered. "You live in penthouse accommodations!"

Maddock didn't reply and avoided looking at me as he stroked his chin again. Finally, after several silent moments where I nearly tied my hands into knots waiting for him to come up with a brilliant plan, Maddock looked up at me. "Well, I suggest we get that young fella and bring him in here so we can question him."

I opened my mouth to immediately discredit what I was sure to be a stupid idea, but I stopped.

In all my panicking, I hadn't thought of that. While I hated to follow any idea that came from Maddock, who would never let me live it down that he was smarter than me, I had to admit to myself that it was actually a really good idea. Annoyance curled in my stomach that I didn't think of it myself. However, anxiety overruled the irritation, and so I put away my pride and stood up, brushing the dirt from the seat of my jeans.

"Do you have rope down there?" I asked.

"Linens will have to do," Maddock sighed. "Although I hate to wrinkle my good silk sheets."

Rolling my eyes, I marched to the door and pulled it open. My four-wheeler was still idling near the building where I had jumped off while the engine was still on, and the ATV that the stranger had used was in a tangled heap outside the perimeter of the pillars.

But the man was nowhere to be seen.

My heart stuttered, and I ran to the edge of where I had laid the magical barrier and scanned the area. No sign of the stranger. I gripped my hair with both hands, feeling the stupidity break over me. The talk with Maddock had been too long, and he had recovered from his crash enough to get away! *Stupid!*

Heart hammering, I ran back inside the hut.

"Maddock, he's gone!" I shouted, coming to look down into the trapdoor. Maddock peered up at me from around the corner of the stairs.

"Well, you're in a pickle now, aren't you?" he called back, as if I had said I'd gotten wet in a rainstorm.

"Maddock, you have to help me! He'll be back, with more people, and they'll take you!" I shouted.

"What's one master compared to another?" he repeated, and he disappeared back downstairs. I charged down the stairs after him, fuming.

The ungrateful little imp!

I reached the bottom of the stairs. Maddock had turned on the TV and was pouring himself a large tumbler full of sparkling apple cider.

"What are you doing? You have to help me! It's not only *you* they'll take!" I shouted. "They'll take *me* too! You have to help me!"

"I don't have to do anything except give you gold. I swear, you're the most demanding of all my masters." He gave me a smirk as he flopped down in a recliner and took a slurp of his drink, smacking his lips. "Ahhh, not bad. It's not whiskey, but it's still good. I will say, though, your parents do get the expensive stuff for me. I guess that is the only thing I will miss about them." He took another measured sip.

I gripped my hips, determined to remain calm. "Maddock, please! They have my parents! I don't know what to do," I said, frustrated that the tears were obvious in my voice. Tears wouldn't soften him. He would only ridicule me for being weak.

"So what?" he asked, lazing back into his chair. "You're better off. I'm certainly better off, but I suppose you'll be my newest master. Besides, your parents weren't that attentive to you anyway, were they? You've said so yourself. Many, many times, in many different irksome tones." He picked up the remote and began flipping channels.

I was about to agree with him about how my parents were so inattentive to me, but, reflecting on my vain, silly parents made me pause. Sure, my parents were greedy, seeming to only care about when Maddock would give us more gold. And they were always running off to "charity balls," or private vacations, or holding parties with important people, while I was up in my room.

But still, they were my parents. I didn't have anyone else; both of my parents had been only children, just like me. I didn't have cousins, or aunts or even grandparents, anymore.

I suddenly felt very alone. Not even Maddock cared about me, except when I was late delivering his food. I watched Maddock as he flipped idly through channels on the TV until he came to a cooking show. He settled deeper into his seat, watching the TV with hungry eyes.

I felt myself deflate.

Maybe Maddock was right. Maybe I should leave him here to be taken, and I should just take all the gold I could carry from the house and start on my own, as those people who had my parents would always be after me. It really wouldn't be any different than how I lived now—alone.

I turned, leaving Maddock to watch his show and wandered up the steps, a few tears slipping down my face. I didn't really want to leave my parents to their fate, but I was just a kid. What could I do? They wouldn't expect me to rescue them. Would they?

Maybe I could call the police and report the kidnappings, and then run away, hoping someone else would find my parents. And once they were found, I could come out of hiding. But those people would probably still be after us. If I could just have a tiny bit of hope. A tiny bit of help.

I exited the hut and stepped into the sunlight, a breeze cooling the tear tracks down my cheeks.

Suddenly, my phone in my pocket buzzed, and I pulled it out, heart hammering.

The time on the notification told me that I had just missed a call from a number I didn't recognize, but they had left a voice message.

I internally kicked myself for not being up where I had reception. I knew my parents' cell phones were back at the house, all smashed up, but maybe they had burners, or found another phone to call me.

I opened it with trembling fingers and pressed the phone to my ear, praying the message was from my parents, telling me that they were safe.

Tears of hope sprang to my eyes as I heard my mom's recorded voice.

"*Mallory, honey, we hope you get this message soon and will follow our instructions. If you're home, and have seen the state of the house, I want you to know that your father and I are alive, and well enough. If not, hurry home. We're not there, we've been taken hostage by a radical—*" There was scuffling, and then someone barked, "*Keep to the script!*" My mom's voice came back on, this time more tremulous. "*We've been kidnapped. They're letting us call you to give you instructions. Now, before that happens, I just want you to know—*" my mom's voice broke for a moment, and when she came back on, her voice was thick with emotion. "*That we love you very much, honey. And we're so, so sorry that—*"

More tears burned my nose and throat as the other end went quiet, then someone's loud voice snarled, "*Maybe* he'll *get to the point!*" and then my dad's voice came on. I wiped away the wet trails on my cheeks, listening hard.

*"Hi Peanut. We love you so much."* In the background, I heard someone bark, *"Enough with the chit chat! Tell her what we told you!"*

My dad's voice came back on. *"Now, Mallory, these people want us to tell you to take Maddock and wait for a group of people to come get you at the house."* There was a slight pause, then my dad began speaking so fast I almost missed what he was saying. *"But don't do it, take Maddock and run or they'll—"* There was the sound of scuffling, and then the line went dead. I pulled the phone away from my ear, my heart hitched in my throat.

I didn't want to think about what those kidnappers were doing to my parents right now for disobeying their orders. My parents had risked injury to keep me out of the hands of these dangerous people. I wasn't sure if it was because they wanted to keep their investment safe, or save me. Maybe it was both. But if they had cared enough to warn me, to keep me from getting kidnapped, maybe my parents actually did love me. Their sacrifice helped me make up my mind. Maybe I could risk trying to save them. My mind focused on next steps.

These HAMMA people took my family and wanted Maddock. Well, if I gave up Maddock, I would be in the same situation as my parents. I didn't know what that situation looked like, but I knew it wasn't good. Giving up Maddock wasn't an option. But if I could get Maddock to help me . . . it might just be possible to rescue my parents.

And I knew how to get Maddock's attention.

Rushing back inside and down the stairs to Maddock's side, I grabbed the remote from his hand and clicked off the TV.

"What do you think you're *doing*?" Maddock bellowed, whipping toward me and trying to swipe the remote back. "They were just showing how to make bourbon beef!"

"You are going to help me find my parents," I demanded, matching his volume.

"Says you," he scoffed, straining for the remote that I held out of his reach.

"*Yes*, says I."

"Nothing doing, lass. I'll stay right here." Maddock jabbed the arm of his recliner in emphasis. "If that bloke is coming back, I'll have no choice but to go with him, won't I? Can't be any worse than here. You can run along now, if you're so afraid for your life."

"You can stop it with the 'it can't be worse than here,' crap," I snapped. "It's not true, and you know it."

"I *don't* know any such—" Maddock began.

"What if I told you that if you help me, I'd free you?" I interrupted. He definitely wouldn't help me if he thought he had nothing to gain from it, and I knew that this would be the only thing to catch his interest. Maddock looked at me for several moments, for once without any snide comments.

"What did you say?" he growled.

"You heard me," I said, trying to keep my temper down. "If you help me, I'll release you."

I had imagined that upon hearing this news his face would have started to glow with joy and thankfulness. Instead, his eyes narrowed, and he seemed even more clammed up and surly than before.

"Why would you do that?" he sniffed, studying his buffed nails. "There is magic that can bind me to you so I have to go anywhere you want to go."

"Yes, but it doesn't make you *helpful*," I replied. "I can't make you *do* anything if I dragged you along with me."

I'd learned from the books my parents and grandparents wrote about leprechauns; the only requirement when a leprechaun is caught is for him or her to give of his gold that he has stockpiled all his life, fair and square. My parents added me doing his chores to make him more amenable to that fact. "I mean, I know you can't hurt me while you're under the spell, but I also can't trust you without it. 'A leprechaun holds no loyalties except for his gold, unless he's captive of a human,'" I recited.

Maddock gave a disdainful snort. "Yes, it sounds like you know *all* about us."

"But I don't want to drag a whining, petulant child around," I continued, ignoring his remark. "I have enough trouble as it is."

He stared at me, eyes mere slits, still silent.

"I need the help of a cunning leprechaun," I pressed, almost breaking the remote in my hands. He wasn't reacting at all the way I imagined, and I was starting to wonder if my plan was dissolving before it even began.

"I'm sure your parents won't be pleased by this little offer you're making, young miss," Maddock said, his tone careful.

I shrugged. We had plenty of gold and investments and properties in different countries. I hoped it would be enough for us to live on, as I really had no idea how much money we really had, or how much it cost to live. And if I saved my parents, I was hoping that they didn't care if I let Maddock free in the process. In all honesty,

I hoped they were alive after this was all through to have something to be displeased about.

"Well, they'll have to," I sighed. "All this gold has made them insane anyway; and if they lose their beloved pet, it might make them more human, and not so leprechaunish," I said with a pointed look.

"Hey, you leave gold and my personality out of this," he hissed, pointing a finger at me.

I continued, ignoring his comment. "*But*, if you promise to help me find my parents, and are cooperative and proactive with finding and releasing my parents and we're all safe at the end, I promise, I will set you free. But any slip, or misdirection, or betrayal, and I withdraw my promise."

Maddock now had the look on his face he got whenever I brought him apple cider instead of whiskey.

"How do I know you won't consider some tiny thing I do wrong as a reason to break your word and withdraw your offer? Humans are all about *take, take, take*. How do I know you won't double cross *me* once we find your parents?" he demanded.

It was a good question. I knew he had the lowest opinion of humans that could exist, but it was a strange question he would ask of *me*.

"Maddock, you've known me since I was eight. Am I the type of person to go back on a promise? I'm not like my parents, who, yes, would probably do something like that. But you know me, even if neither of us like that fact." He still stared at me with snake eyes. I sighed. "At the very least, you'll be able to get out of here for a while. But I promise you, I *will* set you free."

We stared into each others' faces. His grave expression didn't change, and I felt my heart drop. Did he really hate me so much that he would miss out on a chance of freedom just to spite me?

"Please," I whispered. "You're the only person I have left in the world."

Something flickered in Maddock's eyes as we stared one another down, then he sighed in a very melodramatic way.

"You're right about one thing, lass. It is embarrassing that I know you. It would be nice to get away from you and try to forget your face and your grating personality," he drawled. They were the most wonderful words I had ever heard him utter, if he meant what I thought he meant. I looked at him, hardly daring to breathe.

"So, you'll help me?" I asked, hoarse. A small smile flickered on his face. Not a pleasant smile, but it was a smile nevertheless.

"Aye, you useless lass. For my freedom, I'll ruddy help you."

# Chapter Seven

While Maddock packed a bag of clothes and necessities for himself, I looked through the book of spells that my parents kept hidden in a locked chest, under a rock inside Maddock's atrium. I found the one my however-great-great-grandmother had used to first capture Maddock and bind him to her, so that he always had to return to her if she called him. There were other spells that bound him to my side so that he was always beside me, but I didn't like the idea of him always by my side. A little distance between us was good.

My parents had made me practice the binding spells over and over again when I was younger, taking time to bind and unbind Maddock to me, so that in case of emergencies, I could move Maddock to a more secure location without losing him. I never imagined I would need them, and so I somewhat forgot the incantations. Thankfully, my parents kept copies of the spells all over the property. The spell I chose allowed Maddock to go wherever he pleased, he could leave my sight, for days and weeks if needed, but if I summoned him, he had to return immediately to my side.

We had to work quickly, as I had no idea when this man would come back with reinforcements. Perhaps he was back at the house now, waiting for more wackos to come steal me and my leprechaun away.

I half wished the man was still here, unconscious, so that we could've tied him up and used some truth spells on him to get information, but having a leprechaun was the next best thing. Besides being clever and sneaky, I had a feeling that once they got fired up on a subject, they would be hard-pressed to let the matter go. While Maddock wasn't exactly bound and determined on finding and saving my parents, I hoped he was fired up on gaining his freedom, and that was all I needed to work with.

After I found the right spell, I followed the instructions, and grudgingly took Maddock's hand tightly in mine, which he also grumbled at, and I read the words aloud.

Maddock, surprisingly, helped me with the pronunciation of some of the words, which made me wary that it was a trick, but once I stated the last words in a clear voice, I felt the familiar, hot burn deep in my chest; a quick flash that made me gasp. Maddock quickly slapped a hand to his chest too, looking as though he had eaten something sour.

"Ooh," he said, still grimacing and rubbing his chest. "That brings back dreadful memories."

I was still gasping for air as the sensation faded. It had been the feeling of a painful air bubble stuck in your ribs when you breathe in, only more intense, and with that strange heat.

As I closed the spell journal, a thought hit me, making me gasp again. "Wait! This spell also connects you to my parents! Could you follow that connection and find out where they are?" I turned eagerly to Maddock, who shrugged then closed his eyes, his expression pinched in concentration.

After several moments, he exhaled. "Odd. I can't feel a connection with them anywhere. I know there's a connection there, but it has a dead end."

The hope in my chest burst, and I tried not to cry out in frustration. I knew I had done the spell correctly, I felt the connection with Maddock myself. So what was blocking them? Now we were back to square one, with no leads.

"Well, let's get going. I want to be miles away before those psychos get back," I replied, upset but eager to get on our way.

"Wait a moment, lassie," Maddock said, pulling me up short as I tried to move towards the stairs. "Those pillars up above keep me in here, remember?"

"Oh yeah. How do these pillars keep you trapped?" I asked. Was the spell going to be too archaic and difficult for me to break? I wasn't well versed in magic, and it would be just my luck that it would be necessary to use a lot of it before this mess was over. Was my grandiose quest over before we even left my backyard?

"Some arcane, druidic magic that we haven't the time for me to explain, ye daft cabbage." Maddock rolled his eyes. "You just have to destroy more than half of them, otherwise I can't leave."

"How do I destroy them?" I asked, glowering. They hadn't been cheap, and I didn't know how much damage it would take to dismantle them.

"The tops just need to be smashed off, is all." He made it sound like it was as simple as plucking flower buds from their stems. The problem was, these columns were seven feet high, and made of pure granite.

"How am I supposed to do that? I can't go back to the house to get a sledge hammer, and they're too tall for me to just knock off the tops anyway."

"Well, then maybe try tipping them over?" he asked, his expression innocent.

"And you'll just sit there watching me do this, won't you?" I frowned. He gave me an oily smile in return.

Back upstairs, out in the air, I took down the protective wall that surrounded the hut, and locked his trapdoor behind us.

I made several failed attempts, including one where I tried to climb a pillar like I was climbing a palm tree for coconuts, and slid back to the ground, bruising my backside. Maddock had to use the doorframe to keep from rolling on the ground with laughter.

I was finally able to use the undamaged four wheeler and Maddock's silk sheets to pull off five of the eight granite Celtic cross toppers. All the while, Maddock watched me, silent, from the safety of the shed doorway. After several close calls of nearly getting smashed by flying, one-hundred-fifty pound hunks of stone, the final Celtic cross fell, splitting in half as it met with the ground. Maddock walked up to the perimeter of the pillars.

"And here I thought you'd be smarter than that, lass," he replied, studying my handiwork.

"What do you mean?" I asked, looking down at him from my ATV as I cut the engine.

"You can use magic. You could've blasted the tops off with said magic." He gave me a crafty grin. "Also your ancestors had a special spell that momentarily lowered the defenses of the pillars so I could slip past them without having to destroy those historic obelisks. Shame they never taught it to you."

I met his eye, gritting my teeth against the anger rising within me. My parents forbade me from ever using magic unless dire circumstances required it, and my infrequent training dropped off as I got older, so I was rusty, but I didn't remember ever learning a spell to lower the pillar's defenses. I'd never used magic outside of training before today, so using it to simplify tasks was still a new concept for me.

"Oh, and you couldn't have mentioned that before I almost got myself killed?" I bristled.

He shrugged, a smile on his face. "I wanted them destroyed."

With a growl, I gripped the ATV handles, trying to calm myself. This was going to be a long, difficult adventure for both of us. Possibly even filled with danger, especially for Maddock, because he was in great danger of me strangling him before our time together was through.

"There, you can come out now, right?" I growled, hopping off the ATV. Maddock took several experimental steps forward, and then gave me a curt nod. "It seems I am free."

He stared, drinking in the view; the tree branches fluttering in the soft air, the lush grass, the birds, the sun. I hated to interrupt his communion with nature, but I had to make sure he was clear on our deal. We were being hunted, after all.

"Well, not free *quite* yet," I said, and Maddock turned to cast a sharp look at me. "Remember, you have to help me to the best of your ability, using gold, or your cunning, or whatever, in my cause to find and free my parents. Only then will I free you, once this mess is finished."

"Yes, yes, I quite remember your needling requirements," Maddock snapped.

"Well, I'm sorry," I groused back, "I just want to be clear."

"So what happens when we free your parents, and the people come after them again?" Maddock asked, his attitude still sour.

I opened my mouth to shoot back some snappy retort, but nothing came. I honestly didn't know. I shook my head. "We'll think of that when the time comes. One problem at a time. Besides, at that time, my parents will be able to help us."

Maddock's expression clearly conveyed that he doubted very much that my parents could help with anything, but he shrugged. "Understood. Now, enough of this. What's next?" Maddock asked, his bitter mood suddenly vanished, replaced with his delighted expression again at being outside.

Thankfully he was studying the clover patches in the clearing, and not paying attention to me, because his second question stumped me. Again.

Now that we were both out, and I had purchased Maddock's help; what *was* next? I had no idea where to start, or where to go, or how we were even going to free my parents, let alone *find* them. Unfortunately, Maddock caught me looking off into space, my face scrunched with worry as I tried to think of what to do. He cleared his throat to catch my attention.

"Listen, lass, leave this to someone who knows how to get things done, hmm? I can take point." He puffed out his chest, his tone dripping with annoying self-confidence.

"You want to take charge?" I asked, heat creeping into my face. He didn't think I could handle this? Be a leader? I didn't want him getting the wrong idea about who was the boss in this situation. I straightened. "No way, Maddock. I'm the leader, I know the area, I'm making the decisions."

Maddock's strained expression conveyed he had a lot to say about that, but he merely clamped his mouth shut and gave me a pained smile.

"Very well, we'll do things *your* way," he said, his voice muffled from his clenched teeth. "Since you think of the most *efficient* ways of doing things." He gave a pointed look at the pillars.

I ignored the jab. "That's right. Good. Now, I think we should go back to the house so I can gather some things up that we'll need—"

"What if that man is waiting there for you?" Maddock blurted.

I bit my lip. I hadn't really thought about that. Of course he might be there. Why would he leave?

"Oh, um . . . Well . . ."

Maddock waved away my trailed-off thoughts. "You have me to protect you. If he's there, I can take care of him, even if he has reinforcements. We'll be fine."

I stared down at him. This diminutive creature, take on that hulking man and his friends? I held back a laugh, as I was trying to use our time with efficiency, and bickering with Maddock usually took up large chunks of time.

"Okay, if you're sure you can handle it." I made a mental note to grab a bat or something while in the house to defend myself when Maddock's bravado came back empty.

"Of course I can," Maddock snorted. "Now, uh, *leader*," he gave a slight bow toward me, "what I suggest we do, is that we go down there, gather your things, and then we can go somewhere safe, and hash out a plan. What do you think of that, uh, boss?" He gave me that same pained smile, and I realized he was trying, and failing, to be pleasant.

Though I didn't care for his forced pleasantries, I felt hopeful. I'd had no idea how cooperative offering his freedom would really make him, and he had some helpful ideas already.

I cleared my throat and nodded. "Yeah, okay. I can, uh, also grab cash and stuff, so we don't have to use credit cards."

"Good idea," Maddock said, giving me a robust thumbs up and an overwide smile. "Your ideas are the best, Mallory."

I shuddered and turned to him, holding up a hand.

"Okay, you can cut the overbearing positivity," I demanded. "It's creepy, coming from you. Our deal is made, there's no need for fake sentiments."

Maddock exhaled as if a huge weight had been lifted from his mind. "Oh, thank the Ever. Dealing with someone as dense as you and pretending to be cheerful 'bout it was going to be a real drudgery. Are you coming, you bag of rocks?" he asked, moving towards the ATV. I caught up to him and gave him a scowl as I heaved his bag up onto the back of the ATV.

"Okay, tone yourself back a little. Some pleasantness is good." I swung my legs over the ATV and turned on the engine as he hopped up behind me, nestling his other bag between us and wrapping his arms around my waist. His fingers couldn't touch around my middle, and I was sure he was going to say it was because I was fat.

He sighed again. "If you say so. You blimpy lump."

I made sure to brake abruptly every so often on the way down the hill so that he faceplanted into my back, and then accelerated wildly so he had to cling to me to stay seated.

By the time we reached my backyard, he was out of smart remarks, and I felt his arms trembling slightly as they held onto me.

We pulled up to the side of the house, and, breathless, I cut the engine. Every nerve in my body crackled, sure that a host of fedora-wearing, trenchcoat-clad neckbeards would come swarming in from all sides.

The house was silent.

"I don't sense anyone inside, magical or mundane," Maddock replied as we both hopped off the ATV. "Tut, tut, hurry up now. We don't know how long people will be gone. They may be back at any moment."

Nodding, I ran inside, Maddock at my heels, my heart wrenching as I stepped over torn family pictures and destroyed furniture. I charged up the stairs, leaving Maddock downstairs.

My room was a literal zone of destruction as I dug a duffle bag out from under the piles of clothes heaped in the closet that someone had torn from the hangers. I picked out outfits from the wrenched-out dresser drawers and shoved them all haphazardly into the bag before running to the bathroom to scoop my toothbrush, makeup, and feminine products into a toiletry bag.

After gathering my laptop, phone charger and a few other electronics, I charged downstairs with my bags and purse, heading to the vault.

My parents kept bonds, gold, and cash, along with property deeds in the vault. The kitchen was torn apart, but the door to the wine cellar and the vault was untouched. Hopefully that meant no one had found it.

Down in the wine cellar, I pressed the button to move the barrel and slipped down to the vault. Hurrying inside, I noticed that the gold I had collected from Maddock the night before was still resting on the desk where my mother had put it, sending golden flecks of light onto the walls. Taking a large leather drawstring bag in one of the desk drawers, I began piling nuggets into it until the drawstring could barely close. I had no idea how much I would need, or if I even should bother with nuggets, but I wanted to cover my bases, and I doubted Maddock would be agreeable to parting with any more bullion.

I then rushed to the wall of deposit boxes. I had to open several before I found the stacks of cash. I grabbed several bundles of one hundred dollar bills, and several stacks of different bills from other countries. While searching through the drawers, I came upon passports for both me and Maddock. Both were under aliases, and were surprisingly up to date. Amazed that my parents had thought of everything, I grabbed the passports and shoved them into the bag as well.

When I felt I had enough money and supplies, I left the vault, taking care to close and lock it again, in case the HAMMA people did indeed come back and search the house again. Coming out of the pantry, I ran into Maddock who was examining the chef's kitchen.

"Well, you took your Ever-loving time. I swear two centuries have passed," he replied, his tone snippy.

"Oh, shut up. Come on to the foyer. I can't drive, so I'll call us a cab," I said as I passed him, not bothering to stop as I went through the kitchen.

"I can drive," Maddock said hopefully, following me through the halls.

"Since when? And *Nitro Rally 3* doesn't count. We're not going to get away just to get arrested for a leprechaun driving without a license," I replied, rolling my eyes. "Besides, we don't want to use traceable vehicles. I'm sure these people have thought of everything. We'll go to a hotel and figure it out from there."

"Very well," Maddock grumped.

We stepped into the ruined foyer, and Maddock whistled low, dropping his bags and looking around the room. "So this is what my hard-earned money bought, eh? Not bad."

I dug my cell phone out of my pocket, and seeing it was dead already from its short charge at Hillary's, I dug out my charger and squatted down beside an electrical outlet. I plugged in my phone, needing just enough juice to call a cab to get us out of here.

If only Santeri were here, he would have driven us. But the house was empty, and I had no idea where Santeri had gone. He too must have been kidnapped.

Finally pulling up the screen and finding a cab company number, I ordered a cab for us. After I gave them the directions, I hung up and unplugged my phone again, wanting to be ready to move the second the cab got here. I would have to charge my phone fully at the hotel.

"Well, they'll be here in about ten minutes," I said, getting to my feet and wandering over to Maddock, who had planted himself in front of our small gallery of ruined paintings on the sitting room wall. "I wonder if I can find some food, I haven't eaten all—"

"Someone's coming," Maddock said sharply, turning away from the slashed painting he had been studying.

My skin crawled with fear, and I involuntarily took several steps towards Maddock, wildly looking around the room. Were they coming from upstairs? From out by the pond? "Where?" I squeaked. I'd never felt more vulnerable, especially in a place that had been my home and refuge. It was like no place was safe anymore.

I looked to Maddock, fear clawing at me. He barely passed my navel in height! Why did I let him pretend he could protect us? I whirled, searching for something in the destroyed room to use as a weapon.

"Coming up the drive. One is the man who attacked you. I can feel my magic on him. And there is someone with him."

I hurried to a window and peered through the glass. Sure enough, stalking up the driveway were two hulking men, each carrying swords and knives. One of the men was limping and had some nice bruises coming in on his face.

"What do we do?" I asked, moving back towards Maddock. I grabbed a broken vase nearby and held it up, wishing for something better.

The door burst open as the two men charged inside, and before they could speak or I could scream, Maddock bounded forward, caught one of the men in the neck with both feet in an impressive leap and then brought two of his fists down onto the second man as the first man crumpled to the floor.

I gawked as Maddock nimbly somersaulted in the air and landed on the floor with a roll. The second man hit the floor as Maddock straightened and brushed off his house robe, looking at me as I stared back at him, slack-jawed. Both men were knocked out cold.

"Will that do?" Maddock asked, eyebrows quirked impishly. I blinked, then realized I probably looked like an idiot, standing there with my mouth open.

"That . . . was incredible," I said, suddenly aware that if Maddock decided to attack me, I didn't stand a chance.

Maddock snorted. "I'm Irish, lass. Of course it was."

There was a burst of static, and a voice started calling out the names Kevin and Axel, repeatedly telling them to pick up. Maddock went over and nudged a walkie talkie out of one of the men's over-coat pockets with a toe.

"Well, I would've said to take these dolts and question them," Maddock sighed, "but I don't think we have time for that. They will no doubt have people coming to look for them."

"Maybe we should meet the cab at the street," I said, fear pummeling my chest. "To make a quick getaway."

"Good idea. You head out and wait, I'll follow you," Maddock said.

I gave him a suspicious look.

"Oh, it's not like I can run off, can I?" Maddock said impatiently. "I promise, I'll follow in a moment. And I'll even bring one of your bags." As if to show his sincerity, he grabbed his own cases and hefted my electronics bag over his shoulder, the bag brushing the floor. He gave me a wide grin. "Go, I'll not be a minute."

On impulse, I scooped up the walkie talkie rasping on the floor beside the men, then stepped over the motionless bodies and hurried down the drive.

The wait for the cab, and Maddock, was horrible, as I imagined men and women in fedoras and black trenchcoats ambushing me and stabbing me with swords. Of all the ways to go, being sworded by role-playing vigilantes would be the most embarrassing.

The cab would be here any moment, and there was no sign of Maddock coming down the driveway. I didn't want to summon him, to show that I could be trusted to trust him, but still; he made me anxious. I fiddled with the walkie talkie, but it had gone silent. The silence was unnerving, like the person on the other end knew Axel and Kevin were indisposed. Like they knew I had the walkie-talkie.

"Snack?" Maddock asked, appearing out of thin air near my elbow, holding out a bag of trail mix. I shrieked and nearly smacked him flat to the stone drive, but instead staggered away from him.

"How did you do that?" I gasped, clutching my bags to keep my hands from trembling.

"What, they don't call leprechauns sneaky for nothing, you know. Hungry?" He held up the mix again, and I took the bag with a wary hand, blood roaring in my ears.

"Is that what you were doing? Getting food?" I panted, incredulous.

"Well, yeah," Maddock replied, as if stating the obvious. "You said you were hungry, and I knew *I* certainly was, so I figured I let the human deal with waiting for the cabbie while I got the fun stuff."

I looked down at him and saw that he was not only carrying my electronics bag, but another bag bulging with food. I shook my head.

*Well, at least I won't go hungry with Maddock by my side.*

"Hold up, lass," Maddock said, squinting across the street. "I think I see . . . wait here." All the bags he was holding tumbled to the ground as he disappeared into thin air. My mouth fell open. I'd never seen him do that before. I mean, I knew the spell that bound us drew on the fact that leprechauns could essentially teleport short distances, but seeing it for the first time was shocking. And kinda cool.

I looked across the street to where he had been staring. Something dark glinted in the sunlight that dappled through the branches of a thick copse of trees. A car?

A few moments later, Maddock reappeared.

"Done. There was another person in that car, watching us," Maddock said, scooping his bags back up. "I think he was a sentry. He's out cold now, but he had this on him, and the other walkie-talkie." Maddock handed me a stack of stapled papers. "Nothing else in the car though, except a lot of fast food wrappers."

The papers turned out to be lists of my family's monthly expenses, our identities, where I went to school, schedules of where my mother went every day, and several pictures of each of us and our house, taken from different angles.

"How long have these people been watching us?" I asked, horror filling my chest and turning into a shiver that raced along my skin.

"Weeks, by the look of it," Maddock replied, looking up and down the street.

There were several pictures of Santeri as well, with the letters *M.A.* stamped in red on the corner of each of his pictures, but no other explanation or information on what that meant.

I ran my fingers over the embossed logo of the same fiery dragon that had been on the kidnapper's shirt. "Who are these people?" I whispered.

# CHAPTER EIGHT

The cab came in good time, and I directed the driver to take us to the nearest hotel, which happened to be a fairly decent one on the Charles River a few miles out of Boston. After I paid the driver at the curb of the hotel, I gathered my bags and turned to Maddock, who was rubbing his hands together as he stared up at the hotel, a genuine grin on his face.

"I've never seen any of the United States before," he said, staring around at the towering buildings around us. "Unless you count seeing the shoreline from our steamship, and bits of Massachusetts as your ancestors traveled around, trying to find their new home. But that was all before the technological wonders of today existed. Things are so different now." He gazed at the crowds of pedestrians and the many cars that zipped by on the busy street.

"You've seen plenty of modern cities on television," I pointed out, still shaken by the stack of papers in my hand.

"It's different in real life, lass. When I arrived, there were no cars, no electricity—" Someone bumped into him, making him stagger. "And not so many people," he groused.

I looked at him in amazement, for a moment forgetting my own worries. I hadn't really realized that he had lived in times before all of this: the busy, car-filled street, people walking down the sidewalk with headphones blaring music, purses and pockets full of modern creations.

"Yep, women couldn't vote and gas lighting in houses was new. It was a different time," he continued, staring up at the buildings towering over us.

A sudden urge to ask him more about what the past was like flashed through me, but I put the thought away. We weren't here to get to know one another.

"Let's go, we look like tourists, standing around here," I replied.

We headed toward the front doors, and I whispered, "So, we'll need to register with different names."

"And how do you expect to do that? I'm pretty sure you need ID to get rooms," Maddock demanded out of the corner of his mouth as a group of people exited the doors.

"Well, I have your passport," I replied, fishing the passports out of my purse. "It looks like you're a Mr. Charles Smith," I replied, handing him the passport for him to look over. Maddock took it with a frown. His real last name was O'Bannon. "Not Irish enough," he grunted.

I opened my passport, where I gaped at my photo with the name Mary Smith typed beside it. Though it was my face, the name made it feel like looking at a stranger. I shook my head, still amazed at my parents' foresight in obtaining these documents in case something like this happened, and I needed to travel with Maddock.

"Looks like you'll have to pretend to be my father."

He gave me a look as if even pretending to be related to me made him rethink this whole idea of getting his freedom.

"It will look suspicious for a minor to be getting a room," I snapped. "So, you need to do this. We need to be incognito."

"Yes, since a three-foot-five inch man has a daughter that can jump clean over him won't raise peoples' eyebrows." Maddock rolled his eyes.

"Hey, little people can have tall children, thank you very much. Just do it," I said through clenched teeth. "We have the ID to 'prove' our relationship."

We walked through the doors, the air conditioning flushing over us. The lobby was noisy, as it was Saturday, and people were busy checking out or in, so we had to wait for a moment in line. When we got to the receptionist counter, the man gave us an awkward smile, having to bend over the counter to greet Maddock.

"Hello," said Maddock solemnly. I didn't like the evil shadow in his eyes. "I'm Mister Charles Smith. I would like two rooms, one for me and one for my unfortunate-looking daughter here. We're related, you see. Can you believe it?" Maddock asked, grabbing a hotel brochure and flipping through it.

I bit the inside of my cheeks, trying to smile naturally but felt my face flame. I couldn't react; if I strangled my "father" in public, it would raise questions. I merely rolled my eyes and gave a pained smile to the poor guy behind the counter, who was frowning at us in confusion.

"Identification, please," the receptionist replied, looking between us.

Giving Maddock a swift glare, I handed over the passports. The man took them, checking the pictures against our faces.

"Ooh, muppet, dear! Presidential suites! Let's get those," Maddock said, his nose in the brochure as he ogled at the pictures of the luscious suites.

"No, *father*," I said forcefully, pulling the pamphlet from his hands, while trying to copy Maddock's Irish brogue. "Mummy will get mad."

I quickly turned to the man before Maddock could say anything, and said, "Two queen rooms, please."

"Would you like balcony bedrooms that overlook the river?" he asked.

"Yes, that will be fine," I replied, ignoring Maddock's frown.

"And for a small fee, you can have breakfast delivered to your room as well," the man said, looking between Maddock and myself, clearly unsure of who to speak to.

"Yes, breakfast," Maddock barked immediately, and I sighed.

"Yes, we'll both take the breakfast," I agreed. Better than eating down here and drawing unwanted attention by Maddock's small stature and enormous appetite.

"Excellent. Just the one night?" he asked, again looking between us.

"Um, for now," I said for Maddock, as he was presently distracted with watching the people passing through the lobby.

"Excellent. Checkout is at 11:30. How will you be paying today?" the clerk asked.

I dug into my purse, where I had stored the several thousand dollars in cash, and quickly counted out the amount for our rooms. If the desk clerk thought it was strange we didn't pay with a credit card, he didn't say as he printed out keys and handed them to us as a bellboy with a cart came and gathered up my luggage. We were led to the elevators—where Maddock made sure he got to push the button to the top floor—and then directed down the hall.

I opened the door to one of our rooms, tipping the bellboy generously before ushering Maddock inside with my luggage. The room was spacious, with a good view of the river beyond the balcony.

"Okay, here's your key," I said, turning to Maddock, handing him the white plastic card. "Do not eat anything out of the mini fridge or the mini bar, okay? They charge a fortune for that stuff," I said, giving him a stern look.

"If I recall correctly, you have a small fortune in these bags," Maddock pouted, frowning.

"I'm serious," I warned. "Do not eat anything. We need this money to last. You brought snacks, that will have to suffice until we order pizza or something."

Maddock snatched the key card from my hand with an ill-tempered look and a muttered "Killjoy," before he marched out the door, making sure he slammed the door behind him as hard as he could.

Rolling my eyes, I dragged all my luggage into the room and pulled out a few of those luggage racks. I wanted to be as organized as possible, because it was the only thing that was completely in my control right now.

When everything was organized to the best of my ability, I laid down on the bed, sighing.

The questions that filled my mind back at Maddock's home came back in full force now that we were out of the house and had taken the first step. I didn't know what the *next* step would be. What was I going to do? How was I going to find and save my parents? I had no clue where to start. I had never heard of HAMMA, and what their purpose was. All I knew was that they had enough members to attack and destroy my house, and kidnap two adults as well. And they knew about magical creatures.

But where to start? I needed to bounce ideas off someone, just so I didn't go crazy sitting here. No time like now to plan on saving my family.

Because Maddock and I were bound, he had to come immediately at the command that accompanied the tether spell. "*Teacht Maddock.*"

Without so much as a sound, Maddock appeared on the bed beside me, wearing nothing but a hurriedly placed towel around his waist that he'd brought with him.

With a scream, I leaped up from the mattress with my hands clapped over my eyes.

"What in the *blazes*, lass?" Maddock hollered, trying to secure the towel more firmly around himself. "I was about to take a bath!"

"I didn't realize you would be undressing as soon as you got into your room!" I shouted, still turned away with my hands over my eyes. "We've only been here for like, thirty seconds!"

Maddock blustered and puffed behind me.

"Hold on," Maddock finally grunted, and I heard him hurry into my bathroom. Although I was still standing in shock, I at least felt thankful that Maddock had been able to grab a towel with him on his way to my summons. Because of the binding spell, unless he was prevented from coming by someone else's magic or he was thousands of miles away, the summons were near instantaneous.

"Alright, I'm decent," he said grumpily after a few minutes, and I peeked through my fingers. Maddock had taken another towel from my bathroom and draped it over his shoulders like a cape, his other towel firmly tied around his chest, the ends tickling the floor when he walked.

"Heavens, I can't have two minutes in my room without you barking for me like a mad seal?" Maddock snapped, clutching the towel closer to his chest.

I almost laughed. There was no way he was more horrified than I was at his appearance. The sight of his extremely hairy, bare chest was going to be burned in my brain forever. However, I was not in the mood to be lectured.

"We're not here on vacation," I retorted as Maddock went and sat on one of the chairs next to the television, taking care that the towel kept him covered as he sat. "We're here to find a way to save my parents, remember?"

He merely grunted.

"When you're free, you can lounge in a hotel room as much as you want," I said.

"So, what do you want?" he growled.

"Well, first, what kind of pizza do you want delivered?" I asked, still feeling huffy, but realizing that both of us being in a bad mood wouldn't get anything accomplished. But I knew what would raise his spirits.

He perked up at the mention of food. "Everything."

"Great. I want pepperoni. You know how to order pizzas, right? Why don't you call and order the food, *within reason*, while I get my computer out."

I knew it was a task he would gladly do, and with a whistle, he hopped off the seat and waddled over to the phone next to my bed, pulled out a directory of the restaurants around the hotel from the drawer, and dialed the number.

I dug out my computer and plugged it all in. By the time it was booting up, Maddock was chatting on the phone with the nearest pizza joint, ordering pies and soda.

When my computer was up, I typed in *HAMMA*, *kidnapping*, and *organizations that destroyed houses*, but there wasn't much info. Well, that wasn't exactly true. There were a *lot* of reports of destroyed houses and arson and kidnappings, but nothing mentioned HAM-MA or magical creatures—no surprise there—or anything that gave a hint of the organization that took my parents.

"Anything promising?" Maddock asked as he hung up the phone, twirling a finger through his curled beard.

"Nothing. Some of these creepy, goth-like websites mention mythical creatures, but I'm not trusting those. How is it that the mainstream media has no useful information?" I asked, glaring at my screen.

"Well, that's your problem right there. Mainstream," Maddock replied, hopping back onto his chair. "Do you really think that if the media knew of unicorns and fairies they would keep it hushed up? Especially if money was to be made? If you've never heard of this group before, it's obvious that they are very clandestine. What you need are underground informants."

"Like, the black market?" I breathed.

The black market was something that had always intrigued me, because I knew that magical creatures had to be swapped there, but I didn't even really know how one found or sold on the black market. Was it a literal place, or you just had to know the right sketchy people?

"Yes, the black market is part of it, but I'm saying people who know things, you know? People whose job is to know information about groups and societies that work in secret."

"Like the mob," I gasped. Dealing with the mob sounded like a terrifying option.

Maddock snorted. "Nothing so well known, you dolt."

I bristled. "Ok, so where *would* we go? Where do we start looking?" I snapped. The thought of walking down dark alleyways asking for unknown people didn't seem very safe. Or smart.

"Good thing you have a sneaky leprechaun on your side, right?" Maddock asked, looking pleased.

"What, you'll go searching?" I asked, surprised at his initiative. "Do you even know what you'll be looking for? Because I don't have a clue what we're even trying to find."

"You look for the people who know things about everything, magical and non-magical." Maddock replied, as if speaking to someone dimwitted.

"And you know where to go?" I asked with a raised eyebrow.

Maddock shrugged. "Not really, but it seems like something a leprechaun would be good at; gathering and spreading information. Especially if it was for money." He gave me a wicked smile.

I shook my head in disbelief. "So, tonight, you'll roam the alleyways of downtown Boston, looking for news on magical movements? Sounds like a dead end."

"It's all we have to go on," Maddock insisted.

I gave a reluctant nod. "But it still sounds sketchy. I mean, how many people know about magical creatures?" I asked.

"I guess we'll find out tonight." Maddock shrugged.

# Chapter Nine

After Maddock had eaten two whole pizzas, two packages of breadsticks, four apple turnovers, and a liter of soda all by himself, he showered and dressed. Reappearing in my room, Maddock held out his arms as if presenting himself.

"I believe I'm ready for my late night stroll."

I stared at him in his leather jacket and dark pants, his hair smoothed back, with a cocksure expression on his face, and I exhaled. "Are you sure about this? What if news gets back to HAMMA that a leprechaun is looking for them? Or you ask someone who is a member of HAMMA, and they capture you somehow and you can't get back to me?" Hundreds of scenarios ran through my head, most of them horrible.

"Don't sweat it. I'll be very inconspicuous; asking a lot of questions, but revealing very little about myself. I'm no novice to discretion. I did evade capture for several decades before your ancestor came along."

"And she caught you," I said, hoping to dampen his bravado. I needed him to be cautious, not bragging about his discretion to the Boston underworld.

"She *was* a devilishly clever thirteen-year-old," he conceded, and I thought I detected a hint of grudging respect in his tone. "And I doubt this HAMMA has one human in their ranks as brilliant as she was, let alone a whole group. She certainly didn't pass that trait on to you." He curled his beard around his finger, admiring himself in the mirror for a moment before turning to me.

I rolled my eyes.

"I'll be back as soon as I have something to work with," he replied as I slapped away his hand that was inching toward the slice of pizza on my plate.

I nodded. "Be careful."

He snorted. "I'm always careful where I'm concerned." Without a sound, he vanished from my sight.

I spent the next couple of hours flipping through channels, eating leftover pizza, and peering nervously out of the closed drapes. Though I wanted to be proactive in helping my parents, I didn't begrudge Maddock taking point on this part of our operation. I was too nervous to be out doing something that was most definitely dangerous. I could almost hear Paz's bossy voice saying I shouldn't be letting a man take care of the danger while I sat at home doing nothing, but I was honestly fine with it. Maddock was clever and sneaky, and with my inexperience with all things magic, I didn't want to make things worse, so I was happy to have someone else handle the scary task of wandering the city streets, interrogating people.

It wasn't until I was checking my emails that I remembered that my phone was still dead from this morning, and I hurriedly plugged it into the charger. Maybe one of my mom's messages had more info in it.

Once the phone had enough battery to open all my apps, I saw that I had several texts from Hillary, Paz, Felicity, and, surprisingly, Marcus.

My heart wrenched in my chest as I stared at the unanswered texts.

I should be doing normal teenage things right now, not stuck here alone in a hotel with no one but my grumpy leprechaun for help finding my parents who'd been snatched by a clandestine magical group that also wanted to capture me. I almost laughed aloud as I imagined having to explain that to one of my friends.

All the texts were asking me to hang out, including the ones from Marcus, but that wasn't an option. Clearing away the tears gathering in my eyes, I typed the same text to all of my friends, telling them one of my relatives that lived in Alaska was deathly sick, and my family was going to go visit for a few weeks.

That was an outright lie, as I didn't have any more living relatives, but I was hoping that pity would help my friends forget that fact.

It worked. I received several sympathy texts from everyone, with demands that I text them once I got home from my trip.

I warned them that I probably wouldn't have service, so I wouldn't be able to text them much. I didn't know how tech savvy HAMMA was, I was a little afraid that they would be able to find me via my friends' phones somehow. If I cut off all ties, they might be safe, and maybe HAMMA wouldn't find us.

I then quickly created a new email with my father's initials and emailed my school, letting them know of our sick relative, and my absence. My father was a patron of the academy, so I knew I wouldn't have any problems with missing classes.

After I had finished emailing my school, I listened to the message my parents had left me, hoping for hidden clues of where they were, but found nothing.

Clicking the phone screen off and setting it aside, I looked at the clock. Maddock had left at around nine, and it was only eleven-thirty. I decided to watch TV until Maddock came back. Changing into pajamas, I took the pizza box into bed with me and began flipping through channels, anything to keep me from obsessively watching the clock.

I was half-dozing, half-watching a couple remodel a home when someone took the pizza I had been holding out of my hand and poked me hard in the arm.

"Hey, I'm back," Maddock said. I sat up with a grunt, rubbing my face.

"You're back," I yawned.

"Indeed. And I've got good news."

That erased all sleepiness from me, and I brushed my hair out of my face, turning my attention to Maddock, who was stuffing the slice of pizza in his mouth as though it was trying to escape.

"You know who HAMMA is?" I asked, rubbing my eyes. Maddock, his cheeks full, was about to wipe his hands on my comforter but stopped when he saw my stormy expression, and used a napkin instead. Swallowing, he took a long drink from my glass of soda on the bedside table.

"No," he said, smacking his lips. "But I've learned the name of the person who does, and I was right; the spreading of information for a fee is the perfect vocation for a leprechaun." Maddock grinned at me. "Funnily enough, he's an old friend of mine."

"Really?" I asked, then frowned. "Wait, what do you mean? Start from the beginning, tell me everything. How did you know where to start in the first place?"

"Well, I started in a pub—"

"*What?*" I shouted. "*Why*—" A pounding on the wall behind me made me jump, my face flushing.

"We're not in my soundproof house anymore, lassie," Maddock sniggered, "Ye best keep your shrieking tones to a minimum, else you'll anger the neighbors."

I turned back to face him, giving him a blistering look. "You went to a bar? You were supposed to be searching, I dunno, alleyways and stuff for creepy people with information, not enjoying happy hour!" I chided.

Maddock laughed, showing me his open mouth full of another bite of pizza, and shook his head, swallowing. "Do you really think people with info are just hunched in alleyways, whispering for passersby to come exchange secrets with them?"

I didn't want to admit that, yes, that was exactly what I imagined happened, and so instead continued to glare. "Maybe you should explain."

"Well I was, until you opened your bawling mouth." He took another bite of pizza and cleared his throat.

"I searched the city for other magic, as I said before, even though I can't use magic like humans can, I can feel magic; everyone who uses or has magic can do so, and every person's magic feels different."

"Could I do it?" I interrupted, intrigued. I didn't know you could feel magic from others.

"Sure, if you paid attention to it and practiced. You have to know someone really well to be able to recognize their signature, but it's not hard to feel general magical traces. Anyway, I wandered the city for a good while, searching for any hint of magic or anything unusual, and this search led me to a pub, or bar, as you yanks call it."

"I know what a pub is," I retorted.

"It led me to a rather mousy looking man at a table in the corner of the *bar*," he continued, ignoring me, "who had some druid blood in him."

"What's a druid?" I asked. I only knew about leprechaun lore growing up, and so learning there were more creatures out there, more that I'd never heard of, was suddenly fascinating to me. My parents never taught me much about magic, and nothing about other creatures.

Maddock sighed. "A druid is a human born with magic already in them. Most humans can learn to use magic, like you and your family, but you weren't born with it. You have to draw from me or other magical creatures, you don't have power to make your own magic. So, this guy in the bar was like, the great great grandson of a druid or something. Very weak magic."

"How did you get him to trust you enough to talk to you?"

"As I said, he was a very pathetic druid; barely a drop of magical blood in him, and I let him use a bit of mine, and asked him to show me some magic as a show of faith. He ate it up. Humans love showing off. Apparently he hadn't met a magical being in a while, and felt lonely. He opened right up after that, and I just asked him if he was a member of HAMMA. Don't worry," Maddock said, seeing my anxious expression, "He said he'd never heard of it, so I just told him it was a magic club. He was interested in learning more about it. He was a ruddy terrible magic user." Maddock made a face. "All he used my magic for was making breezes flutter dame's skirts. Kind of a creep."

"Eww! *Kind of?*" I whisper-squealed. "You mean *definitely!*"

Maddock nodded. "A bloomin' spanner. He was a dead end on HAMMA, but he did mention someone called the Sewer Fox, and his connections. That got me curious, however my little druid friend was a little reluctant to tell me any more, so I may have bought him a drink or eight." Maddock chuckled. "If you get enough liquor in them, humans will spill anything."

I rolled my eyes.

"Anyway, after he was loosened up," Maddock continued, "the druid told me that the Fox was in New York City. The druid had used his services a year or so back, and said the Fox knew a lot about everything, as he had tons of eyes and ears in the city. He said the Fox was getting pretty powerful, too. When the druid told me it was a leprechaun, I knew it had to be my old chum. I've known Patrick for ages."

"How do you know him?" I asked, wide-eyed. It wasn't like Maddock had been making social calls over the years we've had him.

"We were good mates back in Ireland. He was captured a year or so before I was, and then we actually came over to the Americas on the same boat, believe it or not."

"Really?" I asked.

"Yep. We only saw each other a few times, as I was kept in confinement most of the trip. We lost contact after we reached Ellis Island."

My heart started doing an excited tap dance in my ribs. If they were good friends, then this Sewer Fox would be willing to help an old friend, right?

"So, we're heading for New York tomorrow?" I asked eagerly. Maddock nodded, standing and stretching, and I saw him eyeing the final piece of pizza that rested in the box.

"Seems like it. It might take a few days to track him down, because the druid didn't know which borough the Fox is living in now, but we'll find him."

I looked at the clock beside my bed. It read two twenty-two a.m.

"Oh my gosh, we've got to get to bed," I said, hopping up to brush my teeth. "I want to get up early and be on our way."

"Can't we sleep in tomorrow?" I heard Maddock ask as I went into the bathroom to wet my brush. I came back out of the bathroom, squeezing toothpaste onto my toothbrush and giving Maddock a look.

"No. I want to get to New York as soon as possible. Don't you?"

Grumbling a goodnight, Maddock snatched the last slice of pizza from the box before vanishing.

I clicked off the TV, cleared the pizza boxes and crumbs off the bedspread, and slid under the sheets. After setting my alarm to wake me up at eight o'clock, I settled deeply into the mattress. As I lay in the darkness, nerves twisting my stomach into knots, I took several deep breaths, trying to quiet the myriad thoughts running unchecked around my mind. I tried to think of positives, concentrating on how we at least had a direction, and didn't realize when I had fallen asleep.

# Chapter Ten

The next morning was a blur. I'd slept through my alarm and had to answer the door for my breakfast delivery in a groggy, rumpled state. I packed my bags while trying not to panic about going to New York City by myself, too nervous to eat.

Every other time I had been to Manhattan, I had gone with my parents or my friends' families. I always had a place to stay, free transportation, and knowledgeable adults to help us get where we wanted to go.

Now all I had was a surly leprechaun, and a whole bunch of people after me. Not to mention the weight of responsibility on my shoulders and the doubts I carried.

I shook away the questions threatening to overwhelm me. If I dwelled on them, I knew I would run away from this. No matter how scared I was, my parents were probably more afraid. That alone helped me keep my resolve.

If Maddock and I got them back in one piece, my future would look very different, for better or worse I didn't know.

Once I was showered and packed, desperately fighting the rising unease in my stomach, I called Maddock to my side, making sure to cover my eyes in case there was a repeat of last night.

"What is it?" Maddock griped, his voice coming from beside my elbow.

"Are you decent?"

"You think I would undress again after what happened yesterday?" he grumbled. I opened my eyes, and looked at Maddock. He was glowering at me with a television remote in his hand.

"Are you ready to go?" I asked, gesturing to all my bags that were stacked near the door. "It's almost 11:30." So much for my wanting to leave early.

"You could've paged my room. Didn't you learn your lesson last time you pulled that little stunt?" Maddock asked, folding his arms.

"Well," I said, irritable, "I never know if you are lounging around or not." I stared pointedly at the remote in his hand. "Don't you want this to be over with as soon as possible?" I asked. "Think of your freedom. I want it for you as much as you do."

Maddock's face grew solemn, and with a sigh he threw his remote onto my bed and turned to me. "Okay, lass. I admit I've been cooped up donkey's years, and that I've been running amok and not taking this whole business as seriously as I should. But this calling me to your side all the time has to stop."

"I've only done it twice," I muttered, but fell silent at his expression.

"I mean, blimey, I can't relax or do anything on my own, thinking you'll summon me to your side at any moment. I can't focus with that pressure."

I remained quiet. Maybe he would finally, really get on board.

"I know you're eager to find your parents, and I'm not going to lie, I can barely keep it under control how much I want to be released from your family's hold," he continued. "So, how about a compromise? I promise to stop treating this whole escapade as a vacation, and try to stay on top of times and situations, and you have to stop calling me to you, willy-nilly. It's a sign of trust. I can appear to you on my own, and I promise to come when I have information, or if we have a schedule to keep. If you say we're leaving at two in the morning for someplace, you can expect me to be at your side at one fifty-five, ready to go."

"But what if I need to talk to you?" I didn't really trust him to keep to our scheduled times, but I was willing to try it, especially if it meant I didn't have to see him in only a towel ever again.

"Buy me a cell phone if you must," he said, throwing up his hands. "Just please, respect me, and trust me, and I'll trust *you* to keep your promise."

"I will keep my promise!" I demanded, stung. A shadow crossed over Maddock's face, but he shook it away.

"So we have a deal?" He held out his hand, thick black hairs sprouting from his knuckles.

"You promise to be open, honest, and very helpful to me?" I asked, narrowing my eyes at him. "No more nightly jaunts to the *pub* for fun or anything like that?"

"I went to the pub for *reconnaissance*," he pointed out, his voice surprisingly calm, "But aye, I swear I'll be the embodiment of trust, respect, and ready aid. A massive help, I promise," he said, solemn. There was no glint of malice or unwillingness in his eyes.

"What's changed?" I frowned, suddenly curious. Before, his attitude on helping me was half-hearted to say the least. I had been surprised that he was so eager to go do reconnaissance last night, but suspicious that he wouldn't actually do his job, that it was just an excuse to get out and see a little of the world. Which I didn't blame him for.

Even the promise of his freedom hadn't seemed like that big of a deal until just now. Sure, he was still grumpy and surly, but he was being serious. One of the first times I had ever seen him so.

He shrugged. "It just hit me that this could really be my shot at freedom. Yours wasn't the first promise of freedom that I've been offered from your family. Like an eejit, I helped those who offered it, and then they found a way to discredit my help, and I remained in captivity."

My stomach twisted. Was my family really that deceitful? The thought made me feel sick. I had always thought that, yes, my family was a little spoiled, a little ridiculous, but outright underhanded and corrupt? I didn't want to believe what he was saying, but his behavior made more sense now. I would feel the same way. It wasn't his freedom he was flippant about; it was the so-called promises of my family.

"I'm . . . I'm so sorry," I sputtered. "I had no idea."

"No, you wouldn't," he said, not unkindly. "I very much doubt your family would've crowed about such behavior; it wasn't one of their finest moments. But, they feel they can do it; I'm nothing more than a glorified pet to them, a beast to do their bidding." His bitterness was sharp, and cut me across my heart.

"How . . . How many people in my family promised you freedom?" I asked, not wanting to hear, but I had to know.

He gave me a hard look and scratched his jaw. "Oh, I've had that little promise made to me about nine times," he said, reminiscing.

"Each time, the one making the promise made their situation seem like life or death, just as you did. I fell for it each time, helping them with their problem with all my might and strength, and then I was sent back to my gilded cage. And I swore, no more. And I've kept that promise for the last two offers of freedom that were made to me."

"So, why did you agree to help this time?" I whispered, my throat tight, trying not to ask what the last two offers were about, though curiosity burned within me.

Maddock stopped running his fingers through his beard and looked me in the eyes. And I mean really *looked*. I swear I almost saw his soul. I wanted to look away, ashamed of my mean thoughts, my family, and my current situation.

"I figured I was going to be captured anyway if I stayed, so that's why I went with you in the first place," he said, "However, I realized, *really* realized, last night that you were different from the others that made me the same promise. You got me a room of my own, you ordered me food that I wanted, you made sure I was safe, and you kept reminding me why I was doing this. These were things no one has ever done for me while here in America." He coughed, fiddling with the button on his cuff.

"Even your great-great-odd-grandmother, as much as I admired her intelligence, treated me like a novelty. When we traveled, I was always in the same room as my masters; they didn't trust me out of their sight, even when I was bound to them. They ordered what they liked, and I was left with the scraps.

"Yes, things are different now, I had a lovely flat with all the food I could want; but not my freedom, when it had been promised me time and time over." He looked up at me, and I was struggling with tears. His hatred of my family made a lot of sense. I didn't see him as a dumb animal, but I had seen him as annoying, a chore to be endured. So wrapped up in my own problems and misery, I hadn't fully comprehended that he was a living creature, intelligent and capable of more than just being a pain in my neck. Guilt welled up in me.

"But you," he continued, trying to break the uncomfortable silence. "You gave me a modicum of trust, even in your young age, when you should be most untrusting of a wily leprechaun on your own, and I realized," he grimaced, "I trust you back."

I blushed and looked at the ground, anywhere but at him. That was the highest praise he had ever given me; that he trusted me. And it was awkward.

Maddock looked just as uncomfortable as he continued. "I may not be human, but I have every feeling a human does; pain, hatred, trust, joy, respect. And you treat me like I'm a proper human, even when I'm not.

"*That* is what has changed my mind. I don't trust your parents within a mile." His face grew sour and hard, and I almost stepped back from him, but his expression changed, and he looked at me again. "But you . . . You're different from them. You treated me like I'm my own person. Like your grandfather did. I admired him greatly, you know."

"I didn't know that," I said, timid.

Maddock nodded. "You remind me of him. He was honest and kind. He visited me a lot, and he tried to get your grandmother to free me for a long time, basically since he was married into the family, but he didn't have the power to do so. Your grandmother put spells on him to keep him from doing it, and he had no magical ability in him so he couldn't shake off the magic. She was a piece of work. Then your parents sent him off to the nursing home once he almost managed to set me free, despite all the precautions they had taken. They thought he had gone insane. That's also why they probably never taught you that spell to get me through the pillars, in case you ever had a fit of teenage rebellion. Your grandmother's influence is still clearly felt by your parents, I imagine."

I'd heard stories of my iron-willed grandmother, but I never met her. She died around the time I was born. But my dad did talk about how mean-hearted she was, and how my grandfather was going to go to heaven just because he had to put up with her.

We stared at each other, Maddock in his jacket, dress pants and button-up shirt, his hair brushed back and gelled, and I saw him, truly saw him, for what he was; an intelligent, magical being. I guessed I had taken it for granted before, or rather didn't want to think of it, because I was too wrapped up in my own misery of not having a life because Maddock took up so much of it. I knew my grandfather had wanted to free him, and I felt a burst of pride that Maddock saw me like him. I hadn't known that.

And now Maddock was saying he trusted me. I guess I had to trust him, too.

"So, deal?" Maddock asked again, holding out his hand again.

"Okay, deal. We'll, uh, need to buy you a phone, then," I blustered, holding out a trembling hand. He gave me a brisk shake of the hand, and then we quickly let go of one another. Now that we knew we really trusted each other, things were more awkward than ever.

"So, shall we crack on?" Maddock asked, bowing slightly towards the door. "You little miscreant," he added with a small smile.

# Chapter Eleven

We would have to take a cab to Manhattan. I'd considered taking the train, but the nearest train station was still too far, and I wasn't keen on the security and cameras at the station with all this money in my bags. A cab would let us be fairly incognito. I even had a credit card in Mary Smith's name as a last resort.

I'd asked Maddock why he couldn't just teleport us both there, and he'd shook his head and called me a "bloomin' dunce."

"Leprechauns can't do tag-along transport. We can only vanish ourselves. And we can't go very far, a few miles at most before having to rest, and that's pushing it."

He had offered to transport ahead as fast as he could and scout out for the Sewer Fox while I traveled by myself, but I didn't want to travel alone. He saw my fear, and though he made fun of me about it, he agreed we should stick together. That meant a cab.

We ordered one at the front desk of the hotel, and soon a yellow cab pulled up to the curb. I glared at the yellow vehicle, desperately wishing I had Santeri to drive us the near four-hour trip to the city in one of my parents' luxury cars. Instead, we had to bribe the driver to make the long drive to Manhattan.

Grumbling, we both slid into the backseat, and I immediately felt carsick from the stench of cigarettes and pungent air fresheners that dangled from his rear view mirror.

Not used to traveling by grimy cab, I was unaccustomed to the unfamiliar driver, the jerky movements, and the disgusting habit he had of smoking and blowing the fumes out his cracked window, which did nothing to prevent the back seat from filling with a blue haze.

"Can you please not smoke?" I choked. The man only laughed.

I felt green the whole ride, and kept the window rolled down, which snarled my hair into a wild ball of knots. Maddock snoozed beside me, completely unbothered. It was good that he had told me he had trusted me before we had gotten into the cab, because I might've punched him while he slept for being so unaware of the discomfort.

By the time we reached downtown Manhattan, I was ready to puke. I didn't enjoy the views of the skyline or the excitement of driving into the heart of the city at all.

"Where do you want to go now, miss?" the cab driver asked, pulling his cigarette out of his mouth to speak to me.

I had no idea where to go next. I hadn't thought to make a reservation at a hotel beforehand; someone had always done it for me.

"The nearest hotel, if you please," I groaned, a headache pounding behind my eyes, my stomach churning.

The man guffawed. "Which hotel, miss?"

"Oooooh," I said, holding my stomach. I didn't want to look up stuff on my phone, I just knew I would vomit. Maddock quickly took my phone and showed the cab driver something on the screen.

"Very good." He pulled down a street and came up to an ornate, stately looking hotel that sat across the street from Central Park.

"I think this one has great access to Central Park," the cabby joked, pulling up to the curb of the hotel.

"And great access to getting me out of here right now," I wheezed, staggering out of the backseat as the cab driver unloaded my luggage from the trunk. I let Maddock pay the exorbitant fare, as I was too busy trying to keep from puking all over the sidewalk. The driver saluted us with a cheerful smirk and got back inside his smelly cab, pulling ahead of a long line of traffic.

"My, my, you're looking mighty ill, lassie," Maddock coughed, failing to hide a laugh. "Let's get you into a hotel room to rest, shall we?"

I was too sick to argue, and allowed him to lead the way into the doors of the hotel. I only stopped in surprise for a moment as we entered the gorgeous foyer. Stunning flower arrangements stood underneath a gigantic, glimmering chandelier, while scrollwork and pillars graced every doorway.

Maddock made the arrangements at the desk, again pretending to be my father, while I leaned feebly against one of the pillars. Once he got our room keys, he steered me through the breathtaking lobby to the elevators. On our floor, I learned Maddock had gotten us suites this time, as he opened my room door and helped me shoulder my luggage in. The suite was a vision of gold and crystal opulence. I couldn't even be angry at him for the unneeded expense. With a laugh, Maddock told me to shower and take a nap; he was going to do more snooping to find where the Fox was holed up, and would be back in about three or four hours.

"You had better keep these for me," he said, handing me his room key and a few trinkets from his jacket pockets. I peered at the items, curious. There were several gold rings studded with gemstones, a few hard candies, a necklace chain, and a worn, gold medallion with a faded crest. "I'm going to be snooping around places that are thick with my kind of people. Pickpockets," he clarified at my confused look. I felt too sick to roll my eyes.

"Okay, be safe," I whispered, realizing the phrase was probably becoming my mantra.

"It's New York that should worry about being safe, lass."

I gave a weak laugh, and he grinned.

I exhaled. "Okay. I'll see you in a while."

Giving me a nod, he walked back down the hallway and stepped into the elevator. I put the Do Not Disturb sign out on my doorknob and shut my door, relieved to have some privacy as I put the deadbolt on, just to feel extra safe. Surprisingly, I did as Maddock suggested, and took a long, hot shower, letting the water and complimentary shampoo clear away the smell of cigarettes and cheap car fresheners.

After I had showered, I did my hair into a long wet braid, slipped into pajamas, and slid under the covers of my enormous, downy bed, feeling much better.

I was in New York City.

Alone.

Tears pricked my eyes at the thought. Outside, I could hear the horns of the traffic and the occasional siren of a police car. It was strangely soothing. Since the car sickness had passed, I was no longer sleepy, so decided to flip through channels and order room service. I would hate to leave my room and miss Maddock and any news he would bring.

I pulled out my laptop to scroll through the internet. I wished I was more tech-savvy so that I could do some technical wizardry and maybe track satellites or traffic cameras or something. Instead, I searched the internet on the hotel's free WiFi, looking up more strange disappearances, anything on HAMMA, or sightings of magical creatures found in the United States.

My searches came up with nothing conclusive, and by the time seven o'clock rolled around, restlessness danced along my muscles. I cursed how I had forgotten to buy Maddock a cell phone so that I could call him to check in, or vice versa. The waiting was torture.

I laid against the pillows and frowned up at the intricately molded ceiling medallion as I fidgeted with the remote, not watching whatever was playing on the TV. The gold and crystal chandelier above sparkled, taking me back to my own home, where HAMMA had snatched my parents. I pushed the fear away with a surge of anger. I felt so useless! Everything that I could've researched on the internet about HAMMA had been done, and I couldn't just keep looking at my friend's texts, wondering what they were doing and wishing my life were different.

I threw off the covers and hopped out of bed, moving to gaze out the window. The city thrummed with life below me. Central park was a swathe of open green among the concrete trees. The setting sun was barely visible through the towering buildings. I wondered where Maddock was out there, navigating that metropolis on his own.

At that moment, I was seized with a desire to join him. I would feel so much better if I could do something constructive. Sitting in this hotel room, as luxurious as it was, was no longer appealing. Not to mention guilt swirled in my gut. I should be out there, actively helping him find my parents. I could learn some things from Maddock when it came to reconnaissance.

With a determined twirl away from the window, I quickly dressed and put on my comfiest shoes. I tucked my phone and some cash into a hidden pocket of my jacket, and then took a deep breath. He wasn't going to be happy about this, especially after our talk this morning. "*Teacht Maddock.*"

His expression made me wince as he appeared before me.

"What did we *just* agree upon, lass?" Maddock barked, his arms crossed, anger bristling his goatee.

"I know, I know, I'm really sorry," I hurried on, holding a leftover slice of cheesecake from my dinner out toward him with a placating smile. He snatched the plate, polishing off the dessert in three bites. "But I was getting so stir crazy in here, I couldn't help it. And you don't have a phone, so I couldn't call—"

He held up a small black phone as he put the empty dessert plate down and wiped his mouth. "Just bought it. Be lucky I wasn't in the middle of paying for it when you summoned me."

Anxiety writhed inside me at the thought. "I really am sorry," I said, biting my lip. "I just . . . I want to go out with you and do some searching."

Maddock snorted. "Lass, you'll only slow me down. I can jump from place to place with ease, and you have to walk everywhere, which will take forever, despite you having those gangly legs."

I refrained from casting a snarky reply back at him as I met his eye. "Look, please? Even if just for a little bit? I want to help, and just sitting around in here is driving me crazy."

"Now you know how *I* felt," Maddock quipped. I snapped my mouth shut, horror curdling my stomach. He had lived in palatial accommodations, but he never really got to go outside. I was so wrapped up in my own annoyances and problems before this whole debacle, I never considered what he lacked.

"Oh. I'm so sorry Maddock," I breathed, a chill running through my blood. "I . . . didn't even consider that. You complain about so much, but you never once complained about not going outside, so I never even consid—"

Maddock waved me away, his expression an indifferent mask. "Water under the bridge. Actually, your grandfather let me out all the time while he was my caretaker. We would go get fast food and hang out at parks and museums. He even took me to the movies and shopping quite a bit. That's where I learned to drive, actually. All without your grandmother's knowledge, of course."

"What?" I gasped. "How? Grandpa couldn't use magic, so how . . . ?"

"Well, your grandmother knew your grandad was taking me out, because of the binding spell that she would place on both of us, and she needed to let me out of the pillar's magical hold, but she thought he was taking me to go gold hunting. *Gold hunting.*" He snorted, shaking his head as he stole some cold fries off my finished dinner plate. "He was able to keep that lie up for about fifty years. Until your parents took over my care. Your grandfather was a great man." He was silent for a moment, his cunning look falling to something softer. Tears pricked my eyes at his expression.

Maddock and my grandfather had been friends, by the sound of it. And now my grandfather was gone, and Maddock was still here. How long would he outlive me?

Maddock exhaled in a loud, annoyed tone that made me jump, breaking me out of my thoughts.

"Fine, you know what? I've been cooped up, walking around for a bit won't hurt too much. You can come along, I s'pose."

Pushing away the guilt and sorrow, I gave him a smile of thanks.

"I was just about to head to Central Park. It's big enough that it could hide some secrets in there," Maddock continued, gesturing over his shoulder. "Let's go take a look around. But take care you don't scare away any magical beasts by crashing around with your colossal feet."

"Your belching is more likely to scare them away than I am," I retorted as he stifled a burp. I laughed as he glowered at me.

Out on the street, premature twilight settled across the city, the skyscrapers glimmering gold in the setting sun. We started off down the crowded street toward the looming treetops, the honking of horns and the distant sounds of sirens louder now that I was out in the open air. The energy of the city around me buoyed my spirits, but also I felt a pinprick of unease. This place was so huge, what was lurking in the shadowy alleyways of this vibrant city?

We soon entered the park, which was emptying of crowds as night was gathering. As we walked down the park path, the large, grassy open space gave way to an enormous pond shrouded in trees.

"I was actually searching around here and I felt magic on the air, but then you called me," Maddock said in a low whisper.

"Really?" I asked, my hands clenching in the pockets of my jacket as we moved further into the park. "When I called you, were you—"

"No one saw me disappear," Maddock assured me with an elbow to my side, and I nodded, relief sweeping through me. I glanced around the thickening trees as the path began to follow the curve of the pond. What magical creature was lurking nearby? I'd never seen another magical being besides Maddock before, and excitement wiggled in my stomach.

"I had also felt something magical stirring *in* the pond," Maddock said, "but I doubt it's anything of use. Probably some magical goldfish or something." I bit my lip as we moved down the path, peering down at the water that lapped softly against the muddy banks.

"But I did feel strong signatures coming from *across* the pond, in the more forested—" Maddock suddenly grabbed my arm to stop me, and I tensed, hissing, "What?"

"Look. Do you see that?" he asked, pointing with his eyes across the water. The pond was just losing its golden shimmer from the now-set sun, the water a deep navy, as he pointed to something small and white high in the trees.

"Come on," he whispered, taking off at a run down the park path. Nonplussed, but my heart beating at a wild pace, I followed. As I ran, the lampposts lining the lane flicked to life. Maddock soon slowed, his eyes turned upward.

"Maddock," I hissed, catching up, breathing hard. He was faster than I ever thought he could be. "What is it?"

He came to a stop under a tree and stared up. I followed his gaze. The dark branches seemed to be slightly illuminated where a bright white bird sat.

"Wow," Maddock whispered. "Would you look at that?"

"A pigeon?" I asked, squinting. It was hard to make out what kind of bird it was in the gathering dark.

Maddock slowly turned to look at me, his expression incredulous. "You think I would point out a *pigeon* to you?"

I shrugged, heat blossoming in my cheeks. "Maybe?"

"That bird is *glowing*, you cabbage!" Maddock insisted. "Barely, but it's glowing."

"I just thought it was a really *clean* pigeon."

Maddock guffawed, slapping a hand over his mouth to stifle his chortling.

I huffed. "Okay, so then what is it, if not New York's most hygienic pigeon?"

Maddock wiped away a tear from his eye, his chuckling slowing. "That looks like a caladrius. A healing bird. They can take a disease away from anyone and expel it. Originally, they're from Italy."

"Really? There's one here, in Central Park?"

"Lass, you wouldn't believe the varying creatures that were brought to these shores, when the world still believed in magic. How do you think I got here?"

"Good point." I looked up again, where the slightly glowing bird gave a soft warble that sent a tingle across my skin. "It's so beautiful. It would be pretty useful to keep in a hospital."

Maddock threw his hands in the air. "You learn about one mythical creature and you're already ready to use it."

I gasped, looking at him. "What? That's not true! I'm just saying . . . Oh never mind."

Maddock made a *tsking* noise with his tongue, then turned away from the bird in the tree. "That signature wasn't what I felt earlier. It's somewhere nearby, though. Come on." He led me further down the path, the canopy overhead completely obscuring the sky, a steep hillside blocking a view of the rest of the park off to our left. A little further down the path, he veered toward the waist-high iron fence surrounding a small green area filled with trees. He gestured to the fence. "Come on, it's this way."

"You want me to hop the fence?"

"If you want to come, yeah. There's gotta be some use for those gangly legs of yours."

I studied the fence. "Is that actually iron? Will it hurt you? Fantasy novels talk about how iron hurts magical creatures . . ."

"Nah. Iron doesn't bind leprechaun types." Without another word, he effortlessly leapt the fence and charged into the shadowy undergrowth.

Growling, I gingerly lifted my leg up and over, clinging to the cold metal, then hopped. My other leg cleared the fence, but my supporting leg lost footing on the damp, muddy ground. With a small cry, I crashed to the underbrush on the other side. Spitting out a piece of bark that had been flung into my mouth, I leapt to my feet, brushing plants and dirt from my knees. Thankfully, Maddock was far enough ahead that I don't think he heard or saw. I hurried after him. When I caught up to him, he glanced up at me.

"Felt like kissing the ground, did you?" Maddock smirked. I gave him a sharp shove, the taste of wood still lingering on my tongue. He chuckled. "Guess those ganglies weren't much help after all."

Soon, the undergrowth opened up to a tiny little clearing, and we came to a stop beside an enormous pile of dirt that resembled a molehill. The pond, and the skyline lights, were barely visible through the thin foliage off to our right. Giving me a warning gesture to be quiet, Maddock cleared his throat.

"Greetings, friends," Maddock called. My heart hammered in my chest as I bit my lip. What lived in that pile of dirt?

"I am sorry to bother you," Maddock continued, "But we're in need of some help."

We sat in silence for several moments, and I was about to ask Maddock what the heck he was doing, when a cleverly disguised door, covered in a solid mound of dirt, opened on top of the molehill. Large, hairless white ears and a small head tufted with a little white hair poked out of the molehill, large eyes staring up at us. I stared back, mouth hanging open. I'd never seen so many magical creatures in one day before!

"Good evening, my little pixie friend," Maddock said, giving a small bow, and I perked up. A pixie? As in, fairy? I had to clamp down a gasp, in case it would scare away the little creature. "I'm Maddock O'Bannon. The giant is Mallory McKenna."

The eyes glanced between us several times before it spoke up in a small voice. "Good eve. I'm Gerden." Gerden's head came a little further out of the hole, revealing a button nose and a wide mouth. The city lights filtering through the leaves were reflected in its large eyes. I could see in the dark that it was wearing a piece of dark brown cloth as a type of tunic. "A leprechaun? But you're not the wily Sewer Fox," he replied, his tone curious.

"You're right, I'm not, but he's an old friend of mine, and I've lost touch with him. Do you happen to know where he lives?"

"I—" Suddenly the little creature lurched sideways, dirt from the molehill walls showering down on him as a clamor of small voices broke out beneath the pixie. He grunted in annoyance until finally the pixie cried, "Alright, alright, I'll move!"

The creature clambered out of the hole, followed by several other pixies, all ranging in different states of dress and height and baldness, and soon eight pixies stood before us, the tallest's ears no higher than my knee, or Maddock's waist.

"You mentioned the wily Sewer Fox," Maddock repeated, "Patrick Hayes? If you haven't any info, are there any other creatures around here that might?"

The pixie shook his head. "As far as I know, we're the only creatures in this section of the park, aside from the abaia in the pond."

"What's an—" I began, but Maddock stomped my foot, causing the pixies to burst into giggles as I gasped and doubled over in pain. Wincing, I used Maddock's head to steady myself as I balanced on one leg to rub my foot on the back of my other leg. There were more giggles.

"So, you've heard of the Sewer Fox?" Maddock pressed.

"Aye. We've heard of him. Word travels in the magical world. He offers services if any magical creature needs help, as well as other . . . shady . . . business."

"Shady, huh?" Maddock asked with a grin. "Would you happen to know where this Fox lives? We'd love to find him."

The pixies giggled again, and I nearly jumped out of my skin when one of the pixies, a female no higher than my mid shin, wearing a bright yellow dress, reached out and touched my leg. She stared up at me with wide eyes. I had to hold myself back from crouching down, afraid I would scare her off or hurt her. I merely smiled at her with a small wave. "Hello."

The little thing gasped, and with a giggle, scampered to hide behind the others. I gave her another wave when she peeked back out at me, and she waved shyly back. My smile broadened, and the girl shared in giggles with two shorter pixies.

I turned back to the conversation Maddock was having just as he nodded with a gruff, "Okay, thank you very much, friends. You've been a great help." He turned to me. "Let's go."

I gave the group a small wave, my heart beating erratically, as we made our way through the underbrush again, toward the path. "Those were pixies?" I whispered, ducking under a low branch.

"Garden pixies," Maddock clarified. "They're like little elves that live underground. They cultivate plants and help farmers. Very kind and helpful, but have a care; different types are much more dangerous. They were probably brought over centuries ago to the new world, maybe even with the first settlers, to help the colonists plant crops, but my Grandad told me that the Puritan movement declared all magical creatures evil. Many creatures died, and so most went into hiding and faded into myth. We magical beings figured out right quick that the growing new world didn't treat magic with respect." Maddock snorted. "Anyways, many people mistake pixie mounds for molehills, so they can usually live peacefully out in the wild or in parks until people drive them away."

Lamplight soon filtered overhead through the trees. As we got to the fence, I heard a soft, "Wait!"

I whirled, stumbling backwards with a gasp as the same yellow-dressed pixie stood at my face height, balancing delicately on a tree branch, something tucked under her arm.

She giggled again as I straightened, then she held out a beige, lumpy object the size of a golf ball that was difficult to discern in the dark.

"Here you go!" she announced, and when I held out my hand, she placed the item in my palm. The object, which was covered in dirt, had a familiar aroma.

"Oh, wow," I said, trying to keep the frown out of my tone. What was it? It seemed familiar.

"A white truffle?" Maddock exclaimed, glancing between the item in my hand and the pixie with an awed, hungry expression. The pixie nodded, beaming. The familiarity clicked in my mind. My parents, and Maddock, adored white truffles.

"Oh!" I gasped. "For me?"

"We like to share," she squeaked.

"Thank you so much!" I had to bite back a squeal of delight at her adorable, cheerful little face. Recalling what Maddock had just said, I asked, "Did you grow this yourself?"

The pixie nodded again, swaying slightly as a blush grew on her cheeks.

"Thank you! It's beautiful!"

"That smells finer than the truffles your parents got me, lass," Maddock said, giving the fungus an appreciative sniff.

With another giggle, the pixie waved and scampered down the tree branch and into the darkness.

I turned to Maddock, a giddy, awestruck grin on my face.

Maddock gave me an impatient chortle. "Yes, yes, they're very cute. Stop acting like a ninny. We got what we came for."

I exhaled, trying to stop grinning like an idiot.

"About the Sewer Fox?" I didn't want to admit that I hadn't been paying much attention to their conversation. My mind had been reeling during most of the meeting. The world had more secrets and hidden places than I ever thought. What other magical creatures have I walked by in my day-to-day life, hiding in plain sight?

"Yup. We're heading to Brooklyn. Apparently my old friend has been very busy making a name for himself in seedy circles. I think it's time we pay him a little visit."

# Chapter Twelve

The next morning found us taking the subway to Brooklyn. After the cab from yesterday, I was done with automobiles for the time being. Maddock had said the pixies talked about the Sewer Fox living by the river, so we headed to the docks. Maddock tried to sense any magic in the buildings and warehouses that lined the waterway as we walked up and down the crumbling asphalt. I kept close to Maddock, sure we were going to get mugged at any moment. By three in the afternoon, I was ready to give up the search and go back to the hotel for a snack break. As we passed several tall warehouses on the south-western side of the borough, Maddock stopped up short.

"Hold up. The rascal is here." He gestured toward an alley between two tall buildings, and I felt my courage finally fail as fear and fatigue bombarded me. The alleyway was filled with reeking dumpsters and rusty fire escapes, and I was certain we would be murdered or get tetanus just by walking through there.

Maddock entered, and I followed, reluctant. "Maddock, are you sure . . ." My voice died in my throat as three men stepped out from the shadows, barring our way.

"Yep, this is it," Maddock quipped.

One of the men smoked a cigarette while the other two leered down at us, reminding me of the kind of men I saw in crime movies for a big mob boss, all clichés of hulking muscle and tattoos. But that didn't make them any less scary.

"Maddock," I squeaked. "I think we turned down the wrong—"

"Shhh!" Maddock hissed, cutting me off with a sharp gesture. I fell silent and tried to shrink behind Maddock as best as I could. He seemed so awfully sure of himself, and even though I'd seen him in action, these colossal men were more numerous, and more muscular than the two HAMMA guys back at my house had been.

"Hey," one of the men with a wolf tail haircut guffawed, bending closer to Maddock. "Are you an escapee from the circus?" he asked, getting into Maddock's face. I could smell the alcohol on the large man's breath from where I stood, and I tried to cough quietly.

"No," Maddock replied, his tone testy. "Please get your giant self out of the way."

"Are you sure?" The man smoking the cigarette flicked the glowing butt away and took two steps forward, towering over Maddock, smoke billowing from his mouth. "Cuz you kinda look like a circus freak."

"Are you washed-up football players? Because you definitely look like you've played without helmets," Maddock said, his eyes skirting scornfully up and down the three men.

"Maddock!" I squeaked, cowering behind his tiny frame as the three large men started to swell even larger with rage.

Maddock began to strip off his sport coat. "Not to worry, lass. Boxing is a religion where I come from," he said, throwing the coat over his shoulder and into my arms. "And I am a devout disciple." Maddock began rolling up his shirt sleeves, and I tried not to roll my eyes.

The three men laughed in surprise as the diminutive man took a few practice jabs at the air.

"Now," Maddock commanded, "do I have to fight you three buffoons in an easy victory, or will you let us through? I have business with the Sewer Fox. We're old chums."

One of the men sniffed. "Well, the Sewer Fox doesn't have business with you. Get him out of here."

Maddock sighed as the other two men stepped forward.

"Very well. Remember after I beat you all soundly that I did give you fair warning," Maddock said, raising his fists. I whispered his name again, but Maddock just cast me a sly grin.

One man reached out to pluck Maddock from the pavement as if he were a garbage bag full of rubbish, when Maddock moved so quick he was a blur. He darted behind two of the men and kicked their knees out from under them. As they fell to their knees, he landed punches on their faces, the force of the blows knocking them back onto the pavement, dazed.

The third man, the one with the wolf tail, stepped forward with a shout, and Maddock nimbly leaped up onto a dumpster and began battering the lights out of him. Wolf Tail tried to block the onslaught of Maddock's fists, but Maddock just began boxing the man's ears. The big man swung wide, trying to catch Maddock off guard, but Maddock, fleet as ever, leapt over Wolf Tail's fumbling attack and landed a blow on the man's throat. The man stumbled back, wheezing, his nose bloody and his eyes beginning to swell. The two men Maddock had knocked down were getting to their feet, looking disoriented and angry.

I ducked for cover around the corner, having no desire to get punched by a stray fist.

Maddock stood on a dumpster lid, his expression haughty. He looked down at the men as they tried to reorient themselves. "Are you humiliated enough? Ready to take me to the Sewer Fox?" Maddock demanded. "He knows me. We go way back."

Two of the men bellowed and pounced at Maddock, who sprang off the dumpster and used their heads as stepping stones to launch himself onto the ladder of the fire escape. Again the two men fell backwards and Maddock, seeing the third man reach for a button beside a metal door, jumped off the ladder and landed on the man's shoulder with a resounding crunch. I saw one of the men stagger to his feet and pull out a gun.

"*Maddock!*" I screamed as the man pointed it toward Maddock, who was just stepping off the unconscious man he'd landed on. A disdainful expression grew on Maddock's face as he turned to face the man wielding the gun.

Suddenly, the door burst open, and a short man with a lion's mane of red hair and a finely tailored suit stepped out.

"Whoa, ho! Hold your fire!" the short man commanded in a thick brogue, his voice incredibly deep for his short stature, deeper than Maddock's. "Lower your weapon," the small man called. Reluctantly, the gunman lowered the gun and holstered it as the second leprechaun I'd ever seen in my life turned to Maddock, his expression unreadable.

After a moment, the red haired leprechaun roared and pulled Maddock into a bone crushing hug.

"Mad Dog, you manky brute!" the redhead bellowed. "It's been, what, almost two centuries?"

"Something like that," Maddock replied, pounding the redhead on the back. "Pat, it's good to see you." Smiling and laughing, they broke their hug. Seeing Maddock smile, I felt as though someone punched me in the stomach. In all my years, I'd never seen Maddock smile like that; genuine, unguarded, without any hint of mockery or malice.

"Eh, they should be calling you the 'Silver Fox' by now, mate. You look old," Maddock said, gesturing to the silver streaks in the Sewer Fox's mane.

"Aye," the Sewer Fox said lightly, shaking his long silver-and-red mop off his shoulders. "It's been a real hit with the ladies."

Maddock, looking down the alleyway and seeing me peering out from behind the corner, gestured for me to come closer. I hurried past the bruised and bleeding guards without making eye contact and came to stand beside Maddock, getting a better look at the Sewer Fox.

His upper lip was shaved clean, and he had a vibrant red chin-strap beard that was trimmed short. The leprechaun was a few inches shorter than Maddock, but that didn't take away from his commanding demeanor. If anything, he seemed taller.

"Well, you wouldn't have come to see me unless you wanted something," the Sewer Fox chortled, clapping Maddock on the shoulder. "So, now that you've soundly flogged my front guard, come in, and we'll talk."

"Thank you, Pat." Maddock took back his jacket I'd been clutching, frowning at me over the twisted fabric as he shook it out. "A few bowsies you got working for you, there, Pat," Maddock said, laying the jacket over an arm.

"Aye, they're not very bright, but they do an alright job keeping away smaller troublemakers and whatnot." The Fox shrugged.

"But if any real threat comes, you're in trouble," Maddock pointed out, coming to a stop beside me.

"Nah, I've got a few other avenues in my security," the Fox said, giving Maddock a sly smile. The Sewer Fox's eyes slid to me, as if finally realizing I was there. "Well, well, well, Mad. Is this your oul doll?" the Fox asked, a smirk creeping up on his small face as he gave Maddock a playful dig of his elbow.

Maddock shook his head, his expression neutral. "My master."

"Oh." Pat's smile vanished within a second, and he stiffened as he looked at me again. His expression deepened into a glare, and I saw him puff out his barrel chest, his fingers itching toward a pocket. "And you brought her here?" the Fox demanded. "Why, Mad Dog? Could be bad for business, ye great eejit."

"No, no, the lass is honest," Maddock said, waving his hands at the Fox. "She just wants information about her parents. They were kidnapped."

The Sewer Fox's expression didn't change as he scowled between me and Maddock. I tried to put on an innocent, kind smile, but my mouth trembled. Maddock could've mentioned that the Sewer Fox was even surlier than he was.

"Information? Well, we'll see about that." Still giving me a suspicious glower, the Fox turned to look at Maddock. "She's your responsibility. Keep her in check. I don't want any funny business, Mad. Still in human custody, huh? Shame." The Fox sent me a venomous glance, then sighed. "Well, come in. We'll see what we can do for you." He started through the door, down the dimly lit hallway.

I touched Maddock's shoulder before he followed the Fox, and crouched down next to Maddock's ear. "What's an owl doll?" I whispered, the funny word rolling around my mouth.

"A girlfriend," Maddock whispered back with a snort before following the Fox through the door. My face flared with heat as I straightened, trying not to scream in horror. Maddock was an old man! Literally over two hundred years old! And not in like, the hot vampire kind of way. I stood rooted to the spot as I watched Maddock disappear.

The embarrassment at the Sewer Fox thinking I was Maddock's girlfriend, combined with the outright hostility that the Fox had shown me, made me want to turn around and go back to the hotel. However, the promise of information was too irresistible, and I knew that Maddock would protect me. Besides, I didn't want to stay out here with these even scarier sentinels that were grumbling and casting me bitter looks as they nursed their injuries. Taking a deep breath, I followed both leprechauns through the shadowy doorway.

# Chapter Thirteen

The warehouse, while it had looked so decrepit and grungy on the outside, was decorated in an expensive, industrial style; the brick walls inside were clean and bright, with lots of brass pipes, wooden accents, and open, polished concrete floors. I felt like I had stepped into an interior design magazine.

The Sewer Fox ushered us into what looked like a conference room, a long table with wingback chairs occupying most of the space and an enormous TV screen taking up the far wall. The sweet aroma of fresh flowers from a large arrangement in the middle of the table filled the room, softening the masculine decor.

The Sewer Fox sat, gesturing for us to follow suit.

"So, what are you up to now, you old scoundrel?" Maddock asked, taking a seat beside the Fox. I sat on the opposite side of the two leprechauns. I wanted to put as much space as possible between me and the nasty looks the Fox was shooting me.

"Oh you know, nothing much," the Fox said with a sigh, "just granting favors and 'magic' to idiots, all for a hefty sum, of course."

"Well, aren't you a cute hoor," Maddock said, slapping the Fox on the shoulder. The Fox shrugged, looking pleased, but I noticed he was twiddling the rings on his fingers, as if agitated.

"Hey, a man has to make a living," the Fox replied. Maddock nodded. The door opened again, and two statuesque women entered, bearing a cart with plates of food and drinks.

"I tell you, Mad, I don't know what those idiots that sell drugs are doing," the Fox laughed, totally ignoring the women as they came to a stop beside him and began placing platters of food and glasses in front of us. "You hold out a few shiny gold coins, whip up some 'magic', and you can get any village idiot to do your bidding. Cheaper, and a whole lot more ethical. Not that I care about ethics, mind you," the Fox said, tapping his nose. "Heck, I'd sell my own wife for a thick corned beef sandwich if I had a mot, but being ethical does keep the *human* cops from sniffin' around my business." The Fox turned to me, eyes narrowing. "Speaking of which, this lass you brought looks like a no good sleeveen, she do."

I had no idea what a *sleeveen* was, but I took it as an insult. I drew a deep breath through my nose, trying to keep myself from either shouting or crying out of nerves. I wasn't sure what would happen if I opened my mouth.

"I tell you, Pat, she's clear," Maddock reassured, eyeing the plates heaping with food with a very greedy, leprechaunish expression.

"Well, we ain't going to talk until I'm sure she ain't earwiggin,'" the Fox said, casting me yet another disdainful look. "She could be a spy."

"A spy?" I burst out, unable to help myself. "For what?"

"Any organization," the Fox said, beginning to fill his and Maddock's plate. "Especially the one that might have taken your parents."

My mouth fell open. "Are you kidding me?" I sputtered. "Why would I kidnap my own parents, then ask Maddock to help me find them? Plus, I'm only fifteen!"

"They start them younger than that," the Fox hissed. Maddock leaned forward and put a hand down on the table between us.

"Pat, you trust me, right? Why would I bring enemies of yours here? We're friends," Maddock said, his voice calm.

"Aye, we are. It's *her* I don't trust."

"Pat, her parents were kidnapped. You know she can't be smart enough to pull off a job like that anyway, being human and everything. They barely remember to drink water," Maddock said, casting me a "shut up" look as he spoke. I clenched my fists under the table to help myself keep quiet. He was trying to help me, and if insulting me was going to get the Sewer Fox to trust me, then I wasn't going to say a word. Even if it did make me burn up inside. "We need your help, because I know if anyone has information, it's the Sewer Fox," Maddock cajoled, nudging him with an elbow.

"You think sweet talking will lower my guard?" the Fox said, looking at Maddock, but I saw him smile as he took a swig from a large foaming tankard that had been put in front of him. He was silent for several moments, and I held my breath, wondering if we'd be thrown out. If that happened, I didn't know where we'd go next.

"Very well. You go first," the Fox said, lowering his drink, and looking between us. "If I feel I can trust you, and I like your story, I'll decide if I'll help you or not."

"Deal." Maddock looked to me. "Right?

I nodded. What else could I do?

"Well, go ahead, then," Maddock encouraged as the Fox began to dig into his plate of food, Maddock following suit.

Returning the narrow-eyed look that the Sewer Fox was giving me, I cleared my throat. The women had placed a plate with potatoes, corned beef, bread, and corn in front of me. My stomach gurgled, but I refrained from dishing up and eating as well. I was sure that if I started eating before starting the story—and kept the angry leprechaun waiting—things could get worse.

Ignoring the tempting smells, I began telling him about the party the night before my parents' kidnapping, how I had gone to my friend's house, that I came home to a destroyed house, and had been chased by the man in the HAMMA shirt. At that, the Fox's eyebrows nearly disappeared into his hair, but was silent. I told him about making the deal with Maddock, and how we ended up here.

The Fox continued to glare after I had finished speaking. Not wanting to give him any reason to distrust me, I maintained eye contact, even though his expression was so severe that heat crept into my face.

The Fox cleared his throat, setting aside his fork. "Okay, here's what I'll do. You may have my mate Maddock convinced that you'll set him free if he helps you free your parents, but I need more than just the word of a human. You see, I know something about humans, miss, and they'll stab you in the back the second you've done all you can for them."

Remembering what Maddock said about my ancestors treating him the same way, I blushed and bit my lip, but I still looked the fiery leprechaun in the face. I needed to put on a strong, confident face to show I wasn't as guilty as the Fox thought.

"However, like Maddock said, there was something in your eye while you were telling your story that makes me believe that you might not be half bad. Well, at least you might be telling the truth." His nose wrinkled, like he didn't believe what he was saying either. I tried not to look too hopeful, but I could feel the blush on my face deepen in color.

"But," he continued, and my heart dropped a little. I had tried not to get my hopes up, but despite myself, I had. Was he about to dash those hopes to the floor? "I still want to be extra sure you are on our side, and you're not looking to nab a new leprechaun for your collection. So, I will tell you about this group that has kidnapped your parents, and if you prove yourself even more to me, that you aren't playing my mate Maddock false, I will even help reunite you with your parents."

"Prove how?" I squeaked.

"We'll get to that. It's nothing much." The leprechaun shook back his mane of hair, unconcerned.

"So, that's it? That's all you want from me, I just have to prove myself?" I asked, breathless.

The Sewer Fox snorted in distaste. "The best payment I can get from you is if you actually let my friend Mad Dog go."

This time, I couldn't hide my excitement.

"Of course, I'll do anything for your help," I stammered, trying not to trip over my tongue as my brain tried spitting out thanks, agreements, and promises all at the same time.

He held up a hand to quiet my spluttering, and fell silent.

"We have a deal, then," the Fox said, and I nodded.

"Very well. We don't have much time, if you're to prove yourself to me, so I'll get right down to it. HAMMA is an acronym for

Humans Against the Manipulation of Mythical Animals." The Fox gave a small, disdainful sniff. "Their objective, in essence, is to stop humans from using magic or owning any magical creatures, powers, or mythical items, because it's unethical. So, they track down those that use magic or keep magical animals; HAMMA calls them Everbleeders, because they claim humans bleed magical creatures dry—"

My mind jumped to being called an Everbleeder by the man in my house, and I shuddered.

"—then they release the creatures into the wild, and punish the humans. Sounds noble, correct?" the Sewer Fox asked in mock innocence.

I frowned, but nodded, scared that the Fox wanted me to agree with him. "I guess?"

"Well, it *isn't*," the Fox snapped, his face hardening. "The organization, or *Community*, as they call themselves, is a complete sham, a hoax, and a front for something much more sinister." He took a long drink from his tankard. "In reality, the members of this group are being duped. The lackeys, the lowest in the pyramid, believe they are saving magical creatures from captivity, to be released back into the wild, when in fact they are actually just gathering the creatures and unknowingly giving them to the higher-ups in the organization. Those higher up on the pyramid then take these creatures to be sold, traded, or kept for themselves."

"That's awful," I said, feeling sick, and the Sewer Fox's head snapped to look at me.

"Don't patronize me, you hypocrite," he snarled.

"What? I . . . I don't—" I looked at Maddock and my protests died in my throat. Maddock was barely shaking his head, but his eyes were widened, as if telling me to shut up. I looked at my plate, face flushing, trying to hold back my varying emotions, and the Fox snorted.

"Anyway, it appears that HAMMA has taken your family in retribution for owning a leprechaun."

Maddock raised his hand as if claiming responsibility.

"So, do you think one of these higher-ups has my parents?" I asked, my voice restricted to a whisper as I gripped my fork.

"Oh, I doubt it. I reckon the bosses are too important for that kind of thing. Besides, they're just as guilty, so clearly they don't care about the ethics of the thing. The members, however, *do* care about the ethics, so much so that they feel justified in not only kidnapping, but torturing those who have had the gall to own magical creatures or relics. They're all fanatics."

I almost tuned out the rest of what the Fox was saying as only one word registered in my brain, and made me stiffen in horror.

"Torturing?" I breathed, icy fear crawling down my back, making the hairs on my arms stand on end.

The Fox looked at me, his severe expression softening slightly. "Such is the style of radical institutions. I'm sorry."

The burning in my eyes became so great that I had to duck my head as several hot tears dropped onto my lap. I didn't want them to see such a weakness, as they already thought so poorly of me, but the Fox and Maddock began making pointed small talk with each other, allowing me to steady my emotions.

I had always taken my parents for granted. I knew that now, and considering everything they had done for me, and the fact that they were now enduring nameless torture somewhere, made my heart hurt in a way it had never hurt before.

But I had to pull myself together, I couldn't help them as a soggy, puffy mess. I quickly wiped my eyes and looked up at the Fox, who was showing Maddock a small titanium sculpture that he was saying he had made in his private workshop.

"How do you know all this?" I asked, trying to blink away the stinging in my eyes. The Fox looked at me, setting the small figurine, an intricate octopus, on the table beside him, and folded his hands in his lap.

"Well, I'm in the same sort of business. I run a sort of underground service that gets magical creatures out of captivity and back to their homeland. HAMMA has been a thorn in my side ever since I started this mission. I personally don't care about punishing the humans that take custody of these creatures. They're human; little-minded and greedy. All offense," he spat at me. "Humans only think of how they can take, take, take, with little consequence to themselves or how it affects others."

My face burned as I thought about my own family. Sure, my parents behaved a little in the way he was describing. They were vain, and more than a little greedy, and cared more about social standing than their family. I myself had felt the effects of their indifference and neglect, but I partly blamed Maddock for that. I often felt that my mother and father cared more for him, and what he could give, than they did for me. But I hoped they could change.

There was no way I was going to tell the Sewer Fox all this. He wouldn't understand, and more than likely take offense at my feelings, maybe even call me a hypocrite. Again. I knew, in a way, how Maddock felt, but I was obviously also in part to blame for his captivity. It was a messy situation, but I did want to stand up for myself a little.

"No, not everyone is greedy and narrow-minded, you're just in the business of dealing with people like that. But the whole world isn't like that," I said, cursing my shaking voice. "I'm not like that."

"But you are leveraging Maddock's freedom for help. That seems pretty on-track on the road to rotten," the Fox snipped back.

"I am in a pretty tight situation," I said through clenched teeth. "I'm just a teenager, I can't do everything alone. And maybe if *I* could trust Maddock to help me *after* I'd released him, I would've released him before we left to find my parents. I have every intention of keeping my word, but I can't trust him to stick around once I release him."

Maddock nodded, a little chagrined. "She's right. I would be halfway to Ireland before you could say 'Irish coffee.'"

"But," I continued, glancing at Maddock to make sure it was safe for me to keep speaking. He gave me an encouraging look. "I can trust him to help me *before* I release him, because he trusts in me to release him this time," I explained. The Fox perked up, looking at me before turning to Maddock.

"So you've been played like a fiddle before too, huh?" the Fox asked, clicking his tongue.

"More times than I would like to admit," Maddock said, shaking his head.

The Fox nodded in understanding. "It's happened to the best of us more than once. We always feel like we can trust the humans to keep their promises, and then the sacrifice becomes too much to bear for them, the thought of losing their beloved pet, and so they don't keep up their end of the bargain."

I exhaled, annoyed. "Well, I intend to keep my end of the deal."

"You would be the first," the Fox said, his bitterness thinly veiled through his bared teeth.

"So, you actually ship animals back where they belong?" I asked, wanting to change the subject, although I still felt irritable.

The Fox snorted. "Aye, and I don't need to make a big splash about it either, nor do I care about the humans getting their just deserts; I just want those poor creatures freed."

"Well, I can respect and support that, definitely," I hurried on. I just wanted him to stop lecturing me about how horrible humans were.

"Excellent." He also seemed bored of abusing the subject, so he took a hearty swig of some amber liquid that he had poured into a nearby tumbler, his tankard now empty.

"So, in shipping animals back, you've learned about HAM-MA?" I asked.

The Sewer Fox rolled his eyes. "They're a plague to me and mine. I've had to follow them closely for my own sake. I haven't been able to muster the numbers to deal with any of their facilities head on yet, so I've just been trying to beat HAMMA to the creatures we discover. If I can get the creatures into protection before HAMMA gets to them, I call it a victory. Once HAMMA does get a creature in their possession, it's impossible for me to get them back. HAMMA is pretty effective for such an ignorant group of people. They have advanced technology, magic—because they're hypocrites," the Fox snorted, "—and hordes of zealous followers to mind the facilities, go on raids, and monitor any security threats."

"So, what is it you want me to do?" I asked, chewing the bottom corner of my lip. I was seriously hoping he didn't want me to help storm a HAMMA facility and free all the animals inside. The way the Fox was talking, that kind of operation sounded dangerous and pretty darn impossible.

The Fox smirked at my worried expression. "It isn't what you are thinking. As I said, the facility nearest us is way out of my league to try and break into. I just content myself with trying to beat that asinine group to the punch. Which is what I need from you. I know you can use magic. To prove your honesty, for my help, I want you to go get one for me."

"One what?" I asked blankly.

"A creature. A mandagot, to be precise." He said it as nonchalantly as if he were asking me to go pick something up at the grocery store.

"You want me to break into someone's house and steal something from them?" I asked, incredulous. "I mean, release their magical animal?" I backpedaled when I saw the Fox's face. "Sorry, this is all new to me," I said, holding up my hands in defense.

Snorting, the Fox shook his head. "It will be easy. I need you to go to a place an hour or so north of here, outside of New Haven, Connecticut. That is where a man, a Mr. Nathanial Kim, has it."

"What's a mandagot?" I asked, timid. "I mean, the only creatures I've known to exist were leprechauns, and—"

Both Maddock and the Fox began laughing, great roaring laughs, and I frowned in annoyance.

"What?" I asked, hating how whiny my voice sounded. "My parents were only obsessed with leprechauns, they never taught me there was really anything else, and it's not like I could ask anyone." While I said it, I felt stupid. I should've realized ages ago that if leprechauns and magic existed, there was bound to be more out in the world.

"Oh, you absolute cabbage. Every country has their own type of creatures," the Fox snorted. "Ireland itself has not only leprechauns, but selkies, banshees, fairies, and several other inconsequential beasts. The few kelpies in Ireland were cleared out a century or two ago. In fact, that is one of the objectives of HAMMA. They were outraged to learn that kelpies existed and then disappeared, and they're trying to figure out why kelpies went extinct, and to bring them back. But I don't think they'll be successful." The Fox and Maddock shared a secret smile.

"So, back to the point," I said, annoyed at being left out. "What's a mandagot?"

"It's a shapeshifter from France. It can transform into any mid-size mammal, but it usually prefers the shape of cats or foxes. It generates wealth and luck wherever it resides, and so those who possess and take care of it receive the fruits of those magical gifts."

"How do you find these people? How did HAMMA find my family?" I asked.

The Sewer Fox laughed, rubbing a hand through his hair. "I'm ashamed to admit that we may have adopted some of the practices of HAMMA ourselves. I have several defectors from HAMMA that work for me, and they've been invaluable resources of information. Basically, HAMMA monitors acquaintances of those they've already taken magical creatures from—"

My mind immediately went to my friends. Would they soon be monitored as well?

"—or they keep an eye on those who rise to wealth and status quickly. They track purchases of suspects, and if they get wind of strange and consistent purchases, the target's purchase history is monitored, and they are staked out. For example, mandagots feed exclusively on raw chicken. We've discovered that Mr. Kim buys new chicks and feed every year in bulk, yet he doesn't sell the eggs or meat." He gave me a knowing look. "So we work from there. After surveillance and research, we can usually discover what types of animals someone owns, then capture and release the creature into the wild without much fuss. This extraction should be very easy." He turned to look at me. "So, what do you reckon? Want to do the right thing for once?"

I bit the inside of my cheek so hard that I winced, but I didn't shout the choice words that I wanted to. The Sewer Fox, though he hated me, was holding out a lifeline, and I was afraid he would cut it at the slightest provocation.

"What is your plan?" I asked, giving him a pained smile.

"You're willing to do it?" the Fox asked, his eyebrows raised.

"If it means getting your help to free my parents, then yes, of course," I said, trying to steady my shaking voice.

The Fox's eyes narrowed as his lips curved into a sly, delighted smile. I felt my bravado deflate slightly at his evil look.

"Um . . . am I going . . . alone?" I asked, swallowing against the dryness of my mouth.

"Please, I don't trust you *that* much. Obviously Maddock will go with you, not only because of your magical tether, but you need some brains for the operation." The Fox slapped Maddock on his back, and both laughed.

I ground my teeth. Being in the company of one leprechaun was bad enough when it was just Maddock, but two was almost unbearable, especially a powerful one that held my future in his manicured hands. With any luck, once my parents were saved, I'd never have to look at another leprechaun again. The thought made me smile, and I took a deep, steadying breath. "Okay."

The Fox clapped his hands together. "Excellent. Let us not delay, then."

While I ate, the Fox had files brought to the table, where he pulled out pictures of the owner, Mr. Kim. We looked through pictures of Mr. Kim's estate: the extravagant, Tudor-style house where he lived alone, and the sprawling land with lots of forest where his chickens were kept.

"We believe he keeps the animal somewhere nearby, obviously in an enchanted perimeter, so the beast can move around a bit, but it can't escape by accident. Mandagots pretty much stay where they have consistent food and shelter, as they are viciously territorial, but humans are notorious for taking above-and-beyond precautions." The Fox rolled his eyes.

I bit back a comment about how that was a rich statement coming from a guy that had three hulking guards outside just to keep people from talking to him. I needed his help, and I couldn't risk getting kicked out for my sarcastic remark.

"Then what?" I asked.

"Then my team will be releasing it back into the wilds of France, where it will find itself a new home."

We spent the next hour discussing the procedure for extracting a mandagot, which the Fox said we would attempt this evening.

"So soon?" I asked, swallowing my fear.

"Aye, be glad it is, too. Prove to me you're worth it, and you'll have help from me to get your parents back, and Mad's freedom, as soon as we can."

Well, that was incentive enough.

# Chapter Fourteen

"He'll be somewhere where it's dark and confined," Maddock said, peering through the bushes. "Kim's still awake, so we won't be able to scope it out beforehand. We'll have to work quick to find its den once we move." We were hiding in the thick grove of trees near the front of the house. The sun was setting behind us, illuminating the large house between the trees. Several of the lights inside the mansion were on, and we could see an occasional figure walking past the windows. "We don't want to wait too long to set up, because the beast no doubt has food somewhere already, and we need him to gorge on our trap."

We'd stopped at a grocery store close to the target's house to buy chicken, wine, and chervil spice for the magical trap to knock out the mandagot. Phos, the driver the Sewer Fox had lent to drive us here, had parked a block away while we set up our stakeout just outside the property. We just had to wait for it to be dark enough for Kim to go to sleep and then set up the trap before the mandagot came out. I sat against a tree, trying to ignore the churning in my stomach.

"So, are mandagots . . . smart? Humanish? Like you?" I asked, twiddling a twig between my fingers as I watched Maddock stare at the distant mansion. I hadn't wanted to ask Maddock any questions on the drive, in case Phos would report what I'd said back to the Fox.

Maddock shook his head, not looking back at me. "They're animals through and through. Like a dog or a cat."

"So . . . what's so wrong with this, then?" I asked, unable to stop the question. "With Kim keeping a mandagot, I mean? If the animal is being provided for, and it's a dumb animal, and it isn't being hurt, why should we let it go? It would probably die in the wild, since it's been so sheltered," I reasoned as Maddock turned around and sat down on the ground. I was finally able to express the arguments I had kept to myself when I was around the Fox. I trusted Maddock enough to not freak out at me. "It's no different than a human having a dog or a bird as a pet," I said. I watched Maddock carefully, a little worried that I had upset him. To my surprise, Maddock sighed as he tossed a pebble in the air.

"Look, I don't know. Personally, I agree with you on this. It's a glorified pet that seems well cared for. But, then again, that's how your family saw me." Maddock's voice hardened for a second, but then the moment passed as quickly as it had arrived. "But Pat wants this done, and if you want to save your parents and grant my freedom, we have to do this," Maddock said, glancing at me. "We'll wait for Kim to go to sleep, and then we'll set our trap. Once it's captured, we'll take down the barriers."

I nodded, my heartbeat escalating.

I sat back against the trunk of a tree, and Maddock settled himself more comfortably in the bush, still staring at the house with a pair of binoculars.

The thought of sitting here all hours of the night sounded like the least fun of all the options, but it was better than the one Maddock wanted; of charging in and knocking out the poor man with magic—or Maddock's foot—and then setting up our trap for the mandagot without fear of interruption. It reminded me too much of what had happened to my parents, and I couldn't do that to someone else. Besides, based on what I'd learned about Mr. Kim, he probably had lots of security inside the house. I didn't want to be caught on some indoor security camera and have my face plastered all over the news.

The seat of my pants was starting to get damp from the grass. I sat forward and brushed the loose bark from my ponytail.

"When is he going to go to sleep?" I asked. "This is getting tedious."

"We can still act on my idea . . ." Maddock's toothy grin shined at me through the dwindling light.

"No, no. Waiting will be okay."

I stood, brushing off my jeans and stretching while taking care to remain hidden behind the tree. "How long has the Sewer Fox been free from his masters? Do you know?" I asked. "It must've taken several years for him to set up all his contacts and his place of operation."

"Pat told me a lot of stuff while you were out of earshot today. During our catch-up, he told me that it's been about . . . twenty-three years, maybe? He's been loving it." Maddock's voice sounded wistful.

"Well, you'll get yours soon enough, once this is all over," I reminded. "How did he get free? Did his masters let him go?"

Maddock snorted. "Pat wasn't in a setup like me, confined to one location. His owners kept him on a magical tether so he could go with them everywhere. They died in a car wreck. They didn't have any kids that he was also bound to, so he was instantly released. Speaking of which, what are you going to tell your parents? About your deal with me, I mean?" His voice sounded excited as he stared up at me.

I kicked at the grass. "I'm not exactly sure. I've been trying to think of other things, because it . . . won't be a pleasant talk."

"I wish I could be there to see it," Maddock said, smiling, a far-off look in his eye as he fiddled with a leafy branch dangling in front of his face.

"Yeah, that probably wouldn't be a good idea. You should be as far away as possible when I tell them," I said with a grimace.

"Well, obviously," Maddock replied, coming back to the present. "But still, it would be a beautiful sight, seeing their expressions. Film it for me, won't you?"

"No," I countered, giving him a hard look.

Maddock sighed and shook his head, grumbling.

We fell quiet as the sun disappeared, the shadows of the trees melting into the graying night. Our silence was punctuated with the noise of crickets and the occasional hoot of an owl. I hugged myself tighter, shifting my position against the tree and sending bark raining down on my shoulders. I was watching the branches above us nod with the breeze, the stars peeping through the leaves, when Maddock said, "I don't get it."

"What?" I asked, looking down at my shoes and tightening a loose shoelace.

"Captivity must've softened the Fox. The Pat I knew was impatient and impulsive and self-serving; didn't care for anyone but himself and his interests."

"Wow, no wonder you two get along so well," I drawled.

Maddock made a noise that almost sounded like a laugh before he continued as if I hadn't spoken. "The fact that he's still living here, helping others escape?" Maddock shook his head "It's an amazing transformation. Hardship can do that, I suppose."

"Did he really have a hard time of it?" I asked.

"Well, he didn't divulge all of the details of his captivity to me, but from what he has said and some of his expressions have hinted that his stay with his masters wasn't a particularly pleasant one. Now if it was a dank dungeon or the same type of situation I was in, I don't know; but I know that Pat feels things deeper and longer than most. Makes lasting impressions, I guess."

I rocked back and forth. I was bursting to ask him questions, but I was scared of making Maddock angry. Although, I reasoned, it wasn't like he could stomp off if he did get mad.

"Maddock?" I asked slowly. He had pressed the binoculars to his eyes again, watching the house.

"Hmm?"

"What are you going to do with your freedom?" I asked.

It was a moment before he lowered his binoculars, and in the deepening dark, I saw him turn and stare out over my head.

"I'm heading back to Ireland."

"Why?"

"If you were kidnapped and later released, wouldn't you want to go home?" he asked, a little scathingly.

I blushed, glad it was dark, and didn't reply.

A horrible thought hit me, and before I could realize it was probably a very personal question, I blurted out, "Were you married?" We didn't much get into personal lives; I certainly hadn't asked him before, and I doubted very much he would've ever replied.

Right when I said it, I felt stupid. Did leprechauns marry? I wanted to disappear as Maddock turned back to look at me with a bemused stare, but he merely grunted, a pensive look on his face.

"I didn't exactly have a woman there for me back home, but there was one I would've liked to have known. She's probably settled now with another lad, with several fat *leanbhs*. Babies," he explained, looking at me. "I'm not too old yet, for a leprechaun. I was taken when I was a young lad." He must've seen the surprise on my face; I'd never thought about how leprechauns came into the world.

"We aren't born from gold nuggets, lass," he said, smirking. "We're red-blooded animals as much as you." I felt my face grow hot, and I quickly began pulling clumps of grass from the ground, trying to quickly think of something else to say.

"How old are you, then? And how does that compare to humans?" I asked.

"Well, I was probably considered still a young teenager when I was captured, even though I'd been around for about fifty years."

"So, you're . . ."

"Eh, 'bout two hundred and some odd years, give or take a decade. Early forties by human reckoning."

"Wow," I breathed, trying to do the math in my head. "How long do leprechauns live?"

"I had a great-great-grandfather that was still alive at five hundred and seventy when I was taken. Who's to say if he's still alive. Probably not."

"So you'll go back to Ireland?"

"Yep. Try to pick up where I left off."

I felt sick to my stomach. Maddock had had a life before he was taken. Family, friends, who had no idea what had happened to him. Well, I conceded, they probably had a good idea about what had happened. But he'd been alive more than two hundred years, and he had been stuck underground for most of that time. I stared at him as he peered through the binoculars again. I could understand why he was so bitter, but somehow he didn't seem bitter enough.

"I'm sorry, Maddock."

He looked at me, eyebrows raised.

"For what my family did to you. I . . . you were underground for so long, I don't . . ."

His expression softened, and he chuckled. "Apology accepted. Besides, I had it better than most. Believe it or not, it was hard for magical creatures out there when I was born, being driven almost to extinction. I saw my fair share of bloodshed, family being senselessly killed. Ever help me, I could have had it worse. Because I was taken so young, I missed a lot of the horrors my family probably experienced living out in the wilds."

We fell silent for a moment before something struck me.

"Wait," I said suddenly, stopping my attack on the now-piled grass before me. "If you were taken so young, how is it that you've been able to provide gold for my family for so long? Where did it come from?"

"None of your business," Maddock said with a stern tone. "Nosy."

A horrible thought at his reaction struck me, and I gasped, "You don't . . . you know, excrete it, do you?"

His outraged expression made me quickly wave away what I'd said.

"Sorry, sorry," I replied, chagrined. We sat in silence for a moment, and, wanting to get back on good terms, I brought up a subject I hoped he'd enjoy talking about, because now I was interested. "So, how many creatures *are* there in the world? I've now heard of pixies, caladrius, mandagots, kelpies, and leprechauns."

"Oh, there are hundreds of thousands, on every continent. At least there were, before the daft humans began decimating them. The majority of them probably fled to the Ever, before it was sealed."

"The Ever?" The word alone made the hairs on my arms stand on end. I'd heard Maddock and the Sewer Fox reference it several times. "What's that?" I whispered.

"It's . . ." He paused, his face scrunched in thought. "I've never been there, obviously. But it's the realm where magic and magical creatures originated."

"Oh wow," I breathed, the goosebumps doubling on my arms. "Like another dimension? Can people go in?"

"Be thankful it's no longer accessible to anyone, really," he said, his tone surprisingly stern. "Especially a human like you."

"What? Why? I've used magic."

"Not magic like this, lass," he chuckled, his tone wry. "This is where raw, deadly power resides. You would be eaten alive or worse. Believe it or not, magical creatures like myself didn't learn barbarity from humans. There's one thing to be said for humans, they have learned something of society and decency and laws. The Ever is a lawless, cutthroat place, where the human-like creatures are more likely to kill you than the animalistic ones. For sport. You'd make a very fun toy. Most magical beings probably sought refuge there when the world began to become aware of magic, but that doesn't mean there aren't still millions of creatures here, trying to survive in an Ever-shrinking world. All the wild places are disappearing fast."

For some reason, that thought made a sadness seep into my chest.

"But the Ever was sealed millennia ago by someone very powerful," Maddock continued. "My uncle tried to get into the Ever once. His wife had been captured by humans, and he wanted to escape his sadness, but he couldn't get in."

Shame burned my cheeks as I noticed his pointed look, and said, "How was it sealed? Is there just one entrance point or something?"

Maddock shook his head. "I haven't the foggiest. Like I said, I've never been there, nor would I try. Stories of the Ever travel around the magical communities, and it's not a place to be entered into lightly."

We lapsed into silence, the chills on my arms refusing to settle as my mind lingered on thoughts of the Ever. A barbaric place? It sounded like it was a good thing it was sealed.

After a while, Maddock cleared his throat. "Well, I think he's asleep now. The lights have been off for about an hour."

I nodded, my nervousness returning. Now for the hard part.

Maddock rustled around in the bushes and pulled out the sacks of supplies we'd brought. The bags contained bowls, spoons, lighters, and candles. The Sewer Fox's limo was supplied with every need; including iron collars and a cage for carrying the creature.

"First, we douse some raw chicken with the wine and spice," Maddock read off the instructions the Fox had given him. "We don't want to do all the meat, as just a few enchanted pieces will do the trick, but mandagots are notorious gluttons—"

"They're not the only ones," I muttered.

Maddock harrumphed and continued, "—and it'll eat all the chicken we have, but we need to hide the smell of the enchanted chicken under the mundane, raw stuff."

He pulled out a metal bowl while I struggled to get the cork off the wine bottle. Maddock watched me wrestling with the bottle with disgust on his face, and then he snatched the bottle from me.

"You get the chicken," he said.

I pulled one of the sacks towards me and peered inside. The raw chicken flesh was soft and limp, the skin slimy with grease and blood. I stared at it, wishing for gloves; I hated touching raw meat.

"Hurry up. You aren't squeamish about a bit of dead chicken, are you?" Maddock asked, holding the bottle of wine poised for pouring into the bowl.

Grimacing, I stuck my hand into the bag, pulling out a handful of slippery thighs and bones, and threw the meat into the bowl.

"More," Maddock said.

I had to reach into the bag three more times before Maddock said we had enough to knock the mandagot out.

I wiped my hands on the grass— wishing for hand sanitizer—and turned to see Maddock drizzling the wine over the chicken and tapping the open glass bottle of spices over the bowl, green flakes drifting into the mixture.

Setting the bottles down, Maddock picked up the bowl and swirled the contents around a bit.

"Okay, hand me the other bowl, and you handle the lighter," he instructed. "I'll cover the bowl after you finish your incantation. Be quick about it, we don't want to cook the chicken at all." He held the empty bowl up, poised to drop it over the other to snuff out the wine-fed flames. "Do you have the spell ready?" Maddock asked.

I nodded. Lighter in one hand and the paper with the incantation in the other, I began chanting. The words were in French, and though I stumbled over a few pronunciations, I could feel the magic settling on the chicken in the bowl. The moment I uttered the last words, I ignited the lighter and set it to the wine. Colorful flames erupted and began creeping around the bowl, greedily sucking up all the alcohol.

"And I cover it now," Maddock said, quickly placing the other bowl on top of the first, covering the flames completely.

"Why not just use like, horse tranqs or something?" I asked as we waited for the flames to die.

"You really don't know anything—" he began with a scathing tone, then shook his head, stopping himself. "Tranquilizers really don't work on us; that's why leprechauns and amazons and the like have to be bound and sedated with magical spells."

He lifted the bowl off, and studied the chicken. "Good, no problems here. Let's get it set up out there. Pat said that Kim probably keeps the beast under the house somewhere. He would never keep it inside, so it must have a man-made den nearby." He pointed through the bushes. "Do you see that?"

About fifty yards away from us, the air shimmered, barely perceptible, as if with heat.

"Is that the magical barrier to keep the mandagot in?"

Maddock nodded. "Pat told me that when they did recon, his team could slip through it without any problems, and he said it was probably specially fitted to keep just the mandagot in. Mr. Kim must have made it accessible for humans and other creatures to walk through it, for his own ease, and to avoid awkward questions. Idiot."

"So we'll have to take it down to get the mandagot back out?" I asked. Maddock nodded again, looking a little impressed, and I rolled my eyes.

"Just because the Sewer Fox believes I don't have a brain doesn't mean I don't have one," I retorted, then paused. "Wait, that means I'm the one that will have to take it down!" I immediately felt stupid. Of course it would have to be me. Maddock could only do "leprechaun stuff."

"Yes, very good lass," Maddock replied with a snort, "You do have a brain, I suppose."

"But . . . I don't know how to take down a specialized magical barrier!"

"The Fox covered that as well," Maddock said, handing me another piece of paper. I stared at it with pursed lips, reading over the spell.

"He really doesn't trust me at all, does he? When did he give this to you? Why didn't he tell me any of this?" I asked, frowning.

"He told me a lot of stuff while you were in the bathroom. You took a really long time," Maddock replied with a stifled snicker.

I flushed. "It's not for the reason you think—"

"Mhmm," Maddock said, giving me a wicked grin.

"It's not! I wanted a break from all the leprechauns, so I took my time," I snapped, and Maddock snorted.

"Whatever you say, Mal...oderous."

"Wowwwww, how long have you been sitting on that one?" I said through gritted teeth.

"Not as long as you were sitting on that toi—"

He barely dodged the stick I threw at him, mortification boiling under my skin.

"Okay, okay. Ready?" Maddock asked, choking back a laugh.

I nodded, my face still burning, but I wasn't about to overreact and make Maddock think he won by getting me all riled.

Taking the chicken and a large fleece blanket to carry the mandagot out with us, we snuck towards the house, silently watching for signs of movement inside or out.

Now that Mr. Kim was asleep, we felt safe enough to scour the perimeter of the house, looking closely into pitch-black window wells, around bushes, and in dark corners. Finally, I noticed Maddock waving me over to where he stood. On the far side of the house was a large bush that, on further inspection, was covering a large cement hole that ran into the ground and out of sight under the house.

Together, we laid out the dark blue blanket a few feet from the hole and carefully dumped all the chicken into the center. We hadn't kept the chicken in a cooler while we waited for Mr. Kim to go to sleep, so the smell of raw meat was potent.

As Maddock finished dumping the chicken onto the blanket, a light clicked on above us inside the house. Fear froze me where I stood, nearly standing in the shaft of light. Mr. Kim was awake? How?

If Kim looked out of the window, he would see us running across the lawn to take cover in the woods. I looked at Maddock, terrified, and Maddock motioned me quickly to move towards the house instead. Taking care not to fall into the cement hole, I flattened myself against the wall of the house beside Maddock, my heart nearly bursting with fear.

The light from the upstairs window illuminated a perfect square of grass near our blanket trap, making the blanket almost visible if you looked closely.

I tried to hold my breath, but I was so nervous that it made me dizzy.

The silence was broken by the sound of scraping claws on concrete deep in the hole beside me. I felt an urgent tapping on my arm, and I turned to see Maddock, his eyes wide with alarm. He motioned me to follow him as the scraping noise got louder.

Suddenly, what the Fox had said about mandagots being viciously territorial rang in my head, and my stomach contracted painfully. We were intruding on its territory.

I stumbled away from the hole, trying to be silent as I moved to follow Maddock just as something dark and the size of a large housecat burst from the hole with a snarl.

I turned just in time to see the yellow, cat-like eyes reflected in the light from the window before the beast launched at me, strong jaws latching around my right calf.

With a scream, I stumbled and fell to the grass as needle-like teeth pierced through my jeans and into my flesh. Another light in the house flicked on, and I looked to see the mandagot, in the form of a black fox, its jaws fastened around my calf. Blood was welling up around its lips from my leg, and I dumbly tried hitting at it, but it let go of my calf and snapped at my hand before getting a fresh grip on my other leg, snarling. I tried stifling a scream, but a howl escaped my lips as pain sliced through my legs.

With lightning fast movements, the mandagot moved up my leg, biting and tearing away at the jeans. I tried rolling, but the fox-mandagot tugged on my leg and tried to shake it, making me scream again as it tore away some of my pant leg. Tears streamed down my face. Was this how I was going to die?

Maddock came soaring over my prone figure and landed a flying kick at the mandagot's head. The mandagot released me with an unearthly shriek and landed several feet away, but was back on its feet within a second, flying at us again. Maddock stood in front of me, hunched as the beast leapt at his throat. Maddock dodged sideways faster than a blink, and with a crisp turn, sent the mandagot flying again with a powerful shove. I tried to stand, but my legs couldn't support any weight at the moment, the pain electric down my nerves.

"What do we do?" I moaned to Maddock, who was staring down the mandagot that was circling us warily from a distance, snarling in an unnaturally high pitch. I heard someone shout around the other side of the house.

"We have to get out of here," Maddock growled.

"But we need that mandagot!" I sobbed through gritted teeth.

Before Maddock could reply, the mandagot stopped moving and closed its eyes, its body shaking, emitting a strange, low gurgling growl. We both stopped and stared at it as the growling grew louder, but the creature didn't move, didn't open its eyes.

"What's it doing?" I whispered through my tears, finding it difficult to speak.

The mandagot's fur began to drop to the grass as the creature started to grow, its snout morphing from the pointed nose of a fox to powerful jaws, its shoulders broadening.

"Okay, we're getting out of here. Now," Maddock snapped. He helped me get to my feet while keeping an eye on the mandagot. Its eyes were still closed as the shape of the fox disappeared, replaced with the sturdy, solid frame of a dog, its face wolfish, its teeth long and curved.

"Maddock," I rasped, fear freezing me to where I stood.

"Run. Come on, *run* ye great idiot!" Maddock growled, shoving me so hard with his shoulder that I nearly fell again, but we were moving. I yelped with every step I took on my torn-up legs, and I thought we would make it, but within a few yards, the pain was too much. The strength from my legs evaporated, and I fell to the grass.

I tried to get up, fear drying up my tears as Maddock pulled on my arms to get me to stand, but I could feel the energy draining out of me. I could see by the dark splashes in the grass behind us that I was losing a lot of blood, but my fatigue made me wonder if maybe the mandagots had some sort of poison in their bite.

There was a renewed snarling, a deeper, larger snarl, and we turned to see the mandagot, its shape almost lost in the darkness, shaking the rest of its old fur away. Where there had been a small fox now stood a wolf-sized brute. It howled toward the sky, then began sniffing out for us. Maddock's tugging on my arms became more urgent.

"I'm trying, I'm trying!" I gasped, trying to get to my feet, which were not responding to my brain's screaming demands to move. I hated to think how much Maddock was despising me at the moment for being so weak and helpless.

Maddock cursed. "Let me carry you."

He tried to pick me up, but the movement made me scream, and he had to stop.

A figure came running around the house into view a few feet from us, holding something long and glinting in his hands. The man stopped when he saw us, with the now-giant mandagot behind us, stalking up on us at a crouch, and the man backed away and ran back around the house.

"Why isn't he shooting at us?" I wheezed to Maddock, who was still desperately trying to pull me to my feet.

"I reckon he figures the mandagot will take care of us. It's got us cornered," Maddock grunted.

Glancing ahead, I saw we were still about a yard away from the perimeter. I was just a limp body now, and safety beyond the magical barrier was too far to get to before the enraged beast reached us. An idea sparked in my frenzied mind, and I began to claw at the paper in my pocket.

"Do you think you could punt that thing to the barrier?" I panted to Maddock, who remained near my side.

Maddock, glancing at the mandagot then back at the shimmering barrier, nodded. "With ease."

"Good," I wheezed. "Get in front of me, ready to tackle and throw that thing. Hard as you can," I puffed, my arms turning to marshmallows. I prayed that I had enough energy to work the spell in time.

I pulled the incantation, hand shaking, out of my pocket and began reciting the barely visible words on the paper as my vision pulsed. I felt for the magic coming from Maddock and drew upon it, pushing through the pain that was beginning to lance down my legs. I extended a bloody hand toward the barrier as I said the last words. The barrier rippled as a large hole was torn open in front of us. I held the breach in the perimeter with waning strength, the magic of the barrier pushing against me. It didn't like being open, and a metallic smell seemed to overwhelm me, the cold grass felt freezing beneath me as I strained to keep the barrier open for just one more second.

It all happened in a heartbeat.

The mandagot lunged towards us, and Maddock sidestepped the pounce, wrapped his arms around the snarling beast, and threw it as hard as he could towards the tear in the perimeter. The mandagot soared above me and just barely cleared the opening of the barrier. With the last ounce of strength I had, I slammed the barrier shut, successfully locking out the rabid mandagot. The creature, having landed on its side, was up again, charging at us with snapping teeth and shrieking howls. But the barrier blocked him from us. He threw himself at the barrier, again and again, but the barrier held. Maddock and I watched him for a moment before my head dropped to the grass; I couldn't hold it up anymore. My vision began blurring and coming back into focus. My legs were burning with freezing cold. The movement made Maddock forget the mandagot that was trying to claw at the barrier to get back at us, and kneeled down at my side.

Maddock seemed far away, then he was suddenly by my side, then far away again as my vision danced.

"What did it do to you, lass?" I heard him mutter.

My legs were shooting pain up into my abdomen, and I coughed weakly. My legs, now growing numb, weren't bothering me as much as my stomach.

"They're poisonous, aren't they?" I rasped, Maddock's face coming in and out of focus.

"Nah." But his voice was unsteady. "They're not poisonous, exactly, but their bite does immobilize their prey. It's a magical toxin that makes it impossible for the prey to move. You'll become comatose in a moment."

I gurgled in fear, and Maddock smiled, looking uncharacteristically pale.

"You'll recover. Unfortunately," he joked. "You just have to ride out the pain."

"Is this as bad as it gets?" I whimpered as another stab of pain sliced up my chest.

He shook his head. "'Fraid not." He was careful not to look me in the eye. "Let's take a look at those legs. Not that anyone would voluntarily," he said, trying to sound scathing.

"Har har," I rasped through clenched teeth as my tongue began to feel coated with electricity.

Maddock stood up and went to my feet. I tried to sit up, but all I ended up doing was just rolling around a bit. I couldn't feel the bites in my legs, but the pain in my stomach was killing me.

"Just lay still, lass," he instructed. I felt him tear away at the rips in my jeans, and he gave a nervous cough.

"You're losing a lot of blood. I can bind up the bites, but, like I said, you're going to have to ride out the pain of the venom."

"Well then, just make sure I don't bleed out," I said through clenched teeth as more tears blurred my vision. "Please."

"I'll be right back." He disappeared without a sound, leaving me with nothing but the snarls of the mandagot nearby. Loneliness and fear spiked through me as unconsciousness flickered at my mind. Would he leave me here forever?

"Maddock?" I whimpered. Only the growls of the mandagot answered me, and tears fell fast and thick down my face. I wanted my mom and dad. I wanted to be home.

Soon I noticed that even the mandagot's yowls were growing more and more faint. After what felt like an eternity laying in a miasma of pain and numbness, the sound of tearing fabric jolted me out of my delirious half-consciousness. Maddock had come back. Peace swept over me, and I closed my eyes. He hadn't left me.

"The mandagot ran off, so we—Oy, don't you fall asleep," Maddock snapped. "This might hurt."

I couldn't reply as another cramping racked my stomach and chest. I felt him place his warm hands on my right calf and clamp down hard, winding something around my legs. The pain in my legs returned full force at his touch, roaring up and down my nerves. My vision flashed red and orange, and before I could scream, darkness swallowed me.

# Chapter Fifteen

"Just like a human to screw it up." The sharp voice broke me out of my unconsciousness, but I didn't want to open my eyes. I was too comfortable, lying on soft clouds of dreamy relaxation.

"It wasn't the lass's fault. We were caught unawares."

"Well, it wouldn't be the first time you've been caught unawares, would it be, Mad Dog?" the first voice snapped. They fell silent.

That silence woke me up entirely, like a soap bubble bursting, the blissful oblivion vanished. Blinking, I found I was lying in an ornate four poster bed, the lights dim. A door off to my right was barely open, light scarcely shining through the crack, along with the angry voices I'd heard.

I tried sitting up, but pain awoke at my movement. My stomach convulsed, an angry drummer pounded a tempo against my head, and my legs burned and throbbed like I'd been stung by a million hornets. I exhaled at the renewal of pain. The memory of the mandagot attack filled my mind and I lay back into the mattress, my heart hammering at the recollection. I had escaped that monster. I was alive. Relief—despite the pain—flooded through me.

The silence outside the door lasted for another moment before: "Pat, at least it's free now, right?" I heard Maddock say in his would-be calm voice. "That's all that matters, right? There are mandagot-like creatures here in the US. It will find a new den and be happy."

"You've made a bag of it, Mad!" the Sewer Fox seethed. Again there was silence.

"Pat, what is wrong with you? I've never seen you like this." Maddock sounded angry now.

"I wanted to release the mandagot back into its *homeland*," the Fox shouted, and I heard a shushing noise from Maddock. "What does any animal want? It wants home! You of all muppets should understand that. I'm going to have to send out a second crew to track it down now. I'll have to waste resources because you were faffin' about and couldn't handle a simple mandagot."

"It attacked the lass. I couldn't let it get her. It would've ripped her to shreds."

"Getting a soft spot for your masters, are you, Mad?" the Fox sneered. "If you had let her die, you would be a free leprechaun."

My breath hitched in my throat, and I trembled beneath the blanket. Did he really hate me so much that he wanted me dead?

"That wouldn't have been very sporting," Maddock said, sounding a little disgusted. "Besides, the spell the lass cast on me also connects me to her living blood relatives, so I wouldn't be free until her parents died."

"Well, I'm sure I could've arranged that in some way," the Fox said, his tone slow and deliberate, and I perked up, a shiver of fear joining the flares of pain through me. Horror and curiosity thundered in my chest. He would be willing to kill my parents? Did that mean he knew where they were?

"What do you know, Pat?" Maddock asked, his tone suddenly grave, almost harsh. "You didn't kidnap her parents, did you?"

The Fox barked out a laugh, and I flinched at the ugly sound. "You know I would never do anything so trivial. I would free the *magical* humanoids held captive, certainly, but take up my precious energy with a kidnapping of dullard humans? Honestly, Mad." The Fox continued chuckling.

"Okay, okay, okay, I was just wondering. You're acting very strange, Pat, I just had to ask."

The laughter stopped. "Of course I am acting strange, I'm dealing with incompetence!"

I felt anger and another burst of pain zing through me. It wasn't completely our fault! Our plan had been disrupted in the worst way possible. How had Mr. Kim woken up?

I heard Maddock sigh. "So it really was that group, HAMMA, that kidnapped the parents?" Maddock asked. He sounded tired.

"Aye. They're responsible for more disappearances than you'd believe. That group drives me dense." The voices behind the door fell silent for a moment more, and then Maddock cleared his throat again.

"Now, will you keep your side of the bargain?" I heard Maddock ask, his voice business-like. "Yes, yes, don't look at me like that. I know we didn't exactly bring the mandagot to you, but it's free now. We proved a point, and you got what you wanted. If we don't get her parents, I don't get free."

The Sewer Fox snorted in response. "Do you really think that pint-sized chiseler will keep her promise? If anything, her parents will insist she revoke it, and she will. You're being naïve again, Mad."

Fury joined the other feelings inside me. I wanted to jump out of the bed and march into the room where the two leprechauns sat and shout at the hateful leprechaun, but as I sat up to do just that, my body convulsed and the room began to spin. I slumped back against the pillows, taking deep breaths with my eyes closed, willing my spinning head to calm.

"Will you keep your promise to help us with her parents? Without you, I will never be freed," Maddock demanded, ignoring the Fox's comments.

"I shouldn't, as it would reward you and that holy show you had tonight."

There was silence, and I could imagine both of them, staring each other down. There was a disgusted sound of "Bahh!" and I heard something like someone being punched.

"Fine, ye ol' eejit, I'll help you," the Fox huffed. "I keep my promises, unlike *some*."

"The creature is free, Pat," Maddock said again. The Fox made a noise akin to disgust and I heard him exhale in an exaggerated fashion and call Maddock something too vulgar to repeat. Maddock laughed.

"Thank you, Pat."

"Mhmm. Well, should we see how your *beloved* bure is doing?" the Fox asked, and I quickly closed my eyes again, my heart pounding. Maddock had defended me, and he had successfully got the Fox to help me find my parents, even though we had 'made a bag' of the job. The darkness behind my eyelids lightened somewhat as the door opened, and I heard footsteps approaching my bed. I kept my eyes shut.

"We know you're awake, lassie. We can see you sweating and trembling from here," the Fox snorted.

"I'm trembling and sweating because I'm in pain," I said through tight lips, my eyes still closed. The Sewer Fox and Maddock laughed, and I was happy to hear that the Fox's wasn't the harsh, ugly laugh from earlier.

"How are you feeling? Better than you look, I hope," Maddock said as I sat up. I grimaced as my head spun, but I was able to stay sitting up. I would hate to think what the Sewer Fox would say should I faint in his presence.

"Still hurting," I rasped, rubbing my stomach. Pain zagged across my lower back.

"Well, you'll be coming out of the pain soon," Maddock replied, ignoring the Fox's displeased grunt.

"How did we get back?" I looked between Maddock and the Fox, and back to Maddock. The Fox's expression made me think he didn't want me to talk to him.

"I called Phos on your phone, and I directed him to us. He helped me carry you back to the car," Maddock replied. I wondered why Maddock didn't use his own phone, but I realized that he probably forgot he had one. He'd never had a cell phone before.

"How did we get discovered by Kim?" I asked. It was almost too inconvenient that Mr. Kim should wake up and ruin our plan.

"By being the size and IQ of King Kong, that's what," the Fox replied, a mean smile on his face.

"Apparently," Maddock said, glancing at the Sewer Fox, "Kim had specialty magic alarms set up around the mandagot's den, and anything taller than five feet set it off."

"I told you to be careful of motion sensors, but you didn't listen," the Fox snapped, his attention directed at me.

"So . . . I set it off?" I asked.

Both leprechauns nodded.

Great. Now even my height is going to be a point of hatred for the Sewer Fox.

"Well, I'm sorry about that," I began, "but I don't think that it's my—"

"I should've realized he'd have better security than just inside his house," Maddock interrupted, earning a disdainful glance from the Fox.

"Don't take the fall for the mistakes of her ungainly body, Mad." The Fox elbowed Maddock. "The mandagot escaped because of her, and her alone. But, be that as it may," the Fox sighed, "you did release the creature. Prematurely, it's true, but you held up your end of the bargain. I shall hold up mine. Although, I daresay, you heard all that already." He nodded toward the room where they had had their argument, and I bit my lip, worried he would go off on me as well.

"Oh, don't get in a tizzy," the Fox said. "I'm not going to eat you like that mandagot almost did."

With a small sigh of relief, I sat back into the pillows. I tried to smile, though I was sure it came off more as a grimace. "So, what's next?" I asked, trying to turn the conversation away from the awkward pause.

"Already the demands come in!" the Sewer Fox snapped. He turned and stomped from the room. Maddock and I sat in embarrassed silence for a moment, and I glanced at Maddock, who was looking very much like he wanted to follow suit. But I needed answers, so I cleared my throat, drawing Maddock's attention away from the door.

"So . . . do *you* know what the plan is?" I asked, clenching my teeth as another zag of pain zigged across my stomach. My legs felt swollen and painfully tingly under the blankets, and I had no desire to take a peek to see the damage. Although I noticed I was in my pajamas. Mortification flared in my face.

Maddock shook his head. "Not yet. We need to let Pat calm down before we ask him for anything more, and you need to get better."

"Yeah . . . um . . . where did my pajamas come from?"

Maddock snorted. "Pat said we could stay here until your parents were rescued. I went to our hotel, checked us out, and brought our luggage back here."

I opened my mouth in horror, but Maddock quickly said, "One of Pat's lady staffers dressed you when they were done bandaging you up."

"Oh. Okay. Good."

We both sat in painful silence for a moment, and then Maddock gruffly smacked the mattress near my foot. "Well, get better. The sooner you're up, the sooner we can get back to it."

"And the sooner you're free," I reminded as Maddock turned to go. He paused for a brief moment in the doorway, then slipped out without another word.

# Chapter Sixteen

Over the next few days, to my dread, I was served revolting concoctions at every meal. Maddock called them "healing potions" that he claimed a druid in the Sewer Fox's employ cooked up. I often wondered if there actually was no druid, and both leprechauns were mixing up the most disgusting combinations from the kitchen they could think of just to torture me.

"I'm sick of this!" I burst out, convulsing as I swallowed the last of the noxious potion Maddock had brought me along with my dinner of cream of wheat. Again. I was getting sick of eating mush for every meal too, but Maddock insisted I had to eat porridge for every meal, so as not to upset my stomach while healing.

"I'm trusting you that this is really a healing potion, and not mustard, milk, and toothpaste mixed together," I coughed, my voice muffled as I shoveled the hot cereal into my mouth as fast as I could. "Or else I'm going to fill your bed with my vomit."

Maddock smirked, and I hated how much I played into his enjoyment, but I couldn't help it. The healing potions were beyond vile.

"It doesn't have to be a joke," Maddock replied. "It's a real potion, and I'm loving how *you* have to drink it, and *I* don't. Enjoy your porridge. I'm off to have chicken cordon blues and mashed potatoes and buttered carrots and chocolate cake." He flashed me the smuggest grin his broad face could manage.

Unable to help myself, I scooped up a heaping spoonful of the porridge and flung it at him as he turned to leave. The hot, goopy cereal splattered against his shoulder and up into his hair as he dodged out of the room. His shouted obscenities echoing down the hall made me smile. He would be finding granules of the porridge on his person for hours.

However, it seemed like the vomit-inducing concoctions truly were healing potions, as after only three days, the gashes made by the mandagot's teeth on my legs were completely sealed up, the strength came back in my muscles, and the shooting cramps faded from my upper body.

On the fourth morning, I woke up early, feeling refreshed, and found I barely hurt at all. I slid out of bed and walked around the room, tears pricking behind my smile. My legs barely had any scarring, and I could walk unaccompanied. A few of the ladies that worked for the Fox had helped me to the bathroom over the last several days, and I was grateful I could now do it myself.

I showered and hurried downstairs before Maddock could come in and force me back in bed so he could watch me drink another potion.

I met one of the ladies on the stairs, who was coming to check up on me, and she led me to an opulent, high-ceilinged dining room. The decor was different from the industrial-esque offices downstairs. A very ornate, white dining table and white plush dining chairs dominated the room that had far too much gold filigree on the walls in my opinion. But Maddock and the Sewer Fox were sitting at the far end of the table, talking and eating from an array of dishes that looked like they belonged at a king's feast.

The two leprechauns didn't look up at me as I was seated across from Maddock, and a large white plate with a gold leaf peacock on it was set in front of me by a butler in full dress.

"Help yourself to anything on the table, miss," the butler whispered to me as he helped push my chair in.

"Thank you." I looked at the food, feeling overwhelmed. I always got to eat whatever I wanted—I did have a personal chef growing up after all—but this extravagant display of food was a little overboard. I poured myself some hot chocolate from a shiny silver pot, and filled my plate with a little bit of everything from the steaming platters. I ate quietly as Maddock and the Fox continued their conversation.

"No, no," the Fox was saying, "their Staten Island warehouse is by far the most stocked. I also believe that is where the head of HAMMA resides. Although, from what I remember from the newest report I read, he is on a vacation to Ireland at the moment. Hunting."

"How do you know that?" I asked, spearing the small potato on my plate. It split into two pieces, steam rising from the starchy center.

"I know rather a lot," the Fox retorted, his tone cold. "HAMMA doesn't realize that I've been tailing them, and I've had traitors from their ranks come and work for me, so I have a pretty good 'in' with their operations."

"Traitors?" I asked, sipping my hot chocolate. It was the creamiest, richest cocoa I'd ever tasted.

"There are members of HAMMA that got wise to what was really going on," the Sewer Fox snapped. "Sure, they still believed in the cause, that magical creatures shouldn't be treated as belongings, but they were fortunate enough to find out that HAMMA was not really releasing the creatures back into the wild, but rather putting them back into captivity." The Fox gave me a wicked smile. "You can imagine how angry they got. They tried to find a way to right the wrongs they were a part of, and we found each other. They give me info, and I use that info to do what they have been wanting to do all along."

I nodded, my mouth full of bacon and potatoes.

"So, in light of my recent deal with you," the Fox sniffed, "I sent some of my men that HAMMA still believes are loyal, back to HAMMA headquarters to search for any news of your parents, and they have reported that several people are being kept at their location in New Jersey."

My breath caught. Were they really so close? "So, what's the plan?" I breathed.

"Well, as you're a very rich young lady, I assume you like banks?" the Fox replied, a hint of bitterness in his voice.

"Banks?" I asked, nonplussed.

"That is where the headquarters your parents are being kept is located. A bank in New Jersey."

"So, what do we do?" I wondered aloud.

The Fox, who had been taking several gulps from his glass, put down the cup, a foam line on his upper lip. "Don't get your knickers in a twist, lass," the Fox growled, wiping his mouth. "I'm getting there."

After eating half of a potato and several bites of eggs and steak, he was ready to talk again. "The plan is, my man Travis has been to HAMMA, and he told them to expect a delivery of a leprechaun." The Fox nodded towards Maddock, who was quietly shoving sausages and potatoes into his mouth without hesitation. "HAMMA knows you are going to pick up a load of humans to take to another one of their facilities out west."

"They operate out west too?" I asked, amazed.

"Of course," the Fox said matter-of-factly. "Wackos exist everywhere, after all. Anyways, don't interrupt. It's rude."

"Sorr—" I began.

"Now, you're going to take ol' Mad Dog here, tell the HAMMA workers that you're there to drop off a leprechaun, and to pick up the 'human scum.' You drive away with your parents in tow, and Maddock escapes the minute you're clear."

"How will Maddock escape?" I asked. "Won't they bind him to them before I leave?" I asked, glancing at Maddock, who didn't look worried in the slightest.

"Not necessarily. A spell isn't the only thing that can bind a leprechaun. How did you keep Maddock from disappearing at your house?" the Fox asked.

"His dwelling was surrounded by Celtic crosses."

"Exactly. Celtic crosses and other totems can keep us put if done correctly. The plan is, we'll put an imperfectly traced Celtic cross on him, as a temporary tattoo or henna, so you can hand him over, and they'll think he's not going to be able to escape, and then once you and your parents are back here safely, Maddock can disappear from under their noses and meet up with you all. Then you can free Maddock, and then you and your parents can be home free. Although," the Fox said with a sly smile, "you might want to change residences once you get back, just to be safe. If HAMMA learns of your escape, they'll be coming back for you."

"Won't they double check the cross on him?" I asked.

The Fox shook his head. "They'll think the cross is real. Otherwise he would have escaped already."

I nodded, my stomach dancing in renewed nervousness. This could actually work.

"So, who was this Travis person in HAMMA, and why did he leave the organization?" I asked, picking a donut out of the pile on a platter.

The Fox sighed, glowering at me before turning to Maddock. "Does she ever stop talking?"

I frowned, and Maddock glanced at me.

"What do you expect? Humans are curious. A flaw of their kind." Maddock flashed me a cheeky grin, and I made a face back at him.

Rolling his eyes, the Fox replied, "Travis was a grunt, like a lot of members, but then he was so good at extracting animals that he was promoted higher and higher until he got to the level where the bosses explained the benefits of being a leader; they can keep animals or trade them for cash or other creatures. It's a very lucrative position. Well, he had a little more integrity than the rest, and he wasn't swayed by riches. When he learned what the organization was really about, he left. And he was angry. He wanted revenge for being lied to." The Fox cracked a wry smile.

"Wait, wait," I said, looking across to Maddock, then back at the Fox. "Why would your guys help us if it is to rescue people who go against what they believe? Wouldn't they refuse to do it?"

The Fox shrugged, looking unconcerned. "I'll just tell them we're doing a creature extraction. Then they'll be hopping to go help us, especially if it's to steal from HAMMA, an organization that lied to them."

"But, you're going to lie to them," I pointed out, "doesn't that sound a little . . ."

The Fox gave me an icy glare, and I quickly shut my mouth.

"Girly, my men are still radical activists," the Fox said, his tone steely. "I have to tread carefully around them, or they'll cause me trouble for helping you. Besides, I won't be lying, exactly, because I'll tell them to steal any animals on their way out, if they can find one. Happy?"

I shrugged and looked down at my plate.

"Sheesh, for an immoral human, you sure are nitpicky about morality." The Fox shook his head and began cutting his steak into large bites.

I was aching to shoot a stinging comment back, like I was used to with Maddock, but a wide-eyed warning look from Maddock made me turn my attention back to my food without saying anything, though I gripped my fork so hard the metal imprinted into my skin.

Maddock had come to my room the second day I was awake after our ill-fated mandagot extraction to tell me that the Fox was very near in changing his mind about helping us. The Fox had received more bad news after our little snafu; HAMMA had beaten him to a rather large and powerful creature, and he was under a lot of pressure from some of his people. We were here on his good grace, so we had to tread carefully. I had wanted to ask Maddock why the Fox would be under pressure from underlings, but decided to keep quiet. Obviously, the Fox wasn't the only person at the top of this operation.

"So," the Fox continued, "we're planning to extract your parents tonight, and—"

"Tonight?" I choked, bits of potato flying from my mouth and across the table. I hurriedly drank hot chocolate to clear my throat as Maddock brushed a few flecks of potato from his suit in disgust.

"What, too soon?" the Fox asked, smirking. "Enjoyed your freedom away from overbearing adults, have you? I can reconsider the whole thing, if you like."

"No, no," I backpedaled. "I just didn't realize it would be so soon. I assumed that there would be lots of planning to do." My heart skittered at the thought of seeing my parents in just a few hours.

"We did most of the planning while you were still in bed. It isn't that big of a job, and the bank is nowhere near as heavily guarded as the Staten Island compound."

My heart thudded in my chest. My life would be changing after tonight. Briefly, I wished it wasn't so soon. I would have to try to reconcile myself with the fact that we would be losing a major part of our lifestyle. While that meant no more "chores" for me, which almost made me smile at the thought, it also meant no more gold nuggets every day, no more endless wealth. What would our family do?

I knew my father traveled a lot for "work" but what that work was, I had no idea. Was he actually part of a large corporation? Or did he just travel buying and selling stocks or art? I hadn't a clue.

Would that end once our prosperity and wealth stopped flowing? Did my dad even have any marketable skills? His family hadn't had to work; they'd relied on easy gold that Maddock had provided.

Maybe right at first our gold would hold up our lifestyle, but my parents might have to dig into my trust funds to keep up appearances, and I would suffer. I had been hoping to go to college—for what major, I didn't know yet—but there wouldn't be any college for me if my parents refused to change their spending habits; trips around the world, extravagant parties and charity balls, meetups with celebrities and important political representatives. The vacation homes in Hawaii, different parts of Europe, and the Caribbean. It would all have to go, or we would be ruined. And knowing how money-loving my parents were, I could see difficult years ahead. It just wasn't something I was mentally prepared for yet.

But I would have to face it.

"Reconsidering?" the Fox asked with a snide smile.

I glanced across the table at Maddock—who looked evenly back at me—back to the Sewer Fox, who was watching me with an almost challenging expression.

"Of course not," I said, trying to keep the waver from my voice. "I just didn't realize how prepared you were. I'm very grateful for your help, and the speed with which you've put this all together."

"In case you didn't know, I didn't do it for you." I noticed the grip on his coffee cup was very tight, his knuckles turning white, and I nodded.

"Right, how silly of me," I said, realizing I was talking with a little too much snarkiness, but I couldn't stop myself. I was sick of being treated like I was a stupid cavewoman who didn't know right from wrong. "Still, I wanted to thank you for your help. I'm sure Maddock is grateful for your speedy help as well—"

With a bellow, the Sewer Fox plunged the point of his steak knife into his plate, shattering the china to bits and scattering food, the knife quivering in the surface of the table. The Fox turned to me, his eyes blazing, his face blotchy scarlet. Fear pummeled my rib cage, and Maddock and I stared at him, our mouths open in shock.

"Keep your thanks," the Fox snarled, his red hair standing on end, making him look deranged. "You humans think you're alleviating some of your conscience, doing us a favor by thanking the likes of us. Well, I don't need it, and I don't want it. So keep your guilt to yourself."

I sat in stunned silence for a moment, and I didn't dare look across the table to what Maddock's reaction was to his friend's outburst, worried it would cause another. The Fox snapped his fingers and his butler appeared by his side and began clearing away the broken china.

"Bring me another plate. I'm not done eating," the Fox grunted, and another exquisite plate was promptly produced.

I watched in slight amazement as the Fox began piling food onto his new plate as if nothing happened. "Be prepared to leave by four-thirty," the Fox said, his tone even, but he didn't look at me. "You'll get there in about an hour, just before it closes at six. I'll provide everything you need, and my men will have all the instructions by then. They have orders from me to obey you. They'll know the plan."

I merely nodded, and the rest of breakfast passed in silence. I had no idea what I had said to set him off, and I wasn't about to do anything else. I kept forgetting that the Sewer Fox was a loose cannon, and wasn't as keen to help me as Maddock was. It was scary being around someone who openly hated people like me the way the Fox did. I never knew what to expect.

The Fox abruptly pushed his chair away from the table, making me flinch. Wiping his mouth with a napkin and avoiding my eyes, he said, "Mad Dog, a game of pool?"

"Sure," Maddock said, also averting his eyes from my gaze as he followed the Fox, leaving me alone with all the cooling food on the table.

I poked at the remains on my plate, unease writhing in my now full stomach.

I didn't know what to think. I wanted to talk to Maddock, to see if he knew what I had done, but I didn't want to interrupt their game. In fact, I wanted to avoid the Fox altogether, hopefully never setting eyes on him again once my parents were rescued. I had a feeling only Maddock's presence protected me from the Fox's full wrath.

Sighing, I got up from the table and meandered out of the dining room. I had only ever seen a few of the rooms here, and I wasn't sure if this was an apartment or a lair or what. I wandered the halls, avoiding the direction the leprechauns had gone.

I found myself climbing a set of stairs up and up, only glancing down the hall of each floor before continuing up, until I came to the top floor. I had counted six floors, but I knew there were a few that went deep into the ground.

The top floor was something akin to an observation deck. There were chairs and coffee tables clustered around the floor-to-ceiling windows that spanned three of the four walls. Stands with potted plants dotted the vast room. A bar was tucked along the far end, with bathrooms located near the elevator.

I wandered to a comfy looking chair and sat, staring at the East River and the boats that came in and out of the harbor.

My legs ached slightly from my wounds and the hike up the stairs. I was laughably out of breath when I had finally reached the top floor. My academy gym class was failing me.

I leaned my head back on the headrest, enjoying the early morning sun shining on me. I didn't want to think about tonight and my future. If tonight was anything like our fiasco mission a few days ago, maybe rescuing my parents wouldn't be worth it. I shook my head. No, I needed my parents. I loved them, and I knew, in their own way, they loved me. That message my mother and father had left on my phone was proof of that. I couldn't make this new life without them, and I didn't want to. It would be better to suffer the new, not-as-wealthy lifestyle if someone shared my pain. I nearly laughed; it sounded pathetic, but it was true.

I realized I would probably have to drop out of my private academy and go to public school. I shuddered. If movies were even a little bit true, I was going to hate it. The private academy was bad enough, with all the snobs and mini class divides, but public high school seemed way worse.

I watched the boats through the morning while playing on my phone and staring at the unanswered texts sent by Hillary, Paz, and Marcus. Hillary, who texted me nearly every day to fill in what was going on with everything, just told me she had successfully asked Tom to the Spring Formal, which would be in a few weeks, and he'd said yes. It killed me to not respond and celebrate with her. Marcus also had sent texts, saying he wished I'd been here to ask him to the dance, but he instead had said yes to going with Felicity.

That time thinking about how to win Marcus over felt so far away. The longing to be there with my friends, away from this mess I was now in, was a raw ache in my chest. But I couldn't do anything to endanger them, and I had no idea what would do that. A full-on cut off of communication was easiest. At least in theory.

I shut off my phone and stared at nothing.

After a while, my stomach gurgled with hunger, but I was too afraid of going downstairs and running into the Fox.

The more the sun made its way across the sky, the more nervous I got: nervous of the plan, of the possibility of messing up the plan, *again*, nervous of seeing what state my parents would be in, and how they would react to my deal with their dear pet.

Maybe I wasn't giving them enough credit. Maybe they would be grateful, happy even, that I had made the deal to save their lives. The last message they left me certainly made it seem possible that they would be glad for a new start. Maybe everything would be alright, if everything went well tonight.

Maybe.

# Chapter Seventeen

I sat up, grimacing as I stretched out my sore back from sitting so long without moving. It had to be nearing two o'clock. I stood, ready to go find Maddock and get something to eat. The Sewer Fox had to have calmed down by now.

"If I had to walk up all those stairs I would've been very upset, lass," a voice said at my elbow. I screamed, my voice echoing throughout the cavernous room, and I fell against a table, toppling the potted fern to the floor. Dirt sprayed all over the chair I'd been sitting on as the plant tumbled free from the planter. With a squeal, I dropped to my knees and began shoveling as much of the scattered soil as I could back into the container.

"You think Pat is going to thank you for messing up his decor?" Maddock asked, standing over me with his arms folded.

"Why the heck did you do that?" I snapped, my voice shaky as I replaced the crumpled fern in the planter and got to my feet. "How did you know I was up here anyway?" I sat back down on the chair I had recently vacated. If the Fox wanted to kill me, he could do it without me ever knowing what had hit me. I shivered.

"A place like this and you don't think Pat has cameras all over it? Plus, remember, we're connected," Maddock asked with a raised eyebrow. "I thought you were smarter than that, lassie."

I had no snarky reply for him. Instead, I avoided looking at him, heat creeping into my face as I twiddled with the key around my neck. This was the longest we'd been alone since our disastrous extraction of the mandagot, and I had yet to properly thank him for saving my life. I wasn't sure where to begin. Would he disdainfully brush off my thanks like the Fox had?

I had no doubt Maddock probably wished me all the ill will. I was a mere means to an end. But I didn't feel right just assuming he only saved me because he needed me. And yet, I was still scared of voicing my thanks. I didn't want Maddock to think I was the proud, ungrateful human that the Fox thought I was.

"Listen, Maddock," I finally began. "We haven't had time to chat much lately, but I just wanted to say . . . Thank you for saving my life." The words made me inwardly cringe, but it was too late to call them back, so I stared down at my lap. Did the words sound as stupid and cliché to him as they did me? I continued speaking, hoping to cover my discomfort. "I . . . I have no doubt that mandagot would've shred me to pieces without you there to help me."

There was silence, and I glanced up to see Maddock staring out at the river, a furrowed look on his face.

I bit my lip. "I know you only did it to protect our deal, I know that." I was sorry to see Maddock nod sharply, but I plowed on, "But I really am grateful to you. Your freedom means a lot to you, and it means a lot to me too. So if nothing else, I'm glad you saved me so that I could save you."

Maddock coughed, casting me a pained look. My face flamed, the awkwardness was so sharp I felt like crying. Why was this so weird? It was just Maddock, who I'd known for years; Maddock who insulted me, hated me, tortured me with his endless demands, his smug or disdainful looks, and his famous glares of death. I guessed it was weird because I was being sincere for once. Although part of me wished he would call me a flying dolt and tell me to shut up.

"No, no, that was stupid," I sighed. "I'm saying dumb things because I just don't know what to say."

"Then don't say anything, lass." Maddock was pretending to watch the boats on the river with nonchalance. "You owe me nothing. I'll admit that I helped save you from sheer worry that if you died, so would my chance at freedom. But I also don't want you to think that I'm the heartless beast your parents think I am. Just as you don't see me that way, I don't see you the way the Fox does. I know you're kind and good, which is sickening to an old, wily codger like me." He cast me one of his famous sly smiles, and I found myself relaxing. "You granting my freedom will be worth everything that happens to me on this little picnic of ours, and we'll be even. Nothing owed."

I nodded. "I can live with that. But still, thank you for helping me," I resumed. "You could've run and saved yourself, but you didn't. You trusted in my crazy, toxin-laced plan."

Maddock chuckled. "It *was* crazy."

"Why *did* you trust it?" I asked, cautious. "You could've died too."

Maddock looked like he was holding back a laugh. "Lass, there are many ways to leave this world, but having a *mandagot* take me out was not even in the *realm* of possibility. Besides, we're in this together." He made a disgusted face, and he must've realized that what he said almost sounded kind, because he added, "You nitwit."

"It's always a joy conversing with you."

"I know."

We were silent for a moment more. Things were normal between us now, and I felt comfortable enough to ask him basically anything. Except . . .

"Do the cameras have sound?" I whispered.

Maddock shook his head. "Nah. Just video."

"So, the Fox this morning?" I prompted, glancing sideways at him.

Maddock exhaled. "The Fox this morning," he repeated, trailing a toe through the pile of spilled soil on the ground. "He's tense about something, obviously. He has been for a while, I imagine. Can't be easy, shadowing a rogue organization like HAMMA. They have no scruples, no worry about the law of the land. And now he has to shelter a human, but not just any human, a human who is the very worst kind of human in his eyes: one that is holding captive a creature and friend. Not to mention, I think Pat fears there's a traitor to *him* in his organization."

"Well, he does have traitors from HAMMA here, they're probably triple agents, giving information on him back to the group," I said.

Maddock shrugged. "I'm sure that's it, but the problem is, which one? All are adamant lunatics, they can easily hide their treachery behind their fanaticism. So if it seems he hates you—"

"Seems?" I scoffed.

"—it's because he hates and distrusts all humans. It's not just you he's mad at. He's been pretty short with me as well. Just stress. I think helping you is giving him hysterics."

"Well, I'll be out of his hair by this time tomorrow."

"True. Which is why I came to find you."

"The plan?" I asked, tensing.

"The plan. You ready to leave soon?"

I nodded, though my hands ached from clenching them so hard into fists. "You?"

"Yep. Are you nervous?" His voice wasn't teasing.

"Naturally. What if we *do* screw it up, or HAMMA doesn't believe us?"

Maddock shrugged. "We've got backup, and ins with HAMMA because of Pat's people. If HAMMA is suspicious, they'll call Travis to confirm your assignment, he'll confirm it, and we will be in."

"Can we trust his men to not double-cross us?" I asked, shaking out my hands.

"Pat seems to trust them all, within reason."

"But we can't be sure," I said slowly.

Maddock nodded in agreement. "But knowing Pat, he can read people pretty well. He read you well enough to know your true intentions about freeing me. Maybe he didn't like acknowledging it, but if he didn't totally believe you to be honest, there is no way he would have let us in the door."

I exhaled, nodding in acknowledgement. Maybe the Fox was good at this whole espionage thing, if he really could read people.

"And it's not really you he doesn't trust, it's your parents, and what they represent; the power, the money, the influence," Maddock said, staring pointedly at me.

"Well, I can handle them."

Maddock's face puckered in uncertainty. "You sure?"

I set my jaw, taking a deep breath. I'd be seeing them tonight. Everything would change.

"So, you okay, lass?" Maddock asked, and I nodded. Everything felt right, even though my stomach squirmed with unease that I would mess things up again. I wasn't good at being sneaky or underhanded. I never had to lie much to my parents to get what I wanted, and I was sure my poker face was laughable.

"Oh, what about your fake Celtic tattoo?" I asked suddenly. "Where are you going to get that?" Maddock reached up and pulled down the collar of his shirt a bit, so that I could see his very hairy shoulder. "Already got it."

Underneath the hair was a circle the size of a silver dollar, with an intricate Celtic cross in the middle of the circle.

"That looks real," I breathed, frowning.

"Well, it's supposed to. But it's not. Pat did it himself. He knew how to make it look legitimate, but also knew where to put the flaws so it holds no power. Trust me, I tested it."

"He seems very clever."

"Oh yes. Patrick is one of the more clever leprechauns I've met. I think that's why he's so bitter towards humans. They kept him down for a long time, and he wasn't able to reach his full potential in their custody."

"I guess I understand why he hates me, but still," I grumbled.

Maddock sighed. "Yes. He admired your honesty and, frankly, the only reason he's helping you is to help me, but if you were in a deadly situation, and he could escape, I have no doubt he would leave you to die. Keep that in mind."

That wasn't what I wanted to hear, but at least I knew not to put my trust in him if it ever came down to that.

"Well, I'll make sure to never see him again after this," I promised.

Maddock smiled. "I'm sure he'll greatly appreciate that."

Four o'clock came too soon, and we were loading up in the car. As I was buckling myself into my seat, someone tapped on my window. I looked up to see the tips of the Fox's red hair just peeking up outside the window, and I quickly rolled it down, hands trembling.

"Yes?"

"Some last minute details," the Fox said, handing up a deposit slip with the name Tracy McKinnon scrawled on the top.

"Hand this to one of the tellers behind the counter at the bank, and tell them you're there for a deposit and withdrawal. Nothing else. They'll take it from there. Got it?"

I exhaled. "I got it."

"Good." The Sewer Fox turned to Maddock. "Safe travels then, Mad. I'll have grannie light a candle for you."

Maddock's mouth quirked in a slight smile and he bobbed his head. "Will do, Pat. We'll be back soon."

The Fox pounded on the car, and Phos took off.

The trip was just as long as our last excursion, but I was much more jittery this time. I spent the hour-long drive trading between playing a few games on my phone, rereading my friends' texts, and staring out the window, trying not to think of all the horrible scenarios that could occur if I messed it up, or how my parents would react to everything I had done to get them free. Would they be horrified or proud upon learning I had broken into private property to "steal" someone else's magical creature?

We came into Newark, New Jersey, and Phos slowed and finally came to a stop and grunted twice. Maddock had quietly told me the horrific reason why Phos never spoke: he'd had his tongue cut out during a mission to save a group of rusalki, a type of magical Russian water maiden, from poachers. I still cringed and rubbed my tongue against my teeth whenever I thought about it.

Both Maddock and I looked out the window. We were on a busy city street, parked in front of a large building with Goldleaf Trust Bank in big bronze letters above the double doors. It was a handsome building, and it didn't look like the storage place of a radical organization.

"Is this really it?" I asked. Phos grunted twice again. The Fox had told us it was a bank, but I thought maybe it was going to be an abandoned bank, or under construction and closed to the public. However, the bank was active with people coming in and out.

"Does it function as a real bank?" I asked, tucking my phone away.

"I would imagine so. Let's see, it's about 5:30, now," Maddock said. "It closes at six, so we should wait until they're about to close, and then go in and ask for the deposit. No point in attracting the attention of the entire public," Maddock said gruffly.

"Won't you attract the attention of HAMMA immediately once you go inside, since, well, you know," I said, giving him a pointed look, "You're not exactly the same height as most humans."

"Thank goodness for that, you absolute giraffe," Maddock muttered. "But you're right, they'll probably spot me within a mile. We're hoping they will, and get us to move along with this escapade even faster."

We waited for about ten minutes before I couldn't take it anymore.

"Okay, let's go in. I'm sick of waiting around here," I said a little too loud, my nerves jangling.

Maddock flashed me a grin. "Let's crack on, then." He opened the door and slipped out. Taking several deep breaths, I followed him out onto the street.

The sun was low in the sky, casting lengthening shadows over the streets. This was nothing like New York City, but the three story bank was still towered over by the buildings on either side of it. We entered the front doors and I took in the surroundings. Polished wooden floors ran the length of the room. Across the middle of the room was a long counter that spanned the whole breadth of the space. The counter had cubbies where tellers stood, helping customers with their banking.

Behind the tellers were several closed doors, and at the very end, behind the counter, was a small windowed office that said 'Manager' on the door. Three large brass chandeliers hung from the ceilings, and small tables with lamps lined the walls beside windows overlooking the street. The bank felt warm and comforting, nothing like what I imagined the lair of an evil institution to feel like. I wrinkled my nose at the incongruencies, but tried to shake off my unease.

I stood in line for the next available teller, unsure if these people doing their banking were aware of HAMMA, or if all these people were HAMMA. They all looked pretty normal to me.

When the customer in front of me was done, I stepped up to the counter.

The teller was a petite brunette woman with a pixie cut. She was writing something down on a piece of paper before quickly typing something on the computer, then looked up at me.

"Hello. How can I help you today?" she asked, giving me a kind smile.

"Um, I'm here to make a deposit and a withdrawal . . ." I tried to control my shaking hand as I slid the deposit slip the Fox had given me towards the teller. I glanced down at Maddock, unsure of what to say next. Maddock gave me a wide-eyed look and a sharp jerk of his head back toward the teller. I snapped my attention back up at the woman. She read over the slip, then looked at me. "Okay, a transaction for a Miss Tracy McKinnon?"

"Um, yes," I replied.

The teller typed something into her computer, then looked up at me, smiling. "Yes, of course. Follow me, and we'll take care of you." She scribbled some letters and numbers onto the slip of paper, then walked to the end of the counter. She swung open a small half door, ushering Maddock and me behind the teller stations. We followed her through one of the doors behind the counter, entering into a wide, brightly lit hall, coming upon a desk, where a woman was talking on the phone. The brunette placed my deposit slip on the desktop and then turned to me.

"Starr here will take care of you, just tell her what you need." She smiled at me then left, walking back down the hall, shutting the door behind her.

I turned back to the new woman, Starr, who gave me a brief smile while she waited on the phone, then she turned to rifle through some files in her drawer. The nameplate that rested on her desk said *Starr Williams, Receptionist*. She was a very thin young woman with carrot orange hair that fell to her waist, and large horn-rimmed glasses.

I stood there awkwardly. None of these people seemed to notice that I was accompanied by a very short man. They didn't even stare or seem to know he was there.

Finally, the receptionist was done with her call, and she hung up, looking up at me. "Yes, hi, what have we here?" she asked, grabbing the slip and reading what the brunette had written. She then opened a drawer and began searching through her assortment of pens.

"Yes, hi," I said, feeling a little more confident, and I glanced at Maddock. "I'm here for a deposit and a withdraw—"

Maddock leapt away from me, slapping away a small black blur that fell to the floor, his face horrified as I whipped back toward the receptionist, just as something sharp pierced me in the shoulder. Stumbling back, I looked up in time to see the receptionist lower a very feathery, pink pen from her lips, a cold smile on her face.

"Lass, a trap!" Maddock shouted as he jumped again, but he sounded as if he were down at the end of a very long tunnel.

I looked to my shoulder, where a small black dart was protruding from my blouse. Almost immediately, the sweet-looking receptionist went blurry, and I groped for the dart with sluggish hands as my knees turned to jelly.

Before I knew it, the receptionist was by my side, and Maddock had vanished. With strength betrayed by her slight build, the receptionist helped lower me to the wood floor, where I felt my jaw go slack as I stared at the lights that dimmed, then brightened, before fading completely black.

# Chapter Eighteen

I gasped as the stinging slap jogged me out of unconsciousness. I opened my eyes, then snapped them shut again, blinded by the powerful row of lights glaring down at me. My head felt light and floaty, my body tingling, reminding me of the sensation I'd felt coming down off pain meds after I'd broken my arm when I was seven.

"Call back your leprechaun," a woman's voice demanded.

My cheek smarting, I squinted through the dazzling light. I looked around the room, searching for the source of the voice. The room was small, devoid of any furniture. The receptionist that had darted me was nowhere to be seen. Instead, standing before me was a petite blonde woman. The tips of her short, raggedly cut hair were dyed black, and she was wearing a deep purple corset and black leather pants.

Behind her stood another woman and three men. The other woman, a taller brunette with green stripes in her hair, was wearing a black vest with a lot of buckles, a leather miniskirt, and black leggings. The men wore black trench coats, fedoras, and combat boots. They looked nothing at all like the normal, professional bank tellers that had drugged me and kidnapped me.

The loopy feeling still clouding my mind, I was unable to stop myself from giggling at their ridiculous clothing, earning myself another slap.

My shoulder throbbed, but not as much as my cheek as I stared at the people standing before me. Had I somehow stumbled into some weird wanna-be goth convention? My mind felt sluggish as I tried to get my train of thought back under control. Where was I? It was just then I realized my hands were in iron shackles that had been bolted to the wall above my head. My feet were cuffed to the floor.

*What is this, was I being held captive at a renaissance fair?*

I snorted at my inner joke. In the back of my mind I knew I was in trouble, but on the surface, everything seemed funnier than it should've been. And dizzier.

"Call back your leprechaun, Everbleeder," the blonde demanded again, bringing my attention back to her. The sight of the large men behind her sobered me slightly. I shook my head.

*Focus, Mallory.*

"Who are you?" I asked, then realized what a stupid question it was. I had come to find HAMMA. These people had captured me, chained me up, and knew about leprechauns. And she had called me an "Everbleeder." I had obviously found HAMMA.

"Call back your leprechaun," the blonde repeated, placing her hands on her waist, and it was then I saw a long dagger sheathed at her side. Looking between the group, I noticed all were armed with swords, daggers, and staves.

Were these people for real? I felt a nervous squirm in my gut, and I felt the silly giddiness leave my system as the gravity of my situation began to take hold.

"Listen, I think there has been a mistake," I whispered, fear flickering in my chest. I had to keep calm. I would just stick to the plan and play dumb. "I'm—I'm here to drop off the leprechaun," I said, hating how my voice was wavering. "Travis told me I was to drop off the leprechaun, and pick up a delivery of human scum."

No one in the group responded, and the blonde's face hardened.

"Please," I continued. "I'm just here for a delivery. Didn't Travis contact you?"

The blonde folded her arms across her chest, and one of the men behind her chuckled.

"Yes, he did, and that's how we knew *you* couldn't be trusted," the blonde replied. "Travis has left our little organization and became a traitor to all of us, but he still thinks we don't know of his change in allegiance."

My stomach twisted, and it suddenly became hard to breathe.

"No doubt you're here trying to steal some of the animals that we've rescued from captivity!" the blonde accused.

"No, no," I stammered, wracking my brain for any idea so that I could get out of this. "No, I was just told by Travis to drop off this leprechaun—"

"A leprechaun that disappeared the moment you were captured?" The blonde snorted. "I don't think so. So why don't you tell me who you're working for and how much you know about our inventory before we take you underground?"

I wasn't sure if it was a threat, or if they had some sort of holding cell that was actually under the ground.

"Listen," I breathed, struggling to come up with a new excuse, "like I said to you before, I just—"

Something small and round dropped from the ceiling and plinked off the head of one of the men standing behind the short blonde. With a grunt, he looked up at the ceiling, rubbing his head, and then bent down to pick up something small and gold. Another small gold orb hit the brunette woman in the back of the leg, and she turned around with a shout of, "Hey!" Another gold lump flew and struck the blonde on the side of the face.

"Ouch!" she shrieked, whipping around while drawing the dagger at her waist. I rolled my eyes at the woman's dramatic reaction. While all were busy questioning one another, their backs to me, Maddock suddenly appeared in front of me, silent as a shadow. In his hand, he held several key rings. He put a finger to his lips before disappearing again.

I bit back a delighted laugh. These idiots had no idea what they were dealing with.

Leprechauns were notoriously difficult to catch because they were summoners and vanishers, disappearing and reappearing from thin air so fast the human eye couldn't follow. And these morons probably didn't believe that I had the cooperation of "my" leprechaun. The thought that he was going to free me probably hadn't even entered their minds.

No more gold nuggets were thrown, and so my four captors gathered up the pieces and huddled together, studying them.

"I think it's real gold," the blonde said, a little bit of awe in her voice.

"Yeah," one of the men grunted. "But where did it come—"

With grunts and cries of alarm, all of my captors began stumbling and bumping into each other, as if they were being shoved by unseen hands. Laughter burst out of me as I watched them fall over each other, scrambling to escape the onslaught.

"It's the leprechaun!" the blonde shouted over the yelling as she tipped sideways into one of the trenchcoat-wearing men.

One by one, the group of people fell to the ground, unconscious before even hitting the floor, as if hit over the head by invisible glass bottles. Once they had all slumped to the ground, Maddock appeared in their midst, holding a feathery dart. "This stuff is potent," he remarked, tucking the dart carefully into his pocket. Gathering up all the gold nuggets from the unconscious human heap, he made the treasure vanish into thin air, then hopped over to where I stood shackled to the wall, keys in hand.

"Hurry, hurry," he said, unlocking the cuffs around my ankles. "We have to leave. They know we're not here for a deposit."

"No kidding," I snorted. He straightened and considered my hands locked above my head.

"Give me a leg up so I can unlock your arms, you mog."

I glared at him, unmoving, the drugs leaving my system making me feel cranky. "Maybe I should keep a tally of all the mean names you call me and keep you bound to me one extra day of your sentence for every mean thing."

Maddock laughed nervously. "You don't even know what 'mog' means! It could be flattering."

I stared at him, unmoving. "Is it?"

"We haven't the time for this, lass," Maddock snapped.

We glared at each other, and I paused for an extra few seconds before I planted a now-free foot against the wall so that my knee stuck out. With a small bow, Maddock leapt up onto my leg. I grunted; he was a lot heavier than he appeared. Reaching up, Maddock unlocked my hands and then dropped to the floor, pocketing the keys. Shaking my wrists out of the cuffs, I turned to Maddock, rubbing my hands as blood rushed back into my fingers.

"Where should we go? We can't leave without my parents," I insisted, wobbling now that I didn't have a wall to support me.

An alarm suddenly sounded, and Maddock grabbed my sleeve. "Yes we can. We have to. We'll think of something else. But for now, we have to get out of here, or else we'll all be sunk."

I followed Maddock at a run out of the door, and we found ourselves in a hallway like the one we came down when I had been attacked by Starr, the evil receptionist. Ornamental urns and statues rested on small tables that lined the hallways, and pictures dotted the walls.

"This way," Maddock said, leading me around a corner down another similar hallway. "We're on the top floor. I was able to scope out the place a little while you were unconscious."

"How long was that?" I asked, hurrying after him. I was tempted to break a few of the vases that lined the corridor, but refrained. I didn't want to get caught because I was busy doing something so petty.

"About half an hour. Come on. This way. There's a stairwell to an emergency exit."

We charged down the two flights of stairs, alarm still blaring from all sides, and hit the ground floor, charging toward the exit. The green exit sign shined like a beacon of hope until Maddock slammed into the door and bounced off, tumbling to the floor. I helped him to his feet, then tried the door again.

Locked.

"Who locks an emergency exit door?" I fumed, kicking the door, the sound echoing in the concrete and steel hallway.

"People who don't want anyone to leave," Maddock replied, his tone grim. "No keyhole. They must have it bolted on the outside." He disappeared, then reappeared a moment later. "Nope. Nothing on the outside. It must be vault-type bolts, controlled electronically from an office." The alarm still shrilled, and I felt sick as I stared at that unyielding exit door that wasn't doing its one job.

"Okay, so this is a no," I said, giving the door one last kick. "We're on the ground floor, let's go back into the hall. Maybe we can find a window to climb out of."

Nodding, Maddock went to the stairwell door that looked out into a hallway and peered through the tiny rectangular glass window.

"Hallway's empty for now. Let's go."

Easing the door open, we glanced down the wood-floored corridor. The entire hall had an annoying lack of windows that opened, and the dainty decorative tables would in no way break through the double-paned security glass. The alarms still shrilled overhead, and I wondered if it would attract the attention of the entire city.

We could see an open door at one end of the hallway that led to a bunch of offices and continued on toward the front of the bank. Voices sounded from that direction, so we hurried through another open door nearby, praying for an exit or something heavy to crash through windows.

The room we entered held nothing but boxes and filing cabinets, with another door across the room that I figured was a closet. Part of me itched to go through the files to see if I could find anything useful, but the other part of me cursed the dead end, knowing I had no time to find anything useful. Chills erupted up my spine. We needed to get out of here, and I felt like we were just getting more and more trapped.

"Okay, this room isn't anything," I panted, "let's try—"

"Whoa," Maddock said, grabbing my hand to stop me from leaving, his eyes on the closet door ahead of us. "There is a lot of magic around here."

"Really?" I asked, turning to follow his gaze to the second door. "Where? In that closet?"

He didn't answer, but charged toward the closed door. He turned the knob, but it was locked. Rifling through his pockets, he quickly pulled out the set of keys.

"Where did you get those, anyways?" I asked, coming up behind him and biting my lip.

"They were in the manager's office. There were a lot of key rings in there, and I just grabbed the lot. I figured we would need them if they put you in a cage or a locked room," he said, trying several keys in the lock.

"Maddock, what are you doing? I thought we needed to es-cape!" I hissed, heart pounding as I glanced back at the door that led to the hall.

"You don't understand," Maddock growled, flipping through keys unnaturally fast. "There is a *lot* of magic through this door."

My breath caught in my chest. Could this be where my parents were being held? Maybe this whole fiasco wouldn't be a huge failure after all.

Finding the right key, he opened the door, and it revealed an-other set of stairs. Something more than just air wafted around us as the door opened, and I felt a prickling on my skin. Magic. Was I starting to pick up the knack for feeling its presence?

"Oh yes, it's down here," Maddock breathed, and without hesitation, charged down the stairs. I followed, making sure to shut the door behind me. I was hoping they wouldn't investigate locked rooms.

We followed the stairs down and down, and panic began prickling the back of my mind as we continued to descend, now at least one story underground.

"Maddock, we're going to get trapped down here!" I breathed.

"Oh no, trapped in an underground room? I can't imagine how terrible that would be," he drawled.

"Yeah, but this time you'll be trapped with *me*."

"Blimey, I didn't think about that." he replied, his tone worried. "Best hurry along, then." He hopped down the last few steps and opened the only door at the bottom of the stairs, stopping short inside the doorway.

Coming up behind him, curious, I too stopped.

Cages upon cages lined the walls, like those found in an animal shelter. However, only a few of the cages were occupied. All of the occupied cages shimmered with magic to keep the magical creatures inside.

However, unlike an animal shelter, this room was completely silent.

Maddock wandered into the room, his eyes hard, and I followed, momentarily forgetting that we were trying to escape without getting caught ourselves.

I saw two mandagot-like creatures, both in the shape of a house cat, lying in small cages, eyes trained on us as we entered the room.

A small group of elf-like creatures that reminded me of the garden pixies, but with bluish skin and shimmery wings, huddled in the corner of a cage, watching us with sad eyes. Another cage held a thick, short black snake that snoozed under a light.

"Well, I'll be a poormouthin' poppy," Maddock murmured, and I followed his gaze.

In the far corner, a cage held a short, bipedal creature about two feet high, dressed in leaves that looked like they belonged in a jungle. Its skin was light green, and the hair on its body looked like long, wild grass flowing down its back. It watched us with cunning eyes, and I could almost feel the hate seething off the creature.

The last occupied cage was, strangely, inhabited with what looked like a normal seal, his coat silvery white with a large brown swath of fur across its back and face. The poor creature looked absolutely miserable, and when it saw me, it gave a mournful moan before closing its eyes and laying its head back down, snuffling and snorting.

"Are all of these magical creatures?" I asked, staring at the seal.

Maddock nodded, his fists tightening into balls of knuckle and clenched muscles. "Those are sprites," he said, gesturing to the group of winged humanoids in the far cage, and then he pointed to the single, leaf-dressed being in the far cage, "That's an eloko. A Central African type of pixie. Very rare, very difficult to catch unless you have very powerful magic. That snake is a ladon, a greek guarding snake, and that's a selkie," he said, pointing to the seal.

I studied every creature in their cages.

"How can they think they're doing good for these animals when they keep them in cages that are way too small for them?" I demanded, looking at the seal, which filled the cage so much that some of its body was pressed against the panels, the criss-crossed bars embedding a waffle pattern on his skin. "Can they not even give that poor seal some water to swim in?" The seal turned and stared at us as if it had understood what I had said. I shivered as our eyes met. They were bright with intelligence.

I glared at the cages, anger and sadness burning up my throat. This fate would be mine and Maddock's if we didn't leave soon, but I couldn't move to leave. I couldn't abandon these poor things here.

I gasped as an exciting idea came to my mind.

Maddock whipped toward me and held up his hand. "Oh no, I know what you're thinking, and no! We don't have time."

"We can't leave them here!" I demanded. "Plus they'd cause a distraction."

Maddock rubbed his jaw. "I dunno lass. Opening the cages alone would be a dangerous job. That ladon is poisonous and faster than it looks, and the eloko are vicious to everyone but their own tribe, and they can actually cast spells. He might curse you when you take down the barrier. And you know what the mandagots will do."

I swallowed, nodding as a cold sweat erupted along my palms, but I took a bracing breath. "Well, do you want to leave them all here, then?" I asked, knowing the answer. Maddock glared at me, and I shrugged, annoyed. "Well, that settles that, then. But to get them out safely . . . Wait, wait, wait! I have an idea," I gasped again, hitting Maddock's shoulder, and he pulled away with a scowl, but I grabbed his shoulders with a curt, "Here, hold still."

"Lass, what are you doing?"

"Just trust me." Taking a deep breath, I withdrew magic from Maddock, repeating the words to the protective shield I had used back at Maddock's house when I had been chased on the ATV.

I traced a hand around first Maddock and then myself. A wind whipped around us as I finished saying the words, then the air, and magic, settled.

Maddock looked at me as if seeing me for the first time. "That's not half dumb, lassie."

"Thanks *bestie*," I said, rolling my eyes. I reached out to try and slap Maddock's face, but my hand bounced away before making contact.

Maddock nodded, a small smile on his face. "Not bad. But will this guard us from magic?"

"I think so?" I replied, sounding hopeful.

"You only *think*?" He frowned.

"It stopped a charging ATV," I said, biting my lip. "Besides, it's the only shield spell I know!"

Maddock snorted. "Well, if we get cursed into a jumble of warty frogs, we won't have to worry about anything else ever again. Take down the barriers," Maddock said, his tone resigned. "And be quick about it. Like you said, we could get trapped down here."

Hoping that my ancestors were thinking of magical protection as well as physical when they created the shielding spell, I reached out with the magic toward the cage of the sprites and searched around the impenetrable forces of the barrier spell. I didn't know exactly how I would take it down, but after a minute, I was able to feel a sort of seam where the barriers connected, where the magic was weakest. Using a solidified ball of magic, I rammed at the seam, and the edges broke apart fairly easily. Once the seam was broken, the magic seemed to melt away.

I looked at Maddock, pleased. "I think I did it."

"Huh. They must not be very strong barriers if the likes of you can dispose of them so quickly," he mused. "Well, stop standing there like a muppet and hurry with the rest."

Moving from cage to cage, I tore down the magical barriers from the cages in quick succession. The moment I took down the barricade guarding the eloko, I staggered backwards as the earthy creature extended his hands and shot a blinding ball of yellow light at me. The spell ricocheted off my barrier, but it still knocked me off my feet. Maddock roared with laughter as I got back up.

"You alright, lass?" he chuckled.

Exhaling in relief that my ancestors knew what they were doing, I nodded.

The eloko danced and made a strange clicking noise, and I realized it was talking, shaking his fist at me in anger.

"So sorry your little curse didn't work," I sniffed, shaking my head as I finished taking down the barriers to the seal and the snake. Once the barriers on all the cages were gone, I turned to Maddock. "You're up."

"Good," he said, clapping his hands together. "You go get all those doors to the hallway open, and be careful."

"You too," I said, giving him a nod. He returned it, then jerked his head toward the door. I ran from the room, propping open the door to the cage room as I left. At the top of the stairs, I used a box of files to prop open the door to the stairwell that led to the storage office, then went and cracked open the door that led to the hallway and peered out. The siren was still going, but was quieter than before, as if it had a volume control. Over the noise of the alarm, I heard voices coming down the hallway and quickly slipped the door shut again. I would have to keep the door closed until the creatures got up the stairs, then I could fling open the door so we would all run out in a confusing rush. I only hoped they would ignore me and go for the door.

As I waited, pressed up against the wall beside the door, I heard hurried footsteps coming from up and down the hall. No one tried the door I hid behind, probably because they didn't expect that Maddock had grabbed the keys to down here. As I waited, the seconds ticking by, I grew more nervous. Did Maddock get eaten by that snake? Or was my shield not good enough, and he was cursed into a pile of toadstools by that menacing eloko?

At that moment, something knocked me sideways, and I looked down to see the small eloko battering at my shins with his fists, but he couldn't reach me. I hurriedly opened the door, and the eloko abandoned the futile attempt of punching me and darted down the hall with a small hoot. I rolled out the aching in my shoulders from crouching; so Maddock had been able to open some cages at least. I was watching down the stairwell when Maddock appeared by my side, panting.

"That cage with the selkie was so small, he couldn't get out by himself. I had to pull him out. He's coming now, though. So are all the other ones. Let's get going."

We exited the door, and were making sure it stayed propped open with another box of files, when we heard a sharp scream pierce over the alarm bells.

"I think the eloko found someone to curse," I said, looking toward the direction of the scream.

"Good. Let's get out of here!" Maddock growled, still puffing.

We ran down the hall just as another door burst open, and a wave of people came spilling out. We flattened ourselves against the wall to avoid being noticed, but the horde didn't even give us a second glance as they stampeded down the hallway. A few moments later, another person came running by, crusty-looking growths sprouting from off her neck and spilling down her shoulders. The woman was crying and screaming, and my heart constricted with pity.

"I hope they can get that fixed with magic," I said with a grimace as the woman bolted past, shrieking.

"This is what happens when you don't respect the boundaries and territories of magical creatures," Maddock said, as the eloko rushed past us after the group of people, cackling as he destroyed paintings and smashed windows.

Down the hall, two large dogs burst out from the basement door, snarling, and they turned and ran down the hall away from us, followed by the sprites who flew out the broken window. A moment later, the black snake, which looked down both of the hallways, slithered up the wall and out the window.

Now that most of the dangerous creatures were out of sight, I took the magical barriers down from both Maddock and myself, not wanting to drain all of his magical strength in case we needed to use more later.

"Do you think the seal will be able to get up the stairs?" I asked, imagining the poor creature floundering at the bottom of the stairs, barking for help.

"Don't worry about it, lass. Also, it's called a selk–"

Ignoring Maddock, I moved back toward the room with the hidden basement. If I had to carry that seal up the stairs and out of the bank myself, I would.

Just as I was wondering how the seal would survive out in the city streets, a tall man stepped out of the room. I stopped short. Not only because he was handsome, which he was, with vibrant, tousled red curls, but he was completely naked aside from a silvery gray, spotted pelt he had wrapped around his waist. He looked down both sides of the hall and, seeing me standing stock still in the hallway, he strode toward me.

He came to a stop before me and held out a hand. I hesitantly took it. He gently squeezed my hand, his green eyes bright with unshed tears. His freckled skin was unnaturally pale and dry, cracked and bleeding in some places, his lips chapped.

"Thank you," he rasped, and he bent down and kissed the back of my hand hard. Giving a salute to Maddock, the man ran and leapt out of a broken window the eloko had smashed, running out of sight.

"Who was that?" I asked, flexing my hand. It felt tingly and oddly light.

"That was the selkie," Maddock said, coming to my side. "Looks like you got yourself a magical kiss."

"Magical kiss? . . . Wait, the seal-kie can turn into a *man*?" I asked, horrified. Before Maddock could answer, two men appeared at the end of the hall and, seeing us, began shouting.

"Come on!" Maddock said, moving to the window the selkie had just exited. Giving me a quick boost, Maddock pushed me over the shards of glass and I fell out of the window. He hopped out behind me with ease, and we burst out of the bushes into the street. Twilight had settled on the city, and through the waning light, a crowd was gathering around the front of the bank, looking at the building in wonder as the alarm blared. Coming up the street was a firetruck and a few police cars, sirens wailing.

"Let's get out of here," I whispered. Maddock led the way across the street to where Phos had parked, waiting.

We charged to the car and threw ourselves into the back seat.

"*Go, go!*" Maddock and I shouted at the same time. Phos put the car in gear and jerkily pulled into traffic, bypassing the droning firetruck, and we were on our way to the highway. When we were safely on our way, Maddock and I looked at each other, and we began giggling like idiots.

"Well, that jaunt didn't go exactly as planned," Maddock said, the first to get a hold of himself. "But at least we did some good along the way, right?" He cast me a roguish smile.

"And some bad," I said, gasping. "That eloko caused a bigger distraction than I anticipated." The adrenaline was fading, leaving me tired and weak. Maddock reached into the small refrigerator and pulled out two sodas. Handing me one, he knocked his can against mine.

"Cheers," he said, opening the tab with a foamy hiss.

We didn't say much on the car ride home. Although we made it out alive along with releasing some magical beings, we hadn't found my parents. That meant we would need more help from the Sewer Fox. My stomach churned as I considered the Fox's reaction when he heard about our failure. I could hear the bellowing from here.

Unless . . .

"So, that was an obvious trap," I said, tracing a finger around the bottom of my soda can. "They knew we were coming . . . The Fox didn't set me up, did he?" I asked. Maddock took an extra long swallow from his drink, then came up for air.

"What would be the point of betraying us to HAMMA? He wouldn't just be betraying you, but me too. He wouldn't do that."

"I mean, that blonde lady did say they knew the Fox's contact had betrayed them. There's probably a lot of intel about HAMMA that is wrong. We need to tell him." My stomach squirmed at the thought of having that conversation.

Maddock must've been thinking along the same lines, because he nodded. "*I'll* speak to him. But Pat would never betray us. I can *feel* how much he hates HAMMA. He would never willingly help them."

I stared out the window as we headed back to headquarters. This debacle meant that the Fox wasn't rid of me yet, and Maddock wouldn't get his freedom for a while. My body sagged. We'd been so close. Again.

I couldn't understand why my parents weren't in that secret basement. Was there another secret basement at that bank that we didn't get to check, and so missed my parents? Or did we not find them because HAMMA, knowing Travis was a traitor, gave him bad information?

I guessed we wouldn't know until we got back and Maddock had a chat with the Fox. But for the moment, happiness at releasing all those creatures swelled within me. I hoped they all escaped. At least we knew most had, including the selkie-man. I ran a finger over the back of my hand again.

"What did you mean when you said that selkie gave me a magical kiss?" The tingly sensation on my skin had faded, but it still felt unnaturally warm and light.

Maddock shrugged. "Kisses have magical potency if bestowed by an Ever being. I mean, all your fairy tales talk about kisses breaking curses or whatever, right? Well, humans got the idea from some-where."

"Will this kiss affect me?" I asked, my heart leaping at the thought. What would it do to me?

Maddock shrugged again. "Probably not. I don't know much about them, never having administered one myself, but I reckon since it was just a kiss of gratitude, he wasn't trying to bestow or break any spell on you."

I spent the rest of the drive mulling over what we had accomplished tonight, absently running my finger over the place the man's lips had met my knuckles.

# Chapter Nineteen

We pulled into the garage behind the Sewer Fox's warehouse, the New York skyline glittering in the deepening dusk. It was so weird not to see stars here. Upon entering the building, the Fox met us in a robe and house slippers, looking like a vexed housewife who caught her husband sneaking in late.

I steeled myself, aware that our venture did take longer than was expected; then again, I wasn't expecting to get captured.

As we approached, I could see the anger trembling in his face.

"Well, congratulations," the Fox snarled. "You two idiots made the evening news."

Before explaining what he meant, the Fox ushered us into his sitting room, where he began to tear into us. And by us, I meant me.

"You *idiot* human girl! It was the simplest plan! You were supposed to get in, make the transfer, and get out. Why did you have to go all vigilante and free all those animals? There was news of dogs loose in the bank, and a snake, and several people came out looking like deformed fungi farms? *On the national news!*" the Fox bellowed. I clapped my hands over my ears, more to cover the tears threatening to squeeze from my eyes than the actual noise, but I heard his continued rant despite my covered ears.

"I do not understand the human desire for destruction! Did you tear up the whole place for the fun of it?" he seethed.

"Pat, you don't understand," Maddock interrupted. "It's not her fault at all. It was a trap for us. Somehow Travis was misled into thinking that HAMMA still trusted him. But they were waiting for us, and they captured the lass. We didn't even have a hope that they believed we were there for a transfer. We had to get out. I'll admit it wasn't the most subtle escape, but we got out to tell you Travis has been compromised."

"So you just *had* to make sure you discredited Travis for good, huh?" the Fox seethed. "Now my main contact with HAMMA is no good!"

"Pat, they already knew he was a traitor to them. That's how they caught us," Maddock said, sounding exasperated. "They knew from the start it wasn't a real transfer."

"I'm not blaming you, mate," the Fox said, still breathing heavily. He looked at me, his expression hardening. "It was her idea to free all those creatures, wasn't it?" he asked, the venom in his voice making me flinch.

"It was so we could escape!" I protested. "We needed a distraction! Besides, I thought you wanted creatures freed!"

The Fox didn't reply, but picked up the nearest thing to him, a book, and threw it at the wall. I flinched away as it hit a large, framed pastoral painting, and both book and painting crashed to the ground.

"Pat, there is no reason to be so upset," Maddock barked. "It was unfortunate, but now we know that they've known all along that Travis wasn't true to the cause. It was an unfortunate problem, but at least we're free, and we can try again."

But the Fox seemed too angry to speak. Suddenly, he grabbed at his heart, and for a moment I was afraid he was having a heart attack. Could leprechauns have heart attacks? I had no idea. After a moment, and several deep breaths, the Fox calmed down enough to turn to look at Maddock.

"Do you agree with this bure?" he spat, casting me a venomous scowl. "It was a good enough reason to let those animals go, that the distraction helped you escape?"

"Well, an eloko broke several windows, and that helped us be able to escape," Maddock said, glancing at me. He turned back to the Fox, nodding. "Yes, it was the right decision."

The Fox exhaled and rubbed a hand over his forehead. "Okay. I suppose I'll need to do some interviews with my men. Get to the bottom of this manky mess." He looked up at Maddock. "I'm sorry for losing my temper. It's just that all these problems started happening when you brought this giant bull into my china shop." He gave me a half-hearted sneer.

I glared back, wanting to get off this explosive minefield of dealing with the Fox.

"If you ask me, she's bad luck," the Fox continued.

"Well, you know what they say about girls named Mallory," Maddock said in a low voice, and the Fox let out a laugh like a foghorn, slapping Maddock on the shoulder. Before I could ask the chortling leprechauns what they meant, the Fox waved us toward the door, wiping at his eyes.

"If you want a midnight snack, there's food in the dining room. Help yourself, then go to bed. We'll discuss tactics tomorrow."

"Do you want help interviewing your men?" Maddock offered. "I was there, I can provide—"

But the Fox waved him away, still chuckling. "I want as few men to know about you as possible. Take your muppet bure and go." He didn't even look at me again as he called, "Now! Get going, you manky dog!"

"'Night Pat," Maddock said, grabbing my arm and towing me from the room faster than my legs could keep up.

"Figured we'd get out while Pat was still in a generous mood," Maddock replied to my affronted look as we headed toward the stairs, out of the Fox's earshot.

"Generous? Not even a 'thanks for setting those creatures free, guys!'" I grumbled as we made our way upstairs to our bedrooms. I didn't even want to think about how quickly he'd gone from boiling rage to amicable helper again. Maybe I would have Maddock suggest the Fox see a therapist once this was over.

"I know. I'm sorry lass. This must have been a big blow to him tonight; he learned his main asset has been compromised for a while. Who knows how long HAMMA has known. Plus, our goal wasn't accomplished, and he probably doesn't know the next step on getting your parents out."

I nodded. The Fox had been very helpful—if not very nice—to me through all of this. I felt bad that he had to learn that Travis was compromised this way, but there was no reason to get mad at me. Then again, I was a human, the plague of the Earth; why shouldn't he blame me for every bad thing that happens?

"Well," Maddock sighed, "sleep well, lass. I'm sure there will be a lot of furious planning tomorrow, especially if HAMMA knows they've been hit by a traitor. They'll probably be trying to find who the culprit is, and that probably puts loads of stress on Pat."

I nodded, almost feeling sorry for our actions that night for the first time. But I knew I couldn't apologize to the Fox. He'd just see it as another insult. I would thank him by working my hardest to help him figure out a new plan.

Bidding Maddock goodnight, I went into my room, changed into my pajamas, and slipped into bed, my brain whirling with ideas on what could be our next move to free my parents. I scrolled through my phone, looking up ways to pick locks and disable security cameras. I considered the key to Maddock's home still around my neck. Maybe I could acquire some sort of skeleton key to add to it, in case my parents were in a cage and Maddock wasn't around.

After about an hour of searching around, I darkened the screen and lowered my phone, thinking. What if the Fox decided to kick me out? What if he finally had enough of being around a human that caused him so much stress?

I closed my eyes, gripping my phone tight. I couldn't let that happen. I needed him, no matter how much we clearly disliked each other. He was my only link to the world of HAMMA.

I heard a small sound, like my door being eased open. Thinking it was Maddock coming to discuss an idea, I raised my head slightly, looking into the darkness. The sound of running footfalls over to my bed broke the silence, and out of the shadows, an enormous figure loomed above me and threw something large and soft over my head.

My heart exploded in panic. I screamed, but it was muffled by the blankets pressed down on me. My body was lifted up and flipped over, tipping me sideways until I was totally enclosed inside the covers, before I was lifted completely off the bed and shouldered through the doorway. Quiet voices reached my ears, and I tried kicking at the person carrying me, but they just shifted the blankets and kept walking. When kicking did nothing, I began screaming for help, hoping to wake Maddock or the Fox. Someone struck me hard on the head with a brusque, "Shut up," which knocked out my desire to keep screaming for help.

I fell silent, counting the stars dancing in my vision, gritting my teeth against the pain. I lay huddled and tangled in the blanket bag, fear palpitating in my chest as I was taken away.

# Chapter Twenty

After several minutes of being jostled around inside my blanket bag, I felt myself get set down on a hard surface. The oppressive covering around me parted, fresh air rushing in. I only had the briefest glimpse of a dim streetlight overhead before the dark figure towering over me shoved something prickly-yet-soft, like a small clump of spanish moss, into my face.

Startled at the sudden object pressed against my nose and mouth, I took a gasping breath to begin screaming for help. As I inhaled the tangy smell of the plant, my arms and legs instantly lost their strength. I fell back against the blanket, my vision swaying, and all troubles seemed to fade from my mind. Something cold and hard snapped around my wrist, but I just stared, uncaring and unfazed, as the streetlight above me darkened, a dull thunk enveloping me into blackness.

I heard a car engine roar to life from some faraway place, but I couldn't seem to feel anything about the vague noise. The darkness began to swirl with muted colors. Though I could still hear the engine and feel my body shift with strange turns and bumps, I seemed to also be half asleep, entering a state of relaxed, aware oblivion as my mind began playing soft visions in that halfway place.

Something thumped beside me, and I snapped to awareness. The dreamy place between wakefulness and sleep vanished, and I found myself on my back in oppressive darkness. I blinked several times, and reached a cautious hand up and outwards. My hand bumped against a very close ceiling, and I realized a hard, thick bracelet was clamped around my wrist. Where did that come from? As my fingers brushed the rough, wiry carpet above me, my memories came flooding back.

I had been shoved into a car trunk like some dead body. The effects of whatever they had used to knock me out had faded, and I could think more clearly, despite the small headache from the blow I'd received earlier that night. The fear hitched in my lungs kept the tears at bay as I began to think of possible reasons for my current predicament.

How long had I been out? What had happened? Why had they put this bracelet on me? I tried to pry it off, but it was too tight to wriggle out of. What was going on? Was the Fox getting rid of me for annoying him?

Though Maddock had been adamant about the Fox's hatred toward HAMMA, and the Fox's promises to help me, maybe I'd become too much of a problem for the Fox, despite Maddock's belief that his friend wouldn't play the double-crosser. I shook my head. If I couldn't trust the Fox, I could at least trust Maddock.

A horrifying thought struck me; what if Maddock and I actually led HAMMA straight to the Fox's lair? Sickening guilt burbled in my stomach. Maddock and the Fox were most likely captured, like me.

Cramped and struggling not to cry, I realized that the car engine wasn't running, but there was a low hum of another engine somewhere nearby, and I felt movement. Listening hard, I felt the familiar sensation of dips and crests of waves. I'd been on my parents' yacht many times, but I still got violently sick without medication to prevent it. Like clockwork, now that I was conscious, the motion sickness began to roil in my stomach along with the fear.

Why was I being taken out to sea? Was I going to be dropped into the water like a bag of kittens and killed? The thought seemed to suck all of the air out of my tiny space, the walls around me seeming to close in. Terror surged through me. Unable to hold back anymore, I burst into tears.

As I lay on my back in the darkness, tears streaming into my hair and ears, I let the self-pitying thoughts flood me. I didn't ask for any of this. I wanted to be a normal teen: rebelling against my parents, getting crushes, worrying about school work. Why was rescuing my parents my responsibility? I just wanted my parents back! It was all so unfair, and so beyond what I was capable of taking on.

I cried until I heard the car start up again. The movement of waves stopped. The feeling of seasickness faded, replaced by carsickness and claustrophobia. Now that I realized I wasn't going to be dropped into the sea, the shock began to fade. I had to get a hold of myself. Taking several deep breaths, I wiped my eyes with a fold of the blanket still beneath me.

Crying wasn't going to help me get out of this, even if it did release some pent up emotions and help me clear my mind. I had to try and get free somehow. If I was in danger, I had to try to fight my way out of it. If I got into the most defensible position I could, maybe I could catch them off guard and give myself a chance to escape.

My determination returning, I searched the blanket I was lying on with my hands, the darkness making things difficult. As I turned, trying to wrestle the blanket out from under me, my phone clattered from my lap onto the trunk floor.

Finally, some luck! I snatched it and clicked the home button to wake it up. Blinking at the light flooding the tiny space, I studied the screen.

No!

I hadn't plugged my phone in, and the battery read twelve percent. However, not plugging it in had been the reason I now had my phone with me. I had to look at the positives. Switching to power saving mode, I considered my options. I had a phone, but what should I do? Call the police? That wouldn't work, I had no idea where I was. That was an option better saved until I could actually tell the police something useful.

I shook my head. What was I thinking? I had something better than the police. I could call Maddock to me. He would beat up those guys driving the car, and save me from wherever these kidnappers were taking me. It would all be okay.

I worried a little about the space in here when he arrived, but Maddock was small, and once he realized where I was, he could leave and get me out. Taking a deep breath, I whispered the words to call Maddock.

I waited, frozen in the darkness, but no Maddock appeared. I tried to stifle the panic that flared in my mind.

Maybe I had just mispronounced the words? I tried again, going slower with my annunciation. I waited with bated breath. Nothing happened. No grumbling leprechaun appeared in this cramped space, complaining as to why I woke him at such an unholy hour.

My mouth went dry.

The only reason Maddock wouldn't come to my summons was if he was magically impeded from coming. Maddock had a phone, but if he was in trouble, I didn't want to give away that he had a phone; it would get taken from him. Plus, I didn't want to waste battery on a call he might not answer, and I had no one else to call.

Taking several deep breaths and wiping away stinging tears, I recentered myself. I could get out of this and figure out what was going on. I shut down my phone, hoping to save the battery. Now, somehow, I had to open the trunk.

I wished I could use magic to get out, but I couldn't recall any useful magic spells. Why hadn't I been more diligent in studying my grandparent's journals? But it was a moot point. Without Maddock's magic nearby for me to call upon, I was powerless anyway.

In frustration, I kicked my foot, and the corner of the trunk caved in a bit. A slight glow from the tail lights peeped through where I'd kicked through. That sliver of light was like a beacon of hope, and I recalled that it was possible to kick out a car's tail lights from inside of a trunk. I could try waving for help if I did that! As I shuffled around to get into a more strategic position to kick the brake light out, the car turned sharply and came to a sudden stop.

I was out of time.

I stuffed my phone in my pajama pants pocket, hoping no one would notice the lump, and then searched the trunk for some kind of weapon. Whoever kidnapped me must've used this car a lot for kidnappings, because there wasn't anything in here I could use as a weapon. No tire irons, jugs of oils, or jacks. Nothing except the blanket. I would have to make it work.

The engine died, and I again heard muffled voices and slamming car doors. Moving quickly, I pulled the blanket out from under me and bunched it into as tight of a ball as I could. It was a difficult task, with the blanket being so large and me being so cramped, but I readied myself.

I heard the clicks of disengaging locks, and the trunk popped open a bit. Using my shoulder, I heaved the lid all the way open. As I emerged, I hurled the large blanket as best as I could up and out at the nearest human I saw. The man grunted in surprise as the blanket hit his face and unraveled over his head and shoulders. I jumped up from the trunk, rushing past him, and began sprinting away through the concrete pillars, my bare feet slapping against the cement floor, not even sure where I was running to. An exit sign would have been nice at this moment.

I didn't get very far.

Someone a lot stronger than me grabbed my arm and wrapped a thick forearm around my stomach, pulling me up short. I looked up to see a gigantic man with brown hair and a strong jaw. He was wearing a suit and a wire in his ear. He looked exactly like a Secret Service agent, except bigger.

"Let go of me!" I shouted, struggling to get away, but he pulled me back over to the parked car like I was a two-year-old.

Standing around the car were three other men, all as equally large and intimidating as the man that held me. One of the men, a guy with dirty blonde hair and white teeth, looked me right in the eye.

"Stop struggling or I'll smack you again," he snapped. Remembering the sound blow I had received earlier, I stopped fighting against the iron hold on me, and I contented myself with glaring at all of them. There was no way I was going to be able to break this guy's grip. Why get my brain knocked around for nothing?

"Who are you?" I panted. "I don't have anything you want."

No one laughed or said anything to me, but the blond man gestured to the other men to follow him, and I was hauled over a shoulder like a sack of flour.

I glanced around at my surroundings as I was hoisted away, hoping to see anything that would tell me where we were. We were inside an underground parking lot that was filled with a variety of vehicles: trucks, sports cars, vans, a mix of clunkers, and hybrid cars. I even saw a Lamborghini in one corner, parked next to a very rusty Oldsmobile. What kind of place was this?

We all piled into an elevator, and one of the men hit level four, the top level, and the doors closed. My heart hammered in my throat, and I hoped that since they hadn't killed me yet, they weren't planning on it.

The ride to the top floor was quick and quiet, and I was still slung over a shoulder, it gave me a moment to examine the thick bracelet on my wrist. It was black and heavy, like it was made of metal. I tried to furtively slip it off, but it wouldn't budge. I felt a small keyhole in the side, so I gave up trying to take it off. It was tight, but it wasn't hurting me. Much.

When the doors slid open, I was carried down a hall and into a very modern-looking office. The room was cast in a half light. Only a few lamps were on; the rest of the room was plunged in semi-darkness.

Ceiling-to-floor windows covered two of the four walls. All were draped in dark gray curtains, shielding the view outside. A marble desk was in the corner, where a man sat writing something on a notepad, his face shadowed. Two chairs sat before the desk, and the rest of the room was empty.

I was set down in one of the chairs. The man at the desk didn't even look up, but continued to write. When he finished, he set down his pen, and I gasped as he looked up at me, the desk lamp bringing his features into sharp focus. I was staring into the face of the man that had been at my mother's party, the business mogul she'd been gushing about.

"Hello again, Mallory," Houston Banwell said.

I glared at him to cover my confusion. The famed multi-billionaire, the beloved philanthropist, the illustrious Self-Made man? *He* had kidnapped me? Why? My mother had been making plans to go on vacation with his family!

Houston Banwell continued giving me a kind smile as he held out the notepad he'd been writing on, and one of the men behind me took the notepad from Banwell's hand and withdrew back into the shadows.

"I'm sorry about the rude summons, but you've been quite a surprising little problem for me, so I thought I'd bring you in to have a chat." Banwell gave me another pleasant smile.

I said nothing, my mind blank as I stared at him, trying to figure out how Houston Banwell fit into all this.

"I see you're a little behind, so I'll try to bring you up to speed, so you can understand the gravity of your situation," Banwell said, chuckling, his amiable expression never fading. "You have something that I desire. We were hoping to catch your little leprechaun a few weeks ago, but those idiots absolutely bumbled it. And I was hoping to take him off your hands tonight, but again, your leprechaun is a wily one, and he disappeared when we were about to nab him."

So Maddock wasn't captured! Relief stuttered inside my chest. However, summoning him here to help free me wasn't an option. I was sure Banwell was just waiting for me to pull such a rookie move. But why hadn't he come to my earlier summons?

As my relief about Maddock faded, despite my question, something Banwell had said clicked in my mind. With a gasp, I tried to stand, but one of the men behind me kept me firmly in my seat.

"*You're* the leader of HAMMA?" I cried.

Banwell had the decency to look a little embarrassed, and he cleared his throat. "I suppose you could say that, although it isn't something I would want listed on my resume. Not one of my more dignified accomplishments, but they do get the job done. Occasionally. Now, I'm not an unreasonable man, and I'm willing to help you. We can get all this sorted out, I'm sure—"

"So, you kidnapped my parents?" I burst out, anger burning through my disbelief. He was responsible not only for my parents, but for all those creatures that had been in the bank. He traded in magic and mythical creatures, all for greed and gain. I was dragged into this whole mess because of this multi-billionaire? He was a man who already had everything he could ever want; why did he need my parents and Maddock?

Banwell shook his head. "Not personally. I am sorry about that. Normally I wouldn't condone such behavior, but the members of HAMMA, well, they want someone to blame. And if kidnapping a few, uh, what is the word they use? Everbloods or something?" He gave a light laugh, still looking chagrined. "Terribly tacky. However, if that will make them happy and keep them productive and motivated, I don't see the problem."

"You *don't?*" I choked. "The—the fact that it's illegal didn't make you pause?" Normally talking to someone like Banwell would've made me tongue-tied, but everything I'd seen and learned in the past few days had made me too angry to feel any awkwardness. Behind the money and the fame, he was nothing more than a lying, thieving hypocrite.

He laughed. "I'm not new to skirting that line, young lady."

"Why don't I just invite a few of your HAMMA followers over to your house? Let them see what you've been up to?" I seethed. "I'd like to see how they would react to how you're making money off their hard work! You're worse than anyone they've ever rounded up!"

"And how do you know what I've been up to?" Banwell asked, smiling.

"I have my sources," I said, realizing that there was a chance that Banwell didn't know that his stooges had followed me to the lair of another leprechaun. If I gave away the Fox, then Banwell would be after two leprechauns.

Banwell smiled, and, without a sound, the Fox appeared right beside his desk.

"Is this, by chance, your source?" Banwell asked, suppressing a laugh.

"What are you doing here?" I gasped, trying to stand but again was forced back into my seat by meaty hands. "*Run*, before he catches you!"

Banwell laughed, and I saw a shadow flash behind the Fox's eyes.

"My dear, the Sewer Fox belongs to me. He's been working for me for years. I like to have many different ways of bringing in new assets."

I stared at the Fox, who looked tired and angry.

"H-how?" I looked to Banwell, mouth agape, mind reeling. "The Fox hates humans. Why would he help gather more creatures for someone he hates?"

"Because he has to. He's my little wild card."

"But you can't force a leprechaun to do what you want," I said blankly. "It's impossible—"

"Impossible for those incompetent in magic," Banwell finished, then he chuckled. "You owners of magical creatures amaze me with your ignorance."

Anger flared in my chest, but I didn't do anything but deepen my glare at him as he continued. "You are sitting on a gold mine of power, and most of you don't even realize it. Which, if I'm being honest, is for the best. Those humans that I set HAMMA on deserve whatever they get. They make flippant use of powers they don't understand, and it can be very dangerous.

"The more magical creatures you own, the more magic you can control, and with more control, you can manipulate those you thought were immune to magic." Banwell flicked his eyes to the Fox, and without uttering a word to the redheaded leprechaun, the tiny man jumped up on the table and began dancing a jig, his expression dead. Banwell smiled at me around the Irish-stepping Fox.

"This leprechaun is under my complete control."

I stared up at the prancing leprechaun, horror rising in my chest. Again, without a verbal command from Banwell, the Fox stopped dancing, hopped down from the desk, and walked out of the room.

I had turned in my seat to watch the Fox leave, then turned back to Banwell, my mouth still open.

"Impressive, no?" he asked.

My throat felt so constricted that I couldn't even reply 'no'.

"Why?" I asked instead, my voice a mere squeak.

"Why do I have a leprechaun spy?" Banwell asked.

"Well, yes, but why do you use him like that?" I rasped. "Why . . . Why are you doing *any* of this?"

Banwell sat back again in his seat, looking thoughtful. "Magic is dangerous. If left unchecked, it can harm and destroy. Can devastate." His face fell into a look of deep hurt for a brief moment before shaking it off so quick, I wasn't sure it had actually happened. "Magic, and the creatures it affects, needs a strong handler, so the magic can be reigned in. Magical creatures run amok, and they need to be caged to keep humans safe. Not to mention, they can help me earn a pretty penny."

He looked pensive for a moment, then sighed. "I also hate waste. Wasting resources, energy, money . . . it irks me to no end. If you'd bothered to read in the news lately, I've recently created a new way of recycling that minimizes energy and costs." He paused, glancing at me, no doubt expecting me to look impressed. When I didn't fall out of my seat with admiration, he continued. "Do you know what happens to a leprechaun once they run out of all the gold they've acquired over centuries of gathering and stealing from others?"

I honestly didn't know, but I didn't want to give him another reason to call me ignorant again.

"They become useless. They have absolutely no other purpose than gathering and hoarding gold. They can't use their own magic to cast spells, they're not wise, nor can they see into the future or create things. They can't do anything of worth. Once their gold is gone, they're a waste of space and air."

The door opened again, and the Fox came in, bearing a tray with mugs and a plate of scones.

"However," Banwell continued, smiling as the Fox placed the tray on Banwell's desk and stepped back, waiting for more orders. "I had to discover all magic can do on my own. I learned that most creatures can be controlled absolutely with enough magic. The rest can be controlled with enough money." He laughed as if he had told a joke, then gave a short exhale. "But I hate waste, and why throw out a source of power?" Banwell took a scone and a steaming mug for himself, then pushed the plate toward me, gesturing for me to help myself. I ignored his offer, continuing to scowl at him.

"He's my eyes and ears in the city. He follows HAMMA's movements for me," Banwell continued, seeming to enjoy talking about his 'exotic pet.' "When they find a creature with intriguing magical properties or abilities, I send the Fox to go in before them and take the animal if he can. I only let HAMMA handle a few extractions; they usually make a huge mess and are generally loud and uncouth. They spend far more time and money than they should, making a splash and a show for their own sense of importance." He took a small sip of his drink. "They feel like they deserve to show their authority, so they also spend inordinate amounts of cash on stake-outs, raids, and schmoozing the creatures' owners for months before finally taking action. It makes them feel impressive. But it also opens them up for someone to come in and snatch something out from under them." He shook his head, and then turned to me. "All they care about are their supposed principles, and punishing those they think are unworthy. They can work quickly when riled, though. You should've seen how fast they took down Mr. Kim."

I inhaled so quickly I choked on air. "Mr. Kim?" I coughed.

"Oh yes. They captured him a few days ago. They were upset when they learned his mandagot was gone, but the fact that they got a human prize was enough to settle them down. They're having fun with him now, I assume."

No wonder the Fox was so upset over the mandagot escaping, along with us releasing all those creatures at the bank. Maddock and I were causing more trouble for HAMMA than we had thought.

"What happens to those people they capture? Do they ever get released?" I asked, horrified that I had been a part of HAM-MA's dealings, allowing a human to get captured in the process, but thinking more of my parents.

"I cannot say. I don't usually follow the itineraries of their victims." He took a long gulp from his mug, coming up for air with a loud "ahhh."

"Anyways, to business. I'll ask you, quite politely, to summon your leprechaun and hand him over to me."

"Oh, is that all?" I scoffed, my kindled anger now blazing. "Why should I do that for you?"

"Do you want your parents back?" Banwell asked. "Because I can have that arranged immediately. I mean, heavens, I could have them back to you before lunch today."

For the third time that night, I was stunned into silence as he sipped on his mug.

"It's just that easy?" I spat.

"To a degree. I'm not heartless. I know that a girl like you, young, and ultra-rich, would have a hard time dealing with lawyers and the government over your parents estate. Not to mention, the news of their disappearance would definitely cause a circus with the press, resulting in a manhunt. I certainly wouldn't want you to have to deal with all of that alone."

*Or have me point the finger to him as the culprit. Not that anyone would believe me. And he knows it.* I ground my teeth as I stared at him. The realization that he had all the makings of an actual psychopath rose to my mind. He didn't seem to have any type of empathy, no understanding of loyalty, love, or compassion at all.

"And the fact that maybe I love my parents," I said through a clenched jaw, "and I don't want them to be imprisoned by your rabid followers doesn't enter into your thinking at all?"

"Oh. I guess it didn't," he replied with a shrug. "Your parents don't seem like the kind of people who would care about what their daughter would be doing. I doubt they are even expecting you to try to save them."

The words stung. I knew they were probably true and I had thought them myself, but it still made anger bloom hotter inside me. I could say it, but hearing him say it . . .

"Not everyone is you," I snapped.

"Very, very true," he quipped. "If they were, the world would be a better, safer place. However, we were talking about *you*. I restore you to your parents, let you all go on your merry way, but in return, you call your leprechaun and allow me to restrain him so that he comes into my possession." He gestured to one of the men standing behind me, and the guard stepped forward and unclicked the bracelet that was around my wrist.

"What is that?" I asked, eyeing the bracelet as I rubbed away the sweat on my wrist that had accumulated under the band.

"Oh, just a little device I made that blocks the connection to your leprechaun. Your parents were also wearing one until they were taken to a more 'secure' location." He said it so matter-of-factly that it took a moment for me to register what he meant.

"You . . . you *made* that? With magic?" Now it was clear why Maddock didn't come to me while in the trunk, and why he couldn't go to my parents at the start of all of this, but that somehow didn't comfort me. What else did I not know about magic that could be used to hurt me?

"Of course. I couldn't have him helping you escape while you were being brought to me. But now you can call him to us, and I'll take him off your hands."

I glanced at the Fox, who was standing so still beside the desk he looked like a statue. He stared straight ahead, his face dark. The thought of sending Maddock to such a life was horrifying. However, I couldn't live my life alone. My parents, though shallow, frivolous, and vain, still loved me, and I loved them, no matter how hard it was to remember that fact. Looking at the Fox put to mind things he had said about how prisoners of HAMMA were treated, and my stomach clenched.

"Are my parents being tortured?" I swallowed, watching Banwell's expression closely.

Banwell put down his mug, an overdone look of shock registering on his face. "Of course not! I allow my members to kidnap and to scare, but I would never condone or allow physical torture of any kind!"

"Somehow, I don't believe you," I snarled, digging my nails into the armrests of my chair. *Don't throw up, Mallory.* Though it would serve Banwell right to have to clean up *some* sort of mess.

"Fine." He picked his mug up again. "Torture that I'm aware of, I don't allow. But I have many followers and many points of operation, and many agents all over the US. It's hard to keep track of them all," he said with a sigh, as if hoping to earn my sympathy for his troubles. "I have been working to get the organization global, but it's been difficult, not to mention exhausting, trying to work with these foreign dignitaries to open their borders to tradesmen like me. But I think the fruit will be had soon. You cannot imagine how many people there are around the world that are eager for an organization like HAMMA to join, and it's so exciting thinking about all the different countries we could . . . But I digress," he said when he glanced at me.

I could feel the heat in my face, and my teeth were starting to hurt from clenching my mouth shut. I longed to shout certain words I'd learned in the hallways at school at the monster before me.

"What you should focus on *now*," Banwell said slowly, "is that I know where your parents are being held, and I can give the orders at this very moment to have them sent back to your home."

I was quiet, picking at my nails as I mulled over what to do.

"I promise, if you hand over your mindless little pet," Banwell continued, his tone patronizing, like I was a small child, "Your parents will be returned, and I will never bother you again. You can go back to living your lives, and you won't have to worry about repercussions from me or my people. I'll even repair your house, and give you a large cash sum for your trouble."

I looked at Banwell's smiling face. He knew that if my parents were free, we would never try to press charges against him or open an investigation. No one would believe us, and he was too powerful. His offer was generous. Extravagant, even. But that wasn't what caught my attention. It was how he mentioned Maddock.

*Mindless pet?* That's what he thought?

I would never admit it aloud, but Maddock was smarter than I was, and though he enjoyed watching *The Suitor,* and could drink my parents entire wine cellar in a weekend, it was beyond an insult to think of him as some dumb brute.

I looked to the Fox again, who I saw cast the tiniest, but staggering, look of venom toward Banwell. It dawned on me that Banwell didn't have the Fox under his *complete* control. With just that tiny glance, I could see that the Fox still had command of his thoughts and emotions. Banwell didn't seem to be able to control *that*. Or even notice it. And that made all the difference in my mind. The Fox felt every injustice, every moment of being used as a dancing puppet. He wasn't mindless in *any* sense, and that struck me to my core. I looked down, trying to cover the tears that had sprung to my eyes.

Banwell interrupted my seething revelation with a tone laced with annoyance.

"I see that you have a very simple binding spell that keeps your leprechaun in your possession. I'm a very busy man, but I don't have much more time to sit here indulging a teenager. Having another leprechaun would bring me joy. However, if you don't hand over your pet to me soon, there is a spell I could enact that would sever your ties with your leprechaun. He would go free, and you would lose my generous offer of trading the leprechaun for your parents and a promise to never bother you again."

"You can break *my* binding spell?" I asked, my heart leaping into my throat.

"Of course I can," he scoffed, sounding exasperated. "I've had twenty-odd years of practice with magic. It's a more complicated spell, and would take some time and effort, but trust me, I could do it, and you'd be without a bargaining chip. I'd lose the leprechaun, but you would lose much more, don't you think?" he asked, smiling back at me.

He had neatly trapped me. Either way, I'd lose Maddock. I knew what kind of man Banwell was. He was so confident in his power that he didn't care if he lost a paltry leprechaun, just so long as he held the upper hand. That was all he cared about. But me, I could lose everything if I didn't take his deal.

I slowly raised my head, looking into Banwell's calculating eyes, and nodded. "You haven't given me very many options," I replied, biting my lip.

Banwell clapped his hands together. "Excellent," he said, his expression cheerful. I closed my eyes, my nerves tingling so much I squirmed. My stomach roiled. I had to do this, or forever be plagued with regret. I could feel Banwell tense with anticipation from where I sat. He loved this; the thought that he could bully anyone into what he wanted.

But he wouldn't get what he wanted this time.

"Maddock O'Bannon," I commanded. But I didn't summon him. I could feel the magical connection thrumming between us, wherever he was. Opening my eyes, I locked stares with Banwell and began to chant the words that would sever the magical ties that kept Maddock bound to me and my family.

Banwell's face slipped from pleased triumph to a confused frown. "What . . . ?"

I spoke faster, but was careful not to trip over the words I had read not two weeks ago.

"Wait a minute. *Wait!*" Banwell shouted, standing so quickly his chair toppled backwards. "Shut her up!" he called, scrambling to reach me.

A hand clapped over my mouth, but it was too late. The tale-tell burning in my chest grew almost unbearable, then cooled to an icy cold. I knew the bond between me and the leprechaun was severed completely. Maddock was finally free. I knew he'd felt what I had felt, and wherever he was, he knew he had been released.

Banwell stood over me, his eyes wide, his face full of genuine shock this time at what I'm sure he thought was my stupidity.

"Did you actually mean to do that?" Banwell asked, sounding appalled. "I hope you know you just lost your only bargaining chip."

Despite the pain in my chest, I smiled up at Banwell. He wasn't intimidating to me anymore. I had outmaneuvered him. Giddy at my "victory," a rush of adrenaline erased my common sense. At that moment, I felt invincible.

"I know," I retorted, the heady sense of arrogance at my stunt feeding my bravado. "But that bargaining chip was someone I respected, and who somewhat respected me, and I would rather live alone for the rest of my life than let him live one second in servitude to a cowardly hypocrite like you."

Banwell stared me down for several moments, then his shoulders relaxed, and he actually chuckled. He meandered back around his desk and sat down.

"How incredibly naïve," he murmured as he settled himself into his chair. "I am a very busy man, and though your little misguided antics made me lose an asset, it isn't the most pressing thing in the world. I have other, bigger things in the works, so if you think you've bested or outsmarted me, you are more ignorant than I first thought. Having another leprechaun would've been nice, but it's a drop in the bucket compared to what I'm tracking down."

He studied me for a moment, and I stared back with an insolent expression, not allowing his words to dishearten me.

He sighed. "Well, my dear. I'm afraid you won't be living alone for the rest of your little life. Like I said before, I am not a heartless man. I know how your separation from your parents must be hard on you. So I'm going to reunite you, and *you* will have to explain to them why you wouldn't trade their freedom for some dullard animal," he said, his smile sharpening as he stared at me. My heart rate quickened, but I still felt satisfaction pumping through me. "I'm going to throw you to the mercy of my rabid followers. And please, I hope you don't feel like you've made some grand gesture that will make the leprechaun like you," he scoffed. "You have made an incredibly foolish decision. I assure you, if it had been your life on the line, that leprechaun wouldn't have hesitated to throw you under the bus. He's long gone by now, and he won't look back."

"I know that," I said with disgust. "I'm not an idiot. I know he doesn't care about any of us," I lied. At least I hoped it was a lie. I didn't want to explain my feelings, or the somewhat mutual respect I hoped Maddock held for me, to the monster before me.

Banwell would only think me naïve again. "His life with us wasn't the happiest," I said, sitting up straighter in my chair. "Heck, my parents never really let him outside. We would deserve whatever you throw at us with your pathetic little followers who blindly follow an inhuman monster like you." I laughed, the intoxicating feeling of spiting the man before me keeping my courage strong. "And the funny thing is, you would deserve their torture even more than anyone. And one day, I assure you, it will come to you."

Banwell didn't look at all frightened or upset at my words, he merely sighed. "Well, then, if you're happy with your choice, that's your prerogative. We'll get you to your parents before lunchtime tomorrow."

He gave me a mocking smile that finally punctured through my bravado, wisps of fear curling in my chest. Banwell looked back down at his desk, and didn't give me a second glance as the thugs behind me heaved me to my feet and dragged me out the door.

# Chapter Twenty-One

Something jarred the rickety car and nearly bounced me out of my seat, waking me up. Groggy, I shifted, wincing at the stiffness in my neck and the pain in my arms and wrists. I tugged against the zip ties binding me. I would never get used to the sensation of being tied up. Wriggling to right myself, I looked out the window. Trees arched over the road in a living tunnel as we drove further and further north. We had been on the road for nearly four hours, and the sun was just coming up, casting everything in the golden glow of dawn.

My drivers hadn't said anything the whole ride, which was fine with me. I wasn't looking to get chummy with anyone from HAMMA, though I was bored out of my mind. Fear of the unknown was not enough to fully distract me. The road wound through the tree-filled hills. I was surprised I hadn't woken up earlier, feeling carsick.

After Houston Banwell had dismissed me, I had been taken back down the elevator to the parking garage and shoved into the backseat of an old car, my ankles bound and my wrists zip-tied behind me.

I'd be lying if I said I had the slightest hope that Maddock would come back and bail me and my parents out. I knew his disposition before starting this journey with him. He may have hated me a little less than he hated my parents, but I was still one of his captors. He may have respected me, but I doubted that loyalty was a possibility in a situation like ours had been. He had been willing to help me in the beginning because he had something to gain from it, just as I had. But now, he was off the hook.

I had started to depend on Maddock. Besides my good friends back home, he was the one person I had come to trust. I even trusted him over my parents. He knew about the magical world around us, and I could finally talk openly about it. Plus, he'd gotten me out of some tight spots. Whether it was out of actual friendship, or because he didn't want me to die and lose a chance at freedom, I would never know. He was gone.

But I was happy for him. Everything I had smart-mouthed back to Banwell had been the truth. He'd changed me. Now that he was gone, I realized I would really miss him. I would never see him again. He'd make sure of that. I just hoped that wherever he was, he thought of me without too much ill will.

I wiped a stray tear from my cheek with my shoulder and stared out the window.

The men up front shared snacks between themselves but didn't offer me anything. The only time they spoke to me was when they pulled over to the side of the road, cut off the zip ties binding my wrists and ankles, and told me it was a bathroom break while shoving a small wad of tissue in my hand. Growing up in a house where the most rustic place we'd gone on vacation was a mansion-sized cabin in Alaska for a week, going to the bathroom in the woods did not sound at all pleasant. I began to refuse, but they persuaded me with a handgun in my face. I supposed they weren't in the mood to clean up any messes I might make in the car during our trip.

They followed me a ways into the woods and then waited for me to do my business. It was one of the most uncomfortable, embarrassing things I'd ever done in my life. With growing fear, I realized that this was probably just the start of my discomfort. While partially hidden in the trees, I had tried calling the police on the cellphone the idiots didn't bother to check me for, but when I turned on my phone, I couldn't get any cell service.

"Dang it," I muttered.

"What's taking so long?" A voice behind me barked, and I jumped, turning to see one of the men had come up from behind a tree to check on me.

"Girls take longer to pee than guys," I snapped, hiding my phone behind me.

"Well, you look done now. Let's get going." He waved the gun in obvious encouragement to hurry.

I grit my teeth as my half-baked idea of running for escape in the trees dissolved, and I stomped back to the car.

By the time we reached our destination, my stomach growled with hunger, almost drowning out the carsickness. The men pulled off the highway into a winding drive, and we barrelled down a dirt road for what felt like forever, delving into the heart of the tree-clogged landscape.

The trees suddenly cleared, revealing an enormous gravel parking lot where a vast three-story concrete building sat, bland-looking yet menacing at the same time. There were no windows.

Here we go.

My stomach writhed and gurgled as the car slowed to a stop. I was hauled out of the vehicle, and we crunched across the gravel to a door that buzzed before it opened. We stepped inside a small reception room, where a young man with bright green hair sat at a desk. He was wearing a red uniform with the same flaming dragon sigil patched onto his shoulder that I had seen on HAMMA documents. Upon seeing us, he began to type on his computer.

"We've been expecting you," he said, not looking up from his computer monitor. "Protocol requires you to turn in your car keys, as a security measure." The receptionist finally glanced up and gave my driver a stern look when he refused to hand over his keys immediately. After a silent stare-down and some grumbling, my driver finally handed over the key to his car. The receptionist's expression was a little smug as he placed the key inside a safe in the wall—filled with keys—beside the desk before giving the driver a claim slip just as something began printing off of one of the many machines behind him. The receptionist slid his rolling chair to the machine and pulled out a freshly printed card.

"Take the liability through that door," the receptionist said, standing and using the card to point to a door off to the right. "Strip her down, give her a jumpsuit, and then we'll have our resident warlock check her before someone takes her to the solitary cell, block 2A, until further instructions."

The men holding me nodded and pulled me through the appointed door.

We entered what looked like a dry cleaning shop. Two women were busy chatting behind the long counter, with a large wall of bins behind them and rows of identical gray-blue jumpsuits hanging from a clothing rack. The two women looked up when we entered, both wearing the same red uniforms with the dragon sigil.

Amazement broke through my fear: were all these people getting paid, or were they volunteers? My mother constantly complained about the cost of our maids, chefs, and gardeners. If these people were getting paid, how much money did HAMMA bring in to pay not only all these people, but the people at the banks, and all the other places Banwell had talked about?

One of my guards gestured toward the door. "I'll go find Renzo," he muttered before leaving the room.

"We need a jumpsuit for this liability," the other man commanded, holding me out to them. After a quick look over at me, they went right to work, searching through the hangers of jumpsuits. The guard cut off my zip tie restraints, then turned me to face him.

"Strip down," my guard commanded, thrusting a jumpsuit into my chest. He made no move to leave me with some privacy, and I raised a brow with a sharp snort of, "No way."

"Undress yourself now." He pulled a taser out of the holster that had been hidden under his un-tucked shirt in a casual sort of way, "Or we'll have someone do it for you." I looked between him and the two women, who didn't seem at all concerned about a grown man demanding an underage teen to undress in front of him. In fact, they weren't even listening to the exchange, as they had turned back to their own conversation.

"Will you at least turn around?" I snapped. "Or when I get out of this place, do you *want* me to file a sexual harrassment charge against all of you on top of kidnapping and assault?" I was just blustering, hoping to scare him enough to at least turn around so that I could sneak my phone out of my pajamas into the jumpsuit without anyone noticing. I didn't worry about the two gossiping idiots in the room; they were completely oblivious to us.

The man chuckled. "You really think you're getting out of here."

I folded my arms, glaring. "I'm not changing in front of you." With any luck, he would just get annoyed and turn around.

I had no such luck.

The man whipped his taser up in the blink of an eye and the next moment, pain like I'd never felt before had frozen me in place. Volts of electricity cemented my muscles in place and I felt myself falling forward.

I screamed for him to stop, but I couldn't hear my voice outside my mind as my body slammed against the tile. The air in my lungs left in a rush as I hit the floor, leaving me gasping for air. My vision flashed white with black specks as I struggled to breathe, and my ears rang with the impact. Pain flared as the electricity stopped surging through my body. I moaned, everything throbbing, and I heard the man click his tongue.

"What's this here?" He bent over me to pick something off the ground. He straightened, my cell phone clenched in his hand.

I groaned louder as he handed the phone to one of the girls, who moved to put it in one of the open cubbies that lined one wall. I saw almost all of the cubbies were occupied with other people's personal effects. I felt my last bit of hope drain as she placed the phone inside a cubby. I didn't even have a chance to use what was left of my phone battery, and now I never would.

"Get this Everbleeder undressed," the man barked to the two women, and they jumped to work, lifting my aching body out of my pajamas and stuffing me into the jumpsuit.

When I was dressed, the guard heaved me to my feet with a grunt while the women gathered up my clothes and put them in the cubby with my cell phone, and the key necklace I'd worn for the last six years. My last connection to Maddock.

The man paused to stare at the wall of cubbies, and he gave a low whistle. "Nice. We'll have a lot of items to donate to charity once this month is up. It's been a productive few weeks."

The women nodded, smiling, and before I could finish processing what was implied by his comment, I was ushered out of the room.

"Wow, I bet you make sure to recycle too, don't you? You must be so proud to be such good people," I rasped. He shoved me so hard I almost fell flat on my face, and I kept my burning resentment from spouting out any other smart remarks.

A new person was waiting at the "welcome" desk along with my second guard. The new man, who I assumed was the warlock, was dressed in a nice suit, his salt and pepper hair slicked back, his ample beard bushy and untamed. He came to stand before me and he held his hands out toward me. I counted several gold rings encrusted with jewels on every finger of his hands, and a very nice wristwatch peeked from his suit sleeves. He closed his eyes, his hands still outstretched, then he lowered them, nodding to the green-haired man at the desk. "She's clean. No reserves."

The green-haired man at the front desk gave me a once over, then nodded to those escorting me. I was handed to a new pair of guards who were dressed head to foot in uniform, and I was marched to a steel doorway. With a discordant buzz, the door opened, and I was hurried inside.

The moment I stepped through the door, I heard distant screaming.

The hairs across my entire body stood on end as I heard pleas for help and screams of agony. I stiffened, trying to pull out of the grip of my captors, but they wrenched me forward, making me stumble as I was taken through a different door. Thankfully, the screams were muted once the door slammed behind us. We entered a small room that was lined with four cells, each equipped with a cot, a metal toilet, and a tiny sink.

I was pushed inside one, the steel bar door was slammed with a clang, and I was left alone. The chills across my skin from the earlier shrieks had not gone away, and I rubbed my arms, shivering. I turned, taking in my cell that was just long enough for me to lie down comfortably on my cot, when I noticed that there were cameras in every corner of my cell and two cameras outside, across from my cell.

No privacy.

Why were they watching me? Where were my parents? Why was I here alone?

I sat down on my cot as terror, despair, and confusion fought each other in my stomach. Was this going to be my final resting place? Doubt about my actions now choked me. Had I been right to free Maddock? If I had been faster, or smarter, or older, maybe I could've come up with a perfect solution to rescue my parents, free Maddock, and save myself from HAMMA's clutches forever. But I wasn't any of those things. I should've saved my parents first, then tried to free Maddock from Banwell afterward.

I had been rash and naïve, clearly afflicted with some heady sense of heroism in spitting in the face of the man who had been the source of all my troubles. I didn't know what horrors awaited me, but those screams sobered and terrified me. If those cries had been any indication, it was worse than I ever could've imagined. And now, there was no hope for my parents, or for me. I had screwed everything up.

I couldn't help it. I buried my face in my hands, and despite the obvious audience, I broke into sobs.

# Chapter Twenty-Two

The day passed slowly, punctuated only by the guards, all dressed in the same red uniform, bringing me what looked like a bowl of mashed beans in watery juice. I left the "meal" alone, not hungry enough to tempt fate, or to use that very public toilet should the bean juice shoot right through me.

I inspected the cell for any flaws, but when it was clear escape was impossible, at least for now, I whiled away the hours, fearful questions keeping me on the edge. What was going to happen to me? Why was I in solitary? Were my parents even here? Mr. Banwell had said he was taking me to my parents, but that didn't mean anything. I didn't trust his word for a second.

After several hours, the lights shut off with a loud electronic popping noise, leaving me in darkness. But I couldn't sleep. I lay awake, wondering what horrors awaited me with the clicking on of the lights.

It turned out, nothing at first.

Day came again, and I was served another bowl of food, this time watery oatmeal, and this I did eat, ignoring the watery bean mash they hadn't taken away. I waited all day on tenterhooks until the lights went out again, signaling evening.

This time, exhausted, I did fall asleep.

The third day passed in the same manner, and I was finally getting stir-crazy. And angry. Was this part of the torture? There wasn't even anything to throw to alleviate my anger after I'd thrown the bowl full of old beans at the guard that had brought my next meal, as he had visibly spit into it. The action had given me a sense of satisfaction, especially when I threw the second bowl, as the guard had screamed like a baby as both bowls caught him full in the face. But the feeling was short lived, replaced by boredom once again. I tried doing pushups and situps to pass the time like I'd seen in movies, but I gave up after just a few tries, knowing that somewhere the guards watching my cell were laughing at how weak I was.

It was bad enough that I was forced to drape my blanket over myself when I was using the bathroom for some semblance of privacy, but being held like this, obviously being watched? There was no way what HAMMA was doing was legal in any sense of the word. They obviously didn't worry about legal repercussions, because no one would believe that we got kidnapped by fanatics because we had magical creatures in our possession.

When night came again, I had that gross, lethargic feeling I got during the summers when I sat and watched my streaming shows for days on end. I curled up on the cot, wondering if they were just going to keep me in here until I wasted away. Anger filled me again, making my face hot, and to escape my pent up emotions, I daydreamed of a different me. A me that knew powerful magic and could come down on all of these monsters with the wrath of a thousand spells and curses, cowing that evil Banwell until he begged for mercy. With those wild, silly imaginings playing in my mind, I drifted off to sleep.

Something small but hard and heavy plinked off my ear, waking me. I peered, bleary-eyed, around my tiny cell, then felt along the bed, searching for what had hit me. It had felt metallic. A piece of the camera above me, perhaps?

After a few moments of sliding my hand along the sheet, I felt it. It was hard, cold, and lumpy. All drowsiness left me as I rolled the lump in my hand, my heart rate spiking at the familiar object.

I looked around the cell again and said in a barely audible whisper, "Maddock?"

I felt a breeze, and a piece of paper brushed my lower lip as it fluttered to my bed, along with something small and hard that rolled against my hand.

I scrambled to pick up the items, and realized that what had bumped my hand was a small flashlight. Not wanting the cameras to see me reading a paper with a flashlight that had appeared out of thin air, I pulled my blanket over my head and curled over the flashlight to help block the light with my body. Clicking the light on, I read the note written in a hurried scrawl:

*Mallory,*

*You're being watched. I have an idea to help you escape, but I will most likely be captured in the process, because I'm a gobshite header that doesn't know how to quit while I'm ahead.*

*I'd been suspicious of Pat for days now, but I had no idea this was the reason. I've been trying to keep my eyes peeled for anything strange, and his overreaction to our escape from the bank made me very wary. I didn't go to sleep, but watched Pat, and overheard him planning to trap me. I used the dart I'd gotten at the bank to knock out those trying to capture me, but I was too late to warn you. They had kidnapped you and taken you away, so I followed you to where you met with that snake, Banwell. I didn't free you, because I was hoping they'd take you to where your parents were being held, and I could release you all at once.*

*I heard everything you said, lassie, and I know what you did for me. And at what cost.*

*So I am going to help you, again, and you'll have to promise to help me in return. Again. I have to be touching you for my plan to work, and for that, I will be visible to their cameras, and will most likely get caught. I know they're watching you for this very reason, waiting for me to come help you escape. We'll never get out if I just let you out of your cell. There's too many security-code-locked doors. But I never planned on that route. These dolts can't possibly imagine how I plan to release you, but we'll have to act very very quickly.*

*I will be bestowing upon you a leprechaun gift.*

*Because it's so rare that my kind finds someone we truly respect, this gift has fallen out of knowledge with humans, and even with most leprechauns. Even I don't know all it can do, but it's an instinctual thing in us leprechauns to be able to bestow this gift on you, and you must use it to get yourself and others out. I don't want to share any more about it, in case this note falls into HAMMA's hands.*

*Your parents are here. I've seen them, and others, and they must be rescued. You can't imagine what is happening to them. Free yourself and everyone else from this place as soon as you can, then come for me. I'll have my phone hidden on me, so you can track me wherever they take me. If you agree, and once you've finished reading this letter, and are ready, cough three times. We will have no time to waste once I begin, so trust me, and do what I tell you.*

*Maddock*


A gift? What kind of gift? I shook my head. It didn't matter what kind of gift! If it was going to help me and everyone else get out of here, there was no time for dumb questions! We'd have to hurry, while everyone was asleep.

Taking a deep breath, I snapped off the flashlight, folded the note tight and stuck it and the nugget down my bra, and pulled the blanket off my head. Swallowing hard, my heart stuttering in my chest, I coughed three times.

A shadow appeared beside me in an instant.

"Give me your hands," Maddock insisted without preamble, and I shoved my hands into his awaiting ones.

The moment he gripped my fingers, he began chanting in an unintelligible tongue, his voice barely audible to my ears. An alarm began to sound inside the room, making my heart leap in terror. HAMMA worked fast. Where was this gift he was giving me? Was he summoning it?

The lights in my cell block hummed to life, and I could see Maddock standing on my cot, his eyes closed, his lips moving so fast he looked almost cartoonish. I didn't feel like laughing. My heart was fluttering wildly against my ribs as I heard distant shouts and running feet, my mouth going dry. How much longer till whatever

Maddock was doing would be done? Maybe he should escape now, and try again later?

"Maddock, go!" I tried to pull my hands out of his grip, but Maddock yanked them back toward him with a violent shake of his head, his words never stopping. Was it the light, or did Maddock look a lot paler? I noticed a sheen of sweat on his forehead, droplets trickling down his sideburns. Without warning, Maddock gripped my hands so hard the bones ground together painfully.

All sound seemed to be knocked out of my ears, and I felt as though I was being thrown backwards, though my body didn't move from its spot on my cot. The sensation of flipping head-over-feet continued, and my stomach jolted and heaved, but I didn't vomit. The pitching feeling eased, replaced by the feeling of complete weightlessness, so much so that I could barely feel the cot beneath me. I felt hot chills race over my skin, dazzling darkness veiled my sight, and bitter sweetness rested on my tongue. The weightlessness increased, and as the heady sensations of contradicting impressions reached a crescendo, an overwhelming feeling of fiery itching jolted through me. Then it all disappeared within the space of a blink. My hearing returned, and I felt as though I crashed back down to the cot, even though I knew I hadn't been floating, and my senses returned to normal. I didn't even feel dizzy.

At that moment, Maddock released my hands and reached up with shaky arms, grabbed the sides of my face, and pressed a kiss to my forehead just as a hoard of men carrying strange looking guns entered the block. Maddock moved from my tingling forehead to kiss my left cheek. Just as Maddock moved to kiss the other side of my face, one of the guards shouted, "Fire!"

Two darts hit home on Maddock's body, one on his side, another on his shoulder, and Maddock immediately slumped, his lips missing my unkissed cheek.

Panicking, remembering Maddock telling me about the power magical kisses had, I realized the kisses he was giving me probably finished the ceremony, sealing the magic. If he didn't complete whatever ritual he was doing, I had a feeling the gift wouldn't be received. Maddock slumped to my cot, his eyes glazing over, and I leaned over him to press my untouched cheek to his lips, grimacing at his lolling tongue. As his lips brushed my face, I was shoved away as the men entered my cell, discordant shouting echoing around the room.

"No! Wait! *No!*" I tried to reach Maddock, wondering if he had missed other vital places, like my chin, or maybe even my lips to seal the ceremony? The thought didn't even gross me out as I clawed against the press of uniformed men, screaming for Maddock. The noise and chaos in that tiny cell made my head swim as I shoved against the rough canvas fabric of uniforms. Held back, I watched in horror as Maddock was heaved out of my cell by two men. With one last shove that sent me slamming into the wall, the men retreated, locking the cell behind them.

Ears ringing and head throbbing from the collision, I stumbled off the cot. Kicking away the tangled blankets around my ankles, I pressed my face against the bars. Dread and panic heaved in my stomach as I caught a glimpse of Maddock through the horde of guards, his eyes glassy, his face deathly pale.

"MADDOCK!" I screamed, watching as the men bore him out of the block, leaving me alone. "MADDOCK! PLEASE, NO!"

I shook the bars, screaming for Maddock, when the warlock appeared in the room again. The screams died in my throat as I stared at him, panting. What did *he* want?

The warlock was followed by the same green-haired receptionist from before. The blinged-out warlock held out his hands to me, closing his eyes once more. I leaned away, panting. Did they know what Maddock had done to me? If so, what did that mean for me? Would they kill me?

I watched the warlock with breathless anticipation as he moved his hands through the air in my direction, his face contorted in concentration.

After a moment, the warlock lowered his hands, shaking his head. "Nothing. She's clean."

They both gave me an appraising look.

"Have any idea what he was trying to do?" the receptionist asked in a low voice.

The warlock nodded. "I have no doubt that she had ordered him to funnel all his magic into her or something, but they weren't fast enough." He laughed. "We needn't worry about her, she's no threat. She didn't get any of his magic." With satisfied nods and smug smiles, the two men left the cell block, leaving me alone with fear and horror crushing down on me.

No. Nonononononono.

I slumped against the bars, my breathing shallow, the tingling where Maddock had kissed my forehead and cheek growing cold.

The warlock had felt no magic on me whatsoever . . . Which meant . . . Maddock didn't finish giving me the gift. He hadn't been quick enough. I didn't know what the gift he wanted to give me was, or how I was even supposed to use it, but if that man didn't feel any magic on me, I didn't have it. I didn't feel any different, except I'd never felt more terrified and panicked in my life. Or more sick.

Two guards reentered the block, and through my haze, I heard one say, "Alright, let's move her out."

They moved toward my cell, but I barely noticed or felt anything as I gripped the bars, staring blankly at the door Maddock had disappeared through.

My one chance at escape was now captured, and his way to release me was worthless. We had been interrupted before whatever he was transferring to me could be complete, and now we were all stranded. He would be enslaved again, and I would probably die. My one chance was gone. Maddock had been captured for no reason.

I had failed him.

Nausea hit me like a train. As the guard reached to unlock my door, I vomited where I stood.

With a slew of profanities, the guard at my door jumped back while the other started screaming and gagging as I fell to my knees and vomited again.

After several minutes of emptying my stomach, I came to myself, lying on the floor away from the discharge, feeling empty.

I became aware the two men were still there, and they were arguing.

"No, *you* go in there and get her," the first guard replied, his hand covering his nose and mouth.

"I told you, there's no way I'm going in there while she's spewing!" the second retorted.

Both men considered me, then the second guard continued. "They didn't say she had to be moved immediately. Let's leave her here until we're sure she's done, then we can move her."

"Fine by me. We're off duty in two hours, I say we wait till *after* then so we don't have to do it." The first guard made another gagging noise.

"Agreed."

I stared with disinterest as the two made a hasty exit, leaving me alone once again. After several uncomfortable minutes, I pulled myself to my feet. I washed the sick from my clothes and face as best as I could with the tiny sink, and the lights in the block clicked off just as I crawled into the cot. Pulling the covers over my head, I held Maddock's note and gold nugget in my hands, crying quietly in the darkness.

# Chapter Twenty-Three

Several hours later, the lights in my cell block clicked on again. Worried the guards would take Maddock's note, I hurriedly stuffed it and the small gold nugget down my jumpsuit, my fingers clumsy with fatigue. I hadn't slept at all during the time I was left alone, my mind too feverish, my soul too distressed. I heard the block door open, and violent swearing echoed around the room as several guards entered. I was too numb to laugh about how these idiots felt the need for four guards to look after one teenage girl. I supposed that being in groups helped them ignore their own evil actions. Cowards.

"Hoffman and Alvarez were right, this is disgusting!" one of the guards coughed. "What have they been feeding this girl?"

"I'm glad I'm not on the janitorial crew," another voice answered, his voice nasally like he was pinching his nose.

With sounds of gagging and more cursing, my cell door was opened, and I was ordered out. I stood from my cot, feeling detached from every emotion, and did as my captors commanded. I ignored the profanity and the not-so-creative names directed at me as they put a ragged bag, with two small holes for me to be able to see, over my head, then marched me out of the cell block and down a small maze of connecting halls. Why was this bag necessary? I thought the point of head bags was so that the prisoner could not see where they were going. At least that's what the movies taught me.

Through my numbness and the muffled fabric of the smelly bag, I noticed the screams from several days ago no longer echoed through the building, and relief barely surfaced within me before it evaporated again. I would no doubt be hearing them again, and I would certainly be one of the many voices screaming in pain soon. But for the moment, it was much easier heading to my doom without a chorus of tortured souls accompanying my entrance.

We came to a set of double doors that opened before us, and we entered into what looked like a spacious indoor sports arena, complete with stadium seating on one side of the room. The stadium seats faced the monstrous, circular cage that took up the middle of the chamber. The cage looked to be about half the length of a football field in diameter, with razor wire encircling the top of the twenty-foot-high perimeter fence. Armed guards stood around the circular pen, watching a shockingly large group of prisoners in varying states of destitution. Makeshift beds of ragged blankets and pillows were scattered about the concrete floor.

The guards held up their guns at those inside the cage as I was shoved forward.

"Back away from the doors," a man commanded. Almost everyone inside the pen had scrambled to get as far away from the cell doors as they could the moment we had entered, so the command was unnecessary. The pen door was unlocked and I was shoved inside, the bag ripped from my head as I fell to the floor. On my hands and knees, I turned to glare back at the guards as they locked the door.

So the bag was just for dramatic effect? What losers.

All the guards filed out of the enormous holding room, leaving us prisoners completely alone, except for a small contingent of sentries seated near the doors, who were talking and playing card games.

Exhaling, I then turned my attention to my fellow prisoners. They remained huddled at the back of the cage, eyes wide with terror as they watched me. Most looked emaciated, their jumpsuits filthy and ripped, and many bore scars and scratches. In their eyes were flickers of fear and anger, but mostly emptiness.

How long had they been here?

I stood and started doing a quick count of prisoners as my eyes roved the sad faces looking for my parents. I had counted up to thirty-four people when from the crowd, I heard a hoarse voice call, "*Mallory?*"

Heart constricting, my eyes sought the voice from the press of prisoners.

"Dad?"

From the crowd, my dad stumbled forward, his jumpsuit badly shredded in places, and ran to me. Before I could say another word, he had wrapped me up in a solid hug. He had never hugged me in such a way before; a weighty, ferocious hug that made me feel afraid yet relieved, and I felt a little awkward as I hugged him back.

"No, no, no," he whispered as he held me tightly, "You can't be here," he moaned.

"Dad, what—"

He pulled away and cupped my face in his hands, looking me in the eye, his expression almost hungry as he skimmed my face, running a hand over my hair. "It's really you. Oh, Peanut." He hugged me again, pressing a kiss to my hair. "I've never felt so happy and so horrified to see you," he said, pulling away again. "When I felt the burning of release in my chest a few days ago, I hoped it didn't mean what I knew it meant, but you're here, and . . . and I'm so, so sorry." Tears filled his eyes and he began to sob, pulling me to him again and holding me tightly. I hugged him back, with more conviction this time. He looked like he'd been through unspeakable torment; his outright tears were proof of that. I'd never, ever seen my father cry before.

When we broke apart again, my throat was burning, and I was having a hard time thinking of what to say. I had been picturing this reunion for almost two weeks, but I never imagined it would happen while being imprisoned, with my father in this state, and without my mother.

My mother.

"Dad, where's Mom?" I asked, looking toward the crowd that was starting to disperse, making their way back to their makeshift beds.

"She's here. She's over there with our friend Judith, who's been incredible with helping out with the injured," he said, wiping his eye with a hand that looked badly scabbed. "But Mallory, your mother . . . she's not doing good. She . . . got bitten a few days ago by some creature, and it must've had some kind of venom. I—I don't—" he broke off, looking helpless.

"Dad, what is going on? What happened to you?" I demanded, tears pricking my eyes as the full extent of his appearance struck me. His own eyes were bloodshot, his hair matted with sweat and what looked like old blood, and he was favoring his left leg. His beard was coming in, making his face look haggard.

"I'll explain later. Come, come see your mother!" he urged.

Barely breathing, I followed my dad, who led me to where my mother was being helped down into one of the makeshift beds. An older woman with short, curly gray hair and a steely demeanor was sitting beside her, holding my mother's hand.

"Mallory," my mother's eyes found mine, and my heart constricted at how weak her voice sounded. She struggled to stand, but the woman, Judith, stopped her with a gentle but firm hand.

"Mom!" I kneeled down beside her, the tears now flooding my eyes. My mother's usually perfect hair was cut short, her face was pale and gaunt, and sweat dampened her ragged, filthy clothing. "What . . . what happened?" I choked.

"Honey, we're so sorry," my mom said, grabbing my hand, and I gripped hers tightly back. "We've been so worried about you, and we hoped you wouldn't be joining us. I can't imagine what you've been through these last weeks."

"*Me?*" I whispered. "What about you two? What happened?"

My dad sat down next to me, taking my other hand, and quickly explained to me about how they were ambushed at the house and were immediately brought here.

"We had no idea what was going on, or what these people wanted," my dad said, his voice tight with unnamed emotions. "Judith here explained everything to us, about HAMMA, about their operations." His grip tightened on my fingers. "And how they treat us here. Mallory . . ." My dad took a deep breath, his expression pained. "Honey, they—"

"No, Clark, please, don't tell her," my mother interrupted, her voice urgent.

"We have to, Grace. She needs to be on her guard," my dad insisted, then his face softened at my mother's tearstained look and he whispered, "We have to. It wouldn't be a kindness to keep this from her."

"But she'll be so scared," my mom whimpered. I gripped my mom's fingers tightly as my dad cupped my mom's cheek with a gentle hand.

"We're all together. We'll be okay," my dad said. Even I could see the lie in his eyes. Taking a deep breath, my dad turned to me.

"Every few days, the guards release animals, some magical, some not, into the pen. The animals are obviously starving and enraged, and so they attack us and chase us around until we've all had some contact," my dad explained. I tried to keep my expression neutral, to keep my mother from worrying, but I couldn't help shivering. I'd seen what enraged magical animals could do. "Sometimes the people here get bored of that and switch it up so that the guards can take part in the fun, and they mete out beatings."

I put a hand to my mouth to try to calm my stomach as I watched my father's face grow darker and darker as he spoke. The woman, Judith, looked just as hardened, her eyes fiery as she stroked my mother's head.

"It's enraging," Judith spoke up. She had a strong, authoritative voice that made me feel a little intimidated. "And they don't even give any medicine to help those who have been injured. I've been doing all I can, as an apothekerin, but there isn't much I can do without anything to work with. They're just letting us suffer in here."

"It's just one giant gladiator's arena for them. They get sick enjoyment out of it. All the workers crowd in here to see the *entertainment*," my dad said, his voice strangled with fury.

"Just because we owned magical creatures?" I whispered, swallowing to try and keep down the horror rising in my stomach.

"Or if you had magical items or plants in your home or garden," Judith said between grit teeth. "They believe humans who use magic are evil, that we are somehow stealing magic from those to whom it truly belongs. Their rhetoric is so warped. They don't understand that sometimes, people are born with magic in them!" Judith hissed. "They took my husband because he was one of those people. A druid. I don't know where he is, but they threw me in here, for 'enslaving' him. They—" She clenched her jaw and suddenly got to her feet. "I'll go check on the others' injuries, and leave you all to catch up. I'll be back soon." She hurried toward a man sitting against the cage wall a ways off.

Staring at all of the people in here, I realized that my folly was worse than I could ever have imagined.

"Mom, Dad," I began, fear and guilt pounding in my ears. "I'm so sorry. I tried to save you, but . . . I messed up."

"No, Mallory," my mother rasped. "It's not your fault. We tried to get you to save Maddock, when we should've had you just run. It's our fault they captured you and forced you to hand over Maddock. We don't blame you. I just wish we . . . had been better . . ." My mom began crying so hard she couldn't speak clearly. My dad hugged her, rocking her gently. I clenched my jaw so hard something popped.

I couldn't stand seeing them like this, seeing them worry and be sorry for me. Realizing I had thrown away the chance to save them from this horror made my stomach churn so violently I couldn't keep it back. I leapt to my feet and ran to an area of the pen that wasn't occupied to vomit again. Nothing really came up, having not eaten much in three days, but I let the heaving take its course, not even irritable at the pain in my stomach and throat.

I deserved this pain, and more. I could've saved my parents if I hadn't tried to be so clever! Why was I so stupid and worthless to think I could spit in Banwell's face and come out unscathed? Yes, I had freed Maddock and kept my end of the bargain, but at what cost? He was captured now, anyway, and now I had no chance of getting us out.

My mother was only bitten a couple of days ago. If I had taken Banwell's offer, I could've saved her from being attacked, and I could've worked on saving Maddock *after* they'd been freed. It might've taken years, but I would've done it, no matter what it took.

But everything had fallen through, especially now, since Maddock's capture was all for nothing. His gift didn't take, and so I failed him in that, too. It was very likely we would never make it out of here alive. All because of me.

I retched again, the overwhelming feeling of blame settling squarely in my gut. After I had dry heaved so much that my throat burned and my stomach and back ached, I sat back, panting, but resolute in my next move.

I had to tell them the truth.

If we were going to die here, I wanted to have a real relationship with my parents, not one built on lies. Even if they would hate me till their deaths.

Taking several breaths, I wiped my mouth, wincing at the vile taste coating my tongue, and walked back over to where my parents were waiting.

"Mallory, are you—" my dad began.

"Mom, Dad, it's not your fault I'm in here," I cut him off, clenching my hands to keep them from shaking. "It's mine. And it's my fault you haven't been released, either."

With a rasping voice, I met their curious eyes and explained everything that had happened to me after I had snuck out of the dinner party two weeks ago. I was fully sobbing by the time I got to the part where I explained my meeting with Banwell. Upon hearing his name, my mother cried out in shock and my father forced her to lie down completely, though he looked ready to punch something.

Through my tears, I told them of the meeting, and my subsequent releasing of Maddock instead of releasing them, and how I was immediately sent here.

When I finished, the silence was terrifying. I couldn't bear to meet their eyes. I stared at my hands, trying to calm my torrent of tears. The sound of movement made me snap my head toward the sound, and I saw my father get to his feet, his fists clenched, his back rigid as he turned away from us. I winced, but I couldn't tear my eyes away from the obvious fury in my father's quivering fists.

"How . . . how *could you*, Mallory," my dad said, his back still to me, his voice strained. "*How could you?*"

"Dad, Mom, I'm so sorry," I wailed, my fingernails biting into my palms as I clenched my fists, pain churning my stomach, "I had no idea you were—"

My father whipped around, his eyes wild, his face blotchy. "You—you had no idea? *No idea!* It didn't matter that you had no idea about all this. We were still kidnapped! We were taken hostage! All for that mangy leprechaun! You should've thought about *us* first—"

"*Shhhhhh*, no, no, Clark. *No*, don't talk to her like that," my mom cried, trying to sit up but fell back again. My dad rushed to her side, his expression pained as he stared at her.

"Don't yell at her, please," my mom begged as tears welled in her eyes. "There was no possible way she could have known about this place. *No one* could've known! Please—" My mom began coughing, and my dad held her hand tightly.

"Dad, Mom, I am so—so so so so—" I sobbed. My mom shook her head, trying to catch her breath.

"Mallory, no," my mom insisted, grasping my hand again, tears spilling down her cheeks as well. "No, it's not your fault. It's not. It's *our* fault. I can't imagine how hard things must have been for you."

I could only sob, unable to meet their eyes. I wanted to disappear. I had been struggling to save them for days, and when I was handed the chance, I had thrown it away. I had done it for noble reasons, but at the moment, in the face of such atrocity and the pain in my mother's pale expression, the nobility felt hollow, felt stupid and useless.

My mom shook her head. "And I don't mean just about these last few weeks. I know we're such a cliché, but being in here has made us realize that we've failed you as parents."

"Mom, shhh, don't," I sobbed, wiping my eyes.

"No, Mallory, please, let me say this," my mom urged, panting, even though she was lying still on the makeshift bed. "I've been wanting to say it to you the moment we were abducted. I should've said it before, but the easy life had numbed us. We were horrible parents. We never *showed* you we loved you, and so maybe this is our penance, for all of our bad choices. For the wrong we did you, and Maddock and Santeri."

Santeri? What was she talking about? I shook my head. That didn't matter right now. My mom was dying, and this wasn't the time.

"No, Mom, *no one* deserves this," I snapped. "We were wrong to keep them, but no one deserves *this*."

"And yet we're *still* here!" my dad shouted, and I saw several people behind him turn to stare at us, "because you chose a leprechaun over your own family!" I jerked away at the force of my father's accusation, but clenched my jaw. My mom tried to shush him, but he ignored her as he snarled, "Your *family*!"

I looked my dad in the face, feeling less cowed than before. Maddock may not have been related by blood, but he had felt like family to me.

"We were wrong to imprison him, Dad," I shot back, now feeling a little angry. "He thinks and feels just as much as we do. He helped me! He was more a father to me than you *ever* were!"

I noticed that the background whispering that had been present before had stopped, making the silence seem deafening as my father and I stared one another down, hurt twisting his expression. We glared at each other, and I resolutely braced myself for the storm of furious words from him, but his shoulders just slumped. He was quiet for a moment as he stared at his dirty feet, his breathing labored. The spectators turned back to their own hushed conversations.

"Maybe you're right," he finally whispered, his words barely audible.

Guilt immediately pricked my heart as I stared at his defeated form. Maybe I'd been too harsh.

"Dad, I—I'm sorry, I just . . . I didn't want Maddock to be a slave to Banwell, to force him to be a part of *this*," I said, gesturing around the pen. "He was my friend. He was trying to help me, and I made a decision that I thought was right, but that I didn't know the consequences of. I had no idea this was happening. Please."

My dad stared at me, that dead look still in his eyes, and my mom coughed quietly.

"Clark," my mom said, looking to my dad, "this isn't Mallory's fault. You know this. Please." My dad looked between my mother's tears and my own, and ran a hand over his face, still silent.

"I'm sorry, Dad, I—I didn't mean it," I said, biting my lip.

My dad nodded. "Yeah, you did. But I deserve it." He fell silent, half-turned away from us.

While he gathered his thoughts, my mom looked at me, gripping my hand. "I'm sorry you're here, Mallory, but I'm so happy to see you," she choked.

I wasn't even surprised that I knew she truly meant it, being happy to see me. And I realized I felt the same. I was happy, relieved, to see her and be with her.

It was odd. I'd never felt such conflicting, strong feelings before. I knew we were trapped, but being here with this new version of my mom, who'd always seemed so cold, beautiful, and too important for me, had clicked into place something I never realized I'd been missing. I never understood how some people loved their moms so much, and did things with them. But feeling accepted, wanted, and needed, and being told so, was like nothing I'd ever experienced.

"Me too, Mom," I replied, blinking quickly.

Pulling me to her, she pressed me against her feverish body. As I lay down against my mother, she wrapped her arms around me, rocking me gently. I was hesitant at first, but after a moment, I relaxed into her and allowed myself to cry against her. Her arms tightened around me. I felt a gentle hand on my head, and looked over my mom's arms to see my dad, blurry through my tears, watching me with that same pained look he had when he had looked at my mother. I frowned as comprehension dawned on me. That pained look on his face was a caring expression, though his expression was tinged with hurt as he looked at me.

I reached out my hand, cautious that he might be still furious at me, but my dad grabbed my hand and gripped it tight, forgiveness in his eyes.

"I'm sorry, Peanut. I shouldn't have yelled."

"Yes. You should have. Though not at me." I gave him a tight smile.

My dad made an odd gulping noise, his hand tightening on mine so much it hurt.

"I love you, Mal."

"I love you, too," I whispered, and I realized I truly meant it. "And I'm sorry."

My dad sighed, sounding tired. "We know you did your best, Mallory. There's nothing to forgive."

I laid my head back down on my mom's chest, trying to sort out my confused thoughts. Was this what a family connection was really like? Being truly furious at someone but still loving them? I had said something very hurtful to my dad, I had chosen Maddock over my family, and they still loved me and forgave me.

Love flooded my heart. It was a sensation I'd never truly felt with my parents as we lay there, quiet, holding one another.

# Chapter Twenty-Four

An earsplitting buzzer echoed around the pen, and people began screaming.

I sat up, bleary-eyed from dozing, as did my dad and Judith, who had come back during my drowse, their faces stormy.

"What does that mean?" I asked, my heart sinking to my stomach as my dad helped Judith to her feet.

"It's showtime," my dad snarled.

"What?" I breathed.

Just then, the doors opened, and a press of people came in, chatting excitedly. A hulking man in front of the crowd was carrying a small, zippered dog carrier that obscured what was inside.

"Come on, get up, Love," my dad was saying to my mom.

"Clark, I can't," she whimpered. "I just can't do this anymore."

"You have to!" he demanded.

I rushed to my dad's side and helped my shivering, feverish mother up. "I'll do all I can to shield you, okay? Just hold on to me. I'll protect you," my dad was saying, pressing a kiss to my mother's damp forehead. I stayed by my mother's other side, helping her stay vertical.

"What is it?" I murmured, pointing to the case.

"I don't know. I've never seen this before," my dad whispered.

The room quickly filled with spectators that filed into the stadium seats. While the crowd gathered, several men walked the perimeter, placing different colored rocks and a few pieces of what looked like bark all around the outside of the fence. Once they had finished encircling the entire pen, the man holding the doggy case shouted, "Quiet! Quiet!"

The noise around the room died instantly, a held breath of expectation in the crowd.

"Today we have a new treat," he called, his voice booming throughout the room. "We caught these guys at the house of a witch. She died rather than be captured by us, but we were able to get all of her belongings, and these were in there." He gave the doggy case a violent shake. "The Maori call them *The Endless Night*." He paused to let those in the crowd ooh and ahh and chatter like rabid monkeys. When the noise quieted, he continued. "We're told they're very fast, very potent, and don't like commotion." He shook the case again with emphasis, then looked at us with a sinister smile on his face. "So this will certainly be a show."

The man opened the cell door, unzipped the case, and threw it into the pen, locking the door, shouting, "Shields up!"

The hairs on my arms stood on end as I recognized magic encasing the entire pen, magically locking whatever creatures were in that case with us. My brain nearly scrambled itself in fury. These filthy, foul hypocrites! They made use of magic and magical creatures themselves!

The injustice of it shook me to my core. I reached out, trying to draw magic from the fence, but I couldn't seem to grasp it. It slipped through my fingers like mist. What did this mean? How was this possible? I should be able to draw magic from that magical barrier. Magic that we had been imprisoned over. My rage surged anew.

But my anger was lost the moment I saw the creatures climbing out of the doggy case.

Three spiders the size of my outstretched hand emerged, emitting shrill hisses as they did so. So blue they were almost black, the spiders were speckled with white spots that seemed to glow, terrifying nightmares that looked like they had been dipped in liquid night sky.

My mother's whimpering increased, and I gripped her hand tightly. She was arachnophobic. A few prisoners to our left shuffled backwards, trying to increase the distance between them and the spiders, but distance didn't seem to matter.

With impossible speed, the spiders attacked. People began screaming and running, trying to get behind other prisoners. The spiders darted and leaped toward those that were fighting for the back position and making the most commotion. All three spiders leapt towards the largest group of scuffling prisoners, and suddenly, three people fell to the floor without a sound. They were still for a moment, then began to twitch and seize, howling incomprehensible words and screams.

Terror broke the ranks of prisoners, and they began to outright run from the onslaught.

More people in the largest group began to fall into shuddering, shrieking heaps.

"Don't move," Judith commanded as my dad went to move my mother further from the attacking spiders. "The spiders seem to be drawn to movement and noise."

We stood in terrified silence as others around us scrambled to escape the hopping nightmares.

"Can't we do something?" I urged as a woman before us fell, mouth open in a voiceless scream. "Can't we, I don't know, put a blanket over them or something?"

I felt I could do it. Even though I was scared, I was more scared of my mom getting attacked. I could possibly survive the venom. My mom couldn't. Besides, I was the most physically fit and able here. It was my responsibility to protect them.

My dad obviously realized this too, because he hissed, "Mallory, don't you dare move!"

Outside the cage, beside us, the enormous guard shouted, "If all of you don't run around a bit and play the game, I'm going to pick a few of you to take a beating. Starting with you, leprechaun girl, and your friends," the man said, pointing to me, with his eyes on my mother that was clearly struggling to stay standing, his smile a hungry snarl. Fury and fear thrilled over me.

"Dad, you move with Mom, I'll run interference with anything coming toward us," I said, gathering my courage.

"Mallory, *no*. We are *not* playing their games," my dad hissed.

I had seen the look in the guard's eye. He knew my mother was ill, and probably dying. He could very easily kill her with just a few hits.

I couldn't let that happen. Not when I'd come this far to find them.

Ripping one of the many blankets from my mom's shoulders, I whisper-yelled, "I'm sorry!"

"Mallory, no!" My dad tried to lunge for me, but he couldn't let go of my mother as I darted toward a spider crawling off the spasming legs of a male prisoner. Leaping toward the spider with the blanket outstretched, I tried to cover the hissing arachnid, but it leaped toward my face.

Dropping with a scream, I rolled over, flailing the blanket as much as I could to shield myself or to hit the spider away, whichever worked best. After several rolls, I scrambled to my feet, and my dad shouted, "Mallory, behind you!"

I turned, whipping my blanket up just as a spider came sailing toward my neck. I felt something heavy land on the blanket, and I pinwheeled the blanket with a gasp. The spider was flung upward and away.

"Well, well, looks like we got ourselves a superhero here, folks!" the same guard who had thrown the spiders into the pen shouted. "Let's see how long she can last. Put your bets in quick, because it won't be long!"

I spun in a quick circle, trying to pinpoint the locations of all three spiders. Two were right next to each other, finishing off the last two conscious prisoners, aside from my parents and Judith. The third one, which I had thrown, was busy flailing on its back.

I just had to keep it away from my mother. I saw my dad, mom, and Judith inching around the perimeter of the fence as slowly and quietly as they could.

If I could just get the spiders out of commission, the game would be over. At least I hoped it would be. My stomach was roiling again, and I felt like I might vomit out of fear, but I held it down.

I lunged toward the two spiders as one scuttled toward me while the other vaulted at my face. I dropped again, rolling and missing the scuttling spider as it leapt away, and I felt something thump onto my shoulder. With a scream, I rolled even faster and felt a loud, wet snapping under me. Not stopping, I got to my feet and ran away from my parents, shaking the blanket in case the other spider had crawled onto it.

People outside the fence were shouting, but I was breathing too hard and was so concentrated on my mission of keeping the arachnids at bay that I didn't hear what they were saying. I saw the remnants of the crushed spider on the floor, and I shuddered as I thought of the remains on my clothes.

I fixed my attention on the two surviving arachnids, who were hopping toward me, hissing in unison. I held my blanket out like a matador's cape, ready to fling them away should they come at me, when one of the spiders turned. It had noticed my parents moving about, and began stalking toward them.

Screaming, I lunged toward it, blanket outstretched. I landed on top of the monster with the raggedy piece of cloth and scooped it up, making sure all the corners were closed, then whipped around at an urgent scream from my mom.

The last spider was soaring through the air toward me.

I lashed the blanket bag containing the other spider upward and out, trying to swing the makeshift bag like a bat at the oncoming spider, when without warning, my stomach heaved. I dropped to my knees, vomiting up bile.

I felt the heavy spider land on my hunched middle back, and as I threw myself backwards to crush it, I felt something sharp puncture my skin. Heat blared from the place just as I heard the sickening crunch as I hit the floor. A faint whiff of mossy rocks and wet bark filled my nose, and everything around me went black as midnight without a moon or stars.

Immediately, I felt so cold I began to cry. The sharp pain seeped into my muscles, into the marrow in my bones. I felt so alone yet so overwhelmed that I felt I was drowning.

I couldn't breathe. I was underwater. I clawed toward the surface, my lungs burning, and I emerged from the crushing deep, only to find myself back clambering up through the grass in Mr. Kim's yard, with the mandagot charging at me.

As the mandagot latched onto my legs, I screamed for help, and I saw Maddock standing not five feet away, watching the scene while sipping a tropical drink, complete with a tiny umbrella.

"*Maddock*!" I screamed, clawing at the lawn as I tried to escape the needle teeth of the snarling beast. "Help!"

"Help? Like you promised to help me?" the leprechaun scoffed. "You let them take me away, lassie. You didn't use the gift I gave you. You squandered it. You aren't even deserving of it; that's why it didn't work. I was a fool to trust you. You deserve this, and more." He pulled up a lounge chair out of thin air and sat down, slipping sunglasses from off his head over his eyes, slurping loudly from the icy drink in his hand.

"I tried! I didn't know what to do!" I cried, tears blurring my vision as I kicked away at the frothing mandagot. "I want to help you, but I don't know how! Please, help me! I thought we were friends!" I sobbed, as the mandagot began to tear through my pant legs. Maddock didn't seem at all bothered by the scene before him as he shrugged.

"You're human. Humans are base, disgusting creatures. You think you can change? No one can change, really. You were just using me to help yourself. You're just a bad person, and you always will be. You don't deserve mercy or help."

"*Maddock, please!*" I screamed as the mandagot reached flesh. Pain seared through my legs as they were torn open once again.

"You deserve this and more," he repeated.

"I tried!" I screamed, my throat raw. "I tried to save you!"

"You failed." The voice changed.

Maddock had morphed into my father, who was standing over me. The mandagot had disappeared, and I was surrounded by all the prisoners who were looking down on me. Beside me, my mother lay, her eyes vacant, her skin pale and cold as death.

"You could have gotten her out before she was poisoned. But you traded an animal for your mother's life, and now her blood is on your hands!" my dad thundered. "You murdered your mother, and I will never forgive you!"

I got to my feet, mind swirling as my father advanced upon me.

"But . . . but you said . . . you forgave me. You said you loved me!" I stammered.

"I was wrong. The fact you chose someone else over your own family means you don't deserve love. From anyone."

I turned and ran, but my father kept pace with me by simply walking.

"You can't outrun this guilt," my father commanded. "I won't let you. I will help HAMMA hunt you down wherever you go, to remind you of what you have done. You will be a caged animal for the rest of your life."

Screaming, I ran, pushing myself into a torturous pace, with my father whispering horrid things to me as I went. I continued to tear across the barren landscape, everything a gray horizon, but I couldn't escape the hateful words, the pain, the replaying of horrid scenes that I couldn't look away from.

Up ahead, the landscape looked different, like a wave of night approaching. I ran toward the wall of starry sky, hoping I could hide myself in the darkness. As I neared, the veil of twinkling darkness grew into a hissing roar, and with horror I realized it was a wall of glimmering spiders. I fell into the mass of hairy legs and bodies, swallowed up by the twinkling, hissing night.

I snapped awake, and felt something soft tickling my forehead. With the spiders still fresh in my mind I jerked away, whimpering.

My dad grabbed my wrist with a gentle, "Shhhh, Mal, shhh. You're okay. You're okay."

Gasping, I looked around, fear pummeling my ribcage. Was this real? Was this another illusion the spider's venom had seeped into my mind?

As I looked around, I realized that I was in fact awake and still in the HAMMA cage, and that was a horror I couldn't wake up from.

At the moment, the cage was quiet except for the sounds of a large group of people softly breathing. The room was dim, only a few lights above us were on, casting the room in shadows.

"What? What—" I gasped.

"You're okay? You're okay!" my dad said, half-chuckling, half-gasping as he pulled me into a hug. I yelped, pain flaring as he squeezed where the spider had bitten me.

"Oh, I'm sorry," he said, releasing me, but his face was shining with a tearful smile. "I'm just so happy you're alright!"

"Where's Mom? What happened?" I whispered, wincing at the tenderness of my spider bite. It itched and stung, but I restrained myself from trying to scratch away the pain. "Are you guys okay?" I asked.

"Yes, yes, we're fine. You saved your mother!" my dad whisper-exclaimed because people were sleeping. He hugged me again, avoiding squeezing my back.

"What do you mean? She didn't get bitten?" I asked, breath hitched in relief as we pulled apart.

"No! It was incredible," my dad whispered. "You killed the spiders, even after you got bitten, you actually killed all the spiders!" He looked ready to hug me again, but my back was itching so much I didn't think I could take it, and was grateful when he refrained. Instead I stared at him, trying to make sense of what he'd said.

"How? How did I kill them all *after*—" I asked, looking around the room. The magical barrier, the rocks, and the crowds were gone. Everyone was sleeping peacefully. How did I kill them?

"The one you caught in the blanket got crushed too. Your flailing around in pain smashed it," my dad explained.

"So Mom is okay?" I reaffirmed.

My dad sobered, looking over his shoulder.

I followed his gaze, and through the dimness, I saw my mom tossing and turning, Judith holding her hand.

"I don't know," he sighed. "These monsters won't give her any medicine or antidote to what bit her. But you saved her from the horrors of those spiders. The others described them to us when they woke up. They said they felt like they were being dipped in lava, or being trampled by horses, all while reliving horrible horrible memories and fears. They said it felt like they were being tortured for days or weeks. I can't imagine what you suffered. You were the last to wake up."

I frowned. I didn't experience pain like he'd described. Sure, I'd had the memories, and the feeling of the mandagot tearing into me anew made shivers flare up along my arms, but the comments about being dipped in lava? And the length of the torture? For me, it didn't feel very long, maybe only a half hour, if that.

"How long was I, you know, under the influence of the venom?" I asked.

"Several hours," my dad replied. "It's the middle of the night. We only know the general times of day because they shut off half the lights when it's time for us to sleep."

Shaking off the conflicting information I'd received, I looked toward my thrashing mother again.

Something itched next to my collarbone under my jumpsuit. With a stuttering gasp, I whipped out the thing that was tickling me.

Maddock's letter.

It was all crumpled from where I'd shoved it inside my clothes. Carefully folding it, I slipped it back into my jumpsuit, ignoring my father's questioning look, and considered what Maddock had said.

Maddock's note had been right. I couldn't believe the things that were happening here, even though it was all happening right before my eyes. How could people lose their humanity in such a way as to see all this suffering, to *cause* all this suffering, and not be moved with horror? How did these people find each other?

And why hadn't Maddock's gift worked?

I just felt so helpless, even though learning that I had saved my mother from such torture did help me feel a little better. But she was still suffering, and we were still stuck here.

"Isn't there anything we can do?" I asked, my heart hurting as I watched her, whimpering and writhing.

The tendons in my dad's neck stood out as he watched my mother.

"Try to make her as comfortable as possible. It's all we can do."

I bit my lip. How could I make her comfortable in this horrific place?

A memory of a happier time with my friends sprang into my mind. We'd been waiting for hours at an airport to take us to California for Spring Break last year, and our flight had been canceled. We had to wait in the airport for hours to get the next flight, and we had come up with a system where we laid down in a secluded area of the airport, each of us taking turns resting our heads on the other's belly for naps.

Getting unsteadily to my feet, I gathered up my makeshift bed and hurried over to my mother.

"Help me lift her," I instructed my dad.

"No, Mallory, you need to rest—" my dad began.

"No," I insisted, cutting him off, "She does, to get better. I'm perfectly fine now. I had my rest." It was true. I wasn't tired at all, despite the late hour and the terrible visions of the spiders.

My dad looked at me, silent for a moment, then nodded. With my father's help, we lifted my mother's head and shoulders, and slid as much of her body as we could onto my lap and stomach. Anything to get her off the hard, merciless concrete.

"Huh? No. No, wha . . . ? Mallory? Mallory," my mother muttered as I shifted her, trying to get into the most comfortable position.

"I'm here, Mom. I'm okay," I said quickly, gripping her hand.

My mother's eyes cracked open, and she stared up into my face, her eyes glazed. "Mallory? Oh, Mallory, are you okay?" my mom whispered, her voice slurred from sleep and sickness. I struggled to keep my voice upbeat and natural.

"Yes, I'm perfectly fine now. Are you comfortable?" I asked as she closed her eyes again, tears slipping out of the corners of her eyelids.

She sighed in response and snuggled closer to me, her breathing eased, though her body still trembled, her skin warm with fever. I took the blanket that had been over me and draped it over her trembling form. After a moment, she fell into a deeper sleep, no longer tossing.

My dad clapped me on the shoulders, his eyes misty as he stared down at me.

"Thank you, Peanut," he choked. Sitting down behind me, my dad had me rest up against him, supporting me as we watched my mother sleep, while Judith sang a soft song in a language I didn't recognize. I thought I felt a hint of magic in her songs, but again, I couldn't grasp the magic like I could when I was drawing from Maddock.

After a while, Judith and my father fell asleep, but I felt wide awake. I was helping them all as best as I could. That was all I could do. Not obtaining Maddock's gift wasn't my *fault*, I realized, just bad luck. I didn't have to beat myself up about it. It wouldn't help me, these people, or Maddock. And I didn't need Maddock's gift to help my mother or my father or Judith try to survive in here. I was the strongest and the most agile. I would help them in any way I could. I owed them that. And I would find a way out of here. Whatever happened, I wouldn't stop trying to escape. Ever.

# Chapter Twenty-Five

B y the time artificial morning clicked on, I was feeling weird. I had a strange heat in my entire torso, and I worried my spider bites were starting to fester, seeing as this place wasn't the most hygienic accommodations I'd ever stayed in. Sure, these scumbags had been thoughtful enough to give us buckets for bathrooms in one deserted area of the pen, which I reminded myself to bring my blanket to help cover me when I needed to go, but sometimes, people didn't use the makeshift latrines.

Judith, who had owned a secret sort of apothecary with her husband before being raided, looked at the bite wounds. She said there was no infection and that I was starting to heal. I wasn't so sure. The bites might heal, but the vivid memory of the nightmares still plagued me during my waking hours. I worried they might never truly leave me. Especially if I failed in getting us out of here.

At the moment, I was worried about how else the bites were affecting me, physically. My skin wasn't hot to the touch, and I wasn't sweating, but it was like there was a warm ball of *something* residing in my middle. Judith reassured me all was well, and it was probably just the bites healing, and so we left it at that. We turned our attention to my mother, who was waking.

My mother's condition still bothered me. She had to get better, and that wouldn't happen with us being stuck in here. My mother seemed to have gotten some good sleep during the night, but was still feverish and weak. According to my father, she had been terrified when the spider had bitten me, and her condition had worsened when I had fallen unconscious. Seeing me awake and moving around seemed to lift her spirits, for which I was very grateful.

I was also worried about another attack endangering her already precarious health, until my dad told me that they let animals into the pens every three or four days. So, we had a few days of respite before more torture. I could only hope that my mother would regain her strength before then.

We spent the morning talking, and I went into more detail about what happened to me after they were kidnapped. I told them everything I could remember about HAMMA and Banwell that I'd learned from the Sewer Fox. I wondered how much of it was accurate.

My parents told me about Santeri, who I had no idea was a mythical being. My parents explained that he was a haltija, a house helper and guardian type of elf from Finland, which was why Santeri hadn't been able to be bought off like the rest of my parents' workers right before the attack.

My whole life I thought Santeri was human. I had always trusted him and felt like he cared a little bit about my silly teenage problems. At least he seemed to listen and care. I probably drove him crazy, and he couldn't ever get away from my dramatics. I almost laughed as I thought about him teaching me to drive. I had just been starting to learn how to get onto the interstate. I was still terrible at it. But he had been infinitely patient, and such an amazing teacher. I had no idea he was bound to my family's house. It made me ache for him. I wished I could have helped him, too. But I couldn't help anyone, apparently.

My father speculated that Santeri had been unable to protect my parents from being attacked and kidnapped because HAMMA had put Santeri out of commission first. The thought of poor Santeri, with his soothing voice and kind concern for me, being mistreated somewhere made me boil in anger. Dwelling on all HAMMA had done and would continue to do unchecked seemed to make even my spider bite zing and flare with fury.

Meals came sporadically, and were surprisingly better fare than I'd had in my solitary cell, though it all did seem a little stale. Old bread, packaged lunch meat, water bottles, and even some bruised and floppy fruit and vegetables came sailing through the opened cell door like stadium workers throwing t-shirts to the crowd at a sporting event.

The herd of prisoners stayed a respectful distance from the cell door while it was open, but mobbed the food as it came flying in. I was afraid we wouldn't get anything on my first feeding. My father was holding up my mom so she wouldn't be trampled by the fighting crowds, Judith wasn't as young as she liked to believe, and I was terrible at catching moving things.

However, I had promised myself I would try my hardest to help us survive, and so I braved the starving mob, desperate to catch even a bruised apple or dusty piece of bread.

I surprised myself.

While I did take a lot of elbows to the face, not only did I catch a chicken leg and a partly mashed banana, I managed to jump into the air and snag an entire loaf of bread just before another person caught it, snatching it right between his outstretched hands.

The crowd pushed in closer now that the food was no longer being thrown, and the fighting became more intense as those around me fought for the pathetic scraps.

A man tried to reach over and pluck the food out of my arms from above, but I saw a very narrow path clear in the swarm of bodies. I ducked into it at a run, ditching the vultures who got cut off in the horde behind me. As I pulled away from the mob, prizes still in hand, a couple fighting over several water bottles dropped one, the bottle rolling right into my path. As I ran past, I scooped it up, unseen by the bickering duo, and hurried to my parents and Judith. We feasted on bread, a bite of chicken each, mashed banana, and a few carrots and an orange that Judith had managed to get.

"You were amazing, Mallory!" My dad grinned as he helped my mother take a sip of water. "This is more food than we've gotten in days! We were watching you. It was like no one could touch you! And the way you snagged that bread out of the air like that!" My dad laughed, the haggard look in his eyes lifting for a moment. "That guy was like three feet taller than you! Here, catch!" my dad called playfully, tossing the unpeeled orange at me. Unprepared, I lifted my hand too late, and I ended up punching the orange away from me.

"Oh no!" Heat surged down my arm as I reflexively, but stupidly late, shot my hand out to try stopping the orange from hurtling straight into my mom's nose.

The orange stopped dead, hovering in the air two inches from my mother's surprised face. We stared at the suspended orange, the overhead lights making the dimpled skin shine as it slowly rotated in place, and I whipped my hand away. The orange dropped like a stone into my mom's lap. I raised my eyes to see my parents and Judith staring at me, their mouths hanging open like they were silently screaming. The sight made a giggle burst from me, and I quickly clapped a hand to my mouth. The sound broke their shock, and my dad immediately looked around to see if anyone had seen. I too glanced around, worried at my dad's sudden apprehension. The guards in the room were all busy playing cards or watching things on their phones. The other prisoners were too focused on defensively eating everything they'd caught as quickly as they could. Did the cameras see anything? My dad turned back to me as Judith scooted closer to me, staring intently at me.

"What was that?" my dad murmured, eyes flicking between me and Judith. Judith put her hands on my shoulders, staring into my eyes for a moment before closing her eyes, her face contorting in concentration.

After a moment, she dropped her hands, shaking her head. "I knew it," she whispered, pursing her lips in bewilderment. "You have magic in you that wasn't there before."

"What?" my parents and I asked at the same time. I felt like something was constricting my throat.

"It's very faint, barely there, but it's there," Judith affirmed. "Like you're just starting to accumulate magic or something. It's the same feeling my husband had around him, but of course his magical aura was much, much stronger."

My mind instantly went to Maddock. Had he somehow given me the power to use magic without him being nearby? Or was this something else? The spiders? No, even if their bites did give magic, I doubt it would give very much. Maybe Maddock's gift hadn't failed!

I had been agonizing over Maddock's gift for days at how it would be just my luck that the ceremony had fallen short, leaving us stranded.

But maybe it did take, and had just taken time to fully actualize.

"This is interesting," Judith continued. "They don't put those who have their own magic in here with the rest of us, because they wouldn't be able to contain them. They only have relics, those stones I told you about," she said to my dad, who nodded, "to prevent us all from drawing magic from the mythical creatures they bring in and such."

"How is this possible?" my dad asked no one in particular, but was staring at me in a pointed kind of way.

For half a moment I was tempted to share with them about Maddock and his gift, but I shook it away. Maddock had given his gift to me in confidence, and I didn't want to spoil anything by sharing where I got my new magical reserve.

"I don't know, really," I replied as honestly as I could. I didn't know exactly what Maddock had done or what all was included in his 'gift', but the possibilities it now presented made my heart beat a mad tempo against my ribcage.

"Well, we can't let anyone know," my dad whispered, quickly looking around to see if anyone was listening, but everyone was too busy huddled away in their own groups, eating like ravening beasts. "This may be our chance for escape."

We all stared around at each other, all of us no doubt wondering the same thing. How soon could we be free? It would all be on me to get us out. The thought made my heart tremble.

"Do you know any spells?" my dad whispered to Judith. "You know, that could help us escape?"

"Possibly," Judith whispered, then paused, a thoughtful expression on her face. "My husband taught me some things, even though I can't use magic myself. We'd have to plan it. You saw the amount of guards and bolted doors there are in this place. However, Mallory's . . . *reserve* is so tiny that it's barely there. It could take several days for it to accumulate to a quantity that would be useful."

My dad sat back, thinking.

"Well, we can wait out a few more days," he whispered, glancing at my mom. "It's better than thinking we will be here forever! But Mallory," my dad said, his tone grave as he looked at me. "No more daredevil stuff. You will keep out of sight and try to stay away from any attacks they put on us in the future, do you hear me?"

I rolled my eyes. I had taken care of myself for a long time. I wasn't stupid. "Dad, don't worry, I'm not going to jeopardize our chance to escape by wasting my . . . *reserve*." I whispered the word. "Besides, it isn't going to be ready for several—"

"I'm not worried about the *magic*, Mallory," my dad snapped, his voice low. "I'm worried about *you*. I don't want *you* to get hurt. I don't want these monsters to find out you have magic and take you away from us. Seeing you take on the spiders by yourself was bad enough, but no more. Yes, you're our one chance to escape," he whispered, "But you are more important than that. Keep low, keep out of sight, and if you see a chance to get out without us, you take it, do you understand?" His expression was almost angry.

My eyes found Judith, who had a torn expression on her face, but she ultimately nodded with a soft, "For now."

Stunned, I looked to my mom, who nodded her head.

"Your father is right. If you see a chance, you take it, even if you have to leave us." Her voice trembled. "I can't bear the thought of them taking you away from us again."

"What? No way—" I began, but my father cut me off.

"No. You stay close to your mother for now," my dad insisted. "I will protect you from now on until we can try to get out, but you leave if you can. You've done your part protecting and trying to save us." My dad's expression gentled, and he gave me a warm, proud smile. "It's our turn to save you."

# CHAPTER TWENTY-SIX

Over the next two days, we whisper-planned our escape. We thought about unlocking doors and letting everyone run wild to cause a distraction while we slipped out, we talked about stealing uniforms, and about knocking out or possibly killing guards, but we couldn't really come up with a solid plan.

I tried not to practice my magic, but it was difficult. At first my dad wouldn't allow me to help him catch food, so I stayed on the sidelines and watched, magic ready to help with my limited knowledge of spells. A lot of magical stuff, the really small stuff, felt intuitive, and I had to practice a lot of self control not to waste it, draining my already tiny reserves on seeing what I could do. But I couldn't help myself from nudging a loaf of bread out of the reach of a greedy man who already had three loaves all to himself, or when I saw a one-sided fight of two men against one smaller man as they tried to take all the food he had, and I used a modified version of the solidified air barrier I'd used before to trip the two men, toppling them like dominoes.

The would-be victim took half a moment to try to figure out what happened, but shook it off and hurried away to his wife. I saw my dad watching me with a narrowed look on his face, and I quickly resumed tending to my mother.

Though my dad tried to be the sole provider of food and water, it became clear that my magic was a huge advantage. On the second day, he allowed me to join him when his previous attempts availed nothing more than a crumbled protein bar and a crushed pear.

The next time meals came around, I was catching and gathering more than anyone. My father helped gather while Judith stayed by my mother, who was trying so hard to be strong and not be a burden.

By the time the guards finished throwing food, I had caught a small chunk of ham, three apples, four carrots, two loaves of bread, seven protein bars, six bottles of water, and a pack of crackers in a blanket that I had brought with me to hold whatever I caught.

My dad was ecstatic once I showed him what I had gotten, and he added his contribution of an orange and two very limp celery sticks. We'd both worried that maybe the lack of food had been what was keeping my mother from getting better, and now she had more than enough to eat.

However, I had caught all this food, not for our group alone, but for a part of an escape plan that I'd been formulating in my mind. I'd been mulling it over for some time, and more than anything I realized we needed to win the trust of most, if not all, the people in here if we really wanted to escape. Maddock had been right. Everyone, no matter what they'd done, deserved to get out of here. This wasn't justice.

But for everyone to escape, everyone needed to act as one. That was where the food came in. More people would definitely make it easier, and if they were in on the plan and were getting food, there was less chance of them ratting us out in hopes of some kind of food reward, or even the hope of being released.

I stopped my father before we reached Mom and Judith, and I quickly whispered to him a very rough draft of my plan. My dad looked unconvinced, but I held up a hand to stop his rejection. "Just think about it. We don't have to share with anyone exactly how we plan to escape, but these people deserve freedom too, and I want them all to come with us. For that, they need to trust us."

I hefted the food bag up in my arms in a pointed way. "We'll take what we need, then I'm going to go around and hand out to those who are suffering the most. They'll be the most likely to trust us first."

He was staring at me with an incredulous look on his face.

"What?" I asked, annoyed. "We need to all work together, or we'll never escape, and I really think this is the way to get cooperation!" I looked around the pen. Everyone was in their own little groups, angry, scared, starving. They'd all been so starved of kindness, seeing the worst of what humankind could do, I could understand why it had been hard for people to start working together to form an escape plan. This place could crush one's soul, and I was determined to ease the burden and help while my magic gained in strength.

Things worked so much better when I'd had Maddock's help trying to find my parents, and I knew teamwork would work here, too. My fellow prisoners were all potential allies, they just needed to be encouraged.

"No, no, it's not that," my dad replied, backpedaling at my tone. "You're completely right, and I think that's a good plan. No, it's just

. . ." He paused, his chin trembling. "How did you grow up and become so wise, so fast? You're just my little girl."

I huffed out a sigh. "Dad. Come on, stop it."

"No, I'm serious." He placed his hands on my shoulder and looked me in the eye. "You're a much better person than I could ever hope to be."

I felt myself smile, a little embarrassed. "Thanks, Dad."

He straightened. "Well, let's start putting your plan into action, then. Those people over there look like a good place to start."

"The plan" came to fruition faster than I had anticipated. Once we began sharing food with those in most dire straits, it immediately opened the hearts of those around us. It was an amazing transformation. The people around us were so starved for a little compassion, a little hint that *someone* in this hell-hole cared for them, that they jumped at a chance to be part of something bigger. Once word got out that we were forming an escape plan, everyone was eager and willing to join in.

It seemed like every hour after our first round of handing out food, someone decided to brave the gap of solitude and suffering between us and joined our group. It was amazing that as the days progressed, every time the guards fed us, we had more hands to grab food, and then we distributed it evenly among our growing group of friends, my heart swelling with hope.

Three new people were placed in the cage on my third day.

The first two were a married couple, Miguel and Jessica Juarez, that arrived soon after lights on, and we quickly took them under our wing. We filled them in on everything that was happening, and my father asked how they had come to be here.

Miguel and Jessica had been desperate to cure a strange bubbly rash that had started growing on Miguel's skin after he'd been out hiking Mount Washington. They'd been to several dermatologists, but no one could give them answers, and no medication helped. Finally, they had turned to the strange medicine shop that they'd heard about from a reluctant friend. Their friend, they said, was hesitant to share the address, which they had found very odd. Once he did share the location, they were informed of lots of rules about going there; they could only go at night, there were secret code words, etc. They had tried looking up the business, but there was no listing anywhere. It was all very hush-hush.

They had arrived at the shop of the apothecary where a nice, older gentleman had just told them about what was causing his complaint and telling him to make a paste out of powdered aglaophotis, which they'd never heard of, and goat milk, and the man was even handing them a bottle of light green powder, when the shop was raided by HAMMA. The older man was carted away, and Miguel and Jessica were rounded up and sent here simply because they had been inside the shop.

The Juarezs had had no idea that magic or mythical creatures even existed before coming to our cell, and still didn't believe it.

They had no idea why they had been brought here. They were simply trying to find a cure for Miguel's skin issue.

Despite all of our explanations, they refused to believe that magic was real. As they were so scared and confused, we didn't press them.

Unfortunately, we all knew that our captors would make sure they knew magic was real soon enough.

The third person arrived a few hours after Miguel and Jessica.

When the guards entered and called the prisoners to move away from the door, they shoved a tall, muffled-shouting prisoner into the cell, ripping the cover off his head as they did so.

"I'm telling you, I want my lawyer!" Grayson First shouted, red-faced, turning back to face the guards. "I don't know what you're talking about!"

My mouth fell open as the guards left the room, leaving Grayson First to continue shouting at no one.

The feeling of being starstruck flared inside me again as I stared at him, but the feeling only lasted for a brief moment as incredulous fear replaced it. How was *he* here?

After a while, Grayson seemed to get bored of shouting, and he turned back to face all of us, finally seeming to realize we were there. Surprise widened his green eyes, one of which was blackened, with a ragged cut splitting his lower lip. He stared around at us in silence, and we stared back, nonplussed.

After several painfully quiet moments, my dad hurried forward, and began murmuring to Grayson, who seemed to recognize my dad by the softening of his expression.

They moved towards us, and part of me felt so embarrassed that I was seeing Grayson again in this disheveled state, but the other part of me realized that was stupid, and only felt pity and confusion as to why he was here.

"I don't know," Grayson was saying as they neared. "They said something about how I had entrapped a mythical creature? I have no idea what they're talking about!" They came to a stop before us, and he glanced at us. Grayson paused as he looked at me. "Wait, I recognize you, too. Weren't you at that party at that really nice mansion a few weeks ago?

"That was our party," I replied, my face warming that he seemed to remember me just a little bit.

He nodded, comprehension blooming on his face. "Oh. Oh yeah, it was your party wasn't it." The expression froze. "Wait. *You're* here too? You—you did this!" he accused, looking around at all of us. "All this trouble came after I went to your stupid party!"

"What are you talking about?" my dad urged.

"My girlfriend began complaining that people were following her, ever since your party, and I noticed people were following me, and I just brushed it off as paparazzi. Then, yesterday, they broke into my house and kidnapped us! I don't know where they put my girlfriend, but they said that *I* had imprisoned her against her will? What do they mean about that?" Grayson demanded. I bit my lip, trying to stifle the gasp that was rising in my throat. Did that mean that Sofia was some sort of mythical being? How many other celebrities were magical entities?

My father and I glanced at one another, then my father put an arm around Grayson.

"You hungry? Come eat some food. We'll explain some things."

However, the look of dread on my father's face told me he was thinking the same thing I was. If HAMMA could recklessly kidnap a movie star from the spotlight with no fear, what else were they capable of?

# Chapter Twenty-Seven

On my fifth day, an hour or so before the lights usually went out, I was busy helping my mother eat her food while Judith, Grayson, and my dad handed out the rest of the provisions to our growing group of allies. The appearance of a movie star advocating for our cause was really helping our numbers grow.

I was still worried about my mom. She should have been getting easier to help around, but she was still very weak and feverish, not getting better, not worsening. Would she be able to hold on until we escaped and found someone who could help her?

I looked up from taking a bite of half an apple we were sharing to see my mother watching me, a small, pained smile on her face.

"What is it?" I asked around my mouthful. "Is your wound hurting?"

I'd seen the large gash on my mother's side where the unknown animal had bitten her. Judith had tried keeping it clean and dry, but it weeped and oozed constantly.

"No, no, it's nothing like that," my mom said, shaking her head. "I was just remembering something. Do you remember the time we went to Maui for my birthday, and how we played on the beach all day and saw that manta ray swimming right next to us?"

I bit my lip, unsure how to respond. "Um, I wasn't there for that," I said. "You had me stay at Hillary's house while you went with your friends."

My mother's wan face flushed a weak pink.

"What about all our trips to California during Spring Breaks? We spent time together then," she insisted, looking a little desperate now.

I shook my head, biting my lip. "You had Santeri take me to the theme parks in California with my friends that came along."

My mom gave me a helpless look, then stared down at her hands, her expression crushed. "No, I swear we . . . did we really not go with you? Mallory I . . . I'm sorry."

My heart hurt looking at her trying to keep her emotions under control. I knew she was trying, and I hated to see her look so crushed. We did have some good times together. Didn't we? I tried to think of a memory we had in common, and quickly held out a part of the apple we were sharing. "Remember that time in New York, when we tried to go see *The Lion King* musical for my eleventh birthday, but we took the wrong train?"

My mother looked up, tears trailing down her cheeks, but her eyes were hopeful. "How could I forget? I was complaining the entire time, naturally. *Wow*, was I spoiled." She exhaled, her expression breaking for a moment, then she laughed. "I remember that after we had dinner, I wanted Santeri to take us by car to the theater, but you wanted to feel like a 'real' New Yorker, and insisted that you, me, and your dad take the subway." My mom looked at me with a soft smile on her face.

"And I made us miss the show," I replied, still feeling the pinch of shame in my chest. "You were so mad, but Dad said we'd go again." And we had, a few weeks later.

"I remember you were so happy, even though we missed the show," my mom continued. "Instead of going to a different Broadway play, you made us walk around, look at the boutique windows, and you even made me eat a hot dog." My mother shuddered.

"Dad liked his!" I insisted, and my mother laughed with another little shudder.

"They had been sitting in that water for who knows how long! I remember I took one bite and almost threw up."

I laughed at the memory. She had drawn quite the attention as she gagged and spat the hot dog on the sidewalk. I remembered being so embarrassed by her exaggerated complaints, but my father had laughed and poked fun at her for how soft she was.

My mom stopped laughing, her face pensive. "What I wouldn't give to be eating one of those hotdogs right now," she said, glancing at me. "I was so rotten. I didn't realize how good I had it." She paused, making an odd gulping noise. When she spoke again, her voice was trembling. "Mallory, I'm so sorry. I don't know anything about you, and that's my fault. I have all these memories of fun times and fun vacations, and I didn't even share them with the people I care for the most. I've tried to impress people like the Banwells, who not only don't even care about us, they aren't even good people! I neglected you. You're the one I hurt most with my selfish ways. And you tried to come and save us, even after everything we did to you." She choked on a laugh. "Actually, everything we *didn't* do. We failed you."

She collapsed into herself, sobbing, and I scooted to her and wrapped my arms around her. I could feel the heat of her skin through the blankets around her shoulders. She clawed at me, clinging to me and rocking me as she cried.

"I'm so sorry, Mallory. I haven't been the mother you deserve," she whispered.

I felt my eyes sting, and I felt almost relieved. I'd never thought I'd hear my mother apologize for how she'd lived her life. She had loved her life, or so I'd thought. I didn't realize she'd had any regrets, including the memories she made without me. But hearing her apology made me feel heard, and more importantly, love bloomed in my chest toward my mother. I hugged her even more tightly.

"Mom, please don't cry. I forgive you. And things will get better," I urged, looking into her face. Her cheeks were splotchy red, and her eyes were swollen as she gave me a weak smile, smoothing a trembling hand over my temple.

She nodded. "We're definitely going on that girls' trip I promised before . . . all of this happened."

"Oh, yeah. That will be fun!" I paused and bit my lip, remembering that night, and something else my mom had said right before the party. "There's something I've been wondering about," I said, and my mother cocked her head in question. "You also said I was supposed to attend a meeting or something that night. What was that about?"

My mom's face puckered in thought for a moment.

"Oh, right." She shook her head. "Your father and I had wanted you to start being part of discussions about investments and how to run the finances in our household. Since your father was going to be leaving for Japan in the morning, we had wanted to have that discussion right after the party." She shook her head again. "Seems so trivial, now."

She met my gaze, and her expression became fierce. "But I'm going to do better. I promise you, Mallory, I'm going to do all I can to get you out of—"

The doors connecting the arena to the rest of the building swung open, cutting her off as the blaring alarm sounded above us. The jabbering sounds of an excited incoming crowd echoed across the concrete.

I felt the blood drain from my face as I saw, at the forefront of the crowd of workers spilling into the room, a hulking man dressed in what looked like hockey goalie gear. He had a hefty club in one hand, and a leashed pole in the other. A ferocious-looking beast strained on the end of the pole. At first I had no idea what I was looking at as the beast yowled, but as they came closer, the horror of the animal came into view.

It was a feline the size of a large, fawn-colored bobcat. It had a small mane of barbed, dangerous-looking quills that wreathed down its spine, ending in a long, swishing paintbrush tail that bristled with feathery-looking spikes. On the back of the beast's front legs, two sharp, bony growths protruded from behind the wrists. A large purple stone with a square symbol on it was tied around the beast's neck. Judith had called those stones relics, objects that sucked magic from a creature into itself so that no one could access the animal's power.

The cat's tail wagged low to the ground, its ears pressed against its head. It reminded me of Paz's cat, La Morena—who hated me—who I called La Morena del Diablo when Paz wasn't in earshot.

Her cat always looked exactly like this spiny cat did now, teeth bared and tail wagging, right before she would pounce on me with outstretched claws, drawing blood. Only this cat did not look like it would be scared off with a simple shout and a pillow thrown at it.

I looked over at Miguel and Jessica, worried about their reaction to this proof that there was magic in the world around them. They were both pale, with Miguel whispering, "No lo creo. No es verdad," over and over as they stared at the otherworldly cat, which was growling low in its throat. It would occasionally try to lunge at HAMMA bystanders that were standing a little too close. Its sturdy, metal-poled leash kept it from going too far, but the bystanders would shriek and jump backwards before dissolving into laughter once the cat was reigned in.

I doubted those of us inside the pen would be laughing, because there was no way this guy was going to reign in this cat on us.

As one, our group backed up to the furthest point of the pen, my dad whispering strategies.

"Those spikes might have toxins, so keep clear. We should draw them away from all the injured and sick," my dad instructed our group as several guards outside the fence began lining up the relics around the pen. Several people nodded. My mom wasn't the only one that was injured. The other two severely injured were Delmar and Kamaria, who both got broken bones when a pair of guards with clubs came into the pen three weeks ago. Kamaria's husband Rakim refused to leave her side.

"Mallory, Judith, and Rakim will stay back with them and try to shuffle everyone away from those that are fending off the beast. If we work together, we might be able to keep anyone from getting hurt too badly. We have to have each other's backs, got it?" my dad instructed, while Grayson made sure everyone understood. Everyone in the group nodded. "Miguel, Jessica?" my dad barked, making the couple jump as they tore their eyes away from the terrible cat. "Stay with us, okay? Just stay with us. And remember, dodge and distract so it looks like we're running around crazy, but remain calm," my dad reminded everyone.

The door to the cell opened, and the man with the vicious, raging cat entered.

"Shield up!" someone from the crowd shouted, and with the buzz of magic, the magical shield enveloped the pen.

The door clanged shut behind him, and he strode forward, tapping his club against the heavy plastic of his chest guard. The sound echoed in the concrete-and-steel arena, the cat's spitting and snarling joining the sound.

"Who wants to come and pet my kitty?" the guard called, and the crowd laughed. "This here is a cactus cat. Fearsome beasts found in the Southwest United States and Mexico. Check out those spines. Like a porcupine's. They use those front bony growths on their forelegs to tear into cactuses, as well as other predators."

My stomach churned as I huddled closer to my mom. She put a reassuring arm around me, hugging me tightly to her, her sweat-sticky cheek hot against my temple. "You'll be okay. I won't let anything happen to you," she soothed, a hard edge to her voice.

I saw my dad cast a quick glance at those in our group, which was now more than half of the prisoners, and they nodded back with grave expressions.

Without warning, the guard darted forward toward a group of captives, scaring the already incensed cat, and it leapt forward with a screech, almost pulling out of the guard's grip. The cat ran toward the nearest cluster of prisoners, who tried to dart away, screaming. The guard yanked the cat back but swung his club at a prisoner who came too close to him, and sent the shrieking captive sprawling, the man clutching his side. My dad and the others spread out, running around and shouting, while my little group moved around the outside of the commotion, trying to remain unseen and unnoticed in all the chaos.

Unfortunately, the panic was contagious, and those who were part of the plan began to lose their cool as the armored guard cleared huge swathes of people with his aggressive cat and dangerous club.

Soon, my dad's well-laid plan was falling to pieces. The guard lost control of the cat. It pulled free from his hand, and began charging around the pen, poled leash clattering along the ground, unrestrained. People scrambled to get away. The guard ran to batter those who tried to pick up the pole dragging behind the savage cat, no doubt not wanting any prisoner to have a weapon.

With a panicked scream, Delmar broke away from our group, dodging away from the yowling feline, but was clotheslined by the quick reflexes of the guard, who was no longer encumbered by holding onto the enraged beast.

The guard was now going out of his way to knock down those who were running around the pen, felling those he could reach with his club, while the demonic cat chased others down. Rakim and Kamaria had also left our group, not wanting to move as slowly around the pen as my mother required. Miguel and Jessica simply cowered by a heap of already injured prisoners, taking cover.

Soon, it was just a few handfuls of stragglers, including my dad and Grayson, left standing. Dad continued to distract the cat while

Grayson drew the attention of the guard, while my tiny group of me, my mother, and Judith tried to dodge around the chaos.

People screamed and cried, lying helpless and crippled on the floor as the cat ravaged any and all it could, filling prisoners with spines or using its claws and teeth to tear into those it saw as a threat. We had been lucky, as we had kept near the larger groups, and the cat had avoided them for the most part, but now the numbers were dwindling. We ducked past several people shoving to get away from the guard, and I was debating on which way to go, with not much choice to be had, when my mother screamed.

I turned to see the beastly feline standing before us, his stare fixed on the three of us, blood staining its face, paws, and swishing tail.

My heart nearly stopped. With my mother already weak as she was, I couldn't let her get hurt. I wouldn't. I stepped forward, ready to head the cat off, when Judith shouted, "Protect your mother!" then dashed past me, screaming and shouting, drawing the attention of the cat.

"NO!" I shouted as Judith only got about five steps away before she was met, not with the claws of the cat, but with the club of the guard.

The weapon smashed into her shoulder, and she fell, clutching her arm. My breath caught in my throat as she fell onto her side before the guard, and as he moved to step over her, Judith kicked out at the guard's ankle, making him stumble and fall to one knee.

The cat, noticing the falling movement, lunged at the stumbling guard. He scrambled to his feet with a lot of cursing as the cat latched onto his padded arm, shaking it so much he fell back onto his butt. The guard shooed the feral cat away with a wild swing of his club, then got to his feet. He turned to Judith, who was lying groaning on the ground, his anger clear in his heavy breathing. She bared her teeth at the guard, then spit at his feet.

The crowd oohed really loud, making me jump. I hadn't been paying attention to the reactions of the crowd, too busy focused on surviving. I heard the guard chuckle behind his mask. It was a brittle sound, and I could see the growing rage in his rigid stance. I instinctively knew what was going to happen as I saw the guard's fist tighten around the club.

I felt an urge to help Judith as she lay there defenseless. She had done so much for my parents, for everyone in here, but I knew I couldn't leave my mom undefended. Torn, I glanced at my mother just as she looked down at me with a hoarse, "Help her!"

Giving my mom's hand a quick squeeze, I dashed from her side, skidding to a stop in front of Judith, fury pumping through me so much that I swore I felt electricity crackle through me as the man raised his club.

"*Filthy coward*!" I shouted, and I felt the hair on my arms stand on end. The entire jabbering crowd of onlookers fell silent. Even the yowling cat paused, a growl dying in its throat. I could see the guard's eyes narrow through the slits in his mask.

"Take off those guard pads and let's see how brave you really are!" I demanded, my face growing hot, my skin tingling.

The guard chortled, hefting his club in a menacing sort of way.

"Yeah, hit a teen girl like the brave hero you are!" I gestured to Judith on the ground. "Hit a defenseless old lady like the man you are, you gutless freak," I commanded, heat swirling over me so much I felt stifled.

Magic.

I hadn't felt it this strong in so long that I had almost forgotten what it had felt like. But the feeling was stronger, much stronger than when I drew from Maddock, much more familiar and comforting. It was *mine*. My own magic was dancing along my arms, eager to be released.

With dawning realization, I knew that this was it. I could get us out, *now*. No more waiting, no more hiding. No more pain.

I could use magic to blast this psycho in front of me. I could scare all these people so they wouldn't attack us as I unlocked the doors. I could get us out.

I stared up at the guard, a grin forming on my face as all these realizations hit me all at once.

This was it.

I raised a hand toward him, magic and fury surging up from that warm place in my torso. He was about to get a taste of his own medicine, and he had no idea it was coming.

My eyes were on the bat, so I didn't have time to dodge out of the way as the guard kicked at my leg, sweeping it out from under me. With a strangled squeal, I fell to my hands and knees, the cold concrete biting my palms. I heard a scream of "NO!" and the sound of running feet from behind me, and I looked up in time to see the guard bearing down on me with the club. It was coming so quick I didn't even have time to gasp in surprise.

But the moving blur that vaulted in front of me was even quicker.

Everything seemed to slow as my mother's form hurtled in front of me, her arms curling around me protectively. The club came cracking down as she took the brunt of the blow on the back of her head. The pull of her weight knocked us to the floor, and I stared into my mother's face, horror freezing me in place. Her gaze found mine, and her pale lips whispered, "Mallory," before I saw something leave her eyes and she slumped to my lap.

My brain stopped.

I stared at my mother's face, her mouth slack, blood beginning to flow from the wound in her head.

No.

The world went mute, went empty, as I stared into the eyes of my mother that would never look back at me.

No.

The air inside my lungs grew cold, turned to ice. My stomach shriveled into nothing as warm blood began to seep into my jumpsuit. I slid her to the floor next to me, staring into her vacant face.

No.

I knew she was dead.

But I couldn't believe it.

No.

We were supposed to escape together. I was going to use my magic to get us out. We were going to be free, and my mother, father and I were going to start a new life together. A life getting to know one another, actually spending time with each other, healing the rift that had been between us. The rift that had begun to heal here in this hell, but not enough. It wasn't enough. I hadn't had my mother for long enough. She couldn't have died here, in this underworld of the worst of humanity. Not here, at the hands of criminals and psychos. Not before I had a chance to really know her.

I looked up at the guard, who was still staring down at us, and something shattered inside me.

A feral scream erupted out of me as I surged to my feet. I ripped the club from the limp hand of the astonished guard and swung it as hard as I could, the bat connecting with his masked face and sending him staggering back. I charged at him again, bellowing, a metallic taste on my tongue as I swung again and again until he tripped over a moaning prisoner. As he went sprawling, I began to batter against his plastic armor, roaring against the truth that battered against my brain, tearing at my throat, threatening to tear me apart.

My mother was dead. He'd killed her. They'd all killed her.

The guard huddled in a ball, struggling to protect his head as I pounded the bat against him, and behind me, I heard a yowl.

The cat was still attacking people.

Still screaming, I felt around with my magic for the barbed cat still running around the pen. Using my power, I ripped away the relic that had been tied around its neck. A blast of foreign magic assailed the pen as I threw the relic aside and began to draw the magic from the cat. It ceased mauling a prisoner, and instead backed against the fence, hissing as I bore down on it with magic to stop its attacks.

Invigorated by the new magic, I knew I would need even more power to get us all out of here alive. I turned toward the fence, the magic from the cat filling me so much I could now not only feel the magic along the pen fence, but I could pull it in, the relics not enough to counter my magical strength. I felt along the wall of magic until I sensed the same seam on the magical barrier I'd found on the cages back at the bank. With a flick, I tore down the entire shield, absorbing the power into the warm ball in my middle.

The pen door opened with a *clang*, and I whirled around as several guards filed inside the cage, guns in hand. Fury flared inside me again, magic singing down my arms.

"YOU COWARDS! YOU MONSTERS!" I howled, grief and rage straining against my lungs, swirling down my arms. A buzzing in my ears seemed to drown out all sound as I focused on the enemies before me. Before they could fire their weapons, I thrust my hands out and pushed all my hate and fury outward. A gale force pressure swirled around the armed guards and flung them backward into the fence, pinning them there above the ground. All their guns dropped to the floor, and those prisoners still standing rushed for the fallen weapons.

Chaos erupted in the crowd of HAMMA onlookers on the bleachers, but my mind had become miraculously clear. I knew what to do and how to get us out of here.

Gathering the magic from the now-demolished shield, I pushed the force of magic through the cage walls toward the HAMMA spectators, all who were scrambling to escape the arena. My skin burned as I knocked over several human scum scrambling to get away.

I looked down, surprised that flames were *not* licking across my skin, yet the burning sensation remained. Using inspiration from the feeling of magical fire in my belly, fire flared from my hands and leaped to the doors, where all of the spectators were trying to exit. As flames spread across the entire doorway, the crowds backed away from the inferno. I watched the panicked crowd of HAMMA workers with an intense feeling of enjoyment.

They were trapped.

Now it was time for our escape.

I turned to find my father, but I heard his strangled cry first.

"*Grace*! NO! GRACE!" My father wailed as he clung to my mother's lifeless body, anguish breaking his features, Judith beside him, tears streaming down her face. Rage anew welled up inside me, and I drew more magic from the cat that was cowering in a deserted area of the pen, hissing and yowling in confusion as my magic continued to press down on it.

We were getting out. Now.

"Everyone who can move, help the injured to their feet!" I bellowed, taking charge. "We're getting out of here!" Still sustaining the magic that was holding up the guards along the fence, as well as the fires blocking the exits, I kicked open the cell door that the idiot guards forgot to lock when they came in. Not that it would've mattered much now that I had control of my magic. I exited the pen and held open the door for those who would be helping others.

As one, all the prisoners scrambled to get out, causing a jam at the pen doors.

"Don't push," I shouted, annoyed at how selfish people were acting again. "We won't be leaving anyone behind! We need to stick together!"

"Listen to Mallory! Don't push!" Grayson shouted, bloody with a large scratch down his face.

Though the crowds around me still pushed, the chaos lessened as prisoners filed through the cage doors, some supporting friends, others carrying the injured in groups.

My dad passed me, my mother's body in his arms, his dirty face streaked with tears, and I had to look away.

Once we were all out of the pen, I directed everyone to stand off to the side of the room, having to yell over the crackling of the fires.

Sweat poured down my skin from the combined heat in my belly and the rising smoke of the flames. Making sure all the prisoners were out of the way, I manipulated the fire that was blocking the exits in order to corral the HAMMA workers into the pen we had just vacated, the magic flowing instinctively.

Surprise and relief surged through me at how docile and compliant the HAMMA workers were. They didn't try to dash through the fire or scream for me to let them go. I supposed being surrounded by fire did make one cautious, but I hoped more than anything that what was happening was making these people realize what they had done, opening their eyes to their own atrocities. That, or they were so afraid they wouldn't try to fight me until we were out. Whatever it was, I was just grateful they were making things easier for us.

Once all the workers and guards that had been spectating were inside the cage, I slammed the pen doors shut, using fire to melt the lock. Part of me hated keeping the cat in there with them, for the cat's sake, but it would recover its magic after a while, if my experience with Maddock was anything to go by, and I couldn't waste time trying to coax it out of the pen. All I could do was hope that these monsters wouldn't hurt it.

Alarms began to blare, but I wasn't too worried, as most of HAMMA's force was now locked up. Extinguishing the magic that fed the fires, they instantly fizzled away. I also withdrew the magic holding up the guards inside the cage as I turned away, not bothering to slow their descent as they fell to the floor.

Leaving the arena, I led our ragtag group of injured humans through the small mess of hallways, using raw magic to blast open locked doors as we came to them. I thought that I would feel tired after using so much magic, but the power I'd stolen was keeping me energized. I had no doubt once I used it up, my exhaustion would cripple me.

I had no idea where all these capabilities were coming from. I'd never conjured fire or blasted doors off hinges before, but I had a gut feeling that my rage was fueling these new skills, seeing as the abilities weren't very subtle, requiring no precision or nuance. I felt like destroying things.

I only made one wrong turn that led us to a breakroom of sorts, but I got us back on track in quick order, and under the rage and anguish, I felt rather proud of myself for navigating the maze of corridors without anything worse happening. I blasted the final door that led to the reception area.

As we began filing into the room, the front doors beckoning to us, a group of ten armed guards filled the office, cutting us off and causing gasps and screams of terror to rise from several in our group. Remembering how the shields I'd conjured before had stopped an incoming ATV, I pulled up a magical barrier around us as the guards opened fire. It was amazing how much faster I could pull it up, and how smoothly I could direct it. Bullets pinged off the barrier, and a small, collective sigh of relief swept the crowd behind me. However, we were blocked. The guards were covering the door, and I wasn't sure I would be able to keep the shield up around us while fighting the armed security. I looked behind me. Almost everyone was injured or weakened in some way, and I was the only one with magic.

"How will you get us all away from here?" a woman behind me shouted.

"You can't protect us all individually," a naysaying man called shrilly as the guards fired again, the bullets dropping to the floor. "You're just a kid! You got us nowhere!"

"I'll think of something!" I insisted, my mind scrambling, but doubts clouded my thinking, grief welling up through the cracks in my raging determination. Were they right? Did I bring us all this far, just to fail now because I was out of ideas? Would these bullets soon break through, and we would be killed? And we were miles deep in the woods; how would we get away?

I felt a pang in my chest. At that moment, I wanted my mother to hug me, to tell me I was doing great. Tears welled up, my resolve weakening. *No, you dolt!* I shouted to myself, channeling Maddock. *Don't stop to cry now! You're so close! Get these people out!*

"Every man for himself!" the naysayer cried, and there was an angry outbreak at that.

"Hey, this *kid* just got us out of there, cut her some slack!" Grayson demanded, his expression determined. I met his eye, and he gave me an encouraging nod.

"But she's trapped us!" the man insisted. "She's just some dumb kid who doesn't know what she's doing!"

"Don't you talk about my daughter that way," my dad snarled, shouldering his way forward to my side, my mother's body still in his arms, Judith following behind him. "You're out of that cage, thanks to her! If you don't like it, you're welcome to go back!"

No one responded, and I took a deep breath. I could do this. I just needed a way to contain these guards, too.

An idea sprang to my mind, and, taking the shield from around us, I moved it to instead envelop the entire armed squad, constricting the barrier so much that those inside it were packed together.

But more importantly, the way was open as I scooted the restrained guards to one side.

"Watch out, everyone!" I called, the magic welling up in my hands. Picturing my mother, fury and magic exploded out of me, shattering the front door outward, the debris flinging out into the trees.

"Let's go! Get out of here!" I commanded, motioning toward the now clear doorway, and a relieved cheer went up as the debris cleared. Outside, the dense forest cast long shadows from the setting sun across the gravel.

"How will we get away? We're miles from anywhere!" the naysayer shrilled, and all eyes turned to me. My heart leapt as I remembered my first day here. I was suddenly glad I had locked the HAMMA workers away. I had unknowingly prevented them from taking our means of escape.

I whirled toward the front desk, funneling magic into the wall safe I'd seen filled with keys days before, and wrenched open the safe door with the squeal of twisting metal. Scooping the keys up with magic, I sent them all to Grayson, who caught them with a grave expression. He was more trustworthy than the rest. He and my father would sort it out.

"These people had to have cars to get here, right? Split up and go search for them."

The alarms continued to blare and I heard more stomping feet echoing through the ruined doorways.

"Get outside! Go!" I shouted, moving out of the way of the hole where the door used to be, putting a small shield around myself to protect myself from the crush of people pushing to get out into the fresh evening air. Grayson cast me a knee-weakening smile and wink as he was carried out, and I wanted to follow. But I couldn't leave yet. I had a promise to keep. And for that, I needed to get to the dressing room.

"Where are you going?" my dad called, struggling against the tide of prisoners rushing the exit.

"I'll be right back! Go outside and help Grayson with organizing a car search!" I commanded. My dad didn't hesitate, but gave me a short nod and let the flow of departing prisoners pull him and my mother's body out of sight.

# Chapter Twenty-Eight

I sprinted into the changing room, the heat fizzling down from my arms as anxiety squirmed in my gut. I hated the doubts that plagued my mind as I ran to the cubbies, hoping against hope that my stuff hadn't been donated yet. I dug through the bins, panting. It needed to be here, it was my only lead to finding Maddock.

"Yes!" I cried as I came upon the bin with my possessions. Ignoring the clothes, I grabbed my phone and key necklace from the bin, relief welling inside me as I slipped the necklace over my head. I whipped around as footfalls entered the room and gunshots exploded through the silence. I ducked just as the wall beside my head splintered with bullets. I dove to the floor behind the counter as more bullets rained over my head.

Fury swelled inside me again, my hands growing so hot they began to sweat. Slipping my phone into my bra and drawing a magical barrier around myself, I stood.

Cold seeped through me as I stared at my attackers.

The same well-dressed warlock that had checked me for magic when I first arrived stood before me. Two guards armed with very large, very impressive-looking black rifles were standing slightly ahead of the warlock.

Guessing by his age alone, the warlock was more well-versed in using magic than I was.

It had been easy to overtake the guards that had mundane weapons, as I'd had surprise on my side. But against magic? I'd never fought anyone with magic before.

"I don't know how you snuck your magic past me. I've never been wrong before," the man called, his tone almost whiny, like I'd hurt his feelings. "However, you can't be very strong in magic now, so this should be easy."

I felt him rip my magical barrier away, and I struggled not to panic as the feeling of vulnerability and debilitating grief filled me. I tried to cast another barrier around me, but that got sucked away as well. Gunfire rained around me as I ducked and spun around the corner into the closet full of jumpsuits. I took a breath and quickly checked myself for wounds, but found no bullet holes, no blood. Amazed, I peeked around the corner, back toward the door I needed to get through. The exit was so near. But I couldn't leave yet. I had to at least check if Maddock was here. I doubted he was, but I would always wonder if I didn't at least check before I made my escape. But now my way was barred. I had to get out of this room.

I considered how lucky I'd been so far, and what my chances were if I acted recklessly now. The armed security hadn't even hit me, and I had been about ten feet away from them. If they were that terrible of shots, it was very possible I could use my magic to distract them and then make a run for it. And hopefully the magic would distract the warlock as well. Time was running out. I just had to go.

Taking a deep breath, I started to pull the magic up from that warm place in my belly, when I realized that it was getting harder to conjure the heated feeling. The magic from the cat and the shield had been enough to get me and the rest of the prisoners this far, but I was running out. I shook my head. It didn't matter. I didn't need much, and I would use all I had to get out of here. Igniting the magic, I sent balls of fire toward the guards and warlock as I leapt around the corner at the same time, sprinting for the closed door.

The hail of expected gunfire came, and I dropped to the laminated floor to avoid the bullets, sliding quite a bit as the shards of death sprayed above me. There was incoherent shouting, and the gunfire ceased as I jumped up from the floor and lunged for the doorknob.

A body slammed me into the closed door. My forehead hit the door, and pain erupted in my head as stars zipped around my vision. I was forced around, and through my blurred sight, I felt the muzzle of the guard's heavy rifle get shoved into my stomach.

"Don't move," the man commanded.

The pain in my head immediately disappeared as I stared at the hateful face leering back at me. My body flushed. The heat flowed up through my arms as I brought my elbows down onto the gun barrel. The momentum made the guard drop his gun. Without thinking, I dove for the weapon. The guard grabbed my arm and yanked me back toward him. Falling into his body, I slammed my knee up into his groin. With a mangled yell, he released me and bent double. Freed, I leapt forward, scooped up the gun, and whipped around to point it at him, but I was closer to my captor than I thought. The barrel of the gun slammed into the moaning guard's face, and he was flung backwards.

With a gasp, I cried out, "Oh, sorry!" as he fell into his comrade, who had been rushing forward to help. Watching them both fall to the floor, I frowned. "Wait. No."

Something silvery shot past me, so close the hairs on my body stood on end, and I whirled around to see the warlock muttering, his hands outstretched toward me. His hands began to crackle with energy, and with a cry, I tried to jump out of the way. However, my body didn't jump sideways. Instead, my jump carried me upwards, higher than I'd ever jumped in my life. So high, in fact, I actually hit the ceiling before gravity kicked back in for me and I started falling.

As I hit the ceiling, several bullets screamed past my face as I hurtled back toward the floor. I landed right on top of the two guards who had just gotten up from the floor and had been firing at me. I landed on one of them hard, while the butt of the gun I still had in my hands cracked across the face of the other. They fell to the floor in an unconscious heap.

I landed on the floor, keeping my feet, and stared, open-mouthed, at the two unconscious guards, completely bemused.

I checked over myself, breathless with confusion.

I should be dead, lying on the ground, full of bullet holes.

I looked up at the warlock before me, and saw him staring at me with the same dumb, jaw-agape-stunned look I was sure I was also wearing.

"What are you?" he whispered. "How did you do that?"

Panting, I raised the gun still in my hands and pointed it at his chest. I hoped I didn't look too stupid, and that I looked like I knew what I was doing with this dangerous weapon.

"You don't want to know," I bluffed. Reaching out, I stripped away the shield he had put around himself. I was surprised that the magic I felt on him was way less than even the spiky cat's reserve had been.

"Now, I know you can use magic, but I'm something far more powerful than just any old magic user," I said, hoping the words sounded true. "Do you really want to see if you can survive going up against me?"

He considered me, and he shot something icy and silvery at me, but I sidestepped it, instinctively using my power to circle the spell back around at him, where it slammed into his shoulder. He fell to the floor with a gasping scream as ice began to grow from his shoulder, traveling down his arm, piercing through his clothing. Heart hammering in amazement that I'd been able to pull that off, I came to stand over him, stepping on his wrist that wasn't encumbered by ice. I knew he would probably have a lot of information about HAMMA and what they knew about us, but I didn't want to drag him along with me, mostly because I knew I wouldn't be able to keep him under control. The only reason I had the upper hand right now was because I'd scared and shocked him. I doubted my control could last long. I needed to find out all I could right now, then get out of here.

"Do you have records of everyone here?" I demanded. It was possible I would be able to destroy the records to make it harder for HAMMA to track us. The man shook his head as he made the ice in his shoulder disappear.

"Stop moving! And don't lie to me!" I snapped.

"We don't!" he stammered, true fear in his face. "Their records are processed in a different place. That's all we know. The Everbleeders are just sent here to be educated."

My blood froze at his words.

"*Educated*?" I shouted, and the man flinched. "You call cold-blooded murder *educating* people? You sorry son of a—" I slammed the butt of my rifle against the man's head. Instead of dropping unconscious like I'd seen in all the movies, he clutched his head, yowling in pain. I stared at him, feeling annoyed. Did the movies lie to me?

Growling, I looked around the room. I needed this guy out of commission. I couldn't just tie him up, because he would just untie everything with magic, and I couldn't bring him with me.

Exhaling with a snarl, I motioned with my gun. "Get up."

He scrambled to his feet, his hands in the air, and I motioned toward the door.

"And don't try anything," I warned, "You saw how easily I took out your security. You would be even less trouble," I lied.

Nodding, his upper lip shiny with sweat, he moved to the door. In the office, the other group of armed guards were still encased in the magical shield, yelling, and some even crying, to be released. Seeing the barrier reminded me that I was very, very low on magic. If I had any, it was only enough to keep the shield up. It would be a good idea to get just a little bit more, in case something went wrong.

"Where do you keep your magical creatures?" I snapped. "Take me there." I shoved the muzzle of the rifle into his side, like I'd seen in the movies, even though they lied to me, and he gave a small squeak.

Taking me through a door on the opposite side of the room, we entered another chamber filled with cages. I saw two foxes, a scorpion in a terrarium, a sad looking racoon, a pair of goblin-like creatures, and, for some reason, a rooster. No Maddock.

"Is that leprechaun that you captured here?" I demanded.

The warlock shook his head, his hands trembling. Clenching my jaw, I scanned the room, looking for a way to contain the warlock.

On all the cages hung the same relic stones, drawing in the creatures' magic. They reminded me of the giant pen I'd just left, and it gave me an idea. I could possibly lock the warlock in one of the bigger cages with the relics to suck his magic away. That way he would have a harder time getting out, giving us time to get away without interference.

"Open those big cages," I commanded. "And where did the leprechaun get sent?"

With a wide-eyed stare, his face growing purple, almost as if he was straining to hold something in, the man vanished from my sight.

"NO!" I shouted, spinning around, worried he was trying to get the drop on me, but he was gone.

I cursed, my palms sticky on the gun as I readjusted my grip.

*Okay. Think, Mallory.*

I had my phone, the only thing that had Maddock's number on it. I could go. I should go. Right now.

But as I looked at the cages, a feeling of resolve filled my chest. I couldn't leave these poor creatures here. I felt guilty enough about the spiny cat. I couldn't do that to these guys.

Whipping another shield around me, this one wavering, I ripped away the individual shields from every cage, storing the magic inside me, and I hurried around the room, opening every cage with an animal inside. My magical shield proved unnecessary, as the creatures didn't even bother to attack me, but ran for the door that I had left open. The scuttling scorpion made me shudder as I took a broom and brushed it out the door.

Once I was sure I hadn't left any animal behind, I ran for the door.

I followed the last of the creatures out into the reception room, watching with satisfaction as they swarmed out into the evening, disappearing into the shadows of the surrounding forest. The security guards were still trapped in my shield, and I was surprised that the warlock hadn't freed them yet. I hoped he was hiding somewhere, afraid I was going to come after him. Whatever the case, my work was almost done here.

Before slipping through the destroyed front door myself, I turned and used the magic I'd accumulated from the cages to blast all the computers, printers, and internet boxes I could see. The fire and smoke that rose from the destruction made a second alarm sound, and above me sprinklers began sprouting on.

*Now* it was time to get out of here.

With nothing more to do, I ducked out the door into the open air.

I paused a few steps outside the ruined door, struck by how good the air smelled, how vibrant the gold-and-pink-streaked clouds looked against the darkening sky. The last of the birds were singing lazy songs in the trees before turning in for the night, and crickets were humming in the gathering darkness. Tears sprang to my eyes. I took one last grateful gulp of air, then the overwhelming silence made me snap my attention to the gravel road.

Where was everyone?

As I surveyed the trees plunged in twilight around me, I saw no one, not one prisoner, not one car.

My breath caught in my throat. They wouldn't have left me. Would they? I remembered the loud-mouthed people that had criticized me. I could see them inciting a panicked rush for cars. Maybe my father couldn't stop them, and he had to leave with them, or be left behind.

Incredulous and hurt, I realized I couldn't stand here. I needed to get away.

Just as I started running for cover, I heard the crunch of gravel and the roar of a car's engine off to my right. I whipped around just as a large black SUV pulled up beside me, and I saw my dad waving at me through the darkened windows.

Running to the door, I hopped up into the passenger seat. I hadn't even swung the door shut before my dad was peeling out, tires spitting gravel as we roared down the lane toward the main road.

"Where is everyone else?" I panted, collapsing against the seat as relief and exhaustion flooded through me. I felt as if I'd just run three miles.

"They already left," my dad said, his pale face streaked with tears. "Every man for himself. Grayson and Judith wanted to wait for you, but I told them to go, take their own cars. I didn't want any cars left behind. Which worked out; we took every vehicle in the entire place."

"Good," I said, feeling a vindictive pleasure at the thought of those monsters stranded. At least for a little while. The warlock was probably already releasing everyone from the cage and calling for help. "It's probably for the best we scattered," I said, the numbness returning to my heart. "Safer for everyone."

We were silent for a moment, and I cautiously glanced at my dad, who kept his eyes on the road, though tears streamed down his face.

Through all of the chaos of the escape, I hadn't forgotten what had happened to my mother, the horrid truth in the back of my mind. The frenzy had helped me evade the reality of it, but in the silence, I couldn't avoid it any longer.

I didn't have to ask where he'd put my mother. I had glimpsed a pair of jumpsuits covering something in the seat behind me, and I turned back to look at the front, my eyes burning.

I didn't say anything. Couldn't say anything.

Now that we were out of there, I felt nothing but numbness. The fire inside me had burned everything away, leaving my insides charred and hollow. But the numbness couldn't extinguish the wild thoughts burning in my mind.

What-if's and shoulda-couldas filled my head. If I had been quicker using my magic, or if I hadn't tried to protect Judith, or had been smarter about the gift Maddock had given me, maybe I wouldn't have failed my mother. If I had done things differently, or tried to learn more about magic from Judith, or taken magic from that spiny cat sooner, we would be escaping from that twisted nightmare with my mother here with us, alive. Could magic bring people back from the dead? I didn't know either way, and my incompetence was killing me.

If I had listened to my dad and stayed with my mother, she wouldn't have thought she had to put herself in harm's way to save me. I could feel the blame emanating from my father's quiet form as he pulled onto the main road and pressed the accelerator. We flew down the road, the trees nothing more than dark blurs as night finally settled around us.

I didn't want to think, didn't want to dwell on everything that had happened just a half hour ago. I didn't want to feel.

I leaned my forehead against the window, closing my eyes against the swelling roar of guilt and pain.

# Chapter Twenty-Nine

After about three hours of speeding down the sporadically occupied interstate, my dad released his anger from off the accelerator.

"We need gas," was all he said as he took the exit of a small town that boasted two gas stations. When we pulled into the nearest gas pump, he looked at me.

"You need to use magic to get us gas," he said, his tone dead.

I stared at him. "I . . . don't know how to do that." And I wasn't sure if I would even be *able* to do it. The warm ball that I'd been accustomed to in my belly felt cold and lifeless.

"Try," he snapped.

"Dad, I don't know—"

"*Just do it, Mallory!*" my dad shouted, slamming his hands onto the steering wheel, grief twisting his face. "*Try!*"

My throat felt tight as I stared at him, not wanting to cry, but I couldn't stop my vision from going blurry. He turned to look at me, and the expression pierced me to my heart. His look was so ugly, so full of blame and anger, that I couldn't breathe.

Eyes burning, I twisted in my seat, jumped out of the car, and ran into the trees surrounding the gas station. After several yards into the woods, I fell to my knees, gasping, pain constricting my lungs.

I could never do anything right. I made every bad decision. My bad decisions had killed my mother. I felt like I couldn't catch my breath. My lungs were being squeezed with iron bands of remorse and self-loathing.

She didn't have to die. I had been rash and stupid, and didn't tell her what I was planning on doing. Now all I had was my father. We had just begun to trust one another, to get close to one another, but now even that was ruined. Our relationship was shattered. The look on his face had been proof of that. He would never be able to trust me again. Never love me again.

"Mallory." Behind me, my dad's voice broke through the shrilling voices in my head. "Mallory, I'm so sorry."

I stood, whirling to face him, unshed tears burning behind my eyes. "*Why?*" I snapped. "We both know I'm to blame for—for Mom! I know you hate me! I wasn't smart enough, I didn't do the right thing, I traded Maddock for your freedom, and I got Mom killed—"

My dad stepped forward and pulled me into a hug so tight the air whooshed out of my lungs, and I could no longer speak. He didn't say anything. He just held me fast, momentarily stunning me into silence.

After a moment, I hugged him back, tears erupting from that numb place, sobbing wildly into his ragged jumpsuit. I howled as we stood there in the dark. I couldn't catch my breath, the tears scalding as they coursed down my cheeks.

After a while my tears slowed, and when we pulled away, my arms ached from clinging to him for so long. My dad wiped his face on his forearm and placed both his hands on my shoulders, forcing me to face him, even though his expression was hidden by the darkness.

"I don't hate you, Mallory. You're all I have. Your mother made her decision. She saved you. She *loved* you, though we never really showed you when we had the chance. I don't blame *you*. Those monsters, those bastards—" my dad choked. "But don't you ever say you got your mother killed. Never again." He squeezed my shoulders, and put his face closer to mine. "Do you hear me? Your mother would be so proud of what you've done. You just rescued a whole crowd of people who were being mercilessly tortured. You are not to blame. Besides," he said, his voice thick, "I think she knew she wouldn't survive long, even if she'd gotten out. We didn't know the cure to what bit her, and her body was shutting down. She was dying, Mallory." I could hear the truth of it in his quiet tone. "We'd had many talks while you slept. She kept saying how I was to get you to safety, no matter what. I know she felt guilt for the way she treated you and for the selfishness your mother and I had. Living more unselfishly was something she was aiming for. She wanted to be better. So do I, but I know saving you was the best decision she could've made. I only wish it had been me." He fell silent for several moments before exhaling. "But now we need to be strong. We are all we have. We have to work together, okay?"

I wanted to believe him, and seeing the love in his eyes loosened the pain in my gut. We were all we had.

I nodded, wiping my eyes.

"What do we do now?" I asked, my voice trembly.

"Well," my dad said, looking back toward the gas station. "Home is less than an hour away. We need gas. I say we hurry home, pack up what we can, and go into hiding. They will come after us again because of what happened there."

"Is that a good idea, going home?" I asked, biting my lip. "What if they're there, waiting for us back at the house?"

"We have to risk it. There are things in the vault that are imperative for us to have to start a new life. I have no doubt Banwell will hear about the breakout. He might even know already, and has dispatched people to our house. I have no doubt he has records of who was all at that facility."

"He especially knows *we* were there," I said through gritted teeth, rage flaring in my stomach at the thought of him. "And Grayson." I looked up at my dad. "What's going to happen to him? What's he going to do?"

My dad ran a hand through his hair. "He knows not to say anything about his kidnapping. And who would believe him? It would probably only put him in danger of getting snatched again. He told me he was going to step away from Hollywood and go into hiding, too. This really shook him up. But he told me to tell you 'thanks.'"

I nodded, my jaw tight. These last few weeks had changed all of us.

"So we need to act quickly, before anyone can get to our house," my dad said, changing topics with a resolute tone.

"What do we do about . . . Mom?" I gulped.

He was quiet, then he rasped, "I don't know. The house was trashed. People will ask questions." He shook his head, planting his fists on his hips. "We'll cross that bridge when we get home."

I nodded, and my thoughts moved to Maddock.

I was out now. I needed to free him. He'd saved us from a terrible fate. I had to return the favor.

For the first time in my life, I wanted to be like my mother: I would go out selflessly if I had to.

I acquired the needed gas by using magic to pull it up through the pumping system. It took longer and was harder than I thought, being exhausted as I was, and my magic was mere dregs now from getting everyone out. But after several attempts, I was able to bring up the gasoline and pump it into the car. I felt bad about not paying, but we were in dire straits. As soon as I was able, I would come back and pay somehow.

I debated on leaving the small lump of gold I had kept in my jumpsuit that I had gotten from Maddock, but I figured the workers wouldn't recognize what it was. Besides, the nugget was easily worth two grand. We only stole about one hundred dollars worth. It wouldn't kill the gas station owners.

It was almost midnight when we made it home. My dad rammed open the gate and we left it open for a quick escape. He pulled into the round drive and stopped right in front of the house. It loomed above us, dark and lifeless. The front doors were wide open, and seeing them agape, like the dark maw of a monster about to swallow me, gripped me with a sudden fear.

"What if they're in there, waiting for us?" I shivered, trying to push away the memories of coming home a couple of weeks ago and finding the house destroyed, my parents gone.

An eternity had passed since then.

My dad took a deep breath. "We'll run for the safe room. There's no way they found it. We'll plan after that. We'll leave Mom here for now, okay?"

I hated thinking of leaving her in the car, but taking her wasn't sensible. And, though I felt horrible, it would be a little creepy bringing her with us.

I nodded.

"Okay, ready?" my dad whispered. "Go!"

As one, we exited the car and ran through the front doors. The house was silent, and darker than I ever remember it being, but that just meant it was easier for enemies to hide. We dashed through the trashed foyer, where I almost tripped over a shriveled potted plant that had been thrown in the middle of the room. We ran through one living room, through a hall into the kitchen, and down to the wine cellar, where my father opened the path to the vault.

"Hurry," my dad whispered. "I didn't hear anyone following, but that doesn't mean they aren't here." We ran to the vault, opened it, and only breathed a sigh of relief when the vault door was closed and locked behind us.

The vault looked just as I had left it.

My dad hurried down the steps and began pulling papers and files out of a filing cabinet in the wall. I followed after him, and he pointed to the doors that led to the safe room bedrooms.

"There are spare clothes and luggage for you in there. Pack a bag."

I hurried inside, went to the closet with my name on it, and I flung open the doors. Inside, shirts, jeans, dresses, and underclothes were stacked and hung in neat rows. There were lots of different charging cords, burner phones, and other electronics. I stared at it all with wide eyes. I had no idea my parents were so well prepared. Now it didn't seem so silly. I found a charger that fit my phone and plugged it in to begin charging before I began shoving items into a pair of suitcases.

"Will we have to sell our house?" I asked as I lugged my filled suitcase into the main room.

"No. I can pretend to sell it, but switch the ownership under a different entity," my dad said, moving to the banknote drawer that I had raided weeks before. I had left plenty of cash stacks behind, but my dad still glanced at me as he looked over the contents.

"I took a lot of money," I admitted, coming over to him. "I knew I couldn't stay here at the house, and I didn't know how much I needed, so I went all out."

My dad granted me the ghost of a grin, and said, "That's my girl."

"But I'm sure Banwell has it all now," I pointed out. The barely-there smile on my dad's face vanished, replaced by an ugly look tinged with grief.

"*Banwell*," he snarled. "My company was talking of doing business with him. That's why I thought he had come to our party. I had no idea he was in on something like this."

We fell silent, and as my dad began putting cash and gold into a bag, I noticed a very old-looking journal at the very back of the drawer.

"What's this?" I asked, reaching and pulling it out. My dad looked over my shoulder.

"Oh, one of our ancestor's magic books. We have a few stored away here." He went to the drawer beside the money drawer and pulled out two more journals. "I guess I didn't put it in the right drawer. My parents were very conservative when it came to using magic. We only used it to protect our interests and our assets, like Maddock. Other than that, we weren't to use magic indiscriminately. And I suppose we taught you the same thing. Not that I was any good at it," my dad said, looking at me. "Your mother was pretty good when she had a magical source to draw from. I guess that's where you get it. But we never imagined any of us actually *becoming* a magical being." He handed me the other journals, and I tucked them under the crook of my arm.

"Yeah, it's just my luck I became magical and I know next-to-nothing about what to do with it," I said, feeling dumb. I could practically hear Maddock complaining about how he wasted his gift on someone as magically ignorant as I was. "I'll have to start studying."

We fell silent. I turned to place the magical journals in my suitcase, and then the both of us continued with finishing our own preparations. We each changed out of our shredded, bloodstained jumpsuits into clean clothes—myself desperate for a shower—and finished packing the bare essentials we would need for a few weeks, then piled our bags next to the vault door.

"Here," my dad said, handing me a small, sleek handgun. I took it with cautious fingers, looking nervous. My dad chuckled. "It's not a bomb. We were going to sign you up to take lessons on how to use it in case of a home invasion, but . . . it's funny how many 'we were going to's' your mother and I had. Now it's all too late." He worked his jaw for a moment, then looked up at me, and seeing me holding the gun flat on my palms, he gave me a weak smile.

"Here, you hold the gun like this," he said, showing me how to use it. "Never point it at anyone except an enemy you're willing to kill." He quickly went over everything, how to engage the safety, how to point it without my finger on the trigger, how to load bullets into the magazine and the magazine into the gun, and how to hold the weapon correctly to protect my hands from the kickback.

As he explained everything, I felt more and more nervous. This small gun felt a lot more dangerous and prone to going off than those big ones I had held back at the HAMMA compound. The big ones felt reassuring, like I could wave it around and not be too worried about accidentally pulling the trigger, because there was more space to put my hands. This tiny thing felt like it would explode at any moment because my hands were so crowded around the dangerous bits.

"If nothing else, you holding the gun up at someone could be enough to deter them. If you do fire, remember to take the safety off." He pointed to the safety latch.

"Okay, thanks, dad," I said, gingerly putting the gun into the concealed holster and belt he had given me. With some instruction, I was able to get the belt and holster in place underneath my clothes. He wanted me wearing the gun at all times while we were here, just in case. He had a similar gun that he had strapped onto himself.

"Okay, good. Now," my dad said, his tone firm, "You stay here, lock the door behind me. I'll go up and check for danger. If all is well, I'll come back down and get you, we'll load the car, and be on our way."

"And Mom? We can't . . ." I swallowed. "We can't carry her around with us."

My dad looked away, his jaw muscles looking ready to snap.

"Maybe," I said, hurrying on, pulling my now seventy-four-percent-charged phone out of my pocket, "We should call the police. We can tell them we were on vacation, and when we got home, we can say we caught burglars in our house and they attacked us and . . . killed Mom."

My dad shook his head. "I don't know if we should get police involved at all. Banwell is too powerful, and not just in the magical world. Besides, there will be a lot of questions we won't be able to answer. The police will know Mom wasn't killed here. There won't be enough blood, and they'll know she died hours ago."

He sighed, looking older and more tired than I'd ever seen him. "Let's get loaded in the car, and we'll figure it out."

I nodded, and he gave me a quick hug. "Lock the door behind me," he said, then slipped out the vault door.

I watched him disappear, and was about to shut the heavy door, when a sudden urge for food stopped me. There was food here in the vault, but it was all that emergency storage type stuff, like powdered milk and packaged noodle mixes. Even though the kitchen had been trashed, there was sure to be some edible remains somewhere. Besides, since the kitchen was right next to the wine cellar, if there was any danger I could scamper back down here to the vault and lock myself in. It would be a very quick expedition for snacks. I was suddenly dying for ice cream.

Shutting the vault door after me, I hurried up to the dark kitchen. I was just pulling out some almond fudge ice cream, light from the freezer blinding me to my surroundings, when I heard gunshots echo through the house.

I slammed the freezer door shut, plunging the kitchen back into darkness, and dropped low, clutching the icy carton to my chest. I listened hard over the sound of my galloping heart. More gunshots rang out, and I scrambled for a more defensible position behind the middle island as my mind raced at what to do.

My dad wouldn't shoot at nothing. Someone was here in the house. Chills raced over my skin.

Did my dad kill them, or was he the one that got shot? I heard barely audible sounds of a scuffle, then silence.

Where was he in the house? Why was it so quiet now?

After several breathless moments, I finally heard the voices again. They were coming down the servant stairs, which was in view of the wine cellar.

I'd shut the wine cellar door behind me when I'd come up, thankfully, but that meant that I wouldn't be able to get into the wine cellar without being seen. I slipped around the corner of the island to be more out of sight, then pressed my face to the floor and peered around the corner toward the stairs, to see who would appear.

"We should probably bandage him," an unknown male voice was saying. "He might bleed out."

"Would serve the scum right," a second male voice snarled. "We'll put him in the car, then find his daughter," the second voice continued, an excited lilt to his voice. "She's gotta be hiding around here somewhere. It's a good thing we got the call so soon, or we would've missed them."

"How are you so happy?" the first voice complained as an awkward, three-man-shaped silhouette came into view through the darkness. "It was a call in the middle of the night!"

One of the men had a headband flashlight on, and it shined in the darkness like some horrible searchlight. I ducked back around the island, my heart pounding in my ears. I heard them shuffle across the floor, and I peered back around the corner, where I saw the men hauling my dad between them like a deadweight.

"Those are usually the most exciting ones!" the second voice said. "Besides, it's not like you had anything to do tonight." The second voice laughed.

"Shut up, man. The females always want Chads, you know that. What I can't understand is how these Everbleeders got out? That place is a freaking compound. Did they tell you how? They didn't tell me anything," the first voice pouted.

"The daughter's a witch, supposedly. Those idiots in Vermont didn't bother to check her for magic or something," the second voice snorted. They moved out of sight. I sat up, pulled my knees up to my chest, and leaned against the island cupboards, racking my brain for a plan. Was it just the two of them? Were there more?

We needed help. I knew my dad didn't want to call the police, but I wasn't going to do this on my own. Not again.

Breathless, I pulled out my cell phone and dialed.

"911, what's your emergency?" a young man's voice asked after one ring.

I froze.

I had no idea what to say. How much should I reveal? I just needed police here to help with the intruders, but I didn't want to lie myself into a corner. We needed room to work out a story when the police got here. I exhaled. Why did I have to get stuck in situations where I don't have time to think decisions through?

"Hello?" the young man asked again.

"Please help," I rasped, keeping my voice low so as not to be heard by any other intruders that might be in the house. "People with guns have attacked our house. Please help me," I whispered, my voice gravelly.

"Okay, can you tell me your address, sir?" the man replied, his tone very calm.

I gave him the address, and after another gruff plea for them to hurry, I hung up.

I sat there for a half a second, wondering if I did the right thing in calling the police, or if I just made our situation worse. Something told me I needed to go after Maddock now, but I wouldn't be able to once the police got here, and I couldn't let those criminals take my dad away. I realized I needed to deal with the intruders before the cops showed up.

I ran to the foyer where I saw the two men dragging my father across the room toward the open door.

I pulled out my gun. "Hey!" I shouted, my voice echoing around the cavernous room, making the men jump "Don't move. I have a gun!" Terrified, I clicked off the safety.

The two froze in their tracks, the man with the headlamp quickly clicking it off, and then they turned to face me. I could see them through the dark as they shifted to put my unconscious dad's body in a more prominent position, no doubt to make it difficult for me to hit them. Even if I knew how to shoot this thing, it would be very tricky. I would definitely end up hitting my dad.

But that was before. Before Maddock's gift of magic.

"Put my dad down, slowly," I commanded, grimacing at my shaking voice.

The two men laughed.

"I'm not kidding!" I shouted. "Set him down or I will shoot you."

"Good luck shooting us through your dad," one said, giving my dad's limp body a small shake as if to prove their point.

"I say twenty bucks she hits her father before she shoots us," the other guy guffawed. The other took the bet.

I ran my tongue over my dry lips, my hands clammy.

They were right. Who was I kidding? I didn't know how to use magic to make a bullet hit someone! Blasting doors off hinges was one thing, but the finesse needed to direct a bullet? I didn't trust myself. I lowered my gun a little bit, internally berating myself. This was so stupid. I had no idea how to work a gun! They had called my bluff, and now I was a sitting duck. I should've stayed hidden until the police got here.

I lowered the gun a bit more, and the gun slipped in my sweaty grip. Gasping, I quickly tried to catch and right the pistol, and accidentally mashed down the trigger. The gun went off with a deafening bang, bucking in my hands, the smell of fireworks in my nose. In the darkness, one of the men holding up my dad fell to the floor, shrieking. Something heavy and metal fell out of his belt and skittered away into the darkness. Their gun? I prayed they only had one.

Without the aid of his friend to help hold up an unconscious body, the other man dropped my dad, who fell to the marble floor like a sack of potatoes.

I whipped my gun upright again, my hands trembling. "Don't move!" I shouted. "Or I'll shoot you too!"

Through the darkness I saw the man raise his hands as his friend writhed around on the ground, yelling obscenities.

"Grab your friend and move over here!" I shouted, gesturing for them to come closer to me, but making sure I kept a good distance between us. I also wanted them far away from wherever their gun had slid to. Dragging his swearing friend, the two men came to the middle of the foyer.

"Sit down," I commanded, gesturing with my gun. The man set down his friend, then lunged at me.

Instinctively, I squeezed the trigger again. The gun rocked in my hands as it went off a second time, and the man staggered back, tripped, and then dropped before me, his head making a sickening crack against the marble floor. He lay still.

Breathing shallowly, I didn't consider the fact that I might've just killed someone, even if it was in self defense. I had no time. I needed to tie them up so they couldn't hurt me while I checked on my dad, who I hoped was only unconscious. Then I could get out of here.

On a hunch, I ran out to the driveway, heading straight for their car, which they had parked beside the one we had stolen, and searched inside it. Along with a disgusting amount of burrito wrappers and empty energy drink cans, there was rope and duct tape in the back seat, just as I had hoped. Grabbing all, I ran back into the house. The first man I'd shot was trying to wake his friend by shaking him, clutching his bleeding leg, then turned to me as I approached.

"*You killed him, you witch!*" he roared.

I flinched, not wanting to hear his words, and pulled out my gun again. "Don't move," I choked. "Roll over with your hands behind your back."

Without a word, the man rolled over, and I quickly taped up his hands behind his back. I also taped up his legs and his bullet wound. I had gotten him in his thigh, and I just put enough tape over his wound to stop feeling guilty about letting him bleed out. Then, taking a deep breath, I went over to his friend. With a heavy heart and shaking hands, I reached out and felt around his neck for his pulse. My heart dropped as I felt nothing with my sweaty hand, then leaped as I felt the faint throb in his neck.

"He's alive!" I gasped.

"What?" his friend croaked. "You're lying!"

"He's really alive!" Relief flooded through me, making my legs shake.

"You lying witch!" his friend bellowed as I turned toward him. "You killed him! You murdering—"

I slapped an extra large piece of duct tape over the screaming man's mouth, feeling strangely elated that I hadn't killed the dangerous man that had broken into my house.

I quickly tied the unconscious man up as well, taping part of his shirt over the wound in his side to try and staunch the flow of blood.

After making sure both men were sufficiently tied up, I ran to my father.

Kneeling down beside him, with bated breath, I felt for his pulse. It thrummed against my hand, his skin warm. Sighing in relief, I used duct tape to bandage the bleeding wounds in his leg and shoulder as best as I could. He woke up as I was finishing taping his calf, and he grabbed at me.

"Mallory! You're okay! What happened? Where are they?" he asked, his voice a bit slurred.

"Over there," I said, gesturing over my shoulder. "Don't worry, they're tied up. But listen, okay, we don't have much time. I called the police. They're on their way. You have to stay here, and pretend you're the one who called them, and think of a story to tell them about Mom. I have to go." I tried to stand, but my dad grabbed my arm.

"Whoa, whoa! *Where* do you think you're going?"

"Dad, we only got out of that compound because of Maddock," I explained, trying not to trip over my words. "I promised him I would rescue him."

My dad's face hardened and he opened his mouth, no doubt to shout, and I placed a hand over his mouth. "No, Dad, listen. Maddock gave me my magic, our means of escaping. I have to save him."

He wrenched his face out of my hand. "Not right now!" he snapped. "We just got away from them!"

"Exactly, Dad," I said, exasperated, the breathless feeling of wanting my plan to work making me feel annoyed. "I have to do it now, when Banwell would least expect me to."

"You're not going anywhere," my dad snarled, grabbing my hand. "Especially not alone!"

Anxiety filled my stomach. I had to get out of here. If I was caught here by the police, then the plan I had been forming would be ruined.

"Dad, we don't have time. I can't take you. You're injured, and you need to be here for Mom," I said, my voice breaking, "and the police. They'll have questions. I called them, and they thought I was a man." I tried not to take offense. "You can pretend that it was you who called, and tell them I am away at a boarding school in France or something. You'll have to find some way to explain Mom, but I need to go, now, before the police come and detain me. Please. Once the police get here, the news will get out, and then Banwell will be on his guard, I know it. Please, let me go."

"What makes you think you can free Maddock? You're just a kid," he protested. "*My* kid." He cleared his throat, his jaw working. "You're all I have." In the light of my phone flashlight, I saw tears well up in his eyes. "I can't lose you."

"I freed you and Mom, didn't I?" I asked, pleading. "Dad, please. I have to try. And I'll come back to you, and then . . . we'll start over."

My dad looked at me, myriad emotions on his face, then his grip on my hand relaxed.

"Take the electric car so you don't have to get gas, and you'll be less conspicuous. I know Santeri's been giving you secret lessons." He released me. "You better be careful, and come back."

"Thank you, Dad. What will you do about Mom and them?" My throat thickened as I gestured over my shoulder again.

My dad shook his head. "I'll think of something. What exactly did you tell the police?"

"I kept it very vague. I just said there were bad people attacking our house, and our address."

My dad was quiet for a moment, then nodded. "I can work with that. Good job." My dad's jaw worked for a moment, then he fixed me with a desperate look. "Mallory, please be careful. I can't lose you, too."

I hugged him, and then he shooed me away. "Go, go! Give Banwell hell!"

Sticking my gun back into the holster, I first ran to the vault where I grabbed one of my bags that contained the magical journals and other important items, then dashed out to the garages. Inside, I chose the silver-blue electric car, the least ostentatious car my family owned. I hopped in the driver seat.

As I drove around to the front of the house, I saw my dad hobbling away from the car we had stolen, heading toward the pond, my mother's form in his arms.

I sped down the driveway and pulled into the street, hyperventilating. I was turning a corner when I heard sirens and saw the distant lights of squad cars speeding up the street toward my house.

I took backstreets until I could no longer hear sirens, then pulled the car over to take a breath and think. My hands were shaking, so I gripped the supple leather of the steering wheel.

How was I going to rescue Maddock? My dad's questions were valid. I couldn't explain to him that it was just a feeling, a feeling that I would have the most luck trying to save Maddock *now*. Banwell wouldn't be expecting me to come for the leprechaun so soon after my escape, if he expected me to come at all.

But first I had to find where Banwell was keeping him.

I was no tech wizard, but the answer came fairly easily. The Krazy Ex app that Paz had showed me the night of our sleepover weeks ago surfaced in my mind. The app that could track any phone if you had the cell number of the person you wanted to stalk.

Maddock said he had his phone, even though it was just a cheap burner, but I hoped the app could still track him with that. Hopefully Banwell's men weren't able to find the phone on him and force him to give it up. I doubted it even entered their minds that he had a phone, and I was grateful for Maddock's foresight to keep the knowledge hidden from everyone, including the Sewer Fox.

After downloading the app, I opened it and growled as I had to go through an annoying questionnaire, answering questions of the gender and name of the person I was looking for, before it let me enter in the number of the phone I wanted to track. I typed in Maddock's phone number. As I pressed 'Locate,' a cartoon of a busty blonde lady with huge lips and crazy eyes popped up on the screen. "I'm Krazy Karol! I'll be helping you find that rascal that got away! Calculating location now!"

Wiping my sweating palms on my jeans, I closed my eyes and leaned my head against the leather headrest, taking deep, calming breaths and hoping against hope that this worked. If not, all that brave talk to my dad and the feeling of starting out on a rescue mission would dissolve into humiliation. I wouldn't know what to do. This was my only lifeline.

My phone dinged, and I looked at my screen with bated breath as Krazy Karol said, "I've found *Maddock* for you!"

A detailed map had come up, showing a satellite view of an insanely enormous castle-estate, more than three times the size of my parents' manor, on a lot filled with trees, gardens, several out-buildings, and stone terraces that had an incredible view of the Long Island Sound. The map said it was just outside of Greenwich, Connecticut. I had no doubt this was Banwell's estate home, and that Krazy Karol was correct about finding the right Maddock. The trip would take me about three hours. I looked at the clock on the touchscreen dash of the car. It was one in the morning right now.

If I drove fast, maybe I could get in and out with Maddock before Banwell even woke up. It might be wishful thinking, but it was all I had to go on.

Tapping the button to start navigation, Krazy Karol appeared in a cheerleader outfit complete with pom poms. With a dazzling smile, she cheered, "Go get him, sweetie! Work your magic to win him back!"

"I will, Krazy Karol," I affirmed in a whisper. Taking a deep breath, I turned on the car and accelerated down the street.

# Chapter Thirty

I bit my lip as I glanced between the pages of the magic journals with the dim light of my phone. Looking up, I stared through the windshield and down the street toward the giant, stone-walled property at the end of the avenue. I had made excellent time arriving, and the sky was still dark, but I could see graying near the horizon. I was running out of time.

I had to find a way not only to get into the house, but to also break the spell Banwell had over Maddock. Not much in the journals was helpful, because my ancestors didn't have to deal with stealing *back* a leprechaun from another magic user.

Perhaps I would just have to use the spell I'd used to break the connection between myself and Maddock. It was worth a try. When I found Maddock, maybe he would have an idea of what we could do to break his connection with Banwell. As a precaution, in case things went wrong, I could even bind him to me again, so that I could call him to me. Hopefully. I skimmed over the spell books, looking for useful spells, but I couldn't spend too much time studying. I had to get in there before the household woke up.

According to the Krazy Ex app, Maddock was at the far left corner of the house. Unfortunately, that wasn't very much information—that corner of the house was enormous. He wasn't moving around, so I assumed he was sleeping, hopefully just like everyone else. Reading back over how to summon fire and ice and how to put someone to sleep, I tried to commit them to memory. Okay.

I just had to act. To go. I had magic to help me. I could do this. *Strike now.*

Sliding my cell phone into the black hoodie I'd put on, I slipped out of the car and hurried down the street toward the property, trying to keep to the shadows as much as possible. A gigantic house like this would no doubt have security cameras.

Sure enough, as I got closer, I could see the red blinking lights of several small camera heads peeking up over the stone-and-steel-topped wall. I paused, glancing down along the rocky perimeter, realizing that getting over the wall that was double my height was my first problem. After a quick glance around, I spotted an enormous tree growing on the outside of the wall that had several of its thicker branches stretching over the iron spikes lining the top of the wall.

My way in.

Now I had to deal with the cameras.

Darting across the street, I hid behind the enormous tree, as it had a camera perched right next to the branches that crossed over the wall, no doubt to deter people from using that means of entering the property. Pulling up my magic that had been rapidly accumulating over the hours, I raised a hand toward the camera, feeling a little silly. Whispering the short words to call forth the element, ice began spider-webbing over the camera lens until the entire head was frosted over.

Breaking off the magic, I exhaled, then checked along the wall, making sure no other cameras were in sight before I began climbing the tree. When I reached the branch that crossed over the wall, I paused to take a breath. I would have to scoot my way down the branch, then make the mighty drop twelve feet to the ground. I hoped my skinny ankles could take the impact.

As I inched along the branch, I tried to shake off the chilling sensation of how exposed I was in the fairly bare tree, and the moment I cleared the wall, I swung my body off the branch so I dangled above the ground. Gritting my teeth, I took a short breath before letting go. I fell, and luckily landed in some relatively springy shrubs. Scrambling out of the bushes, I darted along the lightly wooded grounds until I came into view of Banwell's house.

The palatial mansion before me made me feel like my own extravagant house was a peasant's cottage. It was like those castles that modern royalty lived in, but somehow even bigger. Five stories at least, the white granite monstrosity sprawled across the grounds like a fat, lounging cat. I'd seen pictures of it online before, and had even read that you could take tours of it on certain days. I had even seen it in a popular movie about a rich spoiled brat that becomes a superhero. But seeing the sheer size and magnificence of it in person was a totally different experience. I had considered booking a tour as a possible way to save Maddock, but for some reason, doing it today felt right. But a tour would've been helpful.

The grounds alone went on as far as the eye could see, and it felt like the house took up half the lot. An enormous drive off to my right ran up to a wide set of stairs that led to the front double doors. The house had multiple wings and side entrances, and was rumored to have many secret passages and underground rooms. Maddock could be anywhere in that maze.

I froze in panic. This palace-fortress was the physical verification of Banwell's strength and authority, of what I was going up against, and I was half-tempted to go back to my car and drive back home, telling myself I had tried.

As I stared at the darkened estate, fear writhed in the pit of my stomach. How could I do this?

At that moment, my mother came to my mind. She had been scared too, but she had chosen selflessness while in the worst condition of her life, helping us all escape. Saving our lives in exchange for hers.

The man who lived here, who put on a mask of wealth and charity, who was in a better condition than most people could even dream of, was choosing evil, corruption, and hate with all he had. He was nothing more than a coward hiding behind his riches. A murderous villain. A monster gilded in greed. But he wasn't going to scare me anymore. He may have taken my mother, my safety, and my life from me, but I would get my friend back.

He wouldn't beat me again. Now I had magic, too.

My determination surged, though I resolved to remain careful and quiet. I would find Maddock in there, but not make a show of it: an outsmarted monster could still be dangerous if confronted.

Keeping my eyes peeled for security cameras, I ducked into a cultivated shrub maze, then I checked my phone. The app said he was on the other side of the castle-manor from where I was. Taking a deep breath, I tucked my phone in my pocket and darted to the shadow of the enormous estate. Sneaking along the walls, I came to the general area the Krazy Ex app said Maddock was. Maddock was no doubt inside, but he could be in an underground chamber for all I knew. And there were at least six floors in this wing of the mansion. He could be tucked away anywhere.

I turned the corner of the house and paused. Before me lay a vast stone terrace with multiple flights of shallow steps leading to the grounds, with grassy lawns that stretched to the Long Island Sound beyond. I bit my lip as I considered the granite walls.

How was I going to get inside? No doubt all windows and doors were armed with alarms, but maybe I could disengage one with magic. As I debated climbing up the terrace to try the doors or a window, an outside light above the terrace flicked on.

I dove into the nearest clump of flowering bushes and peered out just as a door—recessed under the stone terrace and partly hidden by shrubs—opened, and a troupe of men with rakes and tree trimmers filed out. The last man, busy pushing a wheelbarrow, left the door ajar as they traipsed out into the grounds. I stared at the open, hidden door, my mouth slack.

No.

There's no way I was this lucky. Was I?

I darted toward the door and slipped inside. The room was basically an immense garden shed full of tools, carriage lanterns, stacks of bagged soil, lounge chairs, some statues, and enormous urns. In the dim light, I saw a door that led to a hallway. I prayed that it connected to the house.

Ignoring the fluttering butterflies in my stomach, I crept up the short set of stairs at the end of the hall and came up into a plainly decorated hallway. I was in.

To consider my next move, I ducked into a cracked doorway that turned out to be a sort of utility closet. Shutting and locking the door, I opened my phone to the Krazy Ex app. I was standing right on top of the pulsing red location indicator. Maddock had to be close.

I bit my lip. The only thing I could do was go around searching rooms and try to avoid detection until I found him. I glowered at the vagueness of his location. The creators of this app really wanted to put the "stalk" in stalker.

Silencing my phone, I took a deep breath and unlocked the door. Peering down the hallway, I made my way down to the next door and opened it. A bathroom. Beside the bathroom, another hallway was shadowed in darkness, and an elevator was recessed into the wall opposite the bathroom. Beside that was another door. I tried it, and it revealed a fire stairwell. I stepped inside and looked upward. I could see the stairs winding up and up and up to the very top of the house. I groaned inwardly. There were a lot of stairs.

Not wanting to get caught because I was too lazy to climb some steps, I hurried up the first flight to the next floor. This floor was more opulently decorated than the one downstairs, and I froze as I heard people's voices coming from somewhere.

No, no, no!

People were awake. I hoped that it was just the housekeepers, but I couldn't be too sure. It was Saturday morning, so I could only pray that Banwell and his family slept in. I hurried away from where I thought the voices were coming from, and, looking into an open door of a darkened room, I eased myself inside.

The voices were getting louder, and I slipped behind the door, peering through the crack as two women dressed in matching dark gray, button-down dress uniforms, with aprons around their waists, came into view. Each carried a stack of linens. Chatting in low voices, they passed my door, then stopped beside the elevator.

"Dennis said they're overhauling the south wing basement to turn it into some kind of laboratory," one of the women said.

"What for?" the second woman replied.

I heard the chime of an elevator opening.

"No idea. He wouldn't say. He just told me to get back to work."

"It's probably for whatever Mr. Banwell has spent so much time in Scotland for—" The voices were cut off as the elevator doors closed, and the floor plunged into silence again. I peeked out, then hurried down the hall, checking all doors in the wing, seeing countless numbers of sitting rooms, spare bedrooms, bathrooms, and empty rooms that seemed to have no function.

I made my way to the next floor, constantly checking to make sure I was in the same vicinity that the indicator dot said Maddock was.

I bit back a grunt of irritation. I felt like I was just wandering around. I had tried using my magic to feel for Maddock, but I couldn't feel anything. Was Maddock actually here? Or did Banwell find his phone and set a trap for me? I considered the possibility as I peered into another superfluous room.

Well, I wouldn't run away when there was even a chance to save Maddock. I would stay here until I found him, or I was caught.

That thought made me pause as I entered into yet another empty bathroom complete with a jetted tub, shower, and enormous vanity. I shut the door behind me, taking a moment to rest behind a closed door and consider.

Why *hadn't* I been caught yet?

Something strange was going on. I had been able to sneak over the wall no problem, reach the house, get *into* the house by some miracle, and had been wandering around for at least twenty minutes with no apparent tripping of alarms. I knew there were cameras and security—how could there not be? There were countless priceless heirlooms in the limitless number of stupid rooms in this house. Even by my standards of wealth, all of this was ridiculous. There was a whole army of people that worked here. How had I not been seen or stopped by one of them yet?

Something told me this was more than magic. I reflected on my feeling of coming to Banwell's house *today*. It seemed so out of place, the timing so bizarre, and yet I couldn't shake the feeling of *rightness* I'd had when I decided to come save Maddock. And then there was the door the gardeners had opened for me right when I needed it to. And how I'd remained undetected this whole time.

Pulling out Maddock's note I'd transferred from my ruined jumpsuit to my jean's pocket back at the vault, I glanced over it. I understood that he hadn't wanted information about his gift falling into HAMMA's hands, but I was still annoyed that Maddock hadn't been more clear on what this leprechaun gift was. Leprechauns were known for hoarding gold and instantaneous transportation, and they were thought to be lucky, which was what made them ridiculously difficult to catch.

It wasn't possible that whatever Maddock had given me was linked to *luck*, was it? Was luck something that could be transferred to someone? I shook my head. I would dwell on all this later. I was being stupid just standing here thinking when I could be searching. Maddock had all the answers I needed. I continued my room search down the hall.

Just as I decided to go back to the stairwell and head up to the next floor, I heard laughing behind me, and I whirled, dancing around in place, looking for somewhere to hide. I was just trying to force open a locked door when two bleary-eyed children, dressed in pajamas, came running around the corner into the hallway where I stood. A few moments later, a young woman a few years older than me came around the corner, laughing with a, "Gotcha! I know you're excited, but you need to get ready to go to the jet—" She stopped when she saw me standing there. With a frown, she opened her mouth to speak but the little girl spoke first.

"Hello!" the little girl, who looked no more than five, called. The little boy, about nine, stopped and stared at me, a frown on his face.

I quickly stepped away from the door and waved. "Hi!"

The three were all beautiful, with soft brown skin and curly hair, and looked like carbon copies of one another. Siblings.

They stayed standing where they had stopped, staring at me.

"Who are you?" the little girl asked, as the little boy eased himself between me and the two girls. I smiled, trying to put on a cheerful, nonthreatening air.

"I'm happy to see you! What are your names?" I asked, trying not to show any panic. Were these Banwell's kids? They had to be. I knew designer clothes when I saw them.

"Do you work for my daddy?" the little girl asked, the older girl and boy still staring at me, unsure.

"Yep, I sure do!" I smiled, my heart thundering in my chest. "But your house is *so* big and pretty that I got lost! Is that silly or what?" I asked, raising my shoulders in a question, and I felt my face flush in embarrassment. I was definitely overplaying this;

that eighteen-year-old for sure knew I was being way too obvious. However, the little girl grinned, and I saw the two older siblings relax a little bit.

"Do you like my house?" the little girl asked, and I nodded.

"It is the prettiest castle I've ever been in! Are you a princess?" I asked, starting to feel sweat forming under my hoodie. I had to find a way to get away quickly and naturally, without these kids following me, and without them snitching on me. I was at a complete loss, and it was a struggle just to keep the strained smile on my face.

The little girl giggled and nodded.

"Such a pretty princess!" I rasped, coughing to clear my throat. "Do you know how I can get back down—"

"Imani! Kellan! Where are you? We need to dress you!" A woman's voice called. My heart raced. No.

A woman dressed in a more elegant housekeeper's dress than the two ladies I saw earlier came around the corner. She stopped right beside the children, giving me an accusing stare. "Who are you? What are you doing?"

"Hi, hey," I stammered, my mouth going dry as I rubbed my palms on my jeans. "Sorry, it's . . . it's my first day, and," I gestured around the hallway, "this place is so big, I—I got turned around."

"Why aren't you in uniform?" the woman asked, putting a protective hand on the little boy's shoulder and sharing a glance with the young woman.

"I'm sorry," I said, my mind scrambling and latching onto the conversation I'd overheard from the two housemaids. "Dennis told me where to go, but he wasn't very clear. Plus I don't know the house yet."

"Dennis?" the woman asked, her expression relaxing.

I nodded, taking a ragged breath. Could I really pull this off?

"Well, okay. I can—" the woman began, then I saw her eyes shift to something behind me just as the little girl shouted, "Daddy!"

"Oh, Mr. Banwell," the housekeeper blustered as the girl ran past me.

The bottom dropped out of my stomach, leaving it hollow as I stood, frozen.

So much for the luck theory.

"Mrs. Packer, is this young lady our new hire?" a male voice behind me said, and the woman before me gave a small nod. I slowly turned around, knowing running would do no good.

Mr. Banwell, dressed in casual khaki slacks and a light green polo shirt, was staring at me. His expression relayed no surprise in seeing me standing there, but I could feel some sort of frenetic energy coming off of him as he bent down and scooped up his daughter.

"I suppose she must be," the housekeeper laughed. "Otherwise we would have a major problem with our security."

"Yes, indeed we would," Mr. Banwell said, his eyes hardened shards of ice as he hugged his daughter to him, locking stares with me.

I stood my ground, staring back, though I felt like vomiting. The sweat under my hoodie had turned cold, the muscles in my legs spasming.

Banwell pressed a kiss to the little girl's cheek, then set her down.

"Go with Kellan and Ahni. I have business to attend to." His eyes snapped to me. "I can take her to where she belongs, Mrs. Packer," Mr. Banwell said, his smile easy as he held out a beckoning hand to me. I didn't move, but kept my eyes locked on Banwell's.

"I can take her, Dad," the young woman said, but Banwell looked at her, his face softening.

"No, you need to keep an eye on these rascal siblings of yours, Ahni," he replied, giving her a smile. "Help them get ready to go to the jet. We wouldn't want to miss our vacation."

"Mr. Banwell," Mrs. Packer said behind me, "you shouldn't have to do that, I'll—"

"No, no, I insist," Banwell said, stepping forward and scooping an arm around my shoulders. "I take pleasure in knowing the ins and outs of my household." He laughed as he guided me away, and as we turned a corner, he then whispered into my ear, "And how *you* seem to know them, too." The pointed squeeze he gave my shoulder stung with unnatural heat.

# Chapter Thirty-One

When we entered the elevator, he pushed the sixth level, never taking his iron grip off me as we ascended. His breathing was ragged and harsh as we stood silent in that gilded box, and fear pricked at my gut.

"Something's different about you, young lady. Magic," he said, his voice faint as the elevator door opened and I was pushed forward out into the hallway.

Stumbling, I kept my feet and turned to see Banwell press something on his phone, then tuck it away and gesture for me to go down the hall that ended in a giant office with a commanding view of the Sound.

I entered the office that was well decorated with live plants, statues, masks, and other foreign artifacts that lined the walls and floor, with built-in bookcases full of books filling one side of the room. Banwell pushed me into a chair and stood over me, the cracks in his calm façade finally showing through as he stood over me, his hands shaking as he pointed at me.

"How . . . *how* did you get in here?" he commanded, his voice juddering, his face purple, his eyes bulging. "How . . . how *dare* you—I demand to know! The only reason I haven't blasted you into oblivion is—I need to know how you got in here—How dare you—HOW?" he shouted.

Despite how erratic and scary he was acting, I felt brave enough to spit back, "I demand to know where Maddock is."

Banwell stared at me, his jaw muscles working for a moment, then he looked up past me, and gave a shaky, surprised laugh.

"That's why you've come? For that stupid *leprechaun*?" His breathy laughter strengthened to a chuckle, and he ran a hand through his hair. Still laughing and shaking his head, he went and threw himself into the leather chair behind his desk, looking strangely relieved. "Whew, and here I was thinking you had come to hurt my family."

"*What?*" I shouted, somewhat insulted that he thought I would do something like that. "I would *never* do that. I am nothing like you!" I snapped, the memories of the last several days, and the horrors we experienced, flooding into my mind. "You're a murderer! You murdered my mom!" My voice broke on the last word, and I looked away, straining to keep the burning sensation in my throat from bringing up tears.

He was quiet for a moment, and when I looked back up at him, he was frowning.

"I heard Grace was killed. Though I don't see how you can blame me. I wasn't holding the club," he said, looking offended at my accusation, and I felt my stomach curdle. "Besides, I can't control everything my followers do."

"How dare you say her name!" I seethed, digging my nails into the fine wooden arms of the chair I sat in.

"I don't see how you can blame me," he repeated.

Rage boiled inside me, heat burning down to my fingers, and I ripped the wooden arm of the chair out of its joint, wood splintering, and hurled the jagged wooden arm at him. He waved it away with an almost lazy flick of his hand, a small smile growing on his face.

"Cute," he replied, unfazed at my attack or the fact that I'd ruined his chair. "But now I need to know how you got in here, so I know who to *terminate*."

I ignored the way he emphasized the last word. I had no doubt he would actually kill someone over my outwitting him.

"Where's Maddock?" I demanded, evading his question again, my face flushed from fury and from embarrassment over his reaction to my failed attack. Banwell stared at me, his eyes narrowed, and I tensed, waiting for the blast of magic that was sure to come from this deranged man for trespassing into his sanctuary.

It didn't come.

Maddock appeared instantly beside Banwell's desk. He looked pale and wan, like he was recovering from a bad bout of flu.

"Maddock!" I cried, standing up from my chair.

"Not so fast," Banwell demanded, also standing and silencing his cell phone that had begun ringing. "Now, I feel like I'm being rather generous by letting you see your old pet again, even though you've come into my house and threatened my family," he said, his tone hard.

"Don't like how it feels, huh?" I spat at him, my eyes flicking between Banwell and Maddock, who seemed to be avoiding eye contact with me.

Banwell smiled again. I suppressed a shiver.

"But," he continued as if I hadn't spoken. "I assure you, that your attempt has been in vain. He's mine forever, and the only reason I summoned him here was to assure you of that fact before I throw you back to HAMMA. After you tell me how the hell you got into my house. I didn't get any alerts on my phone, no calls from my security people about any sort of anomalies, which I get even if a strange squirrel crosses the lawn, but your magic isn't powerful enough to outwit my security. And I have a feeling I wouldn't have known you were here had I not seen you with my own eyes. How did you do it?"

I looked at Banwell, another revelation hitting me.

Maybe I *was* lucky.

I was captured by Banwell, but in doing so, it brought me straight to Maddock. I tried to catch Maddock's eye, the unspoken question in my mind, praying for some sort of confirmation from the sickly looking leprechaun, but he just stared ahead, not moving; no smile, no mischievous wink.

Well, there was only one way to find out.

Staring at Banwell, I focused my energy toward Maddock and began chanting the spell of severing bonds as quickly as I could, hoping it would be enough to sever Maddock's hold from Banwell. Banwell watched me, an amused expression on his face, and when I finished my spell, he shook his head.

"You didn't let me finish. You're a very rude young lady," Banwell drawled. "Spoken spell bonds can be broken by other spells, as

I told you back at my office. I've already commissioned his tattoo to be made. You won't ever be able to break him free, because his binding is physical, no messy spells draining me or able to be broken by someone else, and you won't be able to get anywhere near him, because I control where he comes and goes."

Maddock stepped forward and pulled down his shirt collar, revealing a shaved circle in his chest hair, and the same circular tattoo of a Celtic cross the Sewer Fox had, right over his heart, the skin still red, blotchy, and raw.

My stomach fell into my shoes as I stared at the dark, braided ink prominent on Maddock's hairy chest.

With all that had happened in the last week, I had forgotten all about the tattoo I had seen on the Fox.

"Now, maybe this little demonstration will help you realize nothing can be done for your friend. If you tell me how you got in here and then leave immediately without hurting anyone in my family, I will let you and your family go in peace." Banwell's phone went off, and he quickly silenced it with an annoyed sound, not taking his eyes off of me.

"You will, huh?" I looked at Banwell, my resolve dropping. "How generous, seeing as how you already killed half of my family." I put my hands on my hips, considering, and I felt the gun belt there. Maybe my luck wasn't out yet.

I whipped my gun out, pointing it at Banwell. "Take the tattoo off of him. Set him free," I demanded, surprised at how strong and clear my voice sounded.

Banwell's face hardened, and he stared me in the eye. "You know I can stop any bullet you send at me, right?" The air around him shimmered, and I felt a sudden blast of magic surround him as he was instantly encased inside a magical shield. "Pulling that trigger on me won't make any difference except increasing my anger. Now tell me, how did you get in here to threaten my family?"

"Take it off of him," I demanded, my mind reeling as I tried to think of my next move.

Banwell's phone went off again, and again he silenced it.

"Lass," Maddock spoke, his voice hoarse and slow. "Leave, before you make another stupid mistake."

I flicked my eyes to Maddock, who wasn't quite staring at me, and I didn't know if it was really Maddock or if Banwell was manipulating him.

I quickly looked back to Banwell, afraid that he would attack me while I was distracted listening to Maddock. Banwell was still standing behind his desk, his eyes hard, watching me.

Chills erupted down my spine.

Something about this whole meeting was not making sense.

"Why haven't you used magic to stop me or take my gun away yet?" I demanded.

Banwell sighed as if annoyed, but I could hear an undercurrent of strain. "Because I don't want a fuss. My entire family is here for a visit, and I don't want them to know about you, or magic, or that gun in your hands. For the last time, you will tell me how you got in here. I won't ask again."

Somehow, I knew telling him how I got in wouldn't satisfy him. *'I got lucky'* was not a person or thing he could *terminate*. He would just think I was lying.

"Oh, you don't want your family to know about your evil, murderous ways, huh?" I said, still trying to think of something to do to get out of this. Alive. A crazy, dangerous idea came into my mind.

I tried to push it away, but it persisted. I glanced at Maddock again, then back at Banwell. He could strike me down at any moment. I had to act.

"I said, take the tattoo off of him," I demanded, though I knew Banwell never, ever would. The fear continued to stay my trembling hand. I glanced at Maddock. I needed him to move. If I could just provoke Banwell enough . . . "If you attack me with magic, I'll use it right back," I snapped, making my tone as threatening as I could muster, "Then we'll see how much your family hears."

Alarm blinked on Banwell's face, but was quickly masked by amusement. "Well, then, I best not use any magic against you." Banwell clicked his fingers, and Maddock pivoted into an attack stance, his right shoulder now pointing toward me as he planted his feet. He raised his fists. "Let's see how you fare against your 'friend.'"

I saw fear flicker behind the dead look in Maddock's eyes, and panic flared in my chest. I'd seen Maddock in action, and what happened to his enemies. But I'd gotten what I wanted, and I ground out the anxiety in my chest. This wasn't over yet.

"Now, unless you want to be killed by your leprechaun, you will put that gun down and tell me how you got in here, NOW!" Banwell roared.

I exhaled, the shaky grip on my gun steadying. One thing was going in my favor at least: Maddock had moved into the perfect position. "Just lucky, I guess." I turned the gun onto Maddock and pulled the trigger.

As the gun kicked in my hands, the bullet struck the leprechaun, blood spraying onto the floor-to-ceiling window behind him, the bullet lodging into the bullet proof glass. Maddock staggered backwards, an agonized roar bursting from his lips before he hunched over in pain.

As one, all three of us turned our eyes to where the bullet hit the leprechaun.

With fumbling, groping hands, Maddock pulled his shirt away, revealing a bloody gash that traveled across part of his chest, exiting shallowly out his pectoral muscle where the binding tattoo was, mutilating the once-perfect ink. Blood began gushing from the wound.

Maddock looked up at me, shock filling his face. Then, he disappeared.

I took a small, sharp breath. *I'm lucky, I'm lucky, please, I'm lucky. Maddock isn't dead. I didn't kill him. His body would've remained if I'd killed him, he wouldn't have disappeared. He's free. Please say I'm lucky.*

Banwell's phone went off, and he didn't even bother to mute the ringing before it stopped as he stared in mute disbelief at the place Maddock had just been standing.

There was another five full seconds of silence as Banwell stared at the blood-spattered window, and then he erupted.

With a wordless roar, the room seemed to explode in light and wind. There was a smashing sound as I was thrown off my feet and thrown into the doorframe behind me, the back of my head cracking against the wood. Head singing in pain, with stars dancing across my sight, I tried to orient myself as the ringing noise in my ears died down. I struggled to prop myself up as Banwell stomped toward me, fury flushing his face.

"*What did you just do?*" he bellowed.

"It's more like what you didn't do," I panted, trying to scoot away, but I couldn't get around the doorframe without it looking like I was actively trying to get away. "You didn't even bother to put a protective shield around your *pet*." I looked up to see Banwell standing over my gun where I had dropped it on the carpet during the explosion. Banwell was shaking with unsuppressed rage.

*"Did you just kill my leprechaun?"* he bellowed as I sat up. Head still throbbing, I stared up into the purple face of one of the most powerful men in the world. And I wasn't afraid. Not even a little bit.

"No, I didn't kill him," I said, coughing, trying to catch my breath. "I freed him." I gave him the snarkiest grin I could muster. "Lucky shot, huh?" From somewhere down the hall, I heard the pinging of the elevator, but my attention was drawn to Banwell as he stooped down, picked up my fallen gun, and pointed it at me. My smile vanished.

"Well, I'm afraid your luck has run out," he said, his eyes wild, his breathing harsh. "You've made your last mistake."

"Sir!" a voice called, and I heard running feet. "Sir!"

"What?" Banwell roared, glancing up at the approaching footfalls. "What? I'm fine! I've got it under control!"

Two men came to a stop beside my head in the office doorway, panting.

"Sir, you haven't been answering your phone—"

"If it's Mendoza, tell him I said absolutely *no* hybrids!" Banwell snarled.

"No, it's not Mr. Mendoza. Scotland's called. We've found it, sir. They say they've *actually* found the island."

It took less than a second for what the man had said to register on Banwell's face. The rage and murder in Banwell's eyes dissipated as he lowered the gun, staring over me at the men. I sat there, breathless as I stared up between the three men, my heart nearly bursting as it battered against my ribs.

"Are you sure?" Banwell asked, seemingly oblivious to me as I lay slumped against the wall. The men nodded.

Banwell's eyes snapped to me, making me physically jump, and then he clicked his fingers at one of the men.

"Mason, take her down to the security room," Banwell said, handing the man my gun. "I'll be down in a moment to deal with her. Amir, I'll need you to take notes. And Mason," Banwell said as I was heaved to my feet. "Don't take the elevator or the main stairs." Mason nodded and pulled me from the office, the double doors slamming behind us as I was marched down to the fire stairwell I had originally used.

"Move," Mason barked. "And don't even think about screaming."

I gave him a scathing look. Did he think I wanted more people—people who could potentially stop me—to know I was here?

"Of course," the man muttered under his breath, "She had to break in today of all days, when the security system has been bugging out on us. I better not have to be the one to tell Banwell . . ." He clutched my upper shoulder harder and forced me down the first flight. As he turned me to go down the next flight, he clenched my arm so tightly that my hand went numb.

"You're hurting me," I snapped, pulling against his grip.

It happened so quickly I almost didn't follow what came next. Mason was so busy snarling at me, trying to get my arm back in his grasp, that he misstepped and his heel slipped on the edge of the stair. As he fell backward, he grabbed onto me as if he believed I could hold his falling weight, but I crumpled like a paper ladder, my legs splayed across the stairs. I didn't fall down the stairs, but simply sat down hard on the top step as he tried to right himself and find his footing. My leg was extended right where he tried to step. I cried out in pain as he stomped down on my shin with his full weight, and I yanked my leg out from under him.

With a garbled cry, Mason dropped my gun straight into my lap as he sailed head-first down the stairs. I watched, open-mouthed, as he toppled down the entire flight of steps. He landed just shy of tumbling down the next flight, where he lay in a contorted heap.

I stared, dumbfounded, at his motionless body for two heartbeats before I was up and running.

Shoving the gun into its holster, I sailed down the stairs, leapt over Mason's still form, and continued charging down the stairway.

I ran as I had never run before, nearly tripping multiple times as I thundered down the steps, only one objective on my mind: get out of this house alive.

I came to the end of the stairwell and burst into the servant hall. I knew the way I came in was going to be my best exit. I tore down the corridor and through a cluster of several housemaids who were busy chatting. They cried out as I shoved past them, running for the garden cellar stairs, ignoring the frightened yelling. I surged down into the gardener's cellar, burst out the hidden door, and sprinted across the lawn.

My breathing was ragged and my muscles were screaming as I made my way back across the grounds the way I had come. The sun was now up, drenching the absolutely gorgeous grounds in the buttery sunshine of late spring.

But I didn't appreciate any of it. The sunlight was good because I could see my destination better, but it was terrible because people could see *me*, dashing like a madwoman across the perfectly manicured estate. Any moment I expected a tackle from behind or a bullet through my head, but nothing happened as I darted through the trees toward the wall.

A wall, I realized, that I had to get over without the help of a climbing tree. As I neared the barrier, I gathered all my strength and magic, and when I got within a few feet of it, I jumped. Using my magic, I blasted myself skyward so quickly that my stomach leapt into my throat. I vaulted over the stone wall with several feet to spare, and because of my exuberance, I completely flipped head-over-feet, limbs flailing, before I started plummeting back to the ground.

Thankfully I righted myself just before hitting the ground. I landed feet first before the momentum of my landing sprung me forward, my body slamming into the grass on the other side of the wall. The wind threatened to leave my lungs, but I was able to inhale and push myself to my feet.

No alarms rang out, no shouts or sounds of pursuit followed me as I got to my feet, but I didn't stop running. Tearing down the street, I saw my car, now visible in the sunlight, and pressed the *start engine* button on the key fob as I slid to the door. The car roared to life as I dove into the front seat, yanked the gear shift into drive, and spun the car around before stomping on the gas and peeling down the street, my mind concentrating on just driving and breathing.

I drove for ten minutes before I allowed relief to seep into me.

Had I really done it? Had I freed Maddock and gotten out of there? Was I really that lucky?

I began laughing. Laughing so hard I was screaming and whooping and slamming my hands on the steering wheel.

"Will you cut that out? You're giving me a headache," a voice snapped from behind me, and the breath whooshed out of me as I ran my car up onto the sidewalk, nearly hitting a fire hydrant.

"Maddock!" I screamed, craning my body to look into the backseat after I'd righted my vehicle. Maddock sagged against the backseat, sweat beading his face, a bloody rag pressed against his shoulder.

"Aye, it's me. *Watch the road*!" Maddock shouted. I whipped to face forward again, jerking the steering wheel to get back onto the correct side of the street. Thankfully it was still early morning, and there wasn't much traffic.

"What are you doing here?" I squealed, then felt the blood drain from my face. "Wait. You're really free, right? You're not here on Banwell's orders to kill me, are you?" I asked, the thought sending ice through my veins as my eyes darted between the road and the sickly leprechaun reflected in my rearview mirror.

"If I were, you'd be dead already," Maddock said, snorting.

"Well, you almost killed me just now," I snapped, still wary. "Why did you do that to me?"

"Because you *shot me*," he retorted. "I'll live, thanks for asking."

"And I freed you, you're welcome," I returned, still trying to calm my heart. "So, you're really not here to kill me?" I asked.

Maddock held up a hand. "I swear."

"Prove it!" I demanded. I'd been burned before with how easily I trusted those around me, and I wasn't about to push my luck now. Especially when I was just starting to believe I had it.

"How?" he asked, his tone scathing as he inspected his bullet wound.

"Well, I'm pretty sure Banwell would make it so you could only obey him, right? Go out and bring me back . . . a stick."

I glanced in the rearview mirror and saw Maddock staring, dead-pan, into the mirror back at me. "Lass, I'm not going to go gallivanting around the forest to find you a *stick* so that you can feel better about me being here. If I was still working for Banwell, you'd be dead or out cold by now, or I would try to warn you somehow. But I'm not. I'm telling you the truth. I'm perfectly free. Your little stunt with the bullet did the trick. Need more proof?" He opened his shirt to flash the bloody bullet wound at me, and I screamed and looked away from the mirror.

"No! Don't! I don't want to see that! It's so gross!" I squealed, glancing back into the mirror again in horrified fascination.

"You're the one who caused it!" Maddock replied, incredulous. "But look." He splayed his fingers around the bloody gash. "You can see exactly where the bullet tore away the flesh containing the edges of the tattoo," he observed, sounding like he was studying an interesting specimen. "Brilliant work, by the way. I was forbidden to touch my tattoo in any way, there was no way I could break it myself, or even ask someone to touch me. Banwell is so stupid. He had no idea you were coming for me. Nice work. Even though you *shot me*."

"Thanks," I said, ignoring his accusing look. "But I'm still worried that you're tricking me." I would've stopped the car to continue speaking with him, but I was still paranoid that I was being followed, so I continued driving. "And how do I know Banwell didn't put any other type of magical restraint spells on you?"

"Because he's an arrogant gombeen and he thought this tattoo was all he needed, as binding spells can use up a lot of magic. He's very stingy."

When I continued to frown, Maddock exhaled in a world-weary way.

"Fine. Here, I'll give you something better than a stick. Something even Banwell couldn't get from me." A small shower of gold nuggets fell into the front seat. I glanced at the small pile of gleaming nuggets and snorted.

"Oh right, like you're going to be giving that to me," I snorted. "The second I put it in my pocket, you'll just lift it back."

"Nope, I swear," Maddock said, raising his right hand. "Consider it a gift."

"A 'Welcome To Death' gift?" I demanded, glaring at him through the mirror. He rolled his eyes.

"I'm telling you, I'm not here to kill you. Besides, that gold belongs—belonged—to Houston Banwell."

"*What?*" I gasped, fear curling around my heart again.

"Remember when you asked me how I've never run out of gold?"

"Yeah, and you told me to mind my business . . ."

"That's because we weren't friends then. As another token of goodwill, I'll tell you my secret. I've never run out of gold, because your ancestors used to use me to . . . erm, rob banks."

"*What?*" I shrieked, accidentally stomping the gas, the engine roaring for a brief moment before I took my foot off the pedal completely. I gripped the steering wheel to keep from swerving around the road as I glanced back at Maddock.

"They only had me do it the first century or so," he said, his tone placating. "Nothing recent. Neither your parents nor your grandparents ever did it, because I think your generation is the most wealthy of all your lineage due to smart investments. And, well, I didn't steal just from banks. I also went after other wealthy people who kept their gold in home vaults like yours."

My mind immediately went to Banwell again. "Do you think he used the Fox to jump into our vault and steal money from us?" I gulped.

Maddock shrugged. "He might've tried, but I doubt it entered his mind to do it. He earns millions a day just by his enterprise alone; he doesn't need to steal. Besides, your family put magical safeguards around your vault to stop anyone from doing just that. I would know. I tried."

"You tried to break into our family vault?" I demanded, glaring into the mirror.

"Well, yeah. I knew you had one, and I wanted some of my gold back, so when we were at the house, just starting our adventure, I might've peeked around your property, but I couldn't get into any vault. There were similar safeguards like my Celtic crosses, and other spells to keep anyone from magically entering. Banwell did not have such safeguards on one of his home vaults. The gobshite," he cackled. "What I just gave you was a mere drop of what I just took from him."

"Oh great, now he's going to be raring to come after us," I cried. "You seriously took time out of your escape to make a pit stop at his vault? What were you thinking? If there's one thing he loves more than his magical power, it's his money!"

"He cares for his family, too," Maddock pointed out, his tone thoughtful.

"Wow, grant him a good citizen award," I groused.

"Trust me, lass, he won't miss it. This is just a drop in the bucket for him. He makes seventy times what your family makes."

I began laughing again, choking on the air through my wild giggling. "You really just stole a fortune from him?" I gasped.

"Did I ever," he chortled. "Hopefully now you trust that I'm not here to kill you. Besides, you'd be pretty well-matched against me now."

My laughter slowed as his words registered in my brain. "What do you mean . . . Oh, right! Yeah, what did you do to me?" I asked, my heart refusing to still as I kept a suspicious eye on him.

"We'll talk about that once you pull into a drive-through and get me as many combo meals as you can afford," Maddock said, fixing me with a stern look through the rearview mirror.

"Um, shouldn't you go to the hospital or something?" I asked, looking to where he was pressing the rag to his shoulder. "You're bleeding all over my dad's car."

"And you ruined my good jacket, you mog. Besides, I've got myself pretty well patched up now," Maddock said, ignoring my skeptical glance into the mirror. "Food first, then answers."

"Deal." I was feeling pretty ravenous myself.

# Chapter Thirty-Two

We pulled into a large, deserted park and sat at a picnic table concealed by bushes and trees, the both of us enjoying the fresh breeze. Maddock wasn't the only one who had been trapped. I couldn't believe this time yesterday I'd been imprisoned, tortured, and starving. The morning was so beautiful, so freeing that I just sat quietly, drinking in the sunshine as I munched my food, occasionally wiping away a stray tear.

After stuffing at least ten burgers into his mouth, Maddock's color had come back into his face. Surprisingly, his bleeding had stopped.

"Bullet went right through. Shallow and clean. Bandaged it fairly easily," he said. "Even though you shot me so close to my heart!"

"I wasn't worried," I retorted, wiping my mouth. "I knew you didn't have a heart to worry about hitting."

Maddock wagged a finger and grinned at me through a bite of burger, and I grimaced at the mashed meat, tomato, and bun that oozed through his teeth.

"Gross," I complained.

He swallowed, then looked at me. "So, you have questions?"

"Uh, *yeah*," I exclaimed, "like what did you actually *do* to me?"

Maddock held up his hand again, as he had taken another enormous bite, and I rolled my eyes as I waited for him to wash it down with several handfuls of fries and long slurps of his drink.

"You're a leprekin now," he said, wiping his mouth.

Bored while waiting for him to finish eating, I'd been so engrossed in running my fingers over the words *Taylor loves Tamara* carved into the picnic table that I didn't catch what he'd said. I looked up. "What?"

"I made you a leprekin," Maddock repeated. "I gave you the power of the leprechauns."

After a pause, I snorted, and he stared at me.

"What's so funny, lass?" he asked, his eyes narrowed.

"Sorry," I coughed, struggling to regain my composure. "Go on."

"This power of the leprechauns," he continued, glaring at me as if daring me to make another derisive sound, "Saved your life, I'll have you know."

I sobered a little. "You're right. I'm sorry. It's just that . . ." I struggled against a smile, "The 'power of the leprechauns?' Am I going to shrink? Will I become a gold miser now?" I asked, still feeling the giddy effects of our escape.

He stared at me for a moment, not speaking, then planted a finger on the table. "I can't believe I chose to bestow my gift on someone of your mental capacity. Didn't you hear me explain what it was I gave you? You are now armed with something even magicians cannot copy. They can try, but the results are far inferior. Don't make me regret giving this to you, lass. You're now probably one of the most powerful beings in the world. The *world*, lass."

I stopped smiling. "What do you mean?"

"You now can do everything a leprechaun can do. You can teleport around with ease, like us. You are human so you can use magic, but most important of all, you are lucky. And not just the, 'wow, my name was drawn for a free sandwich' lucky."

"Lucky?" I breathed. So it was luck.

"Lass, leprekins are legendarily lucky. They get it from us leprechauns. While we have a little luck, something happens when we transfer our powers to humans. The luck expands and becomes twenty times as powerful as when we have it. It's not fair," he grumbled, "Just like how we can't use magic to cast whatever spells we like, either, but it's how we're built. Unless we become a warped witch. But that's neither here nor there at the moment."

I frowned, trying to grasp what he was saying. "So, I've been using this luck spell you gave me—"

Maddock slapped a hand over his face.

"Lass, it's not a luck *spell!* It's changed your entire being! The Luck of the Irish, the Luck of the Leprechauns, the Power of the Leprechauns! It's all the same, and all very powerful. You are no longer human, not quite leprechaun, but you can do everything we can. You're one of us now, in all but blood and height. And since you're human, who knows what other talents you'll acquire. The gift reacts differently with everyone."

I was quiet, trying to process everything.

"You are now a very lucky young lady," Maddock continued. "But be aware, your circumstances may not seem lucky at times. Just know that whatever happens will guide you to a lucky outcome. For the most part."

We were silent for a moment as I tried to grasp the implications of what he was saying, then Maddock began chortling.

"What?" I asked, my train of thought broken.

"Did you know that the name *Mallory* literally means 'unlucky'? Now that's funny." He continued laughing, despite my flat stare. "I guess I lifted that curse from you!"

"Wait, is that what you and the Fox were laughing about before? You said something like, 'that's what you get with girls named Mallory,' or something, then you started laughing?" I demanded.

He nodded, chuckling.

"Charming. So, how did you give me this transformation?" I asked, annoyed.

Still laughing, Maddock stuffed the rest of his last burger into his mouth, then sighed.

"I'm not exactly sure. Like I said, we can't cast *spells,* per se, but this isn't really like that. It's more instinctual magic, more like part of us, like how I can disappear and reappear, or how mandagots can change shapes, or naiads can sever one of their own from their lake as banishment." He shrugged. "It's just something we can do, though it's very rare, even among our kind. I doubt even Banwell has heard of it. No way Pat would ever tell him about it. And Banwell is a fool to think we cannot offer more than just gold, and robotic service once our gold has disappeared," Maddock growled, suddenly angry. "That arrogant human prides himself on knowing magic, but he doesn't understand the fundamentals of the beings he holds captive. Like leprechauns, for instance. Just because we don't display all our talents in the shop window, doesn't mean we don't have them stored in the back."

I bit my lip. "How was your time with Banwell? If you don't mind me asking."

Maddock shook his head. "Pretty standard stuff. He tried to get all my gold from me before the tattoo was placed, but feigning being weak and sick helped while we were connected with just a spell. He didn't get a single nugget. Though I really was pretty sick. Whatever those psychos at the compound shot me full of really took a toll on me."

"Wait, start from the beginning," I said, waving my hands. "What happened once I set you free the *first* time?"

"Well," he sighed, dipping a handful of french fries into ketchup. "To begin, what you did was something I never expected out of anyone, and I knew your grandfather. He was a good man, for a human. But even he wouldn't do what you did for a leprechaun. I was amazed, but I was also so excited about being free, that I plumb left you for a few days. Though I did stay long enough to hear what you said, I'm sorry to admit that I had been so excited about being freed, I forgot my plan to follow you and release you and your parents. I kind of went off my head a bit with joy."

"So where did you go as soon as I released you?" I asked, smiling despite myself.

"Before the spell was done cooling in my chest, I had hopped on a plane for Ireland."

"But you don't have an ID," I said, remembering how all of my possessions I'd packed for this whole venture, including our fake passports, were left at the Sewer Fox's warehouse. "How did you buy a ticket?"

"Did I say I bought a ticket?" he asked, a sly smile on his face. "There's plenty of space in the belly of the plane, lass. I appeared into the cargo hold right before takeoff, and vanished out right before landing. Easy peasy. Was bloomin' cold, though. But I was finally home." His eyes became shiny, and he quickly began slurping on his drink, trying to cover the emotions that slipped from behind his mask of gruff indifference.

"So what then?" I asked.

He took a big breath. "Well, I was there for exactly four hours when I realized I wasn't even enjoying myself. The beauty of my home island, the food, the booze," he sighed. "I was uncomfortable. I knew it was my stupid conscience working on me, telling me I couldn't leave you to your fate. I knew Banwell was sure to do something horrible to you for what you did for me, so I came back to the States.

"Didn't take me long to find you. We still had a residual connection, so I was able to follow that right to you. I saw the compound and everything that went on there. I couldn't believe it. Something inside of me came alive, and I knew I could make you one of my kind. We accept you as one of our own." He sighed again. "Well, after I made you leprekin and they shot me full of whatever that stuff was, I can't remember much of what happened next. I was so out of it, no doubt they kept me drugged until I was in Banwell's possession.

"He had me run errands, spy for him, etc, etc. He did make sure to keep me from Pat, though. No doubt he didn't want his assets getting chummy and somehow finding a way to rebel. Poor Pat. I had no idea."

"Me neither, nor about what HAMMA did to those they take," I replied, and I saw Maddock's face shift to a darker mien.

"I couldn't believe what I saw. Sure, your parents kept me captive, but my lot was nothing compared to the atrocities HAMMA inflicted. HAMMA, I'm sure, is just the beginning of what the world would look like if magic becomes fully known, unless people get properly educated. Magic just started coming back only a century or two ago. But I don't see that happening, because HAMMA is a force to be reckoned with."

I nodded, anger writhing in my stomach. It had only been a few hours since I'd escaped, yet it felt like weeks, the torture and pain of the last weeks and of my mother's murder had hardened something inside me. "And magical creatures won't be the only ones who suffer. We've seen that," I snarled. "Those murderers are just going to get away with what they're doing, because no police force will believe us!"

"And those who are in the police that know of magical creatures aren't going to say anything to their coworkers." Maddock gave a sardonic chuckle.

"My mother died for nothing. She won't get justice," I choked. Eyes burning, I turned away.

Maddock sobered and looked at me. "I'm sorry about your mother, lass. I had seen she wasn't well before I gave you my gift."

I had no desire to go into detail about how my mother actually died. It hurt too much to think about, along with the what if's that accompanied it. Instead, I redirected to one of my biggest concerns. "My mother wasn't the only one to have been killed by them, and she won't be the last. None of them will get justice!" I said, wiping my eyes.

"It seems no one is safe," Maddock agreed.

My fist clenched the burger wrapper I'd been gathering up, remembering my father, alone with my mother's body, back at home. My mother was dead, all because of HAMMA and their warped, hypocritical ideals.

"Someone needs to teach them a lesson," I snarled. "They need to be taken down! They murder and steal and torture and burn. How can they be stopped?"

Maddock shook his head helplessly.

The sound of a car pulling into the park's parking lot perked us up. We watched from our vantage point as a family of six piled out of the minivan, the kids running toward the distant playground. Looking at the time on my phone, it read eight-thirty. And a Saturday.

It was so bizarre to me that it was a normal Saturday, people going about their daily lives with not a care in the world. Kids could run and play, parents could watch their kids, and a hidden world of magic and mayhem lived beyond their knowledge. And yet, none of those families were truly safe. HAMMA could see anyone as a threat to their warped ideals. And no one could stop them.

The happy shrieks of the children broke my thoughts, sending shivers of unwanted memory across my skin.

"We better get going, before this place gets crowded," I said.

Maddock cleared his throat. "Well, *you* better get going, lass."

I turned to him, a questioning frown on my face. "What do you mean?"

He looked a little embarrassed as he began sweeping burger wrappers into the empty fast food bag. "Well, I'm not going home with you. You realize that, don't you?"

My heart dropped into my feet, and I stared at him for a stupid amount of time as my brain struggled to process his words. He didn't even make fun of the obvious dumb expression I had on my face, but was careful to avoid looking at me.

After several moments, all I could say was, "Oh."

For this last hour we'd been together, I'd forgotten that he was free, our mission was over, and he wasn't coming home with me. I had just been enjoying the moment, the peace I'd felt so much that it felt like old times, back before the Fox had betrayed us.

I had forgotten that we both had our own lives to rebuild.

Apart.

Somehow, realizing this hurt more than when I'd released him the first time. I'd done it in part as an act of defiance and desperation, but now that he had a choice, and wasn't coming with me and was no longer going to be a part of my life, it hurt. Not only that, it felt wrong. We'd been through so much together. He'd been part of my life since I was eight years old. And now I'd be continuing my life without him in it.

Sure, I'd hated his guts for most of that time, and he'd hated mine, but it was amazing how much one's perceptions and heart could change in a short amount of time, and how one's appreciation and kinship towards a person could grow when tested. We'd both been through fire, changing us into new people. Better people.

I shook my head, horrified at the tears welling in my eyes. "Wow, I . . . I forgot. That's so weird," I said, my voice thick.

"You're not *crying*, are you lass?" Maddock teased, wadding up the fast food bag and tossing it into a nearby garbage can.

"Tears of joy," I threw back. "I thought for sure I'd be stuck with you for the rest of my life!" I tried to keep the smile on my face, but my expression crumpled. "But you're leaving—" I covered my face with a hand. I felt a gentle touch on my shoulder, and turned to see Maddock sitting beside me.

His face was softened by a gentle smile. "Hey, don't cry, lass. We'll always have that time I told your mother I wanted you to dress up in a pink bunny suit for me for Easter, and she made you do it."

"That was so humiliating!" I moaned, covering my face.

"Hey, that Easter egg I gave you afterwards was an authentic imperial egg," he reminded me.

I laughed through my tears, quickly wiping them off my face, then blew out a long breath. "So much will change. My home, my friends, my mom—"

I bit down hard on my lip, the memory so sharp in my mind I couldn't breathe. How was that only last night? She had tried to save me. Had saved me. Now she was gone, just like Maddock was leaving me. Was everyone going to leave me?

*Stop crying, you ninny*, I said to myself with Maddock's voice, hoping it would help. It didn't. It only made me cry harder.

"Hey now, lass," Maddock said, tapping my arm and holding a handkerchief out toward me. The sight of the lacy hankie caught me off guard so much that I actually did stop crying.

"You carry handkerchiefs now?" I asked, taking it and wiping my eyes.

"Don't knock it. I always have. Old habit. Listen to me, lass. You survived the last week without me, right? Well, that week was training, now you're prepared for the rest of your life. You survived HAMMA. You can survive anything. Even life without my beauteous good looks to sustain you."

I laughed, and he sobered. "But seriously, lass. You got this."

I blew my nose into his handkerchief, then giggled at his disgruntled expression at the now soggy hankie.

"Hey, that's what happens when you carry a handkerchief and not tissues like a normal person," I admonished. I held the handkerchief out to him, but he shook his head, holding up a hand to stop the return of his possession. "Keep it. Something to remember me by," he said.

"Yeah, right," I laughed, tucking it into my pocket. "You just don't want to have to wash it."

Maddock grinned. "You're catching on to me, lass. Good thing I'm leaving. I can't have a human know *all* my mysteries."

"Yeah," I exhaled. "Good riddance." I cast him a watery smile, then we sat in silence for a moment. I tried not to think of the actual parting. If he would just disappear, it would be easier. "Oh!" I exclaimed, the thought suddenly striking me. I quickly slipped the key necklace from off my neck. "Here. I want you to have this. You're truly free, now."

Maddock took the necklace, his face scrunched as he studied the old key to his underground home. "Thank you, lass. I just want to say—" Maddock began, but I held up a hand, my face contorting in pain.

"No, don't! You'll make me cry again!" I wailed, trying to hide my face.

Maddock chuckled, patting my arm. "Okay, lass, okay. I'll just leave it as 'I'll miss you, Mallory.'"

Before I could react, he was wrapping his arms around me in a tight hug. Screwing up my face against the tears, I embraced him back, my eyes stinging.

"I loathe you, Maddock," I choked.

"I detest you, too, lassie. And don't you believe anything else," he whispered.

We broke apart, and Maddock took my hands, squeezing them briefly. "You're going to be alright," he assured. I nodded, taking a fortifying breath and smiling.

With a wink, Maddock disappeared.

I looked down into my hands, and resting in my palm was a sparkling purple gemstone the size of my thumb. I laughed, shaking my head and admiring the glittering jewel as it reflected the early morning sunlight. "Thank you, Maddock," I whispered.

He was right. I could do this.

Taking several shaky breaths, I wiped my eyes, then stood and hurried back to my car. My dad was probably wondering where I was. I didn't want to keep him worrying any longer.

# EPILOGUE

*Six Months Later*

The bony fingers of winter-bare bushes reached out toward me as I ran down the quiet street, my breath blooming before me as I panted in the morning air.

The stop sign.

I could make it to the stop sign, and then I would have to stop running to take a rest. I pushed harder, my legs and lungs screaming, my feet pounding against the cracked, well-worn road, which was devoid of cars this time of morning. As I ran past the stop sign, I slapped its red face, the metal icy-cold against my skin, and then I slowed to a walk. Gulping air, I planted my fists on my hips and looked up at the cloudless sky, the sun just peeking over the open fields and leafless trees. I was sweating, but my fingers and nose were freezing. I re-adjusted my scarf so that it covered where the cold was biting my face, and after another moment of rest, I pushed myself into a run again.

The nightmares had returned last night.

Whenever they came, the feeling of being trapped, and the stifling helplessness of being in the pen, watching my mother die, made it hard to breathe.

I had rolled out of bed and crept down the stairs of our small farmhouse to go running. It helped the caged feeling go away. At least for a little while. But the realization that HAMMA was still out there, torturing, kidnapping, and killing itched beneath my skin, no matter how much I ran. The thought urged me into a sprint again, and I tore down the street.

After rescuing Maddock, I had gotten back to my family estate just fine. My dad had left me a message on my cell phone to stay hidden, as he had told the police that I had been traveling abroad, and hadn't been present for the break in.

When he gave me the all clear to return to the house, we had to wait for my mother's body to return from the coroner. My father told the police that he and my mother had been tied up for days, and that those who had broken in had taken her outside and killed her late last night. My father had placed my mother's body into the pond to account for the loss of blood that wasn't at the house. He also explained that the two men had been taken into custody, but weren't talking, as well as other details to help fill in the other holes of our story, but I was too tired and too sad to really pay attention.

The next few days were a blur. My father's social influence was able to speed up processes that would usually take a while. He also ensured that the investigation would be short and shallow.

Once we got my mother's body back from the coroner, we had a private funeral. We buried her in the family plot on the estate, and then we went into hiding. I couldn't even say goodbye to my friends. My father wanted us to disappear into thin air, and didn't want any of our friends or acquaintances to know anything, in case Banwell went after them. It broke my heart all over again, the thought of leaving with no trace, with Hillary, Paz, and my other friends wondering what had happened to me. But it was better than them falling into danger.

We left, with the affairs of our finances and estate in the hands of trustworthy lawyers. We moved into a farmhouse in the rural part of New York between Buffalo and Rochester, keeping to ourselves, with our many acres of land to keep neighbors at a distance.

My dad kept me out of school, to avoid the hassle of fake ID's and the possibility of being found. Instead, I focused on learning from the books our ancestors had kept about magic, trying to strengthen my skill and knowledge. It was rough, because all the books were written in cursive, and a lot of the theories and spells were speculation. My ancestors didn't know much about magic. My dad wasn't good at magic, either, so we just had to try the best we could.

I kept to myself. No use putting more people in danger. Besides, since I didn't go to school or hang out with kids my age, it was easy to keep aloof. Our neighbors barely knew we were here.

However, all this isolation made me feel even worse. What was the point of life if I was living in fear the whole time? The helpless, frightened feeling of not wanting to be found, yet not being able to do anything to stop the horrific actions of HAMMA put me into a depression. Banwell had done this to us. HAMMA was out there, running amok under the nose of those able to exact justice on murderers and thieves, yet they would never be caught and tried, at least not anytime soon. And I couldn't do anything about it.

I continued running, a burning, metallic taste in my throat as I pushed myself faster, and I turned down the road to my house. The three bedroom, two bathroom farmhouse was perfect because it was so rural, and my dad figured that come spring he could hire people to work the land to avoid suspicion as to why all this land wasn't being farmed by the owners.

I cut across the dead grass of the front yard and up the steps to the wraparound porch. I collapsed into one of the chairs on the porch, gasping. From somewhere out in the chilly morning, a rooster's crow echoed across the barren fields aglow in the weak winter sunlight.

My heart rate slowed and my breathing evened out as I watched the morning brighten.

I felt cold now, but drained of the fear and itchy feeling of restless helplessness. But it would return. I knew my father felt the same. I'd eavesdropped on a few phone conversations where I heard the name *Banwell* mentioned. No doubt he was trying to keep tabs on the monster, but he would never let me help. He would always change the subject or flat out refuse to have a discussion about what he was doing. It was starting to become more than I could bear. But I didn't press him for answers. I let him redirect the conversation to playing a board game or telling stories about his travels. Being able to spend more time with my dad was the only nice thing that had come from all we had gone through.

Taking one last deep breath of cold November air, I took out my key and let myself in the front door. When I got into the kitchen, I passed the open fridge door that was hiding my dad from view.

"Wow, Pops, you're up early," I greeted, continuing on to the sink to get myself a drink of water.

"And you're a very slow runner, lassie," came a gruff, familiar brogue.

I froze in my tracks as the well-known voice hit me, and then whipped around to see Maddock emerging from the fridge with eggs, cheese, onions, and bacon in his arms.

"Omelette?" he asked, his tone innocent.

"*What are you doing here?*" I squealed, rushing forward to scoop him in a hug.

"Watch the eggs!" Maddock cried as I rocked the leprechaun, omelette ingredients and all, from side to side. "Ach, you're all sweaty!" he protested.

"Am I?" I asked, running my sticky forehead across his cheek. He made a strangled noise of disgust, and fought to free himself from my embrace.

I finally let go of him, grinning, and he piled everything onto the counter, making hemming and hawing noises.

"Ruin my appetite, why don't you?" he grumbled, popping open the lid to the eggs and inspecting them for breaks. "No, wait . . ." He held up a finger, his face pinched in thought. "Yeah, okay, it's back."

"No, but seriously, what are you doing here?" I demanded, leaning against the counter as he pulled a kitchen chair over to the stove, where he lit one of the burners and placed a frying pan over the flames.

"Getting a free breakfast, obviously," he replied, gesturing to the spread before him.

"Maddock, I'm serious," I said. "I'm thrilled to see you, but . . . I kind of assumed we'd never see each other again."

"Well, you know what happens when you assume," Maddock said conversationally. "It makes *you* an ass. Pass me the salt, won't you?"

I pursed my lips, remembering now that I hadn't missed this part of Maddock at all.

"Maddock," I warned as he scooped a large knife-full of butter into the pan, where it began to melt, popping and sputtering. Maddock clapped his hands together, a look of glee on his face.

"Food first. Food always first," he demanded, cracking eggs into a bowl he'd retrieved from the cupboard.

"And run the risk of my dad waking up and finding you here?" I asked, eyebrow raised.

"I'm not worried about your old Da. In fact, he'll need to hear this." He began chopping the onion and bacon.

"What?" I demanded, my stomach clenching. "What is it? What's wrong?"

Maddock pointedly ignored me as he finished dicing the ingredients and mixing them into the eggs. I exhaled.

"Maddock, I swear—"

Maddock sighed in an aggravated way and glared at me. "You're not going to let me enjoy the spiritual experience of cooking omelettes, are you?" Maddock huffed, adding cheese to the eggs.

"If you don't tell me right now, I'm going to put spinach in your omelette," I threatened.

"Alright, alright, no need to get nasty," Maddock snapped. "What do you want to know?"

I made a disbelieving noise. "Well, to begin, what are you doing here? I thought you were in Ireland. What, the Irish weren't as charming as you remembered?" I smirked.

"I was in Ireland," he replied, ignoring my jab. "Until I almost got captured. Twice. Then I decided something needed to be done."

"Done?" I asked, my heart thumping in an odd, breathless sort of way.

"With these HAMMA people!" Maddock said, his tone hot. "Magical people are getting snapped up left and right, all by magic poachers, and I can't stand sitting around anymore, letting it happen."

"HAMMA isn't in Ireland," I said, recalling my conversation with Banwell months ago about how he was having trouble establishing communities in Europe.

"No, HAMMA isn't in Ireland yet, but that doesn't mean HAMMA's influence isn't felt around the world. Magic is getting discovered, and by the worst people imaginable. People that are completely ignorant about the Ever."

"And you came to me why? I . . . I don't know what I can do to help you," I said, biting my lip.

Maddock snorted, turning to look at me with an expression of pure disbelief. "What absolute blarney. You're a *leprekin*, lass! Or did you forget?" he rebuked.

"I've been keeping a low profile!" I argued back, feeling my face flush. There was no way I could forget who I was and how I came to be here, and that knowledge just made the world all the more scary. "Who knows where HAMMA is, always watching." I hadn't used any magic since we escaped, though I could feel its constant, comforting warmth curling in my chest. I was too afraid.

I was sick of being afraid.

"Lass, if *you* can't do anything, no one can," Maddock said, his tone grave as he stared me in the eye. I glanced down at my dirty running shoes as I leaned up against the counter, shame flaming my face.

"You're more powerful than I am. More powerful than any magical creature like me, because you're human and can use magic, and you're luck-blessed. Don't squander such a gift," Maddock entreated. "Use it to help me."

"To do what? Take down HAMMA?" I asked, incredulous.

"Take down HAMMA," he replied, credulous, with a bit of fire in his expression. "And maybe teach the world a little bit about respecting magic."

"I'm barely sixteen!" I said, trying to laugh, to make a joke out of it, because if this wasn't a joke, that meant it was serious.

My sixteenth birthday had come and gone, with little to no fanfare. After our captivity, a party of the caliber I'd planned was the furthest thing from my mind. The party I ended up having was a world away from what I'd dreamed of because we had been so focused on keeping ourselves discreet.

What was supposed to be the biggest party of the decade thanks to my mom's epic party planning skills ended up being just me and my dad. He'd gotten me some shooting targets to practice with in our small range he built on our property, as well as some nail polish, a very frilly, shiny skirt that wasn't my style at all, and a new laptop, since mine had been taken by the Sewer Fox. It had been touching, though it was also clear my dad and I still had some bonding to do. But we had time.

He'd also baked me a cake, something I never thought I'd see him do. The cake came out a little lopsided, but I loved it more than any ten-foot frosted masterpiece.

"What's the big deal?" Maddock broke through my musings. "I'm the great Maddock O'Bannon. I'll help you."

I gave him an exasperated look, though the butterflies in my stomach wouldn't calm.

He shrugged. "So what if you're young? You're a dropout from high school anyway, you're already in hiding, and it helps that you're disgustingly wealthy and can fund our projects."

I was silent, wondering if he was really serious, while trying to ignore the frantic beating of my heart.

Maddock, noticing my silence, sighed. "Lass, HAMMA took everything from you. *Banwell* took everything from you: your mother, your friends, your home, your teenage years, the awesome sweet sixteen birthday party you wanted. Everything."

The truth of his words made the latent anger flare in my chest. I frequently stalked my friends' social media pages from a burner account, watching them live their lives. Watching them not have to worry about what was out there, lurking. Watching them be happy. I paused, then looked up at Maddock, a small smile of disbelief tugging at my lips.

"You remembered about my sweet sixteen party?" I teased.

Maddock cursed, looking embarrassed, then chuckled. "You only mentioned it *constantly*, lass. And I was really looking forward to the leftover cake your mom would send me. Which reminds me, happy late birthday."

Without looking up from the eggs in the pan, he tossed me a tiny parcel wrapped in newspaper. I opened it, a small, baby blue convertible rolling into my palm. He'd even remembered the color.

I smiled as I twiddled the car between my fingers, then shook my head. "So you want to go up against HAMMA? Where would we even start?"

He shrugged. "I say we take a few pages out of HAMMA's book. Establish a headquarters, do reconnaissance, and hit 'em where it hurts. I suppose the most we can do at the moment is just give HAMMA hell. We can figure out other things as they come along."

My lips puckered in thought as I stared at the leprechaun that I'd shared more adventures with than I ever imagined I would. Did I want to share more with him?

The obvious answer was yes. Maddock understood what I was now, and he had become a close friend, and I trusted him above anyone, besides maybe my dad. I wanted to help with the HAMMA problem, but alone, I didn't know how to do it, or even where to start.

The atrocities of HAMMA had been burned into my brain forever. I wanted to make them pay, to hurt them for what they'd done. They needed to go down for their hypocrisy and absolute disregard for life, human and magical. I had seen what HAMMA had done to those poor creatures they claimed they wanted to help. Those they imprisoned deserved justice. Santeri, wherever he was. The Sewer Fox. They deserved to be rescued.

And now, here was Maddock, offering a solution to the very reason I'd been up this morning, running. The helplessness, the anger, the desire to do something had felt inescapable. Here was the answer. Alone, I hadn't known how I could. But with Maddock, it was possible we could really do something great.

Make actual change.

"And you want to be partners?" I asked.

"Partners. Co-founders. HAMMA hell-raisers." He held his hand out to me, and I couldn't stop the slow smile curling on my lips. He grinned back as I slapped my hand into his.

"HAMMA hell-raisers."

# ACKNOWLEDGEMENTS

Every good thing in my life has come from my Heavenly Father and Jesus Christ. That includes my ability to write and the inspiration I have received from them, not just for my stories, but for everything in my life. They have helped me in more ways that I can count. I will always be grateful to Them.

As always, I'm so grateful to my husband, Bryan, who is unfailing in his help, patience, and trips to the store for ice cream when I'm having a hard writing day, not to mention his love that helps me combat imposter syndrome. You are my rock, Bryan, and I'm so thankful for you. And also for your technical writing skills.

A big shout out to my early readers: Mary Locke Jolley, Sarah Lowe, Gayle Burnham, Nicole Burnham, AJ Nora, Brooke Clonts, and my dad, Gary Kitchen (I'm sorry I didn't change that one part you really didn't like, Dad.) All your help with ironing out the story to make it polished was seriously so wonderful, and I'm grateful for you and the time you took to read the early drafts.

To my editor, Mary Locke Jolley, those ten years you spent as a college English professor really were a blessing for me. But you are seriously a wonder, woman. Thank you!

A large thanks to Stephanie Roberson, who talked with me about some of the more difficult themes in this book. Thank you so much for being willing to chat, Stephanie.

To My Lan Khuc Valle, who once again worked magic to make the book cover so gorgeous, and who was so patient with me on getting exactly what I wanted. You're amazing and it's seriously such a joy working with you!

To anyone who has helped me with writing the back blurb, you are the real ones! You know who you are, and you're amazing! Blurbs seriously take more out of me than writing 120k words, so thank you for all your support, and for commiserating with me about how absolutely ghastly it is to write the blurb.

To my nephews Jackson and Maverick, your phone calls to update me while you were reading book one of this series really made my day.

And to everyone who had given me such kind words about my first book, receiving your texts out of the blue, filled with wonderful comments and stories about reading my book, puts me on cloud nine for days! Please keep them coming (lol) and I hope you love this book, too.

To my family, who are so supportive and excited for me to do this crazy writing thing, and who keep me laughing, I love you!

And to those who took a chance on reading my books, thank you so, so much. I appreciate you to no end. Readers make the writer's world go round, and you are spinning mine like crazy.

# About the Author

Chantel Burnham is a writer of Young Adult Fantasy and Sci-Fi, as well as a movie quoter extraordinaire. After spending some time as a film major, she discovered that her true passion is creating worlds of her own through writing.

When she isn't procrastinating writing her next book, Chantel can be found crafting decorations for Spooky Season, listening to music non-stop, reading from her ever-expanding TBR list, or snuggling her dog, cats, and husband, usually all at the same time.

Chantel lives in Northern Utah even though snow isn't her thing, but mountains, forests, and lakes are, so it evens out.

Check out her website at www.chantelburnham.com or scan the QR code.

www.ingramcontent.com/pod-product-compliance
Lightning Source LLC
Chambersburg PA
CBHW020326010826
48973CB00005B/1150